Where The Fruit Falls

Karen Wyld

16pt

Read How You Want
LARGE PRINT BOOKS, BRAILLE & DAISY

Copyright Page from the Original Book

Karen Wyld is a freelance writer and author living on the coast south of Adelaide. Born in South Australia, her Grandmothers' Country is in the Pilbara region of Western Australia. As a diasporic Aboriginal woman of Martu descent, she writes fiction and non-fiction that seeks to contextualise colonisation, displacement, the Stolen Generations, homecoming, resistance and rights. She's currently a Masters candidate, exploring how magic realism is used to articulate time, belonging and Country in Aboriginal-authored text.

An ancient ocean roars under the red dirt. Hush. Be still for just a moment. Hear its thundering waves crashing on unseen shores. This vast ocean was there in the beginning, as it will be in days not yet begun. Alongside gentler comrades, massive creatures once tumbled in the ocean's depths – jaws chasing tails. This harsh water ballet continued until the meek inherited an evaporating body of water. With budding legs, they crawled onto land and spawned. With the passing of time, their descendants and descendants' descendants procreated. Each generation became less like their forebears, as they roamed unhurriedly, populating an ever-changing continent.

Creatures of all shapes and sizes left their marks on terra. Footprints in an empty creek bed, claw marks on fossilised trees, faint impressions of a thumping tail across a gibber plain. Until time circled once again, and the era of colossal rulers was no more. By the time their bones had mingled with dust, others already roamed the earth.

ONE

That distinctive aroma of apples evoked many memories for Maeve, but it was her beloved who lay on the bottom of a distant ocean that she now recalled. This memory had been carried on a wisp of a wind through the orchard outside her door, teasing ripe apples until they'd dropped to the ground. That heady perfume of apples and first love was not the only thing that arrived on her doorstep that afternoon.

As the door closed, Maeve heard a fluttering of tiny wings. Instinctively, the corner of her upper lip rose slightly, with just enough momentum to displace wrinkled skin. That quivering sound took Maeve back to an almost-forgotten moment, when she had intimately known such wings beating against her own chest. Back to a time when a younger Maeve had not yet discovered corporeal yearnings, and foolish romantic notions had sufficed.

And then came an era, many decades past, during which Maeve Cliona Devlin had slowly and surely shed all sense of innocence, through hard times and pleasurable moments. Nonetheless, as life tends to be cyclic, matters of a carnal nature had long since been replaced by a more ascetic existence. Nestled in a wrought-iron bed that had seen better days, Maeve did not often succumb to nostalgic musings on the distant undulations of a life well lived; she appreciated the uncomplicatedness that ageing sometimes grants a woman. It is strange what memories can be stirred, at any given time, by the aroma of apples or the simple act of a door opening.

*

It was Brigid who had opened the door. She entered the room quietly, not wanting to disturb her grandmother. Brigid was oblivious to the fluttering wings she carried, the faint beating that had caught her grandmother's attention. It could be said she was generally unaware of nuances, both the everyday kind and the extraordinary. Despite recently turning eighteen, Brigid Devlin had not yet noticed she was no longer a child, let alone become aware of the perils of fluttering hearts.

Brigid unconsciously shuddered as the coldness of her grandmother's cottage hit her. She didn't notice that shudder squeeze through just a sliver of a gap as she shut the door. Her grandmother had heard that shudder leave but took no offence – she had the good sense to know that not even a shudder would willingly venture too near a fading light.

Putting aside her musings, Maeve patted the bed. 'Birdie, sit. Tell me about your day.'

Brigid walked towards the small kitchen table, placing upon it a well-laden basket. 'Let me open a window first, Granny, to let some fresh air in.'

The older woman nodded. A few moments more of waiting were of no consequence. It was enough that someone had arrived, fleetingly bringing some sunshine. She felt no animosity towards family, even if she sometimes felt they'd already executed their final goodbyes. Only the granddaughter willingly remembered the old woman at the bottom of the garden. Numerous times a day, Brigid brought her granny distractions from the outside world, to dilute the infinite seconds of waiting. The others, when they remembered the old woman, came out of a habitual sense of duty. The three broad-shouldered youths on the brink of manhood, who reminded Maeve of beloved male kin left behind on a distant shore, rarely stepped over her threshold. In the bluntness of old age, Maeve no longer felt any attachment to the sons of her daughter, unlike the fondness she had for the eldest grandchild, Brigid: her Birdie. The grandsons didn't know of Maeve's sense of disconnect. Even Margaret, her daughter, was unaware. Perhaps those bonny boys reminded Maeve too much of home. Of love lost, and lands never to be seen again. Or perhaps the way they filled a room simply reminded Maeve that she was shrinking.

Opening the window, Brigid caught sight of a small black-and-white bird. Maeve raised her head seconds before the bird broke out in song. It was a cheeky tune, alluding to promised embraces and stolen hearts. At least it was to Maeve's well-travelled ears. Birdie didn't hear the same tune. She heard spring blossoms and sun-warmed afternoons. And had a sudden longing to hide in the long grass and watch as wispy clouds made patterns in the blue. Maeve smiled, as the birdsong had brought back cherished memories. In cahoots with an old woman's fancy, a warm gust of wind floated through the open window to kiss Maeve's paper-thin skin, bringing her lost whispers of forever and ever, and then some. It had been decades since her husband had passed away but some things are never forgotten. Kisses on yesterday's skin last forever.

*

If her eyes had not grown milky, Maeve might have cast them over the room where she now lay entrapped. Maeve had built this cottage, not much more than that one room, with her own hands; and some unexpected help. The room served as parlour, kitchen and bedroom. Later, a small attached bathroom had been added by her son-in-law. Not an inside laundry though, as, right up until her sight had completely gone, Maeve had insisted on using the tarnished copper tub in the detached laundry out the back. If she could have looked around the room, she would have found more than a few shadowy memories lurking in corners. None of her husband, as he'd never set foot on this land where Maeve had built a home for the next generation.

Setting sail as a bride, Maeve disembarked as a widow. The anguish of leaving behind her family, knowing she would never again see the emerald island of her childhood, was overshadowed by the loss of her first and only love. His body had been sent to the bottom of the sea mere days before land was sighted. Having recently returned from war, Roan Devlin had been far from robust when they'd left the land of their childhood. He was certainly no match for La Grippe's frenzied tango. This unwanted dance partner had barely raised a flamed hue on other passengers' cheeks before dancing Roan off, to the end of time. Stepping away from the rail, having witnessed their shared dreams become entangled in the shroud that drifted from sight, Maeve had turned her thoughts to staying afloat.

Fortuitously, before his fated last journey, Maeve's husband had the foresight to secure a modest slice of land on the country they had chosen to sow their marital life. When Maeve arrived alone, heavy of heart and womb, she had taken comfort in the realisation that love's legacy was a patch of good earth, with a modest wattle-and-daub lean-to. Using coins that had weighed down the hem of her pinafore during the ocean crossing, Maeve had purchased timber and set to work. Ignoring the strangers who scoffed at her determination, she welcomed extra hands when offered. Unable to pay for their labour, Maeve acknowledged her new neighbours' kindness with lovingly prepared food, resulting in full bellies and warm laughter. This did not gain her any friends among the women in the small town by the coast.

Not to begin with. Then word had spread that Maeve was not only recently widowed but expecting. Primly downturned mouths then became welcoming smiles. And Maeve soon had a one-roomed cottage and caring neighbours to shelter her for decades to come.

With her bridal trousseau finally unpacked, Maeve had set about making her acquaintance with the land. First, she removed a sea of stones, putting them aside for a wall that had since seen many people pass by. All those decades ago she had imagined a simple wooden gate sitting between low stone walls, opening to a path that led to her front door. On either side of the path would eventually grow an abundance of fragrant herbs and flowers, familiar plants from her homeland whose scents carried with them fond memories. These pleasant images had made time pass quickly as she tilled the land, proudly building calluses on her long-fingered hands.

Maeve planted well-sprouted potato eyes that she'd kept damp all through the ocean crossing. Unbeknown to her husband, who had sworn that his wife would never be made to eat another potato for as long as she lived, Maeve had hidden precious peelings in her luggage. She had listened attentively at the feet of womenfolk and knew there are times when the humblest of vegetables makes the tastiest meal. Reassured that a good future crop of potatoes lay nestled in the spring-warmed earth, it was time to prepare her modest home for the little stranger's arrival. Having been so intent on grieving, building and planting, Maeve had put off pondering the new life she'd been growing. Until mild pains in her lower back reminded her that neither death nor birth can be controlled.

At first sight, her daughter's resemblance to Roan had been confronting; she had his eyes. Maeve quickly found comfort in those bluest of blue eyes. The midwife and female visitors had laughed at the inexperienced mother's joy, before kindly informing her that all newborns have blue eyes. Maeve didn't listen to their chattering, as she knew her daughter's eyes would never change.

Maeve had named the babe Margaret, the moniker her Roan had chosen upon hearing he was to be a father. And even though she knew others would think it archaic, Maeve bestowed on their daughter the middle name Boudicca, feeling she might one day need strength from the homeland. There was no saint's name given, for grief had caused Maeve to question, and then abandon, her once deeply ingrained faith. Shortly after mother's milk flowed in abundance, Maeve had returned to working in the field and, with help from her neighbours, she'd brought in the first crop of potatoes.

*

'Granny, are you all right?'

Maeve started. Dragged from days past, it took her a few moments to recognise the voice. 'I'm fine. Quit your fussing.'

Brigid moved away from the open window and perched on the edge of her grandmother's bed.

Maeve reached for her hand. 'How are the apple trees?'

'Father managed to get rid of those woolly aphids. He made up something smelly to wash them away.'

'That man was born with a green thumb. Your mother did right to marry him.'

The apple trees, more so than the other fruit trees in the orchard that surrounded the cottage, were important to Maeve. They connected her to the land and people of her childhood. Maeve and Roan had brought cuttings of fruit trees from home, wrapped carefully in layers of dampened moss and rags. With careful coaxing, Maeve had persuaded those trees to adapt to a new climate, to bear fruit for generations of offspring. In addition to creating the orchard, Maeve had made fruit preserves, pies and other treats in her younger years. She sold the excess to neighbours, and later at the local market. And there were always potatoes to sell. This had enabled her to support her child, without needing a man.

Those earlier years were tough. At first she was lonely, far from family and widowed so young. Then Maeve found warm arms for cold nights. There would only ever be one true love for her, but that had not stopped her from taking a lover whenever she desired. In her cottage at the edge of town, it had been easy for Maeve to be discreet. And she had been firm with each and every lover; she was not interested in keeping house for any man. That dream had floated away when Roan was left at sea.

By the time Birdie was born, Maeve had tired of her lovers and decided to devote herself to her granddaughter, whose arrival had caused a storm. When Brigid's mother was a young woman, it had become apparent that she had not inherited her mother's green thumb. Instead, Margaret had her father's wanderlust, which urged her to leave home too soon. Four years later Margaret had returned with a toddler in tow, setting off the gossips. Despite children out of wedlock being considered wicked, they were not too uncommon in times of war. Margaret, however, had committed an entirely different sin. One the settlers could not fathom. But Maeve hadn't seen things the same way as her neighbours. She was instantly besotted with her granddaughter. She had marvelled at Brigid's curly dark-brown hair, so like her own, and eyes of deepest brown. The first time someone had dared call her little Birdie a piccaninny, Maeve had flashed them such a look of disdain that no one ever uttered that word again. At least not when Maeve was in earshot.

If Margaret had shared her story, then perhaps a few of the vanguard matrons would have sympathised with her. Perhaps if she had spoken of how she'd fallen for the handsomest, kindest, most cherished of men, she could have melted their bias. Margaret might have told them about the tears she'd shed when they discovered that he was not permitted, by law, to marry her. She would then have told the townsfolk how she'd travelled with Edward, her love, to stay with his family. Surrounded by a more tolerant community, their union was declared in the desert, not a church. Margaret could have shared her birthing story with other mothers. And how a few years later she and Edward had moved to the coast with their bonny baby.

If none of that had helped sway the disapproving matrons, then the next part of her story might have. Margaret should have told them how her husband had died a hero. How, against her pleas and advice from his father, Edward had enlisted in the army. And, like too many young men, had died on a battlefield in a distant country, for a cause he did not quite understand.

Margaret never told her neighbours and friends that story because she could never forgive them. They were too similar to the rigid people who had practically forced Edward to don a uniform. He had gone to war in the hope of returning to a different, kinder nation. He'd hoped that if he proved himself to those who were constantly judging him, controlling his life, then they'd accept his relationship with Margaret. And they'd no longer take their prejudices out on her, or the child. Edward had gone to war because he believed in a future where everyone, regardless of their origin story, was seen as equal. Deeply entrenched in grief, Margaret hadn't told this story of love and loss. Instead, she hardened herself to the stares and whispers of those around her.

The whispers faded when Margaret became a more respectable woman in the eyes of others. She was soon expecting another child, this time as a married woman. Maeve had accepted her daughter's choice of husband even before she'd discovered that Frank Browne was skilled in horticulture as well as other trades. Due to the after-effects of polio, Frank had not been deemed fit for war, but nothing could stop him from achieving whatever he set his mind to. He had soon built a modest house next to Maeve's cottage, for his wife and stepdaughter.

Frank's presence had also provided young Brigid protection from the Protector. Not that she really needed it. No one could have stolen the child from under the watchful eye of Granny Maeve. Unfortunately, Granny had taken this protection too far. For she had wrapped that child up so tightly with her love that Brigid had rarely been beyond the cottage gate as a young child. Coddled, she hadn't noticed people who looked just like her: those made to live further out than the edge of town. They had seen her, and encouraged their children to play with the girl from the apple orchard. Maeve shooed the shy children away, and threatened the more courageous. She finally had a word to the parents. Eventually, they all hesitated to even look at Brigid in passing.

Maeve had also buffered the child from curious glances and loose tongues whenever they went into town. When Brigid was old enough for school, it became harder for Maeve to keep a close watch on her. On the first day, Brigid had come home in tears, wondering why the other children teased her. Maeve had told Brigid she was like a little potato; her skin might be brown like the earth, but inside she was just like everyone else. Later, when Brigid had voiced her doubts about dirt-encrusted potatoes, Maeve had told her a tale about apple seeds, which made even less sense to Brigid. She soon stopped telling her granny what the other children said, and eventually stopped agonising over how different she was from them.

Brigid was also different from her brothers, and not just in appearance. After the first Browne brother had been born, a year later another one arrived, and one the year after that. Three blue-eyed, freckled, light-haired brothers. They were Brownes and she was a Devlin, which just added to her troubles at school. Her brothers didn't understand what it felt like to be an outsider, and they never once stood up for her. Brigid never really felt close to them. Nor did she really feel at home in her family's house. She much preferred grandmother's cottage. Maeve and Brigid were more alike. They both had soft curls of the deepest brown, and wide-awake possum eyes. Maeve's were grey and Brigid's deep brown.

*

'How peculiar,' remarked Brigid.

'What is it, child?'

'That bird, the one that was singing, it's now perched on the windowsill.'

Maeve shifted in the bed. 'What does it look like, Birdie?'

'Small. Black and white feathers.'

Maeve nodded sagely. 'So that time has come. Too soon, if you ask me. Bring me that box, lass.'

Brigid fetched the small wooden jewellery box that always sat on her grandmother's dresser, the one whose contents she desperately wanted to discover. She respected her granny too much to peek inside.

Opening it, Maeve took something out. 'Here. This is yours now.'

'What is it?'

'An apple seed dipped in silver. It's from the very first apple that ripened in our orchard. That tree was grown from a cutting I carried across the seas, all the way from my birthplace.'

Brigid held the pendant up by the small silver chain to which it was attached.

'Put it on, go on. Wear it always, so you never forget.'

'Forget what, Granny?'

The old woman patted her granddaughter's hand. 'Never forget that an apple seed may travel far, carried on the wind by bird or folk, but the fruit never falls far from the tree.'

Brigid began to ask what her granny meant, but a sharp trill interrupted her. Brigid noticed the small bird on the windowsill. A bird that seemed quite determined for attention.

***

Before the tale of the little black-and-white bird can be told, other birds must be heralded. Three, to be precise. For a conspiracy of ravens had formed near the small cottage at the bottom of the garden. First one settled in the tall tree out the front of her grandmother's cottage. Then a second. Maeve knew it wouldn't be much longer before the third would appear, but she was not afraid. She was more than ready.

These large carnivorous birds didn't frighten away the smaller bird that had taken up residence in the apple orchard. A willy wagtail goes where it will and does what it wants. And what it wanted was Brigid's attention. It had first appeared at her bedroom window, on an unmemorable morning a few weeks past. It was a couple of days before Brigid noticed it. First by its cheeky song, later by its persistence. That bird sang at her window every morning, greeting her with joyous chirps as she woke to a new day. The novelty soon wore off for Brigid. She had many times opened her window to swoosh it away. That cheeky bird just hopped around a bit, before recommencing its song.

Her brothers then tried to make it to go away, rushing at it comedically with flailing arms. The bird wiggled its tail at them, took a few hops to the left, and started singing again. On the third morning of the third week, that willy wagtail was at the door, waiting for Brigid. When she walked to the washing line it followed, chirping away. When she went to pick apples, it led her to the juiciest in the orchard. When she walked into town, to the general store, it hopped down the lane in front of her. She couldn't go anywhere without that bird. In the fifth week, sick of it carrying on, her stepfather Frank chased it away with a shovel. Not with malice, just frustration. It made the family laugh to see the gentle, tall man yelling at a tiny bird. By the time he'd shut the door, it was already out the front of the house again, singing even louder than before.

That look-at-me bird was annoying the whole family, so it came time for Granny to tell Brigid what that little bird was saying. Because Maeve knew the secret language of birds. She had learnt it from her grandmother, who had learnt it from her grandmother. And so on and so on, through a long line of apple-growing grandmothers. Maeve had discovered the local birds weren't that much different from those in her homeland. And that is why Maeve knew the raven duo was waiting for the third to arrive. Once it did, it would be time for Maeve to leave. Although she'd miss her Birdie, Maeve knew her granddaughter had a journey of her own to go on. Who would be leaving first was still undecided. So Maeve knew she needed to put aside thoughts of her gatherers for a while and have a much-needed talk with Brigid about the birds and the apples.

***

The soft thud of the cottage door closing roused Maeve from a most pleasant dream. Her dreams were full of vibrant colours and sunlight. As the days began to pass even slower, sleep was where she preferred to be. Orientating herself to the darkness of the non-dream state, Maeve felt the presence of Birdie in the cottage.

'Good morning, lass.'

Birdie laughed. 'It's late afternoon, Granny.'

Maeve clicked her tongue, annoyed at being found in a state of disorientation again. With her mind clearing, Maeve remembered she had to tell Brigid why that small black-andwhite bird was so persistent.

'Brigid, come here. Sit for a bit. I need to tell you some things of importance.'

Having loved her grandmother's stories since she was a small child, Brigid eagerly did as she was told. And so Maeve told her granddaughter about the small messenger bird. And how it carried a message just for her. That willy wagtail would not be going away any time soon. Instead, Brigid must follow it. Brigid protested. She did not want to go anywhere, ever. She wanted to stay with her granny. Maeve sternly asked her to stop chattering and listen some more. So Brigid listened as her grandmother told her about birds and destinies.

According to her grandmother, there were two types of birds: those that led you to good fortune, and those that led to no good. It was almost impossible to tell the two apart, usually not until it was too late. Maeve didn't say that she had a feeling this bird was the type that might just escort a young person to find their one true love. What Maeve didn't know was if this would be a harmonious pairing or a whole lot of trouble.

*

The day the third blue-black raven appeared, Maeve didn't need to be told. She'd already felt its presence, and was wondering if she really was ready.

'There's three of them,' Brigid noted as she closed the door.

Placing a warm plate on the bedside table, Brigid removed the cloth that covered her grandmother's dinner. A pungent but pleasant aroma hit Maeve.

'Leave it,' she grumbled.

'It will go cold, Granny.'

Maeve shifted slightly, letting out a faint sigh. Brigid helped her sit up, fluffed the pillow, and resettled her grandmother. Maeve turned her head towards the window, her milky eyes sensing a shadow. Unseen by Maeve, on the other side of the glass the three ravens perched in the oldest apple tree. The first she'd planted.

Brigid raised a fork. 'Have just a little. It's roast lamb, peas and mashed potatoes with gravy. I made it for you. Please, Granny.'

'Maybe I'll just try the mash, Birdie.'

Brigid carefully lifted the fork and placed warm, smooth potatoes on her grandmother's tongue. Savouring the taste, Maeve instantly thought of potato eyes wrapped up in dampened moss and rags. And a husband with eternal youth, resting on an ocean floor. Suddenly, she longed for Roan's embrace. The memory of his strong arms around her shoulders was still as vivid as if it was only yesterday. She knew then that she was indeed ready.

TWO

She left in black. Carrying a small suitcase, she stepped over the threshold. Tears had been shed. Her mother, stepfather and brothers had been farewelled. There was nothing left to do but follow that little black-and-white bird.

Tilting its head, the willy wagtail waited for her.

Brigid nodded. 'Get moving. I'm ready.'

The bird hopped down the road and Brigid followed with sadness weighing down each step. She was leaving behind the place she swore she'd never leave. As she passed her grandmother's cottage, Brigid turned to look at the oldest apple tree in the family orchard across the road. Three ravens let loose sorrowful caw-caws as they flew up into the sky. When they became not much more than dots in the distance, Brigid plucked an apple from the tree, and then turned her sights to the road ahead.

Brigid walked for all of that first day, following that little bird, heading due north until the sun disappeared. Then she made a fire, before falling asleep to the soothing sound of the bird's chattering tales. The next morning, she walked some more. Until it was again time to light a campfire. Days soon became weeks, and weeks turned into months. Still she followed that bird, continuing the journey to an unknown destiny.

Sometimes Brigid would stop in a town for a while, seeking work and a soft bed. She'd stay just long enough to replace worn shoes with new, then pack her suitcase and be off again. As Brigid walked, her vista changed: from coastal dunes to scrubby plains, hilly terrain to rocky outcrops, and finally red sand and spinifex. With that little black-and-white bird as companion.

Just when Brigid felt she could walk no further, the bird stopped where desert stretched out to kiss the ocean. There sat a small town, nestled behind red dunes. At a rusted road sign, on the edge of town, Brigid sat down to catch her breath.

'Where'd you come from?'

Startled, Brigid looked up and saw her reflection in a stranger's hazel eyes.

'Did you come out from the desert, all on your own?'

Brigid turned around, looking for the bird. It had disappeared. 'I walked here from down south. I mostly followed the coast.'

The man extended a hand and helped her up. He gave her the warmest of smiles, so inviting that Brigid thought perhaps she really should still be sitting down.

He shifted his gaze to the west, and with a slight up-nod of his head remarked, 'Did you know there's an ancient sea out there, in a faraway desert? I hear it sometimes, on still nights. It calls for me. Know what I mean?'

Brigid reflected on her long days of walking, with just a little bird for company. On the road she'd heard many types of sounds, including some that frightened her in the dark. She'd never heard the sound of waves in the desert. She'd never even heard of the possibility of interior seas. Not until today, when she'd chanced across this spot, where red desert met blue sea, where a man with the warmest of eyes and strange notions on his tongue was waiting for her.

The young man turned back towards her. 'I'm Danny, by the way. You look like you could do with a cold drink, a warm meal, and a comfy place to rest your weary self. Come on.'

So she went with him. She ate, and she rested. She even stayed the night. Then she stayed another day, and another night, and then another day. Days soon turned into a week. And that week turned into a month, and then another month. Until she called that place home. And he called her *My Birdie.*

***

They were happy for a while. Some might even dare to say they were blissfully content. Until that moment Brigid expressed something carelessly. Despite the look of pain in Danny's eyes, she insisted no offence was intended. It was of no significance. Danny felt it was of great importance. At that moment, a crack appeared. Neither of them knew how to make things right again. They did know how to make things worse. Before either of them could whisper those two words that make wrong things right again – *I'm sorry* – slammed doors and regretted words had filled the space between them.

One morning Danny announced his plans. He was leaving to find that ancient sea. He told Brigid he needed to take some time out, to cool down. To reflect on whether he should or could be with her, now that he was conscious of her views that had sparked the conflict between them. And he had no way of telling if he and she were wrong-skin. This had been worrying him. Danny knew they couldn't properly be together until he knew for sure who his mob were. He still loved her, and wanted to be with her. If she was prepared to talk things out, instead of repeating that meaningless tale of potatoes.

For now, all of that would have to wait, because he'd been offered a few months' work, moving cattle along well-trodden stock routes into the interior. He believed this was his chance to find the inland sea that called to him. As Danny packed, he kept glancing over at Brigid expectantly. She stayed silent. Grim of mouth, he picked up his swag. As Danny walked out the door, whispers of forever-and-evers followed him, drifting away on the wind.

***

Brigid heard word of Danny's travels from his friends. He'd finished the droving job, and was now searching. She was told that he'd headed in an easterly direction, towards the heart country, apparently aiming for the spot where he suspected a sea lay under hot red sands. Reassured that he was safe, Brigid wasn't sure if she wanted him to return just yet. She had her own thinking to do, some of which involved piecing together half-forgotten tales of potatoes and apple seeds. And matching those with older, forgotten stories, when she'd lived with her mother even further up the coast. She'd once overheard her mother and stepfather talking of those years. When Brigid had lived with a different father, one she did not remember. She wondered: *Was he a potato, or an apple?*

Three months after Danny left, Brigid began to feel unwell. At first she thought it was regrets churning her stomach, making her feel sick. Then she realised what was really happening: she had an ocean inside her, with a little boat riding the waves. Brigid couldn't wait to share the news with her wayward beau. She began to wish for his return, prepared to tell him that she was wrong, not him. Each day she sat on the wide sea-view verandah of the home they'd once shared, waiting for him to come whistling out of the desert. Days soon became weeks, and weeks became months. Still he did not return.

And then came the worry-thoughts. No one had heard from Danny for quite a while. No letters, not even a single word had been passed along the road. Brigid imagined all sorts of things: he was hurt, lost, incarcerated, or had simply stopped loving her. No one could console her. She turned her back on everyone and everything.

Until a little white-and-black bird turned up at her bedroom window. Convinced this was her bird, come back to lead her to Danny once more, Brigid immediately packed her battered suitcase. In her haste, she'd forgotten what Granny had told her. Brigid hadn't even taken a good look at that bird. If she had, she would have seen this was one of those no-good birds her grandmother had warned her about.

With no one to hug farewell this time, Brigid left with just her suitcase and that turbulent ocean-within. On this journey, she soon found out the walking was harder and sleeping outside was most uncomfortable. During the day, she carried that watery weight, and at night tumultuous waves gave her no peace. Still she walked, following a little whiteand-black bird.

It didn't take too much longer for Brigid to realise this was not her bird. She noticed it was moulting. A black feather here, a black feather there. That bird was becoming more and more white. Then Brigid surmised that it was a selfish little bird. It didn't even try to slow its pace for her. And Brigid was moving slower and slower. As each day passed, that bird travelled faster and faster, until it was further and further ahead. Brigid had to strain to hear its song in the distance. Until, one morning, she woke to the sounds of silence. That bird had left her.

***

Brigid scanned unfamiliar terrain, trying to recall how far away the last town was. She didn't even know in which direction it lay. In the distance, she saw a shimmering. It was like that flash of light when sun hits metal. With renewed hope, she rushed forwards, stumbling over small rocks, kicking up red dirt, disturbing small creatures hidden in low-lying vegetation. Finally, standing on top of a small sandy hill, she saw what had caught her attention.

A large lake stretched out before her. *Could it be? Might it be?* Perhaps it was. She rushed forward, stumbling towards the waters' edge. Bending with much difficulty, she scooped up sun-warmed water from the shallow lake. Raising a hand to her parched lips, she took a sip. And spat it right back out again. It was salty! *Was this the inland sea that Danny had been seeking? More importantly – was he here?*

Brigid stood and, using a hand to shield her eyes from the blazing sun, peered into the distance, to the other side of the lake. Brigid saw nothing. Only red sand and this shallow water. She knew then it was just a lake, not the inland sea Danny had spoken of so many times. It was just a salty lake of disappointment.

Brigid dropped next to the suitcase she'd flung in the dirt. Tears she'd been holding back could no longer be contained. For the rest of that day, and into the night, she sat beside the lake and wept. The morning found her still weeping. She cried until her tears became a small salty rivulet that drenched the sun-hardened ground. Some of those tears sought out that lake, merging with the salty water. And some of those tears kept on flowing, becoming a stream, then a river. This river of tears snaked its way towards the south-west, leaving the desert behind. Much much later, it flowed past the wooden gate of an empty cottage nestled in an apple orchard. Unnoticed, it went past the house next door. Inside, a mother, father and three almost-men were seated for dinner. Finally, that tributary of tears found its way to the sea. Once there, Brigid's salty tears mingled with a much older brine.

*

Meanwhile, back in a desert far far away, Brigid had dried her face with the hem of her dress. Too busy crying, she hadn't noticed the occasional ripple on the lake. She hadn't noticed ancient eyes watching her from that salty lake. She'd not heard long, sharp fingernails scratching and scratching, in anticipation, on the sides of an underwater cave. Something with an ancient hunger, waiting for the right moment to make its move. She'd not heard anything at all, until the wind picked up. That zephyr quickly became a squall, pushing Brigid, forcing her to leave the lake. Walking away, Brigid remained blissfully unaware of the frustrated wails of the insatiable old one that lurked within those waters.

Feeling lighter from the release of tears, Brigid walked with determination. And even when that resolve wavered, she kept on walking. Until, a few days later, as the sun set behind her, she came to a place of snaking waters. Brigid couldn't see if it was a series of thin interconnected lakes or part of a river. What she could see reminded her of snakes. At a relatively stone-free point in between the two largest serpentine bodies of water, Brigid set up camp.

She made a comforting fire and then, realising she'd run out of food, lay down to sleep. As she gazed up at the cloudless night sky, Brigid marvelled at how bright the stars were. Letting her mind wander, she spied two starry snakes, one smaller than the other. Separated by the Milky Way, these celestial beings reminded Brigid of her quest to find Danny. She also thought of her misspoken words and his dreams of an ancient ocean that had separated them. Nestled between water-snakes, with astral-snakes above her, Brigid fell into a deep sleep. And dreamt of ethereal serpents – of course.

Out in the desert, the line between now and forever is thinner in some places. Much care is taken at such places, so as not to cause offence to the old ones. Unless one is unaware of their existence, as Brigid clearly was. She could not have known any better, having been brought up with tales of dirt-encrusted potatoes and fruit that fell from apple trees. Thankfully, no wind picked up. No prickles on the back of the neck were felt. Nor the sounds of feathered feet on dirt. In this instance, her trespassing was forgiven. Brigid slept peacefully.

She woke sometime before dawn, when the crack between worlds was still slightly ajar. From between her fluttering eyelids, Brigid thought she spied a large slithering mass emerging from the nearby water. She suddenly felt cold. She attempted to enliven the campfire, but even the embers had gone out. So she curled up into a ball, and shut her eyes again.

*

Brigid awoke to warmth. Opening her eyes, she saw flames coming from a campfire that had been stone-cold only a few hours ago. Next to this fire, steam rose from a flat rock. Moving closer, she noticed that whatever sat on the rock had a most appealing smell, and her tummy rumbled in agreement. She lifted a small portion and, taking a bite, guessed that it had once been a bird of some type. A large one, considering the size. She thought perhaps it was a bush turkey, now cooked to perfection. Next to the charcoaled meat was a smaller pile. Whatever it used to be, it was now shrivelled, like tiny raisins. Brigid tentatively bit into one. It tasted a little like sundried tomato, but peppery. She sat by the fire and devoured these offerings, too famished to wonder where they'd come from.

Wiping hands on her dress, she took note of her surroundings. She gazed over the twin lakes she'd seen the previous evening. The morning sun was beginning to warm the cold earth on which she sat. A few clouds were racing across the skies, southbound. Behind her was a low ridge of red rock. She'd not noticed it the night before but was grateful for how well it blocked out the wind as she sat by the fire. With her tummy full, and a fire to warm her, she felt a bit sleepy. Brigid reluctantly stood up. Now was not the time for sleeping. She needed to pack up camp, ready to head off again. *Where to?* It all suddenly felt pointless.

Any chance of finding Danny was slim; and her expanding belly was making travel more and more difficult. Even though the days were warm, the nights were cold. In the evenings, increasingly, there were heavy rains. Brigid knew she was moving further and further away from the coast, and away from people. She couldn't even remember the last time she'd spoken to a real person, instead of imaginary conversations she had with people who'd once been in her life. Brigid wondered if she should turn back. Return to the house she'd shared with Danny, where she'd last seen him. Or perhaps it was time to go home, to her family. Moving further inland would just be foolish. Regardless of this morning's mysterious feast, Brigid knew this terrain would not sustain her for long. *And when her waters broke, what then?*

Unbeknown to her, Brigid was camped in a place that sat comfortably between the here, now and perhaps. Even if she had no idea what to do next, others had a firm vision. And, it would appear, a plan to move her forwards.

*

A short while later, Brigid found herself following an ancient serpent in a southerly direction, almost in the direction she'd just come. And then it changed course. Eastward, further into the desert. Sometimes that serpent was an undulating rocky outcrop. Other times it was dunes of burnt-red dirt. Once it took on the appearance of a narrow lake. Even when Brigid couldn't see it, she knew it was still there, beside her. They travelled together for days. On rocky ground, up and over red dunes, and along dry riverbeds. And every night that gigantic serpent would curl around Brigid as she slept, keeping her warm. Once she woke in the night to find it missing. She looked to the skies, at a river of vivid stars encircling above, and watched as Hydrus courted Hydra. Then she fell blissfully asleep again. In the morning, she woke to the familiar sound of the serpent's rhythmic breath nearby.

As the days passed, Brigid came to feel as if she might soon be drowned by that ever more tumultuous ocean-within. She walked laboriously, stopping often to take a breath. One chilly evening, just when Brigid felt as if she could walk no more, she saw a small cluster of haphazard buildings in the distance. That night, as Brigid curled up to sleep with her travelling companions – the ancient serpent encircling her and the tiny passenger of the ocean-within – she felt a sense of contentment. Brigid knew the time to release that ocean was approaching, and she felt ready. When she woke up the next morning, the ground was particularly cold. And the serpent was gone.

Picking up her suitcase, she walked towards the signs of people she'd seen the day before. As she approached the first building, she became aware of a small crowd looking in her direction. It was not her they were looking at, mouths agape. Brigid turned around just as a gigantic grey sky-mushroom began to disperse on the far western horizon. As she turned back to the people, she realised they'd noticed her. Brigid opened her mouth to shout hello, or some such words to make her arrival less awkward. After many months of not speaking, all she could manage was a series of squawks. With a shrug, she walked towards people.

THREE

Brigid's sudden appearance, and that mysterious cloud, were not quite as big a surprise as her passengers' arrival. As soon as she'd walked into that small outpost, the ocean she'd carried from the coast, across the desert, had gushed onto terracottahued ground. Before Brigid could catch her breath, young feet came forward, guiding her to old hands. And just in time, for those hands skilfully caught the tiny boats that had long sailed on the ocean-within. There was not one boat, but two. Each with its own tiny passenger. Two beating hearts. Two strong wails.

'Well, just look at these sweet bubbas!' exclaimed the old woman.

*

This woman had instantly recognised Brigid, and knew her as kin. As for those passengers, the old woman could already see herself in one of the twins; they had the same nose. Both Brigid and the other baby reminded her of Edward, her only child. It had been many years since Edward had died, leaving behind his woman and a baby daughter, but a mother never forgets the soft curves of a child's face. Edward's partner had lived with the family for a while. She'd given birth right here, on the same spot this woman's waters had just dampened. Despite years having passed by, the old woman knew in her heart that this young woman was her son's daughter. And these babies were her great-grandchildren. This pleased her, even if she still carried the pain of loss. Those missing years of watching Brigid grow up to be this strong woman who stood before her. The stolen years of being with Edward, her son. There would be time to fill in the gaps later. Right now, the old woman knew the new mother needed rest. A bed was promptly made, and Brigid and the babies were soon asleep.

Once they had been left to rest for a day and a night, the old woman entered the room. She silently picked up one of the infants, and walked outside again. Brigid panicked. Hurriedly picking up the other baby, she chased after the woman. The old woman walked away from the small community. Confused, Brigid followed her into the desert. For an elderly woman, she walked briskly, and Brigid struggled to keep up. After a while the woman bent at the waist, baby held tightly to her chest, and entered a cluster of low shrubs. Brigid followed, and on the other side saw women gathered around a fire. The old woman placed the baby into a freshly dug indentation in the warmed earth. She turned towards Brigid and indicated that she should do the same with the other twin. Brigid hesitated at first, until she heard the familiar breath of an ancient serpent. Reassured, she placed her daughter in that shallow hole, next to her other daughter. Brigid thought the twins had briefly smiled, but knew it could just as well have been wind.

Brigid smelt burning leaves and noticed that heavy grey smoke was filling this space behind the line of shrubs. She turned, and saw the old woman place green branches on the small fire. As the leaves caught fire, more smoke rose. Brigid started coughing, and tightly squeezed her eyes to shut out the smoke. When she opened them again, the woman was beckoning her. Brigid could not understand her words, or what she wanted.

'Have you forgotten language?' asked the old woman, in words more familiar to Brigid.

Brigid had no idea what she meant. *Language?* There was only one language she knew of.

The woman saw her confusion, and spat whatever she'd been chewing onto the ground. 'Did she teach you nothing? Not even one word? Never mind, there will be time for learning. In the meantime, come here. You need cleansing. I don't know where you've been or what you've done, but there's something not quite right about you. Come now. And then we smoke the bubbas.'

*

A few days later, with help from the old woman, the babies were named. She insisted that one be named for her. So one twin was gifted the same name as her grandfather's mother: Victoria. Although the old woman was more often known as Vic. Brigid didn't protest; that name was as good as any other. The smallest twin was named Margaret, after Brigid's mother. As that was much too big a name for a sparrow-of-a-girl, Brigid decided to call her Maggie for now. She had plenty of time to grow into her proper name.

Brigid and her twins were quickly accepted into the community in the middle of the desert. After all, they were family. Nana Vic showed her how to care for the babes, and was always close at hand to take them so the young mum could rest. Nana Vic sang to the twins in language. Brigid didn't know what the words meant, although some of the songs were somewhat familiar. Her nana told her that she had sung those same songs to her as a bub, before Brigid's parents had gone away. Brigid didn't remember her father at all, but she thought perhaps she remembered the sound of her nana's voice.

Just as the wet season settled in, Brigid was finally reunited with her grandfather Albert. The similarities between Albert and Brigid were uncanny. He'd been away in the city, on land rights business, and had hurried back when news of his granddaughter and her babies had reached him. The sight of them had instantly made the old man's heart beat with hope once more. Albert had been heavy of heart for too many years. He still missed his son and even now could not fathom why Edward had enlisted to fight under the oppressors' ensign. He did not understand the urge to participate in a war on foreign soil when the battle for their own Country had not yet been won. They'd parted on bad terms.

Edward's leaving, and lack of letters home, had hurt Albert deeply. After a while, though, he felt a sense of pride in what his son was doing. He then asked a visiting pastor to help him write a letter to Edward. In it, Albert told his son how wrong he'd been to criticise his choices. And how proud he was of the man Edward had grown to be. Not long after, news of his son finally reached him. A few words on a piece of paper officially informed him that Edward was gone. *'Deeply regret ... Stop. Credit to the nation ... Stop. Stop. Stop.'* That pain deepened more when the army would not provide any assistance to bring Edward's body home, to kin and Country. Albert feared his son's spirit would never be able to find rest on foreign soil. When the old man had heard this latest news, of Brigid and the twins' arrival home to Country, he'd rushed back. The moment he'd laid eyes on his granddaughter, good memories of his son flooded back. And there was no doubting whose child Brigid was.

*

The ripples of interest around the twins' and Brigid's arrival soon dispersed. The trio fitted easily into the gap Edward had left. Once Brigid had rested from the birth, and those months of walking, Vic clucked over the babies while Albert set to the task of showing Brigid her ancestral lands. The old man had smiled proudly when he'd heard how far Brigid had walked, alone and without any bush training. He recognised that this grannie, although stubborn, had a unique power, and he was keen to help her develop more skills. To his delight, Brigid appeared to be an avid learner.

Hunting and food collecting took up a fair bit of everyone's time. Sometimes Brigid would go out with just her grandfather, other times Nana Vic would join them. Unlike some of the other women, Nana Vic was a confident shooter. Whenever a roo, emu or bush turkey was sighted, Albert and Vic would take turns with the rifle. They hardly ever missed. If Brigid was hunting with just her grandfather, he would let her use his rifle. She rarely missed the target either.

Sometimes Albert would pick up his spear and boomerang, call his dogs, and go out hunting with the men. Brigid soon learnt not to ask to accompany them. There are just certain ways that things are done. When the men and boys were out hunting, Brigid would often leave the twins with one of her sister-cousins and go gathering with Nana Vic and other women. She was shown how to find the fattest witchetty grubs, and soon eagerly searched for them. Brigid watched as the women set fire to spinifex, and then prised open small holes in the ground with wooden sticks and crowbars. Digging deep, they would pull out goannas and blue-tongues that had sought safety from the fires. Brigid was shown which plants were edible, which ones would make her sick, and which were used for medicine. She feasted on quandong, bush currants, rock figs, pig melons and bush oranges. She dug for yams, lily bulbs and bush potatoes. And for a taste of sweetness, she sipped nectar straight from the plant, chewed on sap lolly, or bit into honey ants.

A more tedious task was collecting the seeds that would be ground into flour. Some of these seeds were dispersed on the walk home, to ensure crops for later. Using a large flat rock as a mortar and a rounded rock as a pestle, the women would grind these minuscule seeds. After a long time of grinding, water would be added to the seed-flour, so the women could knead the mix before putting it straight into the coals. The resulting damper was best eaten warm and smeared with jam.

The jam came from a nearby outpost. Women and children would walk there every couple of weeks, to collect rations of jam, white flour, tea leaves and tobacco. The outsiders who distributed these foreign staples would carefully observe the children, recording in their logbooks whenever they noticed a new baby, asking the occasional verifying question: 'Is the father a whitefella?' Brigid had only been to the outpost once, when Nana Vic had been too sick to go but was craving some sweet jam. Her nana had insisted the twins be left behind, warning Brigid that it was unsafe for them to be seen by those white men with their sharp eyes and sharper pencils. Although puzzled, Brigid did as she was told.

*

One day, on the way to the termite mounds, where pythons and lizards often hid, Nana Vic suddenly veered to the right. After a while, they reached a cluster of tall rocks. When they got closer to the rocks, Nana Vic put out her arm to stop Brigid.

'Wait here,' she ordered, before going on alone.

She heard her nana sing in language. A few moments later, she returned.

'Come. I've told them who you are.'

Not understanding at all, Brigid followed until they came to a rock pool at the feet of the tall rocks. Next to the pool was a tree. Brigid recognised its type, having been taught about it before. It was a bloodwood tree. The strange-looking fruit hanging from it were sometimes called apples, other times bush coconut. To Brigid they didn't resemble either; she thought they were quite ugly. She didn't mind the taste of the grub that lived inside these cocoons. This not-really-a-fruit was so very different from her granny's apples. Everything here was different from Brigid's childhood memories. Even so, she felt a sense of tranquillity in this particular spot, beside the rock pool, and an odd sense of familiarity.

'You come from here. This is your place,' remarked Nana Vic, looking closely at her granddaughter.

Brigid turned to her nana, frowning. Was this to be another one of Nana's strange tales, she wondered.

'Here, by this tree, is where you were born. You belong to this Country.'

Brigid turned her back to the bloodwood tree. 'My mother's family has apple trees. A whole orchard of them. Real ones. My granny brought cuttings from across the ocean when she was young, and planted them. When I was little, I liked to climb the trees. And sit up there, eating an apple as I watched the sun move across the sky.'

Nana Vic made a 'harrumph' sound, and turned on her heels. 'Those trees aren't your place. This is.'

***

Sitting out the front of their small fibro house, Albert heard his wife open the door and walk towards him. The old man was engrossed in reattaching a spearhead to a long narrow piece of wood that held the memory of his hands. He could sense that Vic had something to say.

'Those girls are growing so quickly,' she remarked.

Albert looked towards the twins playing on a blanket at their mother's feet, as Brigid hung washing on the line.

With a sigh, Vic said, 'She won't listen. Have you noticed?'

He nodded, returning to repairing his spear. He had noticed. And it worried him. Brigid was a keen hunter, asking lots of good questions. She was also very interested in navigational skills. How to find her way using landforms, or the sun and stars. She had an excellent sense of direction. And she was competent at finding drinkable water. Brigid soaked in all that learning but ignored even more. She seemed to have no interest at all in language. And she would change the subject or just wander off if anyone started to talk about lore, law, songlines or anything related to cultural knowledge. She wasn't even interested in stories of her father.

Albert replied, 'We can't force her to listen. Perhaps once she's learnt all the things she's so keen to know, then she'll be more receptive to the rest.'

'I'm not sure she ever will be. That one is on a mission, all right. It's that fella, the girls' father. All she wants is to learn what she needs to keep on walking, keep on looking. She's not going to be here for too much longer.'

'Brigid is stubborn. Remember what her father was like at that age? I reckon they both get that from you, old woman,' Albert chuckled.

Vic flicked a tea towel at his head, hitting him lightly before going back inside. As the door shut, Albert heard her laugh.

***

Because her granddaughter wouldn't listen, Nana Vic turned her attention to her great-granddaughters. She believed that Brigid had been yearning to leave for some time. Her granddaughter would have left sooner, if not for Maggie. Unlike Victoria who, like a thin-legged colt, had been walking at an uncannily early age, Maggie took her time learning to stand on her own two legs. This gave Nana Vic more time to infuse her sweet bubbas with the fragrance of essential stories.

When bathing them, she'd tell them stories of animals and plants. Each had its own story, of its origin and purpose. As Maggie and Victoria lay down to sleep, the old lady would whisper tales of celestial serpents and seven starry-sisters. She would fill their ears with maps, instructions and long-held lore. If they misbehaved, Nana Vic would tell them about sharptoothed beings that lived in watery caves, and other ancient beings that craved tasty children. The babes' eyes widened, soaking it all in before asking for more.

Knowing that time was against her, Nana Vic took every chance she could to top up Brigid's survival skills. To add to what Albert had shown her. She taught her the signs of bad health, and the causes. Her granddaughter refused to believe there were places where spirits lurked, ones that could cause someone to become ill. She thought being fearful of whistling in the dark was just foolish nonsense. The old woman sighed. Instead, she showed her how to find the right leaves for the smoking that cleansed a person. She told her about dryness and death. She spoke of how to stay healthy, how to be safe, how to care for the young ones proper way. She showed Brigid how to harvest the good plants, the ones used for medicine. Nana Vic showed her all this, and more. Most of it Brigid took in. Except if Nana Vic tried to teach her language or lore. Then Brigid would ignore her. Occasionally, the young woman would still speak of her granny, and retell that most peculiar tale of dirt-encrusted potatoes.

***

Brigid and her daughters stayed through the wet season. And then through months of dust. They stayed for a few cycles of rain and dust. Until one day, as water soaked into the desert and bright flowers bloomed overnight, Brigid felt a warm wind sweep through the community. As that gust flew out over the red landscape, she once more felt that old restlessness for her lost beau. The next time a truck drove into the community, she'd already packed her worn suitcase. And another that had been given to her, for the twins clothes, along with a cloth bag for cooking utensils.

Her grandparents knew it was pointless trying to persuade her to stay. They were well aware of their granddaughter's stubborn streak, inherited from their son. Albert helped Brigid carry the suitcases and placed them in the back of the truck. Nana Vic's favourite digging stick poked out from the cloth bag and Albert pushed it back in. The driver started up the truck, warming the motor before the long drive.

'Wait,' called Albert as he scuttled back inside the house.

When he returned, he was carrying his rifle. He handed it to Brigid, who seemed confused.

Realising what her grandfather's intentions were, she stated,

'No. It's yours.'

'Those young ones will need good tucker to help them grow strong. Digging for small animals and roots is not going to fill them up. You're a good hunter. I know you'll use this well.'

Brigid nodded and took the gun. While Grandfather Albert patted Brigid's shoulder, her grandmother fussed one more time over Maggie and Victoria. The old couple knew they'd never see them again. Brigid gave Nana Vic a quick hug, before climbing into the truck's cabin with her two sleepy daughters. She did not look back as the truck drove out of the small community in the desert.

FOUR

As the last plutonium-loaded cloud settled over the red sands in the south-west, many footsteps away three strangers emerged from a sister-desert, seeking rest from a road now seldom travelled. Even though they had entered the town cloaked in dawn's light, news of their arrival had spread before the last rooster finished crowing. This flurry of curiosity was not because it was unusual on the gibber plains for people to suddenly emerge from out of nowhere. Others had arrived in such a manner. Nor was it unusual to see strangers, even though this town was in the middle of nowhere. The train, in passing, often spewed out adventurers, government officials, wayfarers, those of a missionary bent, and other lost souls. And it was not the shock of seeing a young woman travelling without the company of a man. Independent women were a familiar sight in this terrain. No, the gossip that raced at the speed of wildfire had been fuelled by the peculiar guise of the two girls who walked alongside the woman. For, despite the century showing signs of becoming more progressive in its middle age, it was still unheard of for one of her kind (and this woman's bloodline was quite unmistakeable) to be travelling unaccompanied with a white girl.

And such a pretty girl, a precious rose – many would add in their recounting of the tale. Such a fine little lady, despite marks of a long trek clinging to her clothes – others would remark to their neighbours later that day. Such flawless, milky skin – some sighed, behind sun-withered hands. And what eyes, like precious opals – they all pronounced. Even though her eyes were more akin to the less precious but equally enchanting malachite.

Once they could tear their attention from this child, they took in the other girl. Reluctantly at first. They openly appraised this child, and not with kindness in their eyes or tolerance in their hearts. This other one, wearing the trials of the road too well, brazenly strode into town; or so they thought. With the steadied gaze of a sun-browned cameleer from days long gone, this girl kept her eyes focused on the road, ignoring the rising disapproval. Clearly, she hasn't been taught her place in the world – some muttered. She needs to be knocked down a peg or two – grumbled others. Such arrogance for one so young, and how dare one of them think highly of themselves – verbalised a few more. It was wrong to have granted those people the right to vote, they'll ruin this country, mark my words – others predicted. The girl raised her head high, and the onlookers noticed her eyes for the first time. Recoiling from those eyes of the bluest of blues, the townsfolk fell silent.

*

Meanwhile, their comments had drifted down the street, carried on the wind. Moving towards the town's edge, they floated gently over an unseen boundary, before fluttering around a gathering of makeshift homes. Inside, the men, doing their best to catch a few more moments of rest before they had to start another day's work on the nearby railway tracks, tried to shoo the words away with the flick of a hand. Beside the campfire, women put down freshly baked damper and waved fistfuls of branches at the nonsensical declarations, sweeping the air until those unwanted opinions were encouraged to move on. As smiles of a quick victory began to brighten suntoughened faces, they became aware of a pungent smell in the air. One by one the dwellers at the edge of town gathered outside, trying to locate the source. It smelt a bit like that whiff of smoke that rode the wind before an approaching wildfire, but they could not see any smoke, near or far.

An old man caught the eye of another, and then another, and another. Soon they were walking away from the town with their families, carrying only the essentials. They hadn't needed a second whiff, for they had smelt this odour many times before. Younger kin, refusing to follow, walked closer to the edge of town, allowing curiosity to be their guide.

Standing unseen, in the shadows cast by the rising sun, they saw the town-dwellers staring at a trio of travellers. The fringe-dwellers were also taken aback by what they saw, even if their comments were vastly different from those words that had floated on the air. For rather than seeing what was different, they had immediately noticed similarities.

Eventually, everyone began to see, even the previously aghast townsfolk. It's something in the bone structure, some thought; such high cheekbones. No, it's the way they both move, the way they hold themselves; they have a certain aura. They could see that those girls had shared many secrets, for they were obviously fluent in that clandestine language known only by twins. All in all, these young strangers were the mirror images of polar opposites.

Never before had the townsfolk seen such mismatched non-identical twins: one white and the other brown. Only the fringe-dwellers could see the truth of the matter, as it was so obvious that both these girls were black.

While all this was unfolding, the woman kept on walking, both oblivious and seemingly accustomed to the astonished stares and whispers of strangers. As she walked down the main street, such as it was, the stranger took no notice of fingers clasping at almost-closed curtains; nor did she acknowledge the slack-jawed affliction that her progeny left in their wake. Steadfastly she walked up to the verandah of the only retailer in town, such as it was, dropped the suitcases she'd been carrying and shook the red dirt from her skirt. Leaving the uncanny twins sitting on a pile of road-worn cases, she walked into Adamson's General Store with her head held high enough for trouble to find her.

A short time later, daughters by her side, she turned a rusty key in a dusty lock, entered a pre-loved wooden hut, and set to turning it into a home. Such as it was.

***

Brigid had been quite surprised at how easy it was to enrol both her daughters in the little tin-shed school that doubled as a church on Sundays. When she had enquired, Pastor Thomas outlined his strongly held view that all God's children required a basic education, despite some peoples' belief in a correlation between melanin rating and intelligence. With his wife's support, the pastor also believed in providing a strong dose of preaching mixed in with the rudimentary reading, writing and arithmetic. Even after this conversation, Brigid had still been hesitant to enrol the girls, fearing that she could not protect them if they were out of sight, but Victoria and Maggie had both insisted. They pleaded, and reasoned, until their mother gave in. *They are five-year-olds, not toddlers,* she remembered. *No wonder they're yearning to be with other children. Will they both find friends, or tormentors?* Brigid had strong memories of being teased as a child and worried that Victoria could experience similar bullying. If not worse. Tales of dirt-encrusted potatoes had not helped Brigid as a child. She acknowledged to herself that at least her granny had tried, whereas her mother hadn't even noticed she did not fit in at school.

The morning of the twins' first day at school was one of such excitement that Brigid had difficulties brushing their wayward hair. It was a good thing the twins had no shoes, their last pairs having finally fallen apart from months of walking, because Brigid would never have been able to keep them still long enough to tie their laces. Their dresses had become slightly too short and had seen better days, but Brigid made them oddly attractive with patches of mismatched fabric all over. The girls did not seem to mind that they lacked new shoes and pretty dresses, and for that Brigid was grateful. Once the girls were ready, Brigid walked with them to school and entrusted them to the care of the pastor and his wife. And then Brigid walked down the road to her new job as a shop assistant.

She was grateful that Mr Adamson had offered food and shelter for her family in exchange for a few hours' work each day. Mrs Adamson didn't appear to be quite as generous in nature; if she was around, Brigid would be given laborious tasks that even many men would have baulked at. She did not give Mrs Adamson the satisfaction of seeing her fail because, after all those years on the road, Brigid knew she was capable of far more. And she was not going anywhere. Not until she'd earned enough money to buy new shoes for her travel-weary family.

***

The door slammed once, twice, signalling the twins were home from school. An inviting smell wove its way towards them. Victoria and Maggie ran to the kitchen, where their mother was making bully beef. Maggie pulled at her mother's apron, waving a small piece of paper in her other hand, while Victoria stood back, wearing an apprehensive expression.

'Mumma, it's an invitation. We've been invited,' squealed Maggie.

Brigid reclaimed her apron and wiped her hands. She took the paper that Maggie was offering up and read it slowly before handing it back.

With a frown, she asked, 'Is Susie the red-haired girl who gave you the kitten?'

Both daughters nodded, one with more enthusiasm than the other. Brigid's frown deepened, for within this simple invitation to celebrate a birthday she could sense trouble.

Maggie pleaded, 'Can we go? Please. There'll be cake. And Susie's cat has had more kitties.'

Brigid hesitated for a few moments, unable to shift her feeling of uneasiness. Then, seeing Maggie smile as she re-read the invitation, Brigid nodded.

'Our first ever party,' Maggie said as she skipped around the kitchen. 'Isn't this wonderfully exciting, Victoria.'

Her sister was not at all excited, for she had seen the worry on their mother's face. Victoria also sensed trouble's winged approach, and wondered if they'd soon be packing again.

'I don't want to go. Parties are boring.'

Brigid raised her eyebrows, wondering if Victoria had meant what she said. Victoria held her mother's gaze with all the confidence she could muster. Not for the first time, Brigid pondered how different the twins were from each other. Not just different in looks and personality, but in how much they had changed since planting roots in this town. The girls had coped with the traveller life in very different ways, and likewise with their now-sedentary lifestyle. Before she'd started school, Maggie had followed her mother and sister unquestioningly, but she'd never been able to disguise her many fears – always wondering what danger lay beyond the campfire, imagining frightening sources for the small sounds she heard in the dark. Maggie's apprehension had made her clingy, never far from her mother's side. Now she was outgoing and talkative, always smiling. Maggie had discovered what it felt like to have friends. Unlike Victoria, she was popular and was often at her friends' homes after school. And some locals had even warmed to her, granting Maggie a smile as she skipped to school each morning. Small-town life suited Maggie.

Brigid knew that Victoria was not as content with standing still. She was always mentioning how much she missed travelling. Brigid often joked that Victoria had inherited the family trait of wanderlust. And she was always eager to learn about nature. Victoria seemed to instinctively know how to read landscapes, like her great-grandfather Albert. Where to find food and water, as her mother had shown her, who herself had learnt from Nana Vic. Unlike her sister, Victoria knew that not all was as it seemed in this nowhere town. While Maggie made friends at school and basked in the adoration of townsfolk, Victoria heard what wasn't being vocalised. She saw it in the eyes of Mrs Thomas, her teacher. And those upturned noses of the old ladies who passed her in the street spoke a thousand words, none of them encouraging. Victoria saw it even in the silent gruffness of the men gathered on the pub verandah.

Brigid had also observed the townsfolk's behaviour. And even though she'd never spoken to Victoria about these microaggressions, she knew what her daughter was going through. She had known the pain of not being accepted. She knew what it felt like to be constantly judged for the colour of one's skin. Brigid noted a defiant flash in Victoria's eyes, the proud way she carried herself, and recognised that this was the result of constantly feeling a need to defend herself. As Victoria already had, but was unable to voice, Brigid felt a building heat coming off the town streets. These sons and daughters of settlers had noticed that times were changing, but that didn't mean they had to accept those changes. Out here, far from big cities, too many townsfolk clung to the not-quite-distant past. And they weren't too shy to use a colour chart to determine who their equals were. Brigid read the party invitation again and wondered if this town was ready for such an event. Even if all children were welcomed at the tin school, this type of associating outside the school gate was an entirely different matter. Brigid felt that Susie's mother was playing with fire, but it was not her family that would get burnt.

FIVE

On the day of Susie's birthday party, Maggie had woken before the first bird even thought of catching worms. Too excited to sleep, she wanted to try on her dress for the hundredth time. It was not a new dress but a dress made new. Brigid had bought it especially for the party from the church fair, along with a dress for Victoria and non-travelling shoes for both her girls. And then Brigid had stitched and embellished those simple dresses until they were party-worthy. Putting it on that morning, Maggie still thought it was the prettiest dress she had ever seen. She loved how the full skirt swished around her legs whenever she moved. Dancing around the house in the early morning light, she made enough noise to wake up her mother and sister. After breakfast Brigid did Maggie's hair, securing her ponytail with a pink ribbon she'd brought home from Adamson's store as a surprise. She then stood back and took in the sight of Maggie's joyful expression. Brigid was trying not to let her worry show. And worry she had.

All week, Brigid had felt that heat as it continued to rise from the town streets. She had seen tiny sparks as she swept the store. And, from behind tall shelves, unseen, Brigid had heard the townsfolk talk. Hate-filled words drifted towards Brigid, embracing her with a sticky heat. The words clung to her, still whispering in her ears hours later: it's not right ... this type of behaviour should not be allowed ... they're not like us ... it's been scientifically proven ... shouldn't have allowed them in the school ... they should remember their place ... someone needs to stop this nonsense.

A week after the party invitations had been distributed, the words had become so thick that Pastor Thomas felt it his duty to do something. So that Sunday morning, the day of the party, his sermon skipped around the problem, using lyrical parables of acceptance, hinting at the brotherhood of man but not offering any real directives. There may have been some nodding of heads during that convoluted speech. Not in response to the words but rather the type of nod people do as they drift off for a short nap. A few of the women appeared to be attentive, which encouraged the Pastor, but they were just counting in their heads how many potatoes they would need to peel for Sunday dinner. If Brigid had been at church, she'd have known exactly to what and to whom the Pastor was referring.

When everyone had left the church of rusting tin, they stood just beyond the gate. The agitated townsfolk resumed talking, unconsciously kicking up dust. Small huddles glanced in the direction of the outsider who had started this most recent tribulation. Susie's mother hadn't even tried to understand how things were done around here. Her red-haired, freckled daughter by her side, she behaved as if completely unaware of what she'd done. Inviting those children to a birthday party. Well, that would never do. The trouble-maker talked with the pastor and his wife, her gloveless hand gently resting on her daughter's head, as if she'd done nothing wrong. Poor little girl, some murmured, no one to teach her what is right and wrong. This is so typical of a newcomer, others observed, pleased for another chance to announce that this woman was not from around here. She was not one of them. It's a wonder that no one has set her straight, commented others, alluding to the fact that obviously the man of that house had been neglectful in his manly duties. The huddles slowly broke up as people wandered home to either put on the roast or put up their feet.

As the townsfolk walked away from church, dispersing along dirt-encrusted streets, the mumbling continued until it became just a low rumble. So low that only a few could hear it. In the hut on the edge of town, Brigid heard the rumbling, mumbling voices. As it was a Sunday, she easily guessed the sound was coming from the church. She wondered what had been said to have caused this much upset. Victoria also heard the town's discontent, and immediately knew its cause, as she'd heard similar rumblings at school that week.

*

Others heard it too, those who had held firm to their place on the fringe. The real locals, whose ancestors had been living off the land for many many generations before the arrival of these newcomers, had heard that rumble as it moved through the town.

They didn't need to hear some sermon to know what was what.

Before the sun had reached its midday peak, more had packed up camp. There was no doubt big trouble was coming. The flame that would never be extinguished had been refuelled by the townsfolk's ignorance over a child's birthday party. That flame's name was hate. Neither water nor sand can put that fire out, so they headed further into the desert, to wait for it to burn its way through town. They knew it would eventually die down to a more manageable ember. And then they would return, to pick up their discarded tools and resume work on the rail line. They could wait for as long as this fire took to burn through town. They were experts at waiting.

Just as during the previous exodus, some chose not to leave their hard-won place. They chose not to listen to their Elders or to see the signs. Instead, they thought of the few coins granted at the end of many backbreaking days, minus work clothing, boots and flour. Instead, they invested faith in recent hazy human rights that had been bestowed upon them after noise was raised by some do-good white people in a faraway city. Those who chose to stay in town shook their heads as more relatives left, thinking back to that recent moment, which had been declared historic, when they'd finally been allowed to cast their votes for a game of musical chairs. They weren't going to run any more. For they trusted the words of the city folk who'd driven shiny cars into the desert just to talk with them, bringing news of what they called a brand-new day: a time in which the practice of moving them off their Country and onto missions would be outlawed. And they had been urged to leave the memories of guns and heartache, land theft and headache, in the past. Desperate for change, they chose to believe a white-man myth and not the words of Elders. This time they were staying put. They had jobs. Even if they weren't paid as much as the other workers. This was their land. Even if they had no white-way rights to land. This was home. And their children had finally been invited to a party in town.

Those who walked away shook their heads, as they knew that the colonisers were not done with their tricks. There was no substantial change. No truth-telling. They'd simply changed the flavour of that sugary snake oil they kept peddling. Those who had seen this all before prophesied a new stream of putrid winds from those concrete cities built on the coasts. That wind was headed towards this nowhere town on the gibber plains, to blow on the existing embers of hate. They knew it was best to be far away, somewhere else, by the time that wind arrived.

Brigid, too, didn't need to be at church that day, listening to the sermon, to know what was being talked about in the streets afterwards. She had dropped a blackened pot in soapy dishwater, left the front door swinging in the wind, and walked towards the church. Looking further ahead, she noticed the departing people who were now dots in the desert.

Brigid felt a strong urge to follow them but knew she couldn't. Much as she had stood in silence against the disapproving looks the townsfolk had directed at her and the twins, she'd also sat in silence when they'd spoken nastily of those who lived on the periphery. Brigid had made no effort to form relationships with other targets of bigotry. And had declined invitations to visit the fringe camp on numerous occasions. Maggie and Victoria had not followed their mother's lead, and were often outside the town perimeter playing with friends. And both girls had more than once stepped in at school, fists raised, when a sunburnt child yelled hateful words at their peers. Instead of extending a hand in friendship, Brigid had chosen a place in the centre. A place devoid of convictions. A nowhere place that provided her with no supports. A place most fitting for a potato. And so, Brigid could neither follow nor lead. Like other times when feeling confronted or conflicted, she could still run.

When she saw the huddles of gossipers outside the church, Brigid returned to the hut intending to pack their cases. When she got home, and saw Maggie all dressed in pink and joyful smiles, Brigid paused. *Maybe I shouldn't uproot the girls once more.* Not when Maggie was so happy here. They could stay and see how things panned out. Perhaps it was just her imagination running wild. Brigid hadn't noticed Victoria's expression, for if she had their luggage would have been packed without any hesitation.

Victoria hadn't needed to walk through the town for confirmation. She'd smelt whiffs of smoke on the wind. Wildfire was on its way.

Despite these snippets of insight, at this moment, on this day, Brigid and Victoria tried to quieten the whispering warnings, and instead donned brave smiles for Maggie's sake. When the time finally arrived, Brigid escorted her daughters to the party. As they walked down the street, Maggie was oblivious to the deepening rumbles around them. Brigid heard them and frowned, clasping her daughters' hands more tightly. Victoria heard them too, and walked with a straightened back, chin held even higher than usual. This only increased the unrest, as townspeople saw it as a defiance that was not at all acceptable.

As the family walked to the party, they slowly became a manifestation of all that was bothering the uptight citizens of the town. It's just not right, some said. Why does that woman have that lovely little girl? Where is her real mother? Her white mother. And other thoughts arising on the lips of the many who had long puzzled over this. That can't be her child, surely. How shameful, raising those girls as if they were sisters, others voiced. Something needs to be done, before this gets worse, some said. One person knew just what to do, and scurried towards the police station.

*

At the party, all was not as it should be. Only a few of the invited guests had turned up. Susie, the birthday girl, didn't seem to mind. From across the road, busybodies saw her standing out the front of her house, happily surrounded by happy children. Children in all shades of black, with a redhaired girl in the middle. As Susie laughed with her guests, she did not see anything wrong with the company she kept. Her mother had raised her right. The tears that she fought to hide were for her other friends from school.

What a thing to have happened, such an outbreak of disease and deepest woes on the very day of her party. Fidgeting fathers had knocked on the door all morning. Measles, they had said. A sprained ankle. Her mother is not well, she needs some help today, said at least three fathers. A death in the family, down in the city, said others. While other children were simply not there, with no messenger provided. Well, none that Susie had heard from, for her mother wanted to protect her from what was being said. Her mother was still hurting from her husband's I-told-you-so, as he stormed off to the hotel, leaving his wife to clean up this latest mess. That said, the children who were there seemed to be having a good time.

Like all good times, however, this one would soon come to an end. While the children sang brightly by the light of candles on a cake, black wings were rushing towards the town. Brigid had already wondered whether she had made the right decision letting her children go. She knew she'd made the wrong choice the moment she heard the rumbling of vehicles approaching town. Without pausing to put on her shoes, she rushed outside and ran towards Susie's house. As Brigid ran, from the corner of her eye she noticed moving shadows. Figures walking between buildings unseen, creeping down the streets. Brigid moved faster, worrying that she'd be too late, that it would all be over by the time she got there. With those shadows ahead of her now, Brigid knew she was not the only one who'd heard a convoy approaching. Once they reached Susie's house, these parents politely declined the offer of a slice of cake and quickly grabbed their children's hands. When Brigid got to the front gate, they were already running towards the red plains.

Seeing her daughters, Brigid called out, 'Victoria, Maggie. Come on.'

Maggie didn't hear her, so Victoria grabbed her hand. 'We need to go. Mum is here.'

'No. Not yet. I want to cuddle the kitties some more,' wailed Maggie.

Victoria dragged her sister towards the gate, where their mother waited with worry on her face. In silence, Brigid led her girls towards their house, all the while listening keenly. She pulled the girls into a sliver of shadows cast by the bank. They hid in that narrow laneway, watching and listening. It was from that vantage point they saw the strangers arrive, and the sergeant's look of self-importance as he walked out of the police station to welcome the convoy. When the two sedans stopped, the dust fell from them, revealing glossy blackness. Arriving next was what appeared to be an ex-army truck. In dull grey paint, on the side of the truck was written: *Good Shepherd Aborigine Children's Mission.*

The doors of the cars opened, revealing three suit-clad men and one woman. Like a fish in a tree, she was out of place standing in the dusty street, wearing a floral-print dress, city shoes and white satin gloves. And from the truck emerged a tall, thin man wearing a tall black hat. He removed the hat and shook the dust from it before taking in his surrounds. Ravenhaired, with an elongated chin as sharp as a carrion-eater's beak, and small, dark eyes, he scanned the street. Searching.

Brigid pulled her girls back into the shadows, and whispered in their ears, 'Be still, be as quiet as a mouse.'

She shook her head at the imagery of little mice running from an elongated, sharp-taloned birdman. Then the air was pierced by shouts. Looking out to red dirt country, Brigid saw a small canvas-clad truck driving much too quickly, creating a cloud of dust. From within this red cloud came the shouting. Young voices, and old. The cloud dispersed, revealing two men alighting from the truck's cabin. One grabbed a child and threw them roughly into the back of the truck. One man stayed in the truck, engine running, as the two chased after the children. Bringing one after another, to throw into the truck. Small arms and legs flailed everywhere, holding on to the sides of the opening in an attempt to avoid being put inside that canvas jail.

Brigid covered her children's eyes so they did not see what was happening to their friends. She did not have enough hands to cover ears as well, so they heard every screaming child and every wailing parent. Children were prised from mothers' arms, fathers were knocked out of the way, until the truck was full of writhing children. The white men got back in the cabin and drove towards town. Tear-streaked brown faces peered back at their parents.

*

While this was happening, the three suited men had ordered some nearby townsfolk to bring out a trestle table and chairs from the school. The tall man stayed beside his vehicle, black hat in his hands. The men in suits, along with the woman, sat down at the table. The canvas-covered truck stopped nearby, and three muscular men in overalls got out. One went to the back of the truck and randomly pulled out a child. The others kept an eye on the parents who had finally caught up to the truck.

A man surged forward and called out, 'Polly!'

The child stopped wriggling, and said between sobs, 'Daddy.'

The sergeant stepped into view and stood next to the three burly men. Hand on his government-issued gun, he shook his head at Polly's father, who stopped, unable to do anything other than watch in disbelief. Kin stood beside him, and an older man reached out and placed an arm around his shoulders. Snippets of chattering drifted from front yards as clusters of townsfolk gathered. And eyes could be seen from more than one parlour window along the street. Polly was taken to where the men, and one woman, sat at the trestle table.

One man studied her. 'She looks very small for her age.'

Polly's father called out, 'No, she's tall for a five-year-old.'

The man said, 'Looks small to me. Perhaps even malnourished. What do you think, Mrs Jones?'

The woman stared at Polly. 'Obviously neglected,

Mr Whyte.'

Mr Whyte, nodded. 'Record that in the book, Smith.

Polly ... surname?'

Polly's father answered, 'Walsh.'

Mr Smith read out what he'd written: 'Polly Walsh was removed from her family on this day, due to neglect.'

'Put her back in the truck,' ordered Whyte.

Her father rushed forward, trying to reach his daughter. One of the overalled men held him back, while another carried the wriggling girl back to the truck. He then pulled out another child to bring before the well-dressed strangers.'

Whyte, who appeared to be in charge, said, 'Pull up his sleeve.'

As the guards did this, Mrs Jones got up and walked towards the boy.

She grabbed the boy's left arm. 'Tut tut. There appear to be signs of abuse.'

The boy whispered, 'Mosquito bites, ma'am.'

'I doubt that. There is no need to cover for your parents.'

Whyte looked towards Pastor Thomas. 'What's this one's name?'

His wife answered instead: 'Sam Goodes, sir. And he's a good boy, with caring parents. He often gets mosquito bites because he plays cricket on the pitch next to the town's dam in the evenings.'

'Have you recorded that name, Mr Smith? Good. You, take him back to the truck.'

One of the strong men did as they were told, then dragged back another child to stand before the formidable Mr Whyte. He and Mrs Jones kept making judgements, which Smith recorded in the large leather-clad book, until there were no more children to stand before the table. Eventually the parents stood in silence, accepting that there was nothing they could do. The sergeant had just stood there, hand still firmly on his gun, keeping his sight on them. There was no one who could stop this injustice. Not when the perpetrators were backed by the law of disorder.

As a shadow passed over him, the silent third man at the table quickly stood up.

'Pastor Bertrand,' he sputtered. 'Please, take my seat. Would you like a glass of water?'

The man who had been standing by his vehicle, watching intently, shook his head. Standing above everyone, he looked around. He then beckoned the sergeant with a wave of two fingers.

'Where are they?

The sergeant frowned. 'Who, Pastor?'

'The girls I was contacted about. Twins, I believe. They've not been brought forward.'

'Mrs Thomas,' called the sergeant. 'Have you seen ... what are their blasted names ... those girls?'

Mrs Thomas stepped forward, her husband hovering behind her. She looked up at Pastor Bertrand, and shivered. He had a discomforting presence. Mrs Thomas hoped the rumours she'd heard of him were not true.

Pastor Bertrand scowled. 'I'm waiting.'

'Victoria and Margaret,' answered Pastor Thomas, as he moved to stand beside his wife.

'And they are where?'

'Home, I suppose. Their mother doesn't bring them to church.'

Pastor Bertrand reached for the large crucifix that rested on his chest. He closed his eyes, moving his lips in silence. He opened his eyes suddenly, and looked down the dusty road.

'I will find them. They will be sent away, to join these other brats,' he asserted, waving a hand towards the truck-full of sobbing children.

Mrs Jones and the three men stood up, and gathered the paperwork. With a quick farewell to Pastor Bertrand, they left. The canvas-covered truck and black cars pulled out of town, the sounds of distraught children becoming fainter and fainter. With looks of despair on their faces, and shoulders sagging in defeat, their parents walked back to their dwellings. Talk of petitioning the authorities, of tracking their children, would happen over the next few months, but for now they sat by their fires in silence. Slowly, the townspeople emerged from their homes. With mixed feelings. Some felt it was only right, as these children would now be given a real chance to prove themselves worthy. Others felt empathy for the bereaved parents. Regardless of these twinges of humanity, they still didn't lend a hand to console the families. Instead, they remained compliant witnesses to the theft of a generation. Even if the shouts and tears had nipped at a few hearts, pricked their consciences, they did nothing. After all, it's best for the children, really it is, mused mild-mannered mothers. Can't have them running all around the countryside willy-nilly, stressed the menfolk. Hard work and a firm hand will enable those little ones to grow more god-fearing like us, and less like their faithless parents, muttered stony matrons. It's the law, and the law must be served, stated the sergeant to his puzzled wife. Suffer little children to come unto me, muttered Pastor Bertrand, arms outstretched, as he watched the dust of departing vehicles.

'What will happen to them?' sobbed Mrs Thomas, clinging onto her husband's arm.

'There, there,' Pastor Thomas said. 'We'll find where they were taken. Then we'll help their parents write letters to the authorities. In the meantime, we'll keep teaching and praying.'

Pastor Bertrand looked at the couple, and snorted. 'Hopeless, both of you. I've taken time out of my important work at the mission to do what you should have done. Give the good townsfolk's children a sound

Christian education without those grubby brats taking up space.'

Then, with help from the sergeant, Pastor Bertrand evicted Pastor Thomas and Mrs Thomas from town.

*

Meanwhile, Brigid had urged the girls out of the shadows and onwards, towards their hut. There she took down their patched suitcases from the top of the wardrobe and started to fill them. Victoria helped, collecting both the essentials and little treasures they'd accumulated. Busily recounting the joys of Susie's party, Maggie didn't noticed the flurry of activity around her. When her mother steered her to the fireplace and started to smear ash on her arms, Maggie woke from her stupor.

'Stop it,' she protested. 'What are you doing?'

'Stand still, Maggie. Just trust me.'

'No! You're making me all dirty. And ruining my party dress.'

'Keep still.'

Something in her mother's voice convinced Maggie to comply, so she stood still as her mother rubbed ash all over her arms, legs, neck and face. Even as tears made tracks down her now-sooty face. She stood still when Victoria picked up the smallest suitcase and headed for the back door. Brigid walked towards

Maggie and took her hand. Maggie pulled her hand away when she realised they were leaving once more.

'We have to,' sighed Brigid.

Maggie shook her head until the party ribbons came loose. 'We have a home now.'

'Not any more,' said Victoria.

Maggie glanced over at her sister, then back at her mother. 'Mumma, why?'

Brigid replied, 'We can't stay here. It's not safe.'

Maggie followed reluctantly, still not understanding. As they walked outside, she saw their kitten playing under a bush.

'I have to get kitty,' cried Maggie.

Brigid scanned the street, worried they were running out of time. It wouldn't be too long before someone realised her daughters were not with the others, in the back of that old truck. She knew Maggie was waiting for a reply. Picking up the kitten, Brigid turned away from freedom and walked back down the street. The girls followed their mother in silence, hiding when she indicated, rushing when necessary, until they were back at Susie's house. They crept down the side of the house, into the backyard, and Brigid knocked on the back door. Susie opened the door, and turned to her mother, who was standing in the kitchen.

'I am so sorry,' cried her mother. 'I didn't realise something like this would happen. I just wanted all the children to have fun.'

Brigid said, 'You weren't to know.'

'It's just awful. Why are these people so hateful?'

'I'm sure they're no different from people in the city you come from.'

A tiny meow reminded Brigid of the kitten she had tucked into her coat.

'I need to ask you a favour,' Brigid said, holding up the kitten.

The woman noticed the twin's faces as they stood in her backyard surrounded by battered luggage.

'Of course,' she replied, taking the kitten. 'Where will you go?'

'Somewhere safer,' replied Brigid.

Susie's mother nodded, tears forming in her eyes, her own desire to leave this town now stronger.

*

Brigid crept towards the front of the house. The town's streets were filled with the most righteous and the downright curious. She took her daughters' hands and led them to the train tracks on the eastern side of town. She quickly found a place to hide – the narrow gap between a large rainwater tank and the station platform. As they waited, the girls leant against their mother, and soon fell asleep. Just as the sun was setting, Brigid saw grey steam rising in the north, like a fierce dragon rushing towards them. Brigid gently woke the girls and, rubbing sleepy eyes, they all stood up. When the train stopped, no one noticed three ticketless travellers climb up into a carriage to hide among freight.

When the girls were once more asleep, Brigid gazed out of the open door, watching shadowed country flashing past as the train made its way south. She occasionally pulled her daughters closer, whenever they called out in sleep. She guessed that in their dreams they were reliving the events of the day, trying to find some reason for the cruelty shown towards their friends.

Sometime in the night, Brigid felt a subtle difference in the train's motion. She realised it was slowing. Looking out the door, she saw the first light of day. Thinking this was as good a place as any to disembark, Brigid gently roused the girls. When the train stopped, they were ready. Brigid threw out their cases and then jumped. Signalling in silence, she caught Maggie, then Victoria. They quickly picked up their suitcases and moved away from the train, hiding behind a clump of dried-out bushes. From there, they had a good view of the front of the train. An old male camel stood on the train tracks, refusing to budge. The train driver and other rail workers were trying to coax him off the track. He refused to budge; head held high, he carried on chewing the cud. The bull camel turned his head and caught sight of the three hiding in the bushes. The camel shook his head vigorously, his plant-flecked slobber showering the men. Victoria was sure the camel winked at her, before he casually got off the track and ambled away.

Once the train had left, Brigid urged the girls to get up. It was time to walk – again. Victoria took a deep breath, gathering both familiar and unknown aromas. She'd missed the freedom of open spaces. Maggie stifled an occasional sob, thinking of the kitten left behind and friends she'd never see again. When the sun was halfway through its day's journey, they came to a clearing nestled by stony ridges. They put down their cases, and Maggie collapsed in exhaustion on top of them. Brigid and Victoria gathered kindling. Although hunger gnawed at all three, they were soon asleep beside a crackling campfire.

It's a good thing you're a potato. That makes your daughters potatoes too. Otherwise, they'd have been taken back there.'

'Granny? Is that you?'

'Yes, Birdie.'

'I don't want to be a potato. And I don't want to walk any more.'

'Ask the bird to take you home.'

'The bird left, Granny.'

'Find another one, lass. Or don't. The choice is yours.'

SIX

Curled up beside dying embers was how they were found. Victoria was the first to sense they were not alone. Opening one eye just a fraction, she scanned their impromptu campsite, noticing that the day was almost over. Upon seeing the figure silhouetted in the sunset, she was careful not to move or make a sound. Victoria felt a subtle shift in her mother's breathing and knew that she was also stealthily measuring this intruder. The man stood a few metres away, hat in hand, as if waiting to be invited into their camp, perhaps eager to warm his hands at their dwindling fire. Having assessed him, Brigid rose to her feet. The man smiled in an exaggerated manner and lifted a hand to wave a greeting. Victoria also stood up, and patted dust off her clothes as she gave him a stern side-stare.

Brigid noticed her daughter's glare and, with a partially suppressed grin, sent her off to find wood for the fire. Brigid added a few handfuls of dried grasses to the embers and blew gently, before adding twigs. Nodding towards a large rock, Brigid invited the man to sit down. As he did, his eyes registered the rifle that lay an arm's length from Brigid. She noticed him eye it off and, with a slight lift of her chin, gave him a hard stare. He awkwardly steered his attention elsewhere. She put water in a blackened pot and placed it on the glowing coals. When it was almost boiling, she added a handful of loose tea leaves. She then poured steaming hot liquid into three enamel mugs.

'We have no sugar or milk.'

The man nodded as he accepted a mug. 'Ah, just what I needed. Thank you.'

'Mumma, who are you talking to?' asked Maggie as she rubbed sleep from her eyes.

Brigid turned around and smiled at her. 'Hey, sleepyhead.'

Maggie walked over to the fire just as Victoria returned with an armful of branches. They picked up a mug each and sat down next to each other, Maggie looking curiously at the stranger while Victoria glared at him.

The man chuckled. 'Fine watchmen you have there.'

Brigid loaded the fire with branches. 'A watchful eye is necessary out here.'

'Yes, most certainly.'

'And a stranger is best watched closely, until they become a friend.'

His face reddened. 'Where are my manners? I am Omer.'

'I'm Brigid. Maggie and Victoria,' she responded, pointing to each daughter.

With a broad smile, Omer nodded at the girls. Only Maggie returned his smile.

Turning back to Brigid, he said, 'This is a good cup of tea, and a most warming fire. A nice way to end a hard day's work. Let me repay you, please. You must have supper with my wife and me.'

'Thank you for the offer, but we must get going. We need to find somewhere to make a new camp, near water, before it gets too dark.'

'It's very dry around here, there's no fresh water nearby. Come to my place and I'll fill up your containers while you have something to eat.'

Victoria jumped up. 'Maybe we can find a waterhole, Mum. You know I'm good at finding those. Let's get moving.'

'No. I can't walk any further today,' moaned Maggie.

'You can so walk. You have to,' insisted Victoria. 'Stop being such a baby.'

Maggie stuck her tongue out at her sister, before turning to Brigid. 'Mumma, please.'

Omer said, 'My place is really not far from here. My wife would never forgive me if I didn't extend a warm welcome to you and your daughters. We could even make up a comfy bed for the night.'

Brigid observed Maggie's attempt to hold back tears, and reflected on what her daughters had been through the day before. She looked at Omer. 'We gratefully accept your offer of water and a meal.'

Victoria gave her sister a glare, before kicking dirt onto the fire. Omer helped her extinguish the fire as Brigid gathered their luggage. He offered to help carry the suitcases and, once everyone was ready, led them across the dry plains.

*

A short time later, they saw a rusted corrugated-tin shed planted among a sea of holes in the ground.

'I don't normally like people coming here,' Omer admitted.

'Except for trustworthy folk, such as yourselves.'

'Is this a mine?' asked Brigid.

Omer nodded. 'Opals. Well, sometimes opals. Mostly I dig up dirt and pebbles. Still, I dig, I hope, and I dig some more.'

The girls' eyes widened as they imagined treasure lying all around them, scattered in the dirt. Instead, they saw what appeared to be the outline of gigantic warrens.

'What lives in those holes?' asked Maggie, nervously.

Laughing, Omer said, 'Nothing to be frightened of. Maybe a few bugs, an occasional snake. I made those holes, not a creature. It's getting late. If you like, I can give you the grand tour tomorrow. For now, let's get that supper I promised you.'

He led them to a battered ute and soon they were bumping their way across a darkening landscape, heading towards Omer's house. It was long enough a drive for Maggie to fall asleep.

'Get up. You've made my arm go numb,' demanded Victoria as the car stopped.

Maggie stretched, before peering out the window, into the night. Omer leapt out, and held the passenger door open. The girls followed their mother as she walked towards a stone cottage. Omer rushed to open the front door for them.

As they all walked in, a woman called out, 'Where have you been? Supper is ruined, again.'

'We have guests,' announced Omer.

A small woman appeared at the end of a narrow corridor.

Removing her apron, she walked towards them.

'Bethel, this is Brigid and her daughters, Victoria and Maggie. I've invited them to share a meal with us. That's all right?'

Bethel smiled. 'Of course. Please, make yourselves comfort able while I set the table.'

'Can I help?' asked Brigid.

Bethel nodded, tears forming in her eyes. Brigid caught Omer's eye, concerned that perhaps it was not a good time for visitors after all. Omer shrugged and walked over to his wife. He gave her a gentle hug. She smiled up at him, and wiped away a tear.

'Omer, you can entertain the young ones until supper is served,' said Bethel.

Once in the kitchen, Brigid asked, 'Are you sure we're not inconveniencing you?'

'No, not at all.'

Brigid raised an eyebrow, still confused as to why their appearance had caused this woman to cry.

Bethel noticed Brigid looking at her. 'Please, don't be so concerned. That little tear before was from happiness, because I enjoy the company of guests. Your daughters, they are so lovely. The green-eyed girl, she reminds me of someone.'

Brigid asked what she could do to help. Bethel showed her where the crockery and cutlery was kept, before stirring a pot on the stove.

Meanwhile, Omer led the girls outside. Maggie squealed with delight when he asked if they wanted to help feed the animals. Both girls smiled broadly as they scattered grain for a straggly collection of hens, and stood back hesitantly when a few hissing geese appeared. As the last ray of sun disappeared on the horizon, Omer shut the animals up for the night.

*

After supper, everyone sat in the small parlour in contented silence. From the shelf above the fireplace, Omer took down a wooden pipe and filled it with tobacco. He then sat back in a worn armchair, while thin wisps of smoke filled the air above him. The sound of a creaking armchair broke the silence.

Brigid had stood up. 'Thank you for such a lovely meal. We really must be leaving now.'

A small groan escaped Maggie's lips. She was quickly silenced with a stern look from her mother.

Bethel raised an eyebrow. 'Go? Where?'

'South, I guess,' replied Brigid.

'Oh no, you must stay the night. It's pitch-black outside.

And the nights are so cold here.'

Brigid looked out the small window, and then glanced back at her exhausted daughters.

'No, we can't put you out,' she said.

'Mum, can we stay just for one night?'

Surprised, Brigid asked, 'Why, Victoria? You love sleeping under the stars.'

Victoria shrugged. 'I'm tired. And it's so nice and warm here.'

Brigid hesitated, then shook her head.

Omer put down his pipe. 'Stay, I insist. We have plenty of room, it really is no trouble. I could do with the girls' help in the morning, with the animals, if you don't mind.'

Bethel added, 'I've already made up a bed for you and your daughters.'

'Please, Mumma,' pleaded Maggie. 'The goats were asleep when we went outside, and I really really want to meet them. And Omer told us there's newborn kittens hiding in the hay, so new they haven't even opened their eyes. Please say yes.'

Brigid sighed. 'Just the one night then. We must be on our way by late morning.'

Maggie smiled, happy that they wouldn't be sleeping outside that night, and even happier that she'd get to see kittens in the morning.

Omer asked, 'How about I tell you a story? And then you must tell me one in return. That's how stories go; they must be swapped or else.'

'Or else what?' asked Victoria.

'Or else the stories turn to dust,' replied Omer solemnly.

Bethel smiled, knowing how much her husband loved to share stories. She picked up the sewing kit that sat at her feet, and began to thread a needle.

'Do you agree to this deal? A story for a story?' he asked.

Victoria and Maggie both nodded, before settling comfortably on large cushions in front of the fireplace. Brigid sat back down, sinking into the overstuffed chair, and slowly the warmth of the fire began to quieten her restless feet.

*

Omer leant towards the fireplace and tapped his pipe on the hearth. Shifting slightly in his seat, he cleared his throat.

'As you have probably guessed, the good wife and I are not originally from here,' he said. 'No, like many who live here, our homelands are far away. It had not been my intention to disembark from the boat I arrived on. A little bird told me I should, so I did. I'd been wandering both land and sea for a few years, trying to put the sounds of gunshot behind me. Those were days of hunger and despair. With feet dressed in rags I pushed on, always seeking work in exchange for a few coins or a modest plate of warm food. Amidst the horror of war's remains, the senseless destruction of humanity, hope still existed. It was the kindness of strangers that gave me the strength to go on. There was nothing, no one, left at home for me to return to. As much as I wandered, I found no place to call home, no sense of belonging. One cold evening, I sat at an unwashed table in a dank tavern by an unfamiliar sea, with just enough coin in my pocket for one more ale. When a gent sat himself across from me, offering me a chance to earn money, my ears pricked up. The next morning, I watched the shore disappear from the deck of a ship. It was not my first sea journey, but it was the only ship I'd worked on that carried goods and passengers. It was to be my longest and last journey: travelling to the great southern lands.'

He stopped suddenly, and gazed into the fire. Bethel looked up from her sewing. Putting down the sock she was darning, she reached over and touched Omer gently on the arm. He turned towards her. After a few seconds, the clouds shifted from his eyes and he patted her hand and smiled. Bethel returned to her sewing, and Omer continued the story.

'The excitement of travelling to a new continent was quickly gone. I found scarce moments to myself, as there was so much work to be done on that overcrowded ship. I began to crave solitude, so I sought out places where I could sit and think for just a bit. Such a place was one of the small wooden rowboats. These were only in case of emergencies at sea, so people had no need to venture inside them. They had tarps on top of them, to prevent them filling up with rain and sea water, which made them perfect nests for hiding. I would climb up into a boat and write poetry in my mind. It wasn't good poetry, I'd be the first to admit that, but it helped to calm my thoughts. One day, after climbing into my sanctuary,

I was surprised to see a little sparrow had got there before me. My sudden appearance frightened the sparrow, so I sat quietly, giving her time to become accustomed to my presence. As we sat near each other in the dark, I could sense the sparrow was broken. Feeling a wave of pain, my heart grew heavy with sadness. Having seen this type of injury too many times, I resolved to help this little sparrow to fly again.'

Brigid stirred as a log rolled nosily out of the fire and onto the hearth. Omer kicked the smouldering log gently with the tip of his boot, returning it to the fire. Reassuring herself that the girls were safe in front of the fireplace, Brigid settled again. She glanced at Bethel and saw a tear on her cheek. Brigid watched her as she stooped over the darning; this woman seemed to cry often. Absurdly, Brigid noticed sparrow-like features in the older woman. And she was reminded of her beloved grandmother and her treasure trove of tales, which were mostly of plants and birds from a different country. She missed her granny deeply and had a sudden yearning to be someone's Birdie again. And then it dawned on Brigid. That sparrow, the broken sparrow Omer talked of, was Bethel. The older woman looked up, with the contented smile of knowing what it was to be someone's birdie.

Omer continued his tale of how he'd befriended Bethel during that long sea journey. The more time they spent together, hidden in their wooden nest, the more

Omer's desire for belonging grew. His quest to help her soon turned into a self-realisation – it was he who needed to be helped. For the first time in his life, he wondered what it would be like to love and to be loved in return. Bethel appeared to enjoy his company but did not respond to any hints of affection Omer dared to show. Always, at some point, the blossoming camaraderie would be abruptly shut down by Bethel. And she would make her escape as tears fell silently down her cheek.

One afternoon, Omer had slipped into the boat and found Bethel already there. From the way she sat slumped over, the slight heaving of her shoulders, he guessed she was silently sobbing. He moved towards her, and quietly made his presence known. He sat there, in silence, while she cried. Eventually, he felt a light touch on the back of his hand. Looking up, Omer saw Bethel wipe the tears from her cheeks with her other hand. She smiled just a whisper of a smile as she perched on the rowboat's bench. Omer had turned over his hand, and gently squeezed hers.

'Even before the ship landed, I'd finally found where I belonged – by Bethel's side,' he declared.

Maggie asked, 'How did you get here, though? This is the furthest you can be from the sea.'

Omer smiled. 'Not as far as you'd think.'

Bethel saw the sparkle of mischief in her husband's eye and smiled.

'There's no sea around here,' said Victoria. 'You're being tricky!'

'Oh, there is, little miss,' he replied. 'You are, in fact, right now sitting quite close to its shore. If you want I can show you tomorrow. After you've helped me milk the goats.'

Brigid frowned. 'A sea, here? How is that even possible?'

Omer replied, 'A long time ago, there was an inland sea here. There's no water any more, just an impression of that ancient sea in the dirt. It's why this area is so rich in opals. Opalised fossils of gigantic aquatic beasts have even been unearthed where this sea once existed.'

Brigid made an unusual noise, like a worried cry.

'Nothing to worry about, dear,' said Bethel gently. 'Those beasts are long dead.'

Brigid replied, 'Someone told me about an inland sea, many years ago. Before the girls were born. I've been looking for this sea ever since, and had almost given up ever finding it.'

Omer said, 'Well, you've found it. If you don't mind me asking, why is it so important that you find this sea?'

Brigid stared into the fire, as if she'd not even heard Omer.

Bethel sighed, 'Not now, Omer. Everyone is tired. Look, the little ones can hardly keep their eyes open.'

Brigid hadn't heard. She still had that faraway look in her eyes.

Bethel stood. 'Come, girls, let me show you to the guest room.'

Victoria got up, followed by Maggie. Eager for sleep, they waited for their mother to make a move.

Brigid finally noticed their presence. 'Yes, it's time we were in bed.'

She followed Bethel out of the room then, pausing in the door way, turned back to Omer. 'I'd like to hear more tomor row, Omer. And perhaps you can show me where this sea once was.'

Omer nodded. 'Of course. Until then, sleep well.'

As Bethel led the stumbling half-asleep girls to the spare bedroom, where a warm bed was waiting, Omer reached for his pipe. Once Bethel had bid Brigid and her girls goodnight, she returned to sit beside her husband.

'It's not right,' remarked Omer. 'Something's not right.'

'What, dear?'

'Why is a young woman out here, in the middle of nowhere, with just those little girls for company?'

Bethel picked up her sewing. 'Have you become so settled that you've forgotten?'

'Forgotten?'

'Yes. Failed to remember there are many sorrows that can push a person onto an unexpected road.'

Omer grunted. 'No, I can never forget. Not sure what our past has to do with this young woman, though. There are no wars here, nothing to push one from the safety of one's own home onto the road of despair. So why is she wandering?'

'War comes in many forms. Man's inhumanity towards man wears many cloaks. You have seen for yourself how her people are still engaged in a combat of sorts. The way they're treated, pushed off their lands by wave after wave of settlers, not even counted as citizens of the Federation.'

'Indeed. And it irks me so. Even here, in a town of migrants from many nations, the first people are treated with disdain. You'd think that having seen up close the impact of irrational hate, our neighbours would be less inclined to judge others based on the race they were born into.'

'Sadly, too many have forgotten the impetus of those not-so-distant horrors. However, in this instance, I think it is the aftermath of abandonment Brigid is fighting. There is something in her eyes I can relate to.'

Omer reached for a twig from the fire, and reignited his pipe. 'Perhaps you are right. Brigid does have the look of some one who has experienced a loss. She may find some comfort in finally reaching the inland sea, but I cannot see what importance that could hold.'

'We all seek something, my love. And it rarely makes sense to outsiders.'

Omer chuckled. 'Ah, my little sparrow, so wise as usual.'

'Finish your pipe, old man. It's late, and there is much to do tomorrow.'

*

Brigid and the girls awoke to enticing smells that pulled them from their bed, and down the corridor towards the warmth of the kitchen. Bethel had already stocked the wood stove and prepared breakfast, even though the sun hadn't been up for long. She showed the girls where they could wash, while Brigid cut and buttered slices of freshly baked bread.

'I like mine extra thick,' announced Omer as he walked into the kitchen.

'Any thicker and you'll get stuck in a mineshaft,' laughed his wife, returning with the girls.

Omer winked. 'I'm not thick. There's just more of me to cuddle.'

Bethel laughed again as she set the table. They all sat down to eat, along with much talking and more laughter. Soon their bellies were full and their cheeks glowing from the warmth of the wood stove. While the women cleaned the dishes, the girls followed Omer eagerly outside. As promised the night before, they were going to meet the goats, and Omer would show them how to milk them. By the time they returned, Brigid had their luggage by the door.

Omer walked in, noticed the suitcases and shook his head. 'You can't leave, not yet.'

Brigid insisted, 'We must.'

'You can't. One of you still owes me a story. A promise is a promise,' Omer said firmly.

Bethel smiled, knowing her husband was having a bit of fun, but also hoping their visitors would stay a bit longer.

'Well, we can tell you one now and then be on our way,' answered Brigid briskly.

Omer thought for a while, then replied, 'No, that won't do. I have work to do now. And after that, I have an ancient sea to show you.'

Brigid stopped protesting. 'Can we see it now?'

Omer shook his head. 'Work comes first. You'll have to wait until this afternoon.'

'Well, point the way and I'll get myself there.'

'It's hard to find. Just wait. I promise you'll get to see it today.'

Bethel picked up a battered metal lunchbox, and handed it to Omer. 'Can you stop by the Panagopoulos's place on the way home? Aspasia made feta and has offered us some.'

'Certainly,' he said, patting his stomach. 'Aspasia makes the best cheese, because we give her milk from the happiest of goats.'

'Oh, off with you,' laughed Bethel as she planted a kiss on the cheek he offered.

As Omer shut the door, she turned to Brigid. 'If you don't mind, I could do with some help with the washing. My back isn't what it once was, and damp sheets are so heavy. Some days it's a struggle to hang them on the line.'

Resigned to having to wait just a bit longer to see the inland sea, Brigid asked the girls to return their cases to the back bedroom. She then followed Bethel to the laundry behind the house. Victoria and Maggie hugged each other and danced around the guest room, glad to be staying another day.

The day passed quickly for the girls, and slowly for their mother. Brigid was imagining the moment she'd finally see that inland sea. She thought of Danny, and their last days together. In her heart, she believed that Danny would be there, at the inland sea. He would be pleased to see her; and overjoyed to meet the children he knew nothing of. Her mind, however, told her not to be so silly, running through a list of contradictions to her heart. And then an image of Danny, in that moment he'd walked out the door in search of the inland sea, flashed before her eyes. Brigid began to worry; even if he was there, he'd not be pleased to see her. Not after what she'd said to him.

*

As the sun began to set, Omer finally arrived home and the girls ran out to greet him. He patted them both on the head and walked inside, where he immediately saw Brigid standing at the kitchen door.

'I'm so sorry,' he said. 'Old Panagopoulos needed help to fix his truck. It took us hours to get it going again. Then I rushed back here, hoping to still keep my promise to you. Sadly, it's too late to go today.'

'Is it really too late? The sun hasn't quite set.'

Omer scratched his head. 'You won't see anything once we get out there. It will be dark by then.'

He noticed her forlorn expression. Bethel stood in the doorway, behind Brigid. He walked towards them, and handed his wife the cheese he'd brought home from the Panagopoulos's.

'Your dinner will need reheating,' she remarked.

Sighing, he looked at Brigid. 'Come on then. Grab a coat, it's a bit cold out there.'

Victoria asked, 'Us too?'

Brigid shook her head. 'Maybe tomorrow. Your dinner *is* ready, so you'd best eat it now.'

While Brigid and Omer headed towards the car, the girls followed Bethel to the kitchen. The thought of warm food was much more appealing than another outdoor adventure. Shortly after leaving, Brigid looked anxiously at the sinking sun. She was now doubting she'd be able to see anything. Even worse, she was nervous of what she would, or wouldn't, find by the sea. Omer drove in silence, sensing that she'd rather be left to her thoughts. After a while, he turned onto what was little more than a narrow dirt track. As the sun disappeared, Brigid saw a campfire a short distance from the track. They drove past slowly, and she saw a handful of dogs run towards the car. She heard the shouts before she saw the man. He was waving his arms, indicating the direction they'd just come from, and shouting words that were quickly taken by the wind. A silhouette of a woman rose from beside the fire. Omer slowed the car to pass some large rocks on the track, giving Brigid a chance to look more closely at the woman. She was calling the dogs back. They came reluctantly to her side. Then the woman uttered something to the agitated man. He threw an arm in the air as he turned, and walked back to the campfire.

The car continued along the track, in the now-darkness. Then it stopped abruptly.

'This is it,' said Omer.

Brigid looked around, seeing nothing but darkness.

Omer suggested, 'It's too dark now. I'll bring you back in the morning.'

He began to reverse the car but stopped when Brigid asked him to. She got out and walked tentatively into the night.

'Are we in the right spot?' she asked as Omer got out and stood beside her.

'Yes, the ancient sea is right in front of you. It stretches further than the eye can see. We are standing on its shore.'

Brigid saw nothing. Just blackness.

'The people back there, do you know them?' she asked.

'Some. They're mostly Isabelle's family.'

'Why was that young man shouting at us?'

Omer observed, 'I guess he's protecting this place. I've heard it's an important part of their Country. Also, sometimes townsfolk drive in, looking to start trouble.'

Brigid was quiet for a while, then said softly, 'That woman, Isabelle, she seemed okay with us being here. Was she?'

'I guess so. Come on, let's go home. Try again tomorrow.'

They returned to the car and drove back down the track. As they approached the campfire, which still burned brightly, someone suddenly appeared beside the track.

'It's Isabelle,' Omer remarked. 'I wonder what she wants.'

Omer braked. The woman nodded at him, then walked in front of the car towards the passenger door. Brigid wound down the window. Isabelle moved so close that Brigid could feel the warmth of her breath.

'You came back,' Isabelle declared.

Omer remarked, 'No other way back from the sea, Isabelle.'

She ignored Omer, instead focusing on Brigid. 'You. You came back.'

Brigid said, confused, 'I've never been here before.'

'You have. In his dreams.'

'Whose?'

The woman thumped the side of the car. 'It's late now. Tomorrow. Tomorrow, we talk.'

As the woman walked away, Omer drove off. Brigid turned her head, watching Isabelle make her way back to the camp. A small group of dogs ran towards her, barking as she called out to them.

Back at the house, Brigid and Omer ate the dinner that Bethel had kept warm. Then, with hot drinks nestled in their hands, they joined the girls by the fireside.

'Right, then,' said Omer. 'Where is this story that is owed to me? You do remember our deal, don't you?'

The young girls nodded and Victoria quickly offered to tell a story. When she had finished, Omer sat wordless, tapping his empty pipe on his knee. She watched him expectantly, concerned her narration was not up to his standard.

He stopped tapping and, gazing into the fireplace, remarked, 'A most satisfying story. Yes, it will more than do. It's not often that I get to swap a yarn with such a talented teller of tales.'

Victoria smiled, and jumped up to hug Omer. This surprised Brigid, as it was a behaviour most uncharacteristic of Victoria. Omer grinned at his wife, over Victoria's shoulder. Brigid glanced at the older woman and noticed yet another tear rolling down her cheek.

She then looked at her daughter. 'Did you make that story up?'

Victoria shook her head. 'Nana Vic told me.'

'You remember her?'

'Yes. And Grandfather Albert. He didn't tell us stories, though. Nana told us lots and lots of stories. She whispered them in our ears as we fell asleep.'

'Even scary ones,' added Maggie. 'I didn't like those ones.'

Her mother smiled. 'Knowing you, I'd expect not. I'm surprised you both remember Nana Vic and Grandfather Albert. Let alone stories. It's only been about two years since we left them, but you were so little. Toddlers, almost.'

Victoria admitted, 'I miss them. Can we visit them soon?'

'Maybe one day.'

'Perhaps Omer could drive us. I like his car. I don't like walking,' moaned Maggie.

'It's much too far. And Omer is a busy man. We can't expect him to be driving us around.'

Omer said, 'I've always wanted to see more of this big country. So maybe one day I could drive you there.'

Bethel laughed. 'As if that old car would make it out of town before breaking down.'

'It might look a bit rough, but it's as sturdy as I am,' he replied with a grin.

Bethel grinned back. She stood, gathered their cups and went to the kitchen. When Brigid walked in, Bethel was pouring warm water from the kettle into the sink.

'Can I help?'

Bethel turned around, sleeves rolled up. 'No, it's fine.'

Brigid nodded. 'Okay. I'll go settle the girls into bed.'

A short time later, Maggie walked in the kitchen with another cup and placed it in the soapy water.

'Bethel?'

'Yes, dear.'

Maggie pointed to Bethel's wrist. 'Why are those numbers not washing off in that water?'

Bethel hurriedly pulled down her sleeve. Turning, she noticed Brigid standing in the doorway. She knew Brigid had heard Maggie's question. Perhaps even seen the faded ink on the inside of her lower arm.

'Maggie, don't ask so many questions of grown-ups. It's rude,' Brigid advised.

'I'm sorry. I didn't mean to be rude.'

'You should be in bed. It's late.'

Maggie said, 'I want to help Bethel.'

'That is kind of you,' said Bethel gently. 'I have only a few more dishes to wash. Perhaps, instead, you can help me make breakfast in the morning.'

SEVEN

The next morning, Brigid didn't need any convincing to stay one more day. She wanted to return to the site of the inland sea in the daylight. And to speak with Isabelle. Omer had promised to return early from work, so they would have plenty of time to drive out there. He kept his word, arriving home just after lunch. This time, the girls insisted on coming too. Nothing Brigid could say would dissuade them, so they all got in the cabin of Omer's ute, and headed out mid-afternoon.

As they drove past Isabelle's campsite, Brigid lifted a hand and waved.

'Who's that?' asked Victoria.

'The woman? That's Isabelle. I met her briefly last night. We'll stop there on the way back.'

Soon, Omer stopped the car and they all got out.

'Is this where that sea was?' asked Maggie.

Omer replied, 'Yes. If you walk around, you might find a fossil of a sea creature. The opalised ones are very hard to find, but if you look hard enough you just might be in luck.'

The girls squealed in delight and ran off to find treasure. Omer and Brigid watched them running around, each stopping now and again to pick up a rock to examine.

'It's so big, I can't even see the other side of this indentation,' remarked Brigid. 'I wonder why it was so important for him to find this place.'

'Who?'

'Someone I once knew. He left years ago to search for the inland sea. And I thought, I thought...'

Omer asked gently, 'What did you think?'

'It's so silly. I realise that now,' she said. 'I always thought he would be here. That I would finally find him, beside the sea he sought.'

'Don't give up.'

She shook her head. 'I'm such a fool.'

'Then you're in the right place. We're all fools around here. Spending our days down holes, hoping to find shiny coloured rocks that will make us rich beyond our dreams. The only ones with any sense are people like Isabelle.'

'I wonder what she wanted to speak to me about.'

Omer shrugged. Hearing Maggie shout, they both turned towards the girls. Maggie was hopping up and down in excitement. She ran to her mother, while Victoria ambled behind her.

'Look, Mumma,' Maggie said as she handed her a flat rock.

Brigid ran a finger along white grooves in the grey rock, tracing the outline of something ancient. Omer studied the rock in Brigid's hand.

'You've found a fossil. See. That's the imprint of an extinct marine creature.'

Victoria handed Omer a smaller rock. 'What's this?'

Omer turned it over. 'It's a fossilised scorpion. Not as old as the marine fossil your sister found, but still old.'

He handed it back to Victoria, and she put it in her pocket.

'You both have keen eyes, to find treasure so quickly,' said Omer.

Brigid remarked, 'Or perhaps they're just lucky. Shall we head home now?'

The girls complained, as they wanted to look for more fossils. Omer reminded them there was still a tour of his mine to be had, with an added promise of fossicking for opals. So they got back in the ute, imagining the treasure they'd find in Omer's mine.

Nearing the campsite, Brigid said, 'Don't forget, we need to stop here for a bit.'

Omer nodded and turned the car to the right, gingerly driving off the dirt track, over rocky ground. He stopped close to the campfire, and they saw Isabelle poking the fire with a stick. Omer excused himself and went towards a man who had his head under a car bonnet, while Brigid and the girls walked over to the campfire. Isabelle gestured for them to sit, then sat down next to Brigid.

'Did you find what you were looking for?' Isabelle asked.

Brigid shook her head. 'The sea was empty.'

Isabelle laughed. 'Not empty. Far from it.' She turned her attention to the twins. 'I know these ones.'

Brigid frowned. Having just been bitterly disappointed by a sea that was not a sea, and, after many years of holding hope close to her chest, she was not in the mood for cryptic puzzles.

'I'm Victoria, and this is Maggie.'

'Can I pat that little dog?' asked Maggie, pointing to a small dog lying in the dirt a few steps away.

Isabelle nodded, and the girls got up to fuss over the dog.

'I'm their aunty,' Isabelle announced, inclining her head in the direction of the twins.

'What?'

'Their aunty, long way back. A great aunt.'

'How is that possible? I have no connection to here.'

'The girls do. Through their father.'

'You know their father?'

Isabelle moved her legs, tucking them underneath. 'Daniel was here. Looking for that sea. He talked a lot about you, but never once mentioned those young ones.'

'Where is he?' asked Brigid, jumping up.

'Sit. Sit back down. He's long gone.'

Brigid was on the verge of tears, her shoulders slumped in weariness.

Isabelle reached over and patted Brigid's knee. 'No, not that type of gone. He went back, to you. He'd found what he was searching for, both that inland sea and family. And then realised that his family was still incomplete without you in his life. So he left. And now you are here, not there.'

Brigid started to cry, softly at first, and then she sobbed loudly. Her daughters ran over, surprised by her uncustomary tears. They comforted her with cuddles until her tears stopped.

Isabelle stood and patted the dust off her dress. 'You come back. Tomorrow. We talk more, tomorrow. And bring them girls.'

Omer, having noticed that Isabelle had left, walked towards Brigid. 'Ready?'

*

Next morning, Omer dropped Brigid and the girls at Isabelle's campsite, then, with a quick wave, continued on his way to work. Once they were settled by the fire, an adolescent girl offered them some damper. It was still warm, and the jam they smothered on it melted quickly. Soon the girls were licking their sticky fingers clean. Their chins were not so easy to deal with, so with a laugh the older girl led them to a bucket of water.

'I can see a strong resemblance to family in those girls,' remarked Isabelle.

'Even Maggie? The green-eyed one.'

Isabelle nodded. 'It's in their eyes.' She turned and peered inquisitively at Brigid's deep-brown eyes.

Brigid smiled. 'Neither of them inherited my brown eyes or their father's hazel eyes. I got these from my father. He died overseas, during the war. I don't remember him. I was very young when he left. The girls were born on his community, where my nana Vic and grandfather Albert still live. Victoria's blue eyes remind me of my mother's eyes. She got those from her father, my grandfather. I never got to meet him, neither did she. He died at sea. You see, Granny wasn't from here, she came by boat, just before my mother was born. Her eyes were an unusual grey.'

'You're a chatty one.'

Brigid blushed. 'Not usually.'

Victoria and Maggie returned clean-faced and sat beside their mother.

'Do you want to hear a yarn?' Isabelle asked them. 'About your father's family?'

They seemed unsure. Victoria and Maggie could both remember a time their mother often shared stories of their father. The same few treasured stories, over and over. The girls never tired of hearing about him. As the years went past, though, and more road was trodden, their mother had stopped talking about him. The girls longed to hear those stories again, but the sadness in their mother's eyes made it too hard to ask.

Brigid smiled reassuringly at them and, turning to Isabelle, replied, 'Yes, please.'

Isabelle addressed the girls: 'Last time I saw your father, he sat in the very same spot as you sit now. Many years ago. He stayed here for a while, having finally found the inland sea that had been calling him since he was a little fella.'

Maggie asked in disbelief, 'Our father was here?'

Isabelle nodded. 'The old sea called him back to Country. I'd been waiting for him long time before the day I found him standing on the shore of the ancient sea. He was overjoyed that in addition to the inland sea he'd also found family. You see, he was taken as a bubba, from his mother's arms.'

Brigid nodded, remembering how he had told her that many times. The government and mission refusing to tell him where he was from, or anything about his family, had hurt Danny deeply. Unlike Brigid, he'd always wanted to put the pieces of his puzzle together.

Isabelle continued: 'I'll tell you what I told him, as we're family. Your father is my nephew, being my brother's boy. So you call me Aunty. Okay? I will tell you his story. First, we must start with my parents' story. My mother Nellie was born not far from here. This is her Country. Yours too. My father came from far away, born in a golden desert across the seas. He arrived with three camels and a prayer mat, and quickly set his path as a trader. Once a year he would visit white people's mines and railway workers' campsites, bringing pots and pans, sturdy shoes, cloth, thread and, occasionally, luxury items. They called him many names, the Cameleer being one, but Abdul Ziyad was his name. I called him Baba. He would also stop at my grandparents' campsite, offering whatever the other customers had passed over, at lowered prices. When the white people's campsites became a town, his visits became twiceyearly. And after my baba met my mother, thrice a year. Over a couple of years, Abdul Ziyad shyly watched Nellie. At first, she didn't even acknowledge his presence. She was young and had not yet been told the way of things. It was my grandmother who first noticed the young cameleer's awkwardness around Nellie. Knowing that the girl had never shown any interest in the men who'd been suggested as potential partners, my grandmother had a word with her husband. Reluctantly, he agreed. He could see that Abdul Ziyad was a good man who worked hard.

And so, after Nellie's woman ceremony, my grandmother whispered in her ear. Next time the cameleer came to town, for the first time, Nellie noticed a certain twinkle in his unusual blue eyes. And from then on, she was smitten. Three visits later, Abdul Ziyad nervously approached my grand father. When he rode out of town, Nellie was seated on the smallest camel.'

'Blue,' remarked Victoria. 'Like my eyes, Aunty Isabelle?'

She nodded. 'And you have the cameleer's nose, just like I do. Your sister has your grandmother Eva's eyes. Eva, your father's mother, was such a beauty. That part of the story comes later. When Nellie returned, my grandmothers glanced at her unchanged waistline. Shrugging, they took her away from her husband and asked a thousand questions, the most common being: what did the world look like from the back of a camel? Each time Nellie returned to camp, the older women would glance at her belly and shrug. A few years later, they began to frown. And a few years after that, they began to question her more intently. A different question by then: was he not a proper husband?'

The old woman paused and reached over to pick up a branch. Gently placing it on the fire, she continued the story: 'It took many years, but there came a time when no shrugs or raised eyebrows were needed when Nellie rode into camp, for she was very round of belly. The next time they visited, my mother carried my older brother Abdul Jafar in her arms. A few visits later, Abdul Jafar sat on the lead camel, Baba on the end, and our mother on the middle one. Mother held newly born me tightly in her arms. Baba's blue eyes were not passed down to my brother or to me. Mother would always say: the next one. There were no more. She became unwell, at about the time I had begun to walk. It was decided that mother and I were to stay here, so she could get help with me and some much-needed rest. Abdul Jafar went with Baba. When they returned, mother had been gone a month.

As I was so young, Baba left me here, with family. Baba and my brother came back regularly at first, then less and less frequently. When the railway station was built nearby, and a general store opened, there was no further need for a cameleer's services. Baba stopped visiting. I didn't really mind, as his long absences had made him like a stranger. And although I missed my brother, I had many cousins to play with. When word got out about the richness of the opals being dug up here, Abdul Jafar finally returned. He had aged, as had I, so I did not recognise my brother at first sight. Abdul Jafar told me Baba had died a few years before. Abdul Jafar also told me, in secret, how he'd returned to make enough money to propose to the woman he loved. They had met when he was working on a pearler. Eva was a green-eyed mermaid. Well, the way my brother described her she sounded like one. Eva was quite a bit younger than my brother. He told me that she could hold her breath longer than any of the other divers, male or female. She had told Abdul Jafar it was because she had salt water in her blood. Her mother had come from islands far to the north-east of this continent, and had also been a diver. Eva's father was born here. Brown-skinned, red-haired and green-eyed, which made him stand out in any crowd. When Eva was a child, he'd told her stories of long-ago shipwrecks and red-haired maroons.'

Maggie piped up, 'Green! Like my eyes.'

Maggie and Victoria exchanged thoughts, in the silent way of twins. Until now, they had both wished they had beautiful brown eyes, like their mother's. And like Nana Vic's and Grandfather Albert's. They'd often wondered why their eyes were so different and were pleased to finally find out that they did, after all, have eyes like family.

'My brother never did make as much money as he'd dreamt of. He did, however, unearth a unique treasure from the site of the inland sea, something so amazing he hoped it would sway Eva to say yes. He'd found three perfect pearls.'

'Pearls?' asked Brigid, frowning. 'Out here?'

'Fossilised pearls, the size of small bird eggs. They had been lying in that ancient seabed since the beginning of time and had become opalised. He thought these unique pearls would win him the heart of a famed pearl diver. He did win her heart, but not because of the pearls. It was because Eva had loved Abdul from the moment she'd first seen him standing on the deck of the pearler. So they married. And seven years later, they had three sons. The youngest was Daniel, your father. Your grandfather, my brother Abdul Jafar, was unfortunately killed by a shark the day before your father was born. A week later, white people took your father and his brothers away from your grandmother Eva. She searched for her boys for many years. Even sold the fossilised pearls to hire a lawyer. Not even a whisper of her sons was found. Eva died of sorrow before her hair had time to turn grey.'

Brigid reached out and gathered her daughters closer. Them being taken was still her greatest fear, and the reason she generally avoided staying in one place for too long. She had learnt her lesson at that last town, and was never going to repeat that mistake again.

Isabelle got up. 'It's time for my afternoon lie-down. Don't worry, Omer is on his way.'

Brigid turned around and saw dust in the distance, most probably made by Omer's car. She turned to say goodbye, but Isabelle had already walked away.

Brigid called out, 'You haven't told me how long ago Danny left.'

'Tomorrow. Come back tomorrow. Without the little ones. We will talk then.'

Disappointed, Brigid walked over to the edge of the track to wait for Omer with the twins. She was quiet all the way back to the house, while the girls asked Omer a million questions about his opal mine.

'Stop with the interrogation,' he finally said. 'You'll see for yourselves. I'll take you there tomorrow and give you the tour. That's if your mother agrees.'

'Can we, Mumma?' asked Maggie excitedly.

Brigid nodded, and then turned to look out the window.

*

As it was, they did not get to go to the mine the next day, or the day after. And Brigid did not get to talk further with Isabelle. Omer had come down with the flu and was not fit for working, or even driving. At first Bethel had to order him back to bed constantly, but soon he was too feverish to even think of going anywhere. Every morning, the girls would enquire about him at breakfast, hoping that today would be the day they visited the mine. Every morning they were disappointed. Five days later, they walked into the kitchen to find Omer eating breakfast.

'You ready?' he asked, putting down his cup of coffee.

They scuttled from the room to get ready for the longawaited outing. Brigid made lunch for four, and had almost finished when the girls returned. While Brigid went to put on her shoes, the girls helped Bethel pack up the lunches. Then they skipped to the ute, slowly followed by Omer and their mother.

'Can we stop off at Isabelle's on the way?' asked Brigid.

Omer nodded, but once they got to the turn-off to Isabelle's camp, they saw nothing in the distance. No smoke, no cars, nothing.

Brigid asked, 'Can we go closer, just to be sure?'

'They often go away,' replied Omer. 'Don't worry, they'll be back soon.'

Brigid frowned all the way to the mine, and barely took any notice as Omer showed them around. The girls, on the other hand, found the mine fascinating and had many questions.

The next day, Brigid went again but still the campsite was empty. Instead, she spent the day with Omer. Not wanting to be a burden, she offered to help. For two weeks, Brigid went with Omer every morning and, not seeing any sign of Isabelle, spent the day working at the mine. Brigid enjoyed helping Omer. She'd discovered a liking for working deep underground. It was quiet, just like her many years of travelling through the outback, and not unlike stargazing from beside campfires. But in this new darkness she searched for shining stars in rocks.

'You've stopped packing,' Omer remarked one morning as they left the house.

'I'm waiting until I speak with Isabelle again. I hope you don't mind.'

Omer shook his head. 'Not at all. We're enjoying your company. Bethel is loving having the girls around the house. I've not seen her this happy in a very long time.'

***

Bethel and Omer were content in each other's company; the love and respect they had for each other was obvious. Even so, sometimes Omer would find his wife staring blankly, with tears rolling down her face. Silently crying, just like the little sparrow he'd found hiding in that lifeboat many years ago. And just like all those days ago, Omer would wrap strong arms around Bethel and wait quietly.

Brigid had found Bethel crying on a few occasions, but did not pry. Instead, she hurried her daughters away, keeping them occupied while Bethel took a moment for herself. And there were those numbers. On numerous occasions, Brigid had seen flashes of the tattoo on Bethel's wrist. She knew what it meant. Just like sad tales of sorting people by blood quantum, sharing horror stories of inked numbers should never be forced.

There soon came a time, however, when they were both ready to unwrap difficult stories. One afternoon, Brigid was kneading bread dough and Bethel was dressing a lamb that Omer had killed that morning. The lamb was to be the main dish at a feast the next day, to celebrate Omer and Bethel's anniversary. They had invited all their neighbours and friends, and the women had been busy preparing food for the last two days.

As the sun headed towards the horizon, Bethel declared, 'That's enough for today. The rest can wait until the morning. Let's catch our breath before serving supper.'

After they washed off the flour, blood and sweat, Bethel made them both a cup of tea. They took their cups outside, to watch the sun set. Omer had built a wooden bench under the olive tree in the backyard. It wasn't much of an olive tree, given the harsh environment it had to survive in, but it was a good place to sit. This tree had significance for Omer. He'd carried it, as a small sapling, all the way from his homelands, protecting it like a child until he found a place to settle. Under this tree had become a favoured place for Bethel and Omer to sit at the end of many a day. This afternoon, Bethel sat with Brigid, watching the dying sun. A sharp screech of galahs broke the silence as they took off, then flew overhead. Brigid smiled when she saw what had startled the birds. Victoria and Maggie were helping Omer with the afternoon chores, which included enticing two very stubborn goats in for milking. One of the nannies had taken off, and the girls were attempting to corner the stubborn goat. Omer stood back, laughing while offering suggestions.

Brigid smiled. 'They do enjoy helping Omer with the animals. Although, in this instance, I'm not sure they are actually being helpful.'

'You have good girls. Strong, courageous, willing to try anything. We have enjoyed having them here, bringing an air of wonderment and joy to our home.'

'You've made us feel so welcomed. It's beginning to feel like home. Even this olive tree reminds me of home. My granny also brought treasured saplings from her country. She was so proud of the apple orchard that she started. Granny told me she'd planted them with purpose, to set down stronger roots in a country strange to her. Those trees from her home country helped her create a new home, for a new family. Unfortunately, Granny did not have the chance to watch her fruit trees grow with a husband by her side, but she did create a good home for my mother and me. Later, there was my stepfather and brothers. I really miss my granny. It just didn't feel like home after she died. This house feels like a home. Omer and you have welcomed us in, like family.'

'Omer is a good man. I could not want for a better partner to share my life with. I will let you in on a little secret: he is not my husband.'

'I don't understand. Tomorrow is your wedding anniversary.'

'It's an anniversary, yes. Just not of our wedding. We never had one. It's too hard to make people understand, though. Too much judging and not enough acceptance in the world. Tomorrow, it will be seventeen years since Omer and I first met.'

Brigid waited, sensing that Bethel had more to share.

'I already have a husband. As much as I cherish Omer, my heart belongs to my husband. To be honest, I do not know if Casimir is even alive. I suspect not.'

Bethel put her cup on the bench, and looked up to watch a gentle breeze play in the olive tree.

'It's been so good having the sound of children laughing in my home once more. I had a son and a daughter. Your Maggie reminds me of my Maja.'

Brigid heard her daughters squealing as they tried to catch the rebel goat. She wondered if Bethel wanted to tell her more about her daughter.

'Maja died before the face of evil revealed itself to the world. Despite knowing that the world was turning into a dangerous place for my angel, I tried desperately to anchor her to me. She'd caught a fever. One that even her papa couldn't cure. Casimir was a doctor, and I was once a nurse, and still we could do nothing. Medicine and good food were becoming so scarce. There was nothing we could do. After Maja died, our son Jakub stopped listening to us. Before that, Jakub had been avoiding coming home, finding the sight of his sister's frailness too hard to bare. Instead, in darkened cellars and barns, he listened to brave and angry men who burned brightly with hope, and the weapons of steel and wood they were stockpiling. The day after we buried Maja, Jakub left. Forever I will carry the knowledge that I was unable to protect my children.'

Brigid looked out across the flat, dry earth, reflecting on survival in the face of the cruelty of mankind. Seeing a movement in the corner of her eye, Brigid turned her head to see Omer standing by the side of the house, watching his wife with concern. Brigid signalled with a hand that all was fine. He nodded in gratitude and walked away. Omer knew that Bethel often needed space on the eve of their anniversary, to remember in silence those she'd lost. To remember those who had loved her before he met her. He also knew that later, when they shared the warmth of their bed, Bethel would need his strong arms as she tried once again to make peace with her past.

Bethel commented to Brigid, 'Looks like they've caught that goat. So we should get supper on the table.'

'We can do it in a little while. There's no hurry. If you don't mind me asking, did you see your son again?'

Bethel nodded. 'I saw Jakub one more time. It was in the street outside our home. They had come for Casimir and me. We hardly had any time to gather warm clothing before they pushed us roughly onto the truck. Standing up there, pressed against my husband and too many of our neighbours, I noticed Jakub in the crowd below us. He was pushing people aside, trying to get to me. I knew Casimir had also spotted him, as he took my hand in his. I caught our son's eye and shook my head. Jakub stopped. As the truck drove us apart, he mouthed, 'I love you.' His father and I silently sent our love to him, willing the tears to pause until our son was gone from our sight.'

'I am so sorry, Bethel. He sounds like a son to be proud of.'

'Yes, that and more. Although I was afraid when he joined the resistance, I was also proud of him. I do not know what happened to Jakub after that final sighting I will carry forever. Through the evil of those following years, every day I prayed he was safe. I still do. And I feel his presence. Do you think a mother knows if her child still walks the earth? I feel that, then I tell myself that is foolish.'

'No, not at all. I believe we can feel loved ones' presence, even if their whereabouts are unknown.'

'I'm not so sure about my husband. Although it hurts to say so, I believe Casimir did not survive the camps. We were separated, sent to different places. Once they discovered I was a trained nurse, I was given the job of keeping alive the few they considered of use. Those evil men and women did not value life, but some of them highly valued the pursuit of medical and scientific knowledge. They were cruel to doctors, scientists and inventors of weaponry. They also wanted them kept alive. So they used me for my nursing skills, which meant my time in those camps was not as bad as most people experienced. I hoped, given his medical skills, my husband had at least the same conditions as I. Casimir had always been so determined and wilful, he would not have found it easy to comply. To take orders from demons. When those big chimneys started to spew out heavy ash...'

Brigid put an arm around her. The last bit of sunlight was extinguished as the women sat in silence under the olive tree.

***

On the way back from the mine, Brigid saw smoke rising in the distance.

'Stop!'

'Looks like Isabelle has returned,' Omer remarked.

'That's not where she was camping before. Maybe it's not her.'

Brigid peered anxiously out of the car window as Omer drove off the road and towards the campfire. As they got closer, they saw Isabelle standing near the fire, with her hunting dogs surrounding her. Isabelle didn't pay them any attention as she continued to skin a large roo. After tossing scraps to the dogs, she stood and wiped her hands on her apron.

'This isn't far from your house. I can walk back later,' Brigid said to Omer.

'Make sure you head off well before dusk. Don't want you falling down any old shafts in the dark.'

'I'll be careful,' Brigid promised as she got out of the car.

She approached Isabelle hesitantly, keeping an eye on the dogs that growled and snapped at each other as they devoured the offal.

'Don't mind them,' Isabelle called out.

Brigid walked around the dogs to get to her.

'Is it tomorrow already?' Isabelle said with a grin.

Brigid laughed. As Isabelle removed her bloodied apron and took her rifle inside, she indicated that Brigid should sit outside the makeshift shelter. She came back out and sat beside Brigid.

'You shoot?'

Brigid nodded. 'My grandparents taught me. I still have my grandfather Albert's gun.'

'How long you been walking?' asked Isabelle, handing her a tin mug full of water.

'Way before the girls were born. After my granny died, I left home. Mum had remarried when I was little. To Frank, a good man. I've got three younger brothers. I don't know why, I just never felt close to any of them. Only my granny. She'd started to encourage me to travel, so when she was gone, it seemed the right thing to do.'

'How did you find your other kin? Did your mother tell you where to go?'

'She told me nothing. It's hard to explain; something led me out there. Good thing I found that place, as the twins were ready to be born and I couldn't walk any further.'

Two young girls ran over and placed plates of food in front of Isabelle and Brigid. After thanking the girls, they ate in silence.

When Isabelle had finished eating, she got up slowly, releasing a small groan. 'These bones are giving me trouble lately.'

She went into her humpy and came out with a bottle. Sitting down again, she poured some whisky into her cup and offered the bottle to Brigid. The younger woman tipped out the remaining water from the mug she held, before refilling it with whisky.

Brigid took a sip before speaking. 'Something also led me to Danny. A little bird. Where the desert meets the sea, I met Danny.' She wiped away a tear.

Isabelle offered to top up her cup then said, 'He told me about meeting you. I told Daniel that he'd been living not so far from the town where his parents first met. He didn't believe me at first. Life is like that. Patterns. History. Stories. Mistakes. Whatever. It all just keeps on repeating.'

'Did he talk about me much?'

'All the time. Couldn't shut him up some days.'

'What did he say?'

Isabelle shared some of the conversations she'd had with her nephew, while Brigid soaked up the words, delving deep into her memories for a clear image of Danny. When the bottle lay empty in the dirt, Isabelle stood up. She whistled for her dogs and went to go inside her shelter.

Brigid stood up. 'You've still not told me about the last time you heard from him.'

'Tomorrow,' replied Isabelle.

'But...'

'Tomorrow. Come back tomorrow. It's getting dark, and you need to get walking.'

Brigid watched Isabelle disappear into her shelter, followed by her dogs. Reluctantly, Brigid walked away.

She stopped when she heard a whistle. Turning back, she saw Isabelle.

'Don't forget to bring those girls with you tomorrow. They have cousins to play with. Much better they are here, with family, than under that white woman's feet all the time.'

And then she was gone again.

***

Brigid walked across the rocky plain, towards the road. There was just enough light left for her to see the outline of the roughly tarred road that would lead her to Omer and Bethel's house. Almost tripping, Brigid realised she was a little bit inebriated. It was so rare for her to drink that it was little wonder the whisky had gone straight to her head. Walking with more care, she made it to the road without falling. The moon was full, allowing her to see the road. Halfway to her destination, Brigid thought she heard giggling. She stopped, trying to locate where the sounds had come from. All she could see in the moonlight was piles of dirt left by mining operations, on both sides of the road. Suddenly, her surroundings looked eerie and unfamiliar.

She thought she heard distinct sounds of laughter, and they sounded close. Then she smelt smoke, and a tantalising smell of something cooking. Brigid walked towards where she thought the smells were coming from, and noticed sparks dancing.

'Careful you don't fall in a crater, sis.'

These words were followed by loud laughs, from what sounded like multiple people.

'Don't call her sis. That one is proper too good for us,' said another voice.

Brigid blushed as she heard yet more laughter.

'Leave her be, it's not her fault. Being brought up as a little brown potato has made her a bit silly.'

Brigid kept walking, curious to find out who was talking, even if their words were hurtful. As she carefully manoeuvred her way around the many discarded mineshafts, Brigid felt she might as well be walking on the moon's crater-littered surface, so alien did this landscape suddenly feel to her. She finally found the campfire and stood in the shadows, taking in the figures who sat in the firelight. Brigid counted seven people. All women, she noted with an embarrassed glance at their partially unclad state. As the firelight tickled bare skin, Brigid noticed they were very similar to each other in appearance. Like sisters, or cousins perhaps.

One woman smiled. 'Come, sit. Don't mind my sisters. They were just teasing. You're welcome to join us.'

Brigid walked towards the circle of women, and sat in the gap created when two shifted over. She put her hands up, feeling the warmth of the fire. Brigid looked around, noticing they were all looking at her.

Nervously, she introduced herself. 'I'm Brigid.'

'We know,' they all replied with one voice.

One of the younger women asked, 'What did that bossy one tell you?'

Brigid said, 'Sorry?'

As the others laughed, one remarked, 'I'm pretty sure Isabelle has never even uttered a sorry.'

'True. That one would never say that word, not for anything,' remarked another.

'She'd make you sorry though, if you ever crossed her.'

Brigid frowned in confusion, which made the women laugh harder.

An older one said, 'About your man, silly. What did Isabelle tell you about Danny?'

'How do you know him?'

'He was here once. Long time, now. We often saw him, late at night, standing on the shore of the ancient sea.'

'He was silly lovesick, like you,' laughed one woman, and the others burst into laughter again.

'Good-looking fella. I was almost tempted. Almost,' shared one as she flipped her hair back with a toss of her head.

'As if he even noticed you.'

'Aye, look out.'

The women continued their banter as Brigid gathered her thoughts. One of them handed her a leg of something. Brigid took it and tentatively bit into the warm meat. It was good. Really good. She ate it down to the bone, then started to feel sleepy.

'Hey, you need to get moving. Those daughts are waiting for you,' said one of the women.

Brigid sat up, alert once more. She noticed the women had covered themselves with cloaks of wallaby skin, and were gathering their belongings. The roasted roo they'd been sharing was now a big pile of bones.

One woman turned towards Brigid, and said softly, 'You don't need him, sis. You don't need any man. Look at you, how far you've travelled. You can do whatever you set your mind to, so why set it on chasing a shadow?'

'She been too lovestruck, that one.'

'She been forgot who she is,' affirmed another.

Another looked at Brigid, frowning. 'She's turned her back on the ancestors. Refuses to listen to Country. She only has herself to blame.'

'I reckon she can hear them. How else do you think she got here?'

'She only hears what she wants. Takes only what serves her purpose. Gives nothing back,' replied the frowning woman.

'True,' said another, throwing dirt on the fire.

'Perhaps she'd do better finding herself, and not chasing that man.'

Some sisters nodded and all started talking at once. Each one had a piece of advice for what she should be doing, could be doing.

Brigid shouted, 'Stop talking about me. I'm right here.'

'You are here. We're not.'

And with that, they were gone.

EIGHT

About the time Brigid realised Isabelle had no more to tell her about Daniel, her feet began to itch. At first it was just a little itch, not more than a tingle. Nothing a good scratch couldn't resolve. Too soon, scratching only made her feet feel hot. This irritation was waking her at night with a frantic urge to scratch her soles. Bethel gave her some calamine lotion to dab on them, and it gave some temporary relief. A week later, Isabelle was puzzled by a restlessness she sensed in Brigid. Sitting by the fire, while the girls played chasey with their cousins, Brigid took off her shoes and rubbed the soles of her feet. Isabelle saw the redness and made a clicking noise. She got up, went into her humpy and came straight out again. She handed Brigid a small jar.

Brigid opened the lid and sniffed the greenish balm.

'For your feet,' said Isabelle. 'Rub it in.'

She did as she was told and felt immediate relief.

Isabelle said, 'It might take away the redness from all your scratching, but it won't stop your feet from itching.'

Brigid sighed. 'Will anything?'

'There's no cure to be found around here. Looks like you've got wandering feet. Those feet want to get walking again.'

'I have been thinking it's time to leave. I just don't know where I should go.'

'That's never stopped you before.'

Brigid nodded, remembering that little bird from years ago that she had followed without questioning, without fear and without purpose. In contrast, all those years she'd walked with her daughters was to find Danny. Then she had a purpose. A why, but not a where. And now? Isabelle had asked around; no one had seen or heard from Danny for many years. Not since he'd boarded a train, headed north. All Isabelle knew was that her nephew Daniel, having found the inland sea that called to him, had gone back to the woman he loved. Isabelle now knew that Brigid hadn't been there, waiting. Brigid and Danny had most probably crossed over the same country. Sat by a campfire and gazed up at the same stars. Just not together.

'He's out there somewhere,' remarked Isabelle, as if reading her mind.

'I have a growing feeling that I'll never see him again.'

'Maybe so. Doesn't mean he's not still out there.'

Brigid shook her head, not understanding what Isabelle meant. And then a shiver ran down her back and dug itself into the soft dirt she sat on. Isabelle had seen that shiver and hoped it would not return too soon. She put a hand on Brigid's back, wishing she could protect her from what lay ahead, even though she knew that was impossible.

'Never let fear win,' she said. 'You're not a mouse. That's not who you are. It's not who your people are.'

Isabelle glanced at the apple pendant the younger woman wore. Brigid reached up and grasped it. The smell of apples wafted on the air. Suddenly, Brigid remembered her granny and the stories she had told. Brigid recalled how confused she had been as a child, listening to stories of apple seeds and potatoes. Now she was more conflicted than confused. Brigid then had an image of Nana Vic, standing by the bloodwood tree with an apple in her hand.

Brigid smiled. 'Me, a mouse? Look how far I've come on my own. And then with my daughters. I keep them safe, all on my own.'

'You think walking takes courage? Listening to things that go bump in the night. Leaving family behind, avoiding people. Pfft. What are you running *from?* Face up to what really scares you, and then you'll no longer need to keep walking.'

'If it makes my feet stop itching, I'll try anything.'

'You say that, but will you?'

***

Once more, Brigid stood with suitcases at her feet. Once more, there were people to farewell. Brigid and the girls had already hugged Aunty Isabelle goodbye. The day before, she'd ordered Brigid to stay by the campfire, while she took the girls to the inland sea in a nephew's rusty car. Victoria came back flushed with excitement, whereas Maggie appeared to be disappointed. When Brigid asked her what happened, Isabelle had made it clear that it was something she shared with her great-nieces, and not of her concern. Brigid shrugged, and said goodbye. Just like when she'd departed from Nana Vic and her grandfather Albert, Brigid did not seem to care that she was leaving behind kin once more, most probably never to be seen again. She felt sure her path would never again cross with Isabelle's. Isabelle didn't judge her nephew's woman, who was leaving on her own terms, but Brigid's coldness would not stop her from hugging the girls closely to her chest. Isabelle whispered final words in Victoria's and Maggie's ears, and then released them. As she walked back to her humpy, Isabelle knew Brigid was also walking away without looking back.

From the back seat, the girls watched their cousins chase Omer's car, waving, laughing, calling out. Victoria and Maggie waved back, already eager for the next time they would see their cousins.

*

Out the front of the general store, Omer helped Brigid place their suitcases next to the coach. The driver picked up the largest one, to put in the luggage compartment on the side of the bus, and then paused.

'Are you both boarding?' he asked.

Omer shook his head. 'I'm not going anywhere.'

The driver frowned. 'She's travelling alone?'

'No,' stated Brigid. 'My daughters are travelling with me.'

The driver suddenly noticed Victoria and Maggie. His frown deepened. Omer handed him another suitcase.

Before he loaded it, the driver stressed to Omer, 'Don't want trouble. You tell 'er that, mate.'

Brigid put her hands on her hips. 'You can speak directly to me. I do speak English, just like you. Perhaps even better.'

She sensed ears tingling around her, as onlookers waited to hear what the driver would say next. He didn't reply; he turned his back on her. One woman, of a similar age to Brigid, had that type of expression that indicated she always had plenty to say. Instead, she quietly smoothed down her black linen dress, and pulled her lace-edged gloves just a bit higher over wrists that hadn't been kissed by the sun for a long time.

Brigid returned to Bethel, who was waiting near the car.

Bethel asked, 'Are you sure you should leave like this?'

'It's time for me to go home. I miss my mother.'

'Why not call her? Your mother would help you get home quicker.'

Brigid shook her head. 'I couldn't ask her for help, not after all these years. I've just enough money for this coach to the city, and once there I'll find work. I plan on staying in the city only long enough to earn the fare home. No longer.'

'I do wish you would let Omer and me help you get home. I am sure that is what your mother would want.'

'Don't worry about us, Bethel. I have this all planned out. You and Omer have done enough for me already. Not only sheltering us for nearly two years, welcoming us into your lives. I can never repay your kindness.'

'Oh please, no need to thank us. Omer is going to miss the girls.'

Bethel then noticed the woman wearing gloves on a hot day, who was looking at them in a most unfriendly manner. Bethel thought she recognised the woman as the dressmaker's daughter, who'd left town many years ago. Mrs Todd, the dress maker, had recently taken ill and Bethel heard the daughter had come back to care for her. Sadly, Mrs Todd had been buried last week. Which would explain the daughter's black dress. Bethel couldn't remember the Todd girl's name. It had been years since she'd married that accountant from the city.

'Mrs Smythe,' said the driver. 'Can I load that for you?'

The woman turned away from watching Bethel and Brigid, and handed her suitcase to the driver. A small boy, a few years younger than the twins, ran to her. She took out a hanky and wiped a smudge of dust off the boy's face as he wriggled in protest.

'Mother, there's other children getting on this bus,' he announced excitedly.

Mrs Jones had noticed Victoria and Maggie talking with Omer. She frowned, confused, as the girls walked over to the woman that was with Bethel. Mrs Smythe watched them, lips tightly pursed. If Victoria had seen her face, she would have whispered to Maggie, 'Cat's bum,' and they would both have laughed, for they had seen such a look on a white woman's face too many times. Neither girl had noticed Mrs Smythe's disapproving stare, but Bethel had. It was a look she'd seen before, in her home country. On the faces of coldly distant neighbours, in the weeks before the trucks rolled into her once-friendly neighbourhood.

'Take care, dear,' she advised Brigid. 'Be wary of façades of civility that mask bad intent.'

Following the direction of Bethel's gaze, Brigid saw Mrs Smythe looking at them. That shiver she'd released back at Isabelle's camp a few days earlier caught up with her. It had crawled all the way here, over rocks and through ditches, avoiding abandoned mineshafts and dodging inquisitive lizards, just to find her. Once it had, it crept up her spine and nestled under her heart. Brigid first felt its coldness, and then a heaviness she would never be rid of until her last breath.

**

Brigid kept her distance from Mrs Smythe once on the coach, finding a seat near the back. The Smythe boy, however, kept turning around in his seat and waving to them. Maggie at first waved back, until Victoria pulled her ear and told her to keep still. That made Maggie cry, and Brigid noticed Mrs Smythe's shoulder twitch slightly with annoyance. She distracted Maggie with a story, until her daughter drifted off to sleep. Brigid didn't need to look up to know that Mrs Smythe was glaring at them. And neither did Victoria. They both sat up, just a bit taller, shoulders back and heads high. Mrs Smythe pursed her lips once more, slapped her son's leg and told him to sit still.

Sometime in the night, Brigid and Victoria had drifted off to sleep too. Brigid, alert even while sleeping, felt the coach slowing, and then heard its brakes. Sitting up, she glanced out the window. The sun was only just appearing. Passengers started moving, stretching and murmuring, eager for a chance to move their legs. Brigid saw a sign appear: *Parsons' Tea Room and Garage.* She grinned at the sign, remembering how her grandmother would say that people who used fancy words for simple things often thought they were better than they really were. Using the label 'tea room' for a run-down roadhouse in the middle of nowhere was proving her grandmother's point. The petrol pumps out the front were still in use, but the garage next door appeared to have been closed for some time. Brigid saw a dim light shining in the roadhouse and, as she watched, more lights came on.

The coach driver called out, 'You have thirty minutes, folks. Not a minute more.'

The passengers filed off the bus, hopeful that thirty minutes would be enough. Maggie was desperate to use the ladies' room.

Brigid took them to the browned lawn at the side of the building. 'Let the others go first.'

Maggie did a two-step dance as she waited, while Victoria studied Mrs Smythe. She'd already used the rest room and was looking for her son. She spied him under some trees and called him to her. She gave him a clip behind the ear, before dragging him into the roadhouse's dining room.

The bus driver walked to the roadhouse door and, as he entered, called out, 'Mrs Parsons, have you made my tea extra strong?'

Standing up, Brigid said to Victoria and Maggie, 'Come on, the queue has gone.'

Returning from the ladies' rest room, the girls sat back down on the brittle grass and Brigid unpacked the hamper she'd made before leaving Bethel's house. After eating, Maggie and Victoria ran around while Brigid packed up. She didn't see Maggie run over to the trees, or the boy who waved her over. Brigid hurried to them when she heard Victoria yelling.

'Let her go,' Brigid said sternly.

Mrs Smythe, still holding on to Victoria's ear, asked, 'Can you not keep your brat under control?'

'My daughters are very well behaved. Unlike some children,' she remarked, glancing at Mrs Smythe's son.

Mrs Smythe let go of Victoria. 'She was associating with my William. Obviously does not know her place. Just like her mother, it would appear.'

'Come on, girls, let's get washed up before getting on the bus,' said Brigid, turning her back on Mrs Smythe.

As they walked back to the rest room, Brigid saw the driver moving towards the coach. A woman in a blue dress and flowery apron followed him.

'I've packed you some scones for later,' she said, handing him a brown paper bag.

'You're a good gal, Flo. George Parsons was a fool to leave ya.'

Mrs Parsons flushed. 'I get by well enough on my own.'

'You're now into that women's rights rubbish, ain't ya? No one's perfect.'

Without a word, she went back inside. The driver laughed to himself as he returned to the coach. Brigid hurried the girls along, worried they'd miss his strict reboarding time. When they all came out of the ladies' room, they saw the driver roughly throwing their suitcases in the dirt. Brigid moved towards him, picking up dusty luggage on the way.

'What do you think you're doing?' she cried.

He stood, avoiding eye contact. 'There's been a complaint. Can't have you and that girl on me coach any longer.'

Brigid asked, 'Complaint?'

'Yeah. Knew you'd be trouble. Your type always is.'

Brigid looked up at the row of windows. Of all the faces staring down at her, she only saw one: Mrs Smythe. The look on her face told Brigid all she needed to know.

'I spent nearly all my money on these tickets. We must get back on the coach. We need to get to the city.'

The driver walked towards the bus door. 'Well, you ain't getting there on my coach.'

As the coach pulled out, Brigid watched Mrs Smythe once more. She knew what was behind that satisfied smirk: hate.

Brigid and Victoria picked up their luggage, while Maggie stared at the coach as it disappeared on the highway.

'Mumma?'

'It's done. Nothing we can do about it. We'll walk. Will take us much longer to get to the city, but we'll get there.'

Maggie began to cry. Victoria prodded her shoulder, which only made her cry with more gusto. As Brigid walked towards the roadhouse, she noticed Mrs Parsons standing on the threshold. Pushing a stray hair behind an ear, Mrs Parsons walked towards them. She moved slowly, seeming to struggle in the morning heat.

'Are you waiting to get picked up by family?' she asked.

Brigid shook her head. 'I need to buy a few items, then we'll be on our way.'

The woman looked closely at Brigid, one eyebrow raised. Brigid continued to walk, encouraging the girls to keep pace.

Mrs Parsons addressed Maggie. 'Where's your mummy, little one? Dry your tears. I'll help you.'

Maggie seemed confused. Victoria stood closer to her sister, placing a protective arm around her shoulder.

'I'm her mother,' said Brigid.

'I highly doubt that. Why do you have her? That's what I want to know.'

'It's really none of your business, but she is clearly my daughter. See, these girls are twins.'

Mrs Parsons stared at Victoria and Maggie, unable to see any resemblance. Brigid gathered the girls to her and led them inside. Next to the dining area, there were shelves with snacks and basic groceries. As Brigid selected goods, Mrs Parsons went to the sales counter and picked up the phone. After dialling, she stretched the phone cord long enough to stand in a storage room. While Maggie looked longingly at the cold drinks behind a glass door, Victoria listened to Mrs Parsons' conversation. Brigid saw Victoria and softly called her over.

'That's not polite.'

'She mentioned us. To the police, I think. Said she would keep us here.'

Brigid noticed Mrs Parsons looking too intently at Maggie, while talking into the phone. She appeared to be agitated. Noticing she was being watched, Mrs

Parsons placed a hand over her mouth and lowered her voice.

Brigid went to the counter, and placed on it flour, jam, condensed milk, tea leaves, onions, potatoes and tinned meat.

*

Mrs Parsons hung up the phone and went to serve her. She moved very slowly, while trying to engage Brigid in small talk. Given their previous exchange, Brigid was curt and willed her to move faster. Once she'd been handed the change, Brigid remembered she'd left the luggage outside. She went to fetch a string bag for the shopping. When she returned, Mrs Parsons was talking to Maggie.

'I always wished I'd have a girl like you. You have such pretty green eyes. Would you like a soft drink? I can get you a cold one. You sit at this table, I won't be long.'

While Mrs Parsons went to fetch the drink for Maggie, Victoria went over to her sister. She tried to pull her out of the chair, while Maggie clung to its sides. Brigid had packed up her groceries, and turned to see the girls fighting.

'Let's go,' she ordered.

Maggie whined as she followed Victoria and her mother out of the roadhouse.

Mrs Parsons called out, 'I have your cold drink, sweetie.'

Maggie hesitated near the door.

Brigid took her hand. 'Come on now. We need to go.'

They walked outside, with Mrs Parsons following them.

'Leave that girl here, she's not yours. You have no right to have her.'

Brigid turned around. 'I'm her mother. I don't need your permission to leave. Or anything else. Keep your damn white women's rights. And keep your hands off my daughter.'

Leaving the roadhouse behind, they walked past the padlocked garage, Brigid occasionally glancing back. A car had pulled up to the petrol pump out the front of the roadhouse, and Mrs Parsons was talking to the driver as she filled up his tank.

'This way,' said Brigid, leading the girls down the side of a rusty shed.

At the back of the shed, she noticed a loose sheet of metal. Peeling it back, she motioned to the girls to enter. It was dark inside the shed, and the smell of oil filled the air. Once her eyes became accustomed to the dark, Brigid saw that the shed was full of old cars. She selected the least rusty one and opened the back door.

'Get in. We'll wait here until it's safe.'

Once they were settled on the wide back seat, Brigid shut the door softly, and climbed in the front seat.

Victoria asked, 'Are we hiding from the police? I know she called them.'

Brigid nodded. 'Just remember, we did nothing wrong. It's not us that's wrong. It's people like Mrs Smythe and Mrs Parsons, and that coach driver. Anyone who thinks we're less than them.'

'I hate them all,' declared Victoria.

'Hate isn't the answer. Keep believing you are not less than them. No one is less human than anyone else, no matter the colour of their skin.'

Maggie whimpered, 'What will the police do if they find us? Will they throw us in the back of a truck and take us away from you?'

'No one will ever take you from me. I'm here, by your side, and always will be. Would you like to hear a story?'

Brigid shared some of Granny Maeve's tales, until the girls fell asleep. They loved hearing those stories. The only tale she would never tell them was the one about little dirt-encrusted potatoes.

*

A few hours later, Brigid shook them awake, whispering it was safe to leave. They gathered their belongings, and crept outside. Maggie froze when she heard a dog barking.

'It's okay, it's not nearby,' whispered Brigid.

They walked down the highway, with only starlight to see by. After a while, Brigid led them away from the road. The girls were tired, no longer used to walking long distances. Finding a sheltered spot, Brigid collected kindling. She lit a small fire and put the billy on. She cut up the onion and potatoes and added them to a metal-handled saucepan full of water. Once the pan was steaming, she opened the canned meat and cut it into cubes before adding it. She spooned the stew onto metal plates and handed one to each daughter. They ate in silence, starring into the fire. Brigid noticed Maggie's eyes drooping, so she spread out their blankets by the fire, took the plate from Maggie, and told her to lie down. Victoria quickly joined her sister. After cleaning up, Brigid snuggled between Maggie and the fire, protecting her from rolling too close in her sleep. As the fire crackled, Brigid drifted off.

Brigid dreamt. Not the dreams of a contented person. Not the dreams of a woman sleeping soundly in a warm bed, in a nice house, perhaps a husband by her side. She dreamt the dream of an outcast. And she lived out her deepest fears within this dream. A sharp-faced version of Mrs Smythe held Victoria by an ear, wiggling her in the air. Her daughter became a longeared hopping mouse, frantically trying to break free. Brigid ran towards her daughter, but the ground felt like thick custard. Slowly, slowly, she got closer. And then she heard a scream. Looking back, she saw Maggie in the arms of a grotesquely oversized Mrs Parsons. This monster-woman had put a pink baby bonnet on Maggie's head, and was trying to shove her in into a tiny doll's pram. Brigid was torn – which daughter to save first?

'You need to save yourself first, sis.'

'Wake up. You need to wake up.'

Brigid was confused. Those voices sounded just like the women she'd met that time, walking home from Isabelle's camp. The seven women who looked like sisters. What were they doing here?

'Sister, sister, you're on fire.'

Brigid suddenly felt a burning heat, and opened her eyes in panic. She smelt burning wool before she saw the flames. And then she felt the heat. The shoulder of her coat was on fire. She could not roll forward to extinguish it, as the campfire was there. She could not roll backwards because, as far as she knew, her daughters lay sleeping there. Brigid screamed in pain and began to panic. Then she jumped in shock as the coldness of water hit her. Victoria stood above her, an empty pan in her hand. Maggie was sobbing, while holding a billy full of water. Brigid lost consciousness before water hit her a second time.

She was still unconscious when two men lifted her carefully, having made a carrier from the blankets, and placed her gently on the back seat of their car. Victoria had flagged them down, after walking back to the highway on her own, while Maggie waited by their mother's side. The men promised that it would be okay; there was a country hospital in the next town. One of them offered the girls some boiled lollies and sips of his cola. It was a long drive, and Brigid murmured in pain every time the car hit a bump.

Maggie held her hand, whispering, 'It will be all right. These people are nice ones.'

Victoria half-heartedly watched the passing landscape, wondering if it really was possible to know if a stranger was nice. Or did every one of them harbour hatred for people who looked like her?

'Listen and you'll hear the waves,' that old woman said, as she placed a wind-hardened black hand on a sun-kissed brown cheek.

The girl squinted, trying with all her might to hear this ocean that flowed under her feet. Disappointed, she shook her head.

Isabelle put her other hand against Victoria's other cheek, gently cupping her face. 'Don't try so hard. Everything is as it should be.'

Loosening the tightness in her shoulders, Victoria tried again, but the earth's secret waters still lay hidden. She then wriggled her toes, letting them burrow like grubs into sun-warmed dirt. It felt good. Her mind began to wander.

The girl gasped and opened her eyes wide, blue eyes catching ancient brown eyes.

'I did it. I heard those waves,' she cried.

'Well, close your eyes again, child. And dive right in.'

NINE

The sun had long set when Samuel Bond turned off the road and up a narrow driveway. Brigid wound down the window and peered out, into the darkness. She saw a light, and then a house. Just as the motor fell silent, the front door of the house opened, revealing a tiny woman.

'What are you doing up? Leave it alone, I can handle this,' came a voice from behind the woman.

'I'm fine, really. I'm still quite capable of welcoming visitors to my house.'

'They're not visitors. She's the domestic. If you can't remember that, how are you going to keep her and those piccaninnies in their place?'

Brigid flinched, and hoped her daughters did not understand what the man had said. As it was, the journey had been most unpleasant. And not because the car interior had been cramped. Samuel Bond had made it clear, in no uncertain terms, that they talk only when necessary. And, if they must talk to him, he was to be addressed as Mr Bond. He was only escorting Brigid and her daughters because his younger sister, Grace Small, the only person for whom he felt anything close to affection, had asked him to. Like his parents, grandparents and great-grandparents, Samuel's preference was not to get too close to people like Brigid. At gatherings of like-minded folk, he would often remind everyone that in his great-grandparents' day the natives knew their place and always obeyed the master's orders. Samuel Bond was adamant that both parties could still benefit from such an arrangement. Which is why he volunteered to be a board member of the St Benedict School for Inland Children, which took boys to be trained as labourers in the city. When he had learnt that his sister had given Brigid and her daughters shelter, he'd strongly expressed his concerns. If driving them to the von Wolff's meant they were out of his sister's life, then that was a sacrifice he'd been prepared to make. After spending the past two days with him, Brigid was looking forward to never seeing him again. So she was relieved to be finally at their destination.

Brigid presumed the couple on the verandah were the von Wolffs, of whom she knew little. She helped her daughters out of the car, while Samuel went to shake the other man's hand. Maggie rubbed her eyes, leaning closer to her mother, while Victoria took in the latest strangers with whom they would be living. The man was still partially in the shadows, which contributed to his ominous aura. He didn't seem pleased to see them, and Victoria thought this might be due to the lateness of their arrival. Or perhaps concern for his wife. Brigid had explained to her daughters that the woman they were going to live with was ill. She had cancer and needed looking after. Also, because her husband was a well-known artist, they must be very well behaved and never disturb him when he was working. Victoria observed the woman standing in the doorway, who was surround by a soft glow from inside the house. Not only was she tiny, it was if she was shrinking in on herself.

Looking loftily down upon Brigid and her daughters, the man remarked to Bond, 'I'm not sure this one will do. And those sprogs look like trouble.'

'Stop that nonsense, Stefan. You'll scare her off,' the woman said, before addressing the new arrivals. 'Don't mind my husband, his bark is worse than his bite. Please call me Iris. I won't have any formalities around here. I want you all to feel at home.'

Brigid smiled. 'Thank you, Iris.'

Iris turned to her husband. 'Show Brigid where they'll be staying. It's late, and I'm sure the little ones are eager for bed.'

Von Wolff grunted as he went inside. He returned with an oil lantern and walked down the steps.

Iris said, 'We've set up the workers' cottage for you. It's old but comfortable. Unfortunately, the cottage doesn't have electricity connected. You'll find a lantern on the table, and plenty of candles. The wood oven was lit earlier, that should provide some warmth tonight. And if you're needing supper, you'll find milk, tea, bread and such in the cupboard. In future, you're welcome to join us for meals in the house. If you'll excuse me, I must return to my bed.'

Brigid thanked Iris and, after removing their luggage from the car, curtly bade Mr Bond goodbye. Victoria shouldered the new bag that Grace had given her, glad to no longer be toting around tatty old suitcases. She then relieved her mother of Maggie's bag; her sister was much too tired to carry anything but herself. They followed von Wolff, who'd walked so far ahead with the lantern that he was just a small dot of light in the distance. Soon they were at the front door of a run-down stone cottage.

They stepped hesitantly over the threshold. Von Wolff had placed the lantern on the table. Ignoring him, Brigid glanced around her latest accommodation. Iris was right, the house was comfortable. Compared to many of the places they had slept in over the years, it was almost luxurious. The fire from the stove had made the room quite toasty, and both the beds looked inviting.

As the girls went over to lie on one of the beds, von Wolff grabbed Brigid's arm. 'I won't have you upsetting my wife, so I'll say this clearly: you must not think you can ever be familiar towards her. You are here to cook, clean and tend to her personal needs. Other than that, you stay in here. You will eat in here, and never with us. And make sure those brats of yours are always kept quiet and never go near my studio. I must have silence when I am working. You will start work at six every day, no exceptions, and you are done when I say so. Not before. If you work hard, I might allow you to have two Sundays off every month. Do you understand?'

Even though she was very uncomfortable with her new employer's behaviour, Brigid nodded. She pulled her arm away and, to hide her indignation, lit the lantern and candles that had been left on the wooden table. She placed them around the room, to chase away whatever lurked in the shadows. She noticed von Wolff watching her and almost shivered as he stepped closer.

'What happened to your face?'

Brigid's hand reflexively moved to her cheek, as if she could hide the scars.

'Well?'

'A campfire accident,' she mumbled.

'Pity. I expect you were somewhat attractive before. Now you are not. Still, you could be a fascinating subject to photograph. What with your colouring and those defiant eyes embedded in such a grotesque face.'

Brigid flinched and looked towards her daughters. She was relieved to see them heads close, whispering and giggling, seemingly in a world of their own.

'Mr von Wolff, with all due respect, I'm here to do the housework. Not model.'

'You are far too uppity for your own good. You will need to learn to curb that tongue.'

And with that he went, leaving the door banging in the wind. Brigid shut it and put the inside latch on, wondering if she'd made the right decision. Wearily, she asked Victoria and Maggie if they wanted supper. They replied they were much too tired, so Brigid added wood to the stove as the girls climbed under the bedcovers. Too tired even for a story, they quickly drifted off to sleep. Brigid made herself a cup of tea. As she sat down at the table, she heard Samuel Bond drive off. That was one person she'd be happy to never encounter again. He was so unlike his sister, Grace Small.

*

Brigid reflected on the past few months. Some points she remembered clearly, others she had pieced together from what people told her. People such as Grace Small. Widowed while young, Grace had inherited her husband's considerable wealth and property. She took her position in the community seriously. She was a patron for many local services, including the small country hospital Brigid had been taken to after the accident.

Walking through the women's ward the day after Brigid arrived, Grace had heard a woman wrapped in bandages muttering about children. When Grace asked the matron if that patient's children had been visiting, she replied the woman had arrived on her own. No one knew who she was; she'd been found on the side of the road. Then a cleaner piped up, recalling there had been two girls with the men who brought the woman in. The matron ordered everyone to search the hospital. A young nurse finally found Victoria and Maggie huddled behind a club chair in the corner of the waiting room, where they'd been left the day before.

The matron had no idea what to do with them, and thought it best to call the Protector of Aborigines. Grace convinced her not to and took charge. She sat the girls down, and over hot chocolate found out what had happened. The girls refused to tell Grace their surname, and seemed wary of talking much about themselves or family. Their focus was solely on their mother: when could they see her; would she be okay; did it hurt much? Grace had no experience with children, so she asked the Johnsons, a middle-aged couple who had raised six children of their own, to look after the girls while Brigid was in hospital. Mrs Johnson brought them to the hospital every day to see their mother, and soothed the girls' worries with freshly baked biscuits and plenty of kindness. When the matron thought Brigid was well enough to vacate the bed, Grace stepped in again, inviting Brigid to stay in her unused servants' quarters. Grace enjoyed having company, as her late husband's manor had felt so big and empty since he'd died. So, a week later, Grace agreed to the twins moving in too.

Sipping tea while appreciating the heat from the wood stove, Brigid recalled those three months at the manor as she slowly recovered her strength. She'd also gathered the courage to look in a mirror. At first, Brigid had not recognised the woman who stared wearily back at her. Not because of the scars that covered one side of her face, snaking down her neck, onto her left shoulder and arm. It was her eyes. Dull. Full of sorrow.

While still in hospital, Brigid had phoned home, trembling fingers remembering the numbers to dial. An unrecognisable voice came on the other end. Patrick, Brigid's youngest brother, now had a surprisingly deep voice. She quickly realised he was not receptive to her call. He refused to get their mother and, instead, firmly told Brigid to stay away. It was not for lack of room that Patrick told her to never return. Her baby brother was now a young man with too much ambition, and he had set his sights on a political career. Patrick bluntly told his sister that a re-emergence of the family shame would ruin his chances of being elected. Brigid had been gone so long that neighbours had forgotten the little brown girl who once played in the family orchard. Patrick wanted to make sure they never remembered.

Maggie stirred, pulling the blanket off Victoria as she rolled over. Brigid got up and tucked them both in. Sitting back down, she recalled how hurt she'd been after that phone call. She'd heard hateful words before, in the schoolyard as a child and while

160

travelling through small towns, but never from her own family. She decided never to go home. If Patrick was ashamed of her, then she didn't want her girls around him.

*

A few months after they'd moved in, Grace accepted a proposal of marriage, after a whirlwind romance. Brigid knew it was time for her and the girls to move on. When Grace told Brigid about a live-in carer role, looking after an old schoolfriend, Brigid had immediately shown interest.

She was now regretting that choice. She already knew von Wolff to be an unwelcoming man. A man who would not tolerate noise, was overly judgemental and much too forward. Despite what Iris had told her, Brigid believed that von Wolff's bite would be far worse than his bark. She put her cup in the sink, then extinguished the candles and lantern. Climbing into the second bed, she shivered and pulled up the covers. That shiver, which had wedged itself under her heart the day she'd bid farewell to Bethel, was now making itself known. Brigid closed her eyes, trying to shut out feelings of apprehension and dread. Lulled to sleep by a gentle wind that blew past the cottage, soon Brigid was dreaming of walking barefoot across stony ground, in the company of seven chortling women.

***

It took Maggie a few moments to work out where she was. She sat up and looked out the small window next to the bed. Victoria and Brigid were still sleeping, so she sat for a while, becoming acquainted with yet another new place. It appeared to be quite different from anywhere she'd been before. This location was so green. She could see rolling fields, with a scattering of trees. There were even wildflowers hiding in long, green grasses. She saw a large tree-fringed dam in the distance, with a short pier in a state of disrepair. Maggie then noticed the little birds flitting about. Tiny, chirping rainbows. She felt a strong urge to venture out on her own, something she'd never been game to do before. She paused, hearing a sound behind her. Her sister flipped back the bedcovers, and stretched her arms.

'There are pretty little birds outside our new house,' shared Maggie excitedly.

Victoria looked towards where she was pointing, then climbed out of bed and walked quietly across the floor. Victoria opened the stove's wood compartment and poked the dying embers until a low flame appeared. After loading it with small pieces of wood, she shut the stove again. Victoria picked up the kettle. It felt full, so she put it on the stovetop. She went to the rickety, freestanding cupboard that had a mesh door, and took out a tea cannister and three cups. While the kettle boiled, she cut thick slices of hard bread. Meanwhile, Maggie had got out of bed and was rifling through her bag.

'Not so loud,' whispered Victoria, pointing to their sleeping mother.

Maggie nodded as she put on her shoes. Finding a jumper, she put it on over her nightgown and went to the front door. She opened it just a fraction and peeked out. The von Wolffs' house was a fair distance to the left. She couldn't see any signs of people being awake over there. Maggie stepped outside, hoping the rainbow birds would fly closer. While her sister got breakfast ready and her mother slept, she breathed in the aroma of nearby flowers, listened to the gentle swish of tree branches, and watched tiny birds fly overhead. She felt as if, maybe, everything would be all right.

***

Brigid had been surprised when Iris had given her the rest of the day off. She usually had every second Sunday off. No more, or less. Stefan insisted she be up at the house from daybreak to nightfall, preparing all the meals and doing all the housework. With a quick break in the afternoons, to greet her daughters after they'd made the long walk back from school. And, after feeding them an early dinner, she went back to work in the big house. A free day on a Thursday was most unexpected. At first she declined the offer, as Stefan was leaving for an overnight trip to the city, and Brigid didn't want to leave Iris alone. Iris insisted on Brigid having the day off, once she'd finished washing the breakfast dishes, as it was the twins' tenth birthday. Brigid was appreciative of having more time to prepare for their party. No friends from school had been invited, as she didn't want a furious Stefan von Wolff knocking on her door, complaining about happy children making noise. As luck would have it, though, he wasn't home, so the girls could make as much noise as they wanted. Brigid was planning on making their favourite treats, and decorating the cottage as best she could. And she would take them on a treasure trail at dusk, to find their presents.

As she was cooking, the sound of a car caught her attention. Concerned that Stefan had returned, Brigid peeked out the door. She saw Sally Humphries, Iris's friend, drive up to the house. Sally took out a number of brown bags from the back seat, and went inside. An hour later, Brigid heard her leave. When she heard Iris calling for her, she raced up to the house, thinking she needed some help. Standing on the verandah, Iris was smiling.

'Come look. I hope you like it.'

Puzzled, Brigid followed her inside. Down the long corridor and into the dining room. On the best table linen, and the best crockery, laid a feast. Cupcakes on delicate tiered stands. Flower petals set in jelly, in crystal bowls. Cucumber sandwiches, with the crusts cut off, on bone china. A huge pink-iced sponge cake in the centre, and Iris's favourite tea set sitting to one side of the table.

'What do you think? Will the twins be pleased?'

'You made all this?'

'I ordered it from the café in town, and Sally delivered it. Doesn't it all look so delicious?'

Brigid frowned. 'What is this for?'

'Afternoon tea for the twins' birthday, of course.'

'Why didn't you ask me first?'

Iris sat down, shoulders slumped. 'What was I thinking? Of course I should have asked you. How silly of me not to consider you'd already have something planned. Please forgive me.'

'Nothing to forgive, Iris. I'm worried about you overexerting yourself. You need to be taking things more slowly.'

'I have been a bit more exhausted than usual. How did I ever manage before you arrived? You're a good friend, Brigid. And I'm a fool. This food will all go to waste now.'

Brigid looked down at Iris. She appeared to be folding in on herself. Her face was worryingly pale, expect for a flush of colour on her cheeks. Brigid had been planning her daughters' birthday party for weeks. Putting aside money to buy material to make their presents, and ingredients to cook their favourite treats. In all their ten years, this was to be the best party she'd ever given them. She didn't like how Iris had tried to take over. She also didn't want to upset her friend, who was obviously excited about what she'd organised.

'What if we combine parties?' suggested Brigid.

'Oh yes! They can come up here after school and...'

'No, you come to our place.'

'How? There's too much to carry.'

'You go put on a cardigan, and let me worry about that.'

When Iris returned, the table was bare and Brigid was nowhere to be seen. She opened the front door, and found her. She'd loaded up the wheelbarrow with food.

'What a good idea! Shall I fetch the crockery?'

'I don't want to risk breaking your favourite setting. We can use what's in the cottage. Are you ready?'

'This feels like a grand adventure. Stefan never lets me have fun. He used to, when we were first married. He'd take me to the city, to dine at the best places. Sometimes we even saw a concert. He does love music. I didn't really like the concerts, but it was fun to dress in my finest and go out amongst people. Nowadays, he won't even take me into the local town, unless I urgently need to purchase personal items.'

Brigid picked up the barrow handles, and started to walk. Slowly, so as not to tire Iris.

'I know you probably won't believe me, but he wasn't always like this. I don't know why he changed. Perhaps it's living with someone who's so dull, and always unwell.'

'You're not dull. Maybe sickness scares him. Some people don't cope when loved ones have cancer.'

'You're probably right. Most of my friends no longer visit, either. I thought it was because Stefan has become so unbearable. Maybe it's because they don't like being around sickness. Is it hard being here, with me?'

'Not at all. I consider us friends. And the girls like your company.'

'Then why do you look sad so often? Is it him?'

'To be honest, it's not easy being around your husband. He expects so much of me, and is often far too abrupt with the children. He scares them.'

'He hasn't hurt them? You can tell me.'

She shook her head. 'Not really. Just words. Some of the things he says are extremely hurtful. He makes it clear that I'm beneath him, as far as he's concerned. He's harder on Victoria than Maggie. Even though she's tough like me, I still worry about her.'

'Why do you think he singles her out?'

'Your husband doesn't approve of us because of our skin.'

Iris suddenly went quiet. Brigid thought, *Have I said too much?* It wasn't an easy subject, and she wasn't used to openly discussing what made her different in the eyes of others, or how she felt about that. She hadn't even talked about this topic with her daughters. Brigid didn't know how to. There had been no one in her life to give her guidance to cope with discrimination, especially as a child, when she needed help to deal with schoolyard taunts.

'What do you mean? Your scars are hardly noticeable. And Victoria has beautiful skin,' commented Iris, before she covered her mouth. 'Oh, now I understand. I should have realised sooner. I'm sorry. It's the way he was raised, all that hate during the war, he can't help it.'

'It's not your fault. Your husband's views are not yours. Are they?'

'No, no. I don't see colour. Truly. You and your lovely daughters have brightened up my dreary life. You know I'd do anything for you.'

Brigid placed the wheelbarrow by the cottage door, and started to unload. *Is it even possible not to see colour?* she wondered. Her granny had alluded to something similar, whenever Brigid had come home from school in tears. All she could give her granddaughter were there-there pats on the shoulder, and strange tales of potatoes. Danny was the first person willing and able to discuss what it meant to be seen as different. Only a newborn when he and his brothers were stolen from their mother, he didn't even have a memory of her face to cherish, let alone family stories to keep him warm. Despite the way some people treated him and the attempted indoctrination he'd received at the children's home, he was a proud Aboriginal man. Brigid recalled how determined he'd been to find his family.

Much to his disappointment, she'd never wanted to talk about identity – his or hers. Brigid knew now that by not properly listening to him, she'd not been loving enough towards him. She suddenly realised she'd treated Nana Vic and Grandfather Albert in a similar way. If she'd let them, they would have taught her how to help Victoria and Maggie stand strong against the hate, to be grounded in culture, to proudly carry the stories. Instead, she'd quietly rejected their help and their stories.

At least Danny had found that ancient inland sea he sought, and been reunited with some of his family. He would most likely want to search for his two brothers. Maybe he was even looking for her. Brigid hoped that, whether he was alive or dead, he'd found the inner peace he was seeking.

Iris looked around, bewitched by the butterflies fluttering over brightly coloured flowers. 'You seem settled in the old cottage. I was concerned it would not be comfortable and warm enough for you and the girls. Winter sure gets cold around here. I do like what you've done here, this garden is so pretty.'

'Maggie helped. She loves flowers. And she was hoping a bright garden would attract more finches.'

Brigid walked inside, with Iris following. She removed dishes from the small table, and spread Iris's lace tablecloth. Together, they reset the table. The café food, combined with the more modest homemade food, made a mouth-watering sight.

Brigid noticed Iris was having trouble breathing. 'Sit, rest a while. The girls will be home from school soon, and you'll need energy to deal with their excitement when they see you here.'

'Do they really like my company, or are you just being kind?'

Brigid went to put the kettle on the stove. 'If they had their way, they'd be up at your house every single day. As we both know, Stefan wouldn't be pleased with their chitter-chatter.'

'They are such sweet darlings, I could listen to them all day long. I hope you don't mind me saying this, but I've noticed Maggie doesn't smile as much lately. Is she all right?'

'She's fine. Just a bit embarrassed about her teeth.'

'Her teeth?'

'She needs braces. I can't afford them on my wages.'

'I hope the children aren't teasing her at school.'

'A little. Mostly calling her flopsy the crooked-toothed bunny, and similar taunts. She's coping.'

Iris took a sip from the teacup placed next to her, while Brigid put scones in the oven to warm up.

'I'll lend you the money for Maggie's braces.'

'No, I can't accept your money. Anyway, I'm sure Stefan would never approve.'

'He doesn't need to know. This would be just between us. I have my own money, in my own bank account. Stefan doesn't even know about my nest egg. My father gave it to me, and made me promise to use it if I ever needed to leave my husband. Both my parents came over for the wedding. He encouraged me to travel when I had an offer to teach overseas. And, a year later, seemed happy when I wrote to tell him I was engaged. He and mother were so excited to visit, to witness me getting married. They'd never been overseas before. Once here, and after meeting Stefan, my father was reluctant to leave me in a country without family.'

'He must miss you. And he obviously cared enough to give you that money. I can't take it. You might need it one day.'

'I am slowly dying. What use have I for a nest egg? Let me lend you the money. It will make me happy to help others. Maggie is far too pretty to endure bad teeth for the rest of her life.'

'Can we talk about this later? I can hear the girls. Are you ready for their squeals of excitement when they see the party we've created?'

***

The morning sun peeked out from between dark grey clouds and penetrated the room through half-drawn curtains. Cocooned under a hand-stitched patchwork quilt, Iris saw the sunlight creeping across her bed. If it wasn't impossible, Iris would have caught that warming light and held it close. She was tired of winter. Tired of the way the coldness tiptoed into her bones and made them scream with pain. She suspected her husband was also tired – of her. He was away from home a lot more, spending most weekends in the city. Stefan insisted it was because of his artwork; he had meetings with gallery owners and exhibition openings to attend. And he still attended concerts and operas in the city, no longer inviting his wife. She thought it was because he couldn't stand the sight of her any more.

Brigid entered the room to ask if she'd like to sit for a while on the verandah. Too exhausted for words, Iris nodded. After nearly two years of caring for Iris, Brigid could almost predict her every need. She knew Iris needed sunlight, whatever warmth she could get. Even though her employer had lost so much weight, Brigid still appreciated Victoria's help to lift her. Together, they gently carried the quilt-wrapped Iris outside, trying not to cause her more pain. After placing Iris in the rocking chair, Brigid sat in the chair next to her. A pile of clothes to be darned lay in a basket at her feet.

As Brigid mended a small hole in a child's dress, Iris's hands twitched slightly at the sound of the needle. Her fingers remembered the motion, in and out, in and out – the comforting rhythm of needle piercing cloth, the softness of cloth surrendering to the hard metal. Iris thought back through the years, seeing in her mind the patchwork quilts she'd created, quilts that were now scattered around the globe, being cherished by others. Her husband was not the only artist in this household. Iris was once renowned for her quilts, each one more a work of art than mere bed linen. All Iris had of those beautiful quilts were her memories and the fading quilt she'd always favoured. The one now used to conceal her shrinking body.

Iris pulled the quilt tightly around herself and studied the vista before her. The sun's rays were no longer peeking through dark clouds. Mist had rolled in, concealing the paddocks, closing her off from the world. She felt uncomfortable, as if something was not quite right. Fog always made her feel uneasy, but today there was something more. Something dark lay waiting, concealed in the mist; she felt sure of it. Victoria had also noticed the mist, but not the foreboding presence. She ran back to the house, searching for her sister.

'Maggie, come and see this. Hurry,' she called down the hallway.

Brigid frowned, having more than once instructed her daughters not to be too unruly around Iris.

Maggie walked out the front door. 'What? It's too cold out here.'

Her reluctance quickly vanished when she looked up, past the verandah, at the mist that crept towards the house. Their small cottage had already been swallowed.

Victoria took her sister's hand. 'Come on.'

Maggie pulled her hand free. 'No. I can see it from here.'

Iris caught Victoria's eye. 'Don't be going out there, girl. It's not safe.'

Victoria paused, reflecting on those cautioning words.

'It's okay. Go and play,' said Brigid with a smile.

Iris's eyes widened. 'It's not safe out there. She should be content with watching it from here.'

Brigid put down her darning and considered the fog for a moment. Victoria waited, prepared to defy both adults. While Maggie stood in the doorway, hoping Victoria would change her mind.

'My grandmother taught me about this type of mist,' Brigid divulged. 'It's the breath of dragons. Apparently they were com mon in her homeland. She'd told me they were friendly creatures, despite their appearance. There's nothing in that mist to be afraid of.'

Victoria glanced at Maggie, eyes shining with excitement. Maggie refused to meet her sister's eyes, for she knew Victoria's attraction to adventure. And her skills of persuasion.

'Are there really dragons out there?' Victoria asked.

'Of course not,' opined Iris. 'It's just a myth. Dragons aren't real. Not here, not anywhere.'

Victoria sat heavily on the verandah steps, shoulders drooping.

Brigid said, 'My grandmother knew they were real. When I was little, she told me lots of stories about dragons. You'll just have to work out what's the truth for yourself, Victoria.'

Victoria glanced over her shoulder, and saw her sister shaking her head.

'Come on, there's nothing to be afraid of. Mother wouldn't let us go in there if it was dangerous. Anyway, you know I'll always protect you,' pleaded Victoria.

Maggie stepped backwards, letting the screen door close, hoping to place a barrier between herself and her sister's persuasive ways.

Victoria walked over to the door and put her face to the mesh. Maggie could feel Victoria's warm breath on her face. The sisters stood, face to face, neither willing to give in to the other's needs.

'That's a good girl,' muttered Iris. 'Don't listen to your foolish sister. Stay here, where it's safe.'

Maggie blinked, just once, and Victoria knew who'd won this stand-off. Despite her fears of what might lie beyond, Maggie was not going to tolerate anyone calling her sister foolish. Victoria opened the door and took Maggie by the hand. With a wary glance at their mother, Maggie allowed herself to be led towards the mist.

Brigid smiled at her shy finch and fearless eagle as they walked towards the thick fog. She still remembered her own childhood adventures after listening to her grandmother's colourful tales. Stories carried across the sea, from a faraway place, in a time long ago.

'You shouldn't encourage them with their nonsense, Brigid. Maybe you should be insisting they put more energy into their homework, rather than playing childish games.'

'Eleven is not too old for make-believe. And they're both doing well at school.'

Brigid ignored Iris's scowl, and returned to her darning. She thought about how much Iris had changed recently. She knew it was the pain. And perhaps fear of death. Before the beginning of the year, Iris hadn't appeared to be very sick, even though she was. Then she began to slow down dramatically. Painkillers no longer helped her sleep at night, so she was always tired. Brigid had overheard the doctor say to Stefan that she'd not last much longer. She missed how close they used to be, before the pain got unbearable. And remembered the affection Iris once had for the twins. Soon after arriving, she'd confided in Brigid that she'd never been able to have children of her own, despite yearning to be a mother. And that she'd always imagined having a pretty daughter, like Maggie. Now, Iris no longer tolerated the girls. *They are too noisy and impertinent,* she'd often say. Sounding more like her grumpy husband each day.

Iris was also becoming like her husband in another way, which concerned Brigid more. She remembered that first encounter with Stefan, and his instant disapproval of her appearance. Not the scars from the fire, the colour of her skin. He'd not let up, all these years. He took any chance to mock her intelligence, to lecture her on the inherent inadequacies of her people, to tell her that she'd never do better than this type of work or the meagre pay he provided. She felt like she was back in the schoolyard. Different, othered, never enough. Iris had always expressed more progressive views than her husband.

*

Insisting she didn't see colour. That her husband was wrong, so don't mind him. Then Iris changed. She began to repeat some of her husband's views on the righteousness of Western settlement, and dying races being an unfortunate consequence of progress. Not in front of Brigid, or the girls. Whispered to her husband, when she thought they were alone. The friendship the women once shared was now gone.

When Stefan had found out about the money Iris lent Brigid, he had insisted she sign a repayment agreement. She'd thought the new terms most unfair, so had asked Iris to intervene. Iris had refused to help, and told Brigid not to come complaining to her about trivial problems. And that Stefan was now solely dealing with that debt and Brigid's ongoing terms of employment. With Iris no longer acting as a buffer, Brigid had to bear Stefan's unfair treatment and insults in silence. She told herself it was the pain causing Iris to withdraw, and perhaps the cancer was somehow changing how she viewed the world. She tried to convince herself that surely Iris didn't see her as less-than. It still hurt. Brigid knew she wouldn't keep the promise once made to Iris: to care for her husband after she died. As soon as that debt was paid off, she'd be gone.

*

As they walked through the mist, Maggie and Victoria held hands. Droplets of water clung to their skin and hair, but they no longer felt cold. All sounds outside the mist had stopped. The girls felt as if they had walked over a threshold, into a different world. They walked cautiously, unable to see too far ahead. Maggie concentrated on where she placed her feet, looking intently at the ground for obstacles that might trip her, while Victoria looked around, not wanting to miss anything that might lie obscured within the thick fog.

Victoria stopped suddenly. 'Can you see it?'

Maggie lifted her head, her heart beating faster, little puffs of smoke accumulating in front of her.

She giggled. 'My breathing makes a trail of smoke, just like dragon's breath.'

'Look over there. Is it real?'

Maggie looked in the direction her sister pointed to, fearful of what she would see. She saw nothing.

'Can't you see it?'

Maggie shook her head, glad for once that she couldn't see what Victoria saw.

'It's more like a huge serpent than a dragon,' Victoria observed. 'I can see how people would get confused. She's frighteningly large and very beautiful. A rainbow, just like those little birds.'

'Stop it. You're just trying to trick me.'

'No, I'm not. Can't you see her?'

'Let's go. I don't like it in here.'

'Okay. Come on then, scaredy cat.'

As they wandered back through the mist, taking each step with care, far away a man was making leaps of abandonment. While his colleagues observed, the bubble-suited man jumped over moon craters and the world held its collective breath in astonishment. Maggie and Victoria wouldn't hear of that historical adventure for some time. Emerging from the haze, the girls were greeted by their mother – holding a finger to her lips. Quietly they stepped up onto the verandah, knowing their world had somehow dramatically changed. Once more.

'She's gone,' whispered their mother.

The girls beheld the empty rocking chair, watching as it made one last movement. They then noticed him on the stiff-backed chair next to Iris's rocking chair, a faded patchwork quilt at his feet. Von Wolff had a dark cloud around him, and a half-empty bottle in his hand. Brigid led her daughters to their cottage, where she helped them select more fitting clothes. Now clad in black, they were told to stay away from the von Wolffs' house. And to always, always play quietly. Out of respect. And fear.

***

Brigid washed the dishes, listening to her daughters chatter as they played knucklebones on the grass out the front of the cottage. She sighed as the sounds of breaking glass came from von Wolff's studio, thinking of the mess she'd have to clean up later. Brigid would have left after the funeral, if not for the increasing debt. The interest Stefan kept adding didn't seem right, but there was nothing she could do. As he'd reminded her only yesterday, she'd signed the repayment agreement and if she even tried to leave without repaying him in full, he'd call the police. Stefan mentioned that could result in the girls being removed and put in an institution for mixed-race children. He somehow knew this was Brigid's greatest fear, and took pleasure in taunting her.

She flinched as more sounds drifted over from the studio.

'Angry man is angry again,' muttered Victoria.

Maggie said, 'He's sad.'

'I don't care if he is sad,' Victoria replied. 'He's mean and angry. And no one likes him.'

'Mr Stevens and Constable Peters must like him, they visit all the time. And Father Paddy. I like when Father Paddy visits, because no one drinks as much.'

'I wish we could leave. This is not a good place. Von Wolff is a bad man.'

Brigid put down the pot she'd been scrubbing and walked over to the cottage door. She saw the back of Maggie's head as her daughter stooped over a flower, plucking off its petals. Victoria was looking towards von Wolff's studio. If a stare could set something on fire, that is what it would look like.

Brigid called out, 'What do think about going back to school?'

Maggie said, 'Really?'

'Yes, really.'

Brigid looked at Victoria, an eyebrow raised. 'Well?'

'I'm not sure. Wouldn't you get lonely with us gone all day, Mum?'

'I might, but I think it's time you both returned to school. I can only teach you so much.'

Victoria stood up. 'I'm not leaving you here, on your own.'

'I'll be fine. Honestly. Wouldn't you like to have more books to read?'

'I want to see my friends again,' said Maggie.

Victoria muttered, 'You have those annoying finches. We don't need school.'

'Don't be mean. It's not safe for your sister to walk to school on her own. What do you say?'

Victoria sighed. 'Okay then. If you think you'll be all right.'

'I will, don't worry.'

Maggie squealed, 'Can we start tomorrow?'

'Silly, tomorrow is a Saturday,' said Victoria.

'We'll all walk there on Monday, and talk to the headmaster,' Brigid suggested.

***

Von Wolff had not objected when Brigid informed him she was sending the girls back to school. It would mean less noise during the day, when he usually worked in his studio. Also, now that Iris was gone, he had begun to feel uncomfortable around Brigid when she was with her daughters. That motherly aura was distasteful to him. Stefan had been raised by a series of cold women; not one was his mother. His father, General Franz von Wolff, was an important man, or so said young Stefan's nannies. Which is why the General had no time for his son. He did have time for the men in business suits and army uniforms who frequented the family mansion. The sounds of their raised voices had wafted out of the dining room, along with the smoke from their expensive cigars. There were no goodnight stories and kisses for young Stefan. Not with such a busy and important father. The sound of his father storming through the house, barking orders at servants and occasionally demanding they keep the boy quiet, was as close as Stefan came to being in his presence. His mother had died of a fever when he was just a baby, before he was old enough to gather memories of her. All he had was portraits in the hallway.

A succession of nannies tended to his every need. They never stayed long. Not because the General ran the house like a military barracks. They left because they would all eventually grow to fear Stefan. From a young age, the boy with the penetrating stare showed most worrying tendencies. At first it was his habit of ripping wings off the butterflies that dared to land on his dead mother's beloved roses. Then the cruel whipping and kicking of hounds. When the nannies reported this to the General, Stefan was given a beating, for his father would not tolerate cruelty towards his dogs. The sacks of kittens the gardeners pulled out of the lake didn't even raise an eyebrow when reported to the General. They did result in one more nanny's quick departure. No one wanted to be around such a malevolent child.

When the cobbled streets of the local village echoed with the footsteps of marching soldiers, the General thought it best to send his adolescent son away. Stefan was the last of the von Wolff bloodline, and the carrier of future generations must be protected so the General's legacy would survive the looming war. Stefan was sent across the sea, to a maiden aunt of his mother's. There was no love to be found in that house either. Even if there had been, the boy would not have been receptive to such a foreign emotion. The war was over on the eve of Stefan's twenty-first birthday. Surrender was marked by the death of his father. Not on the battlefield, a heart attack in a brothel. Stefan had no interest in returning to either his family's residence or the land of his birth. Instead, he packed his trunk and travelled further and further east.

His inheritance meant he'd never need to work. Instead, he took up photography, at first to amuse himself. It soon became an obsession. His fixation on photography drove him to perfection, and he soon became an internationally renowned artist. Eventually, Stefan von Wolff turned towards the southern continent. Locating suitable land and an agreeable woman, neither of which he deserved, he settled. The property he'd purchased was a day's drive from the city. Von Wolff found the pace of country life enabled him to concentrate on his art. In the early years, he'd venture out, taking photos of the landscape. He found many suitable subjects to photograph in local towns, with a preference for labourers and farmers. There was something in the lines of those weather-hardened faces that appealed to him. For relaxation, he'd fish for trout off the small pier over the dam. His love of music drove him to the city every so often, to attend concerts with Iris. Other times, he'd go alone, to meet with gallery owners and international buyers. As his wife became more unwell, he increasingly went to the city without her.

Since her death, Stefan spent more time in the city, followed by long days in his studio. When Brigid said she intended to send her daughters to school again, von Wolff was pleased to hear those noisy pests of hers would be elsewhere during the days.

TEN

Victoria and Maggie sat at the table doing their homework, while Brigid finished making dinner. She was pleased with how they had resettled at the local school. And relieved they were away from this place during the day. Away from von Wolff. After Iris died, he didn't make her work such long days, so she was able to have breakfast and dinner with her daughters. Sometimes he let her go early, and she'd walk towards town, to meet them along the road. Occasionally, Mr Stevens, one of the teachers, would drive Maggie and Victoria home. And then stay late, drinking with von Wolff. He was a regular on card nights, along with Constable Peters.

'Victoria has made a friend,' Maggie remarked.

Brigid turned towards Victoria. 'Do you want to tell me about your friend.'

Victoria's face reddened, and she didn't reply.

'It's a man,' Maggie disclosed.

Victoria slapped her sister lightly on the arm, which made her cry.

'Victoria,' said Brigid sternly.

'Sorry, Maggie.'

Brigid asked, 'This friend works at the school?'

Victoria pretended to be busy with her homework.

Brigid sat down at the table. 'Victoria, who is this man?'

'Crow. He works at the timber yard,' Maggie offered.

Brigid frowned. 'Crow? What sort of name is that?'

Maggie said, 'It's his last name.'

'Gabriel Crow,' mumbled Victoria. 'I chat with him sometimes, on the way home from school.'

'What do you talk about?' asked Brigid.

'Just stuff. Hunting, finding wild foods, things we did when travelling.'

'He promised to take us fishing,' said Maggie. 'Mumma, can we go?'

Brigid grinned. 'Since when did you like fishing, Maggie?'

'I don't really. I just want to go anywhere that Mr von Wolff isn't. And Mr Crow is real nice.'

'I think I should meet this Mr Crow. Victoria, will you invite him to afternoon tea this Sunday?'

Victoria nodded as she got up to set the table for dinner.

***

Maggie had been in the flower garden since they'd finished lunch. Brigid asked her a few times to help set up for their visitor, then gave up. Maggie was worried she'd miss Mr Crow's arrival. She wanted to make sure he saw their flower garden. Mid-afternoon, Maggie's excited squeal alerted Brigid that their visitor had come. Brigid wiped her hands on a tea towel, and went outside. Her first impression was: *Gosh, he's tall.* Brigid was taller than average for a woman, so Danny had only been slightly taller than her. From a distance, Gabriel appeared to be almost a foot taller. As he got closer, she noticed he had dark brown hair, like Danny's. Only difference was the lack of curls. He reached out a hand, in greeting. Brigid smiled, and looked up. His eyes were a warm brown, with copper streaks. As if shooting stars had exploded in his irises.

He smiled too. 'You must be Brigid. It's good to finally meet you. The girls have told me so much about you.'

Brigid blushed. That radiant smile of his had made her knees weak. She'd not felt this way in such a long time.

'And you must be Mr Crow. I've hardly heard anything about you.'

She noticed Victoria and Maggie standing behind Gabriel. Victoria had on her *Oh Mum, don't be so embarrassing* expression. Brigid looked back at Gabriel; he was still smiling.

'Please, call me Gabriel. I didn't mean for the girls to keep me a secret.'

'Looks like you were a secret that couldn't be kept.'

Victoria let out a groan, and left. Brigid paused: *Is Victoria embarrassed because she saw me flirting? Was that flirting? If so, did he start it?*

Maggie said, 'Come this way, Mr Crow. We've set up a tea party outside, with a view of the dam.'

She grabbed his hand, and practically dragged him away from her mother. Brigid followed, and blushed again. She couldn't help herself. He was just so fine-looking, from every angle. Victoria was already sitting at the table, book in her lap.

'Sit here, Mr Crow,' insisted Maggie. 'In between Victoria and me.'

Brigid took the only seat left, across from Gabriel. Keeping her eyes averted, she hoped her cheeks were no longer flushed. She concentrated on pouring the tea, while Maggie piled his plate with food.

'Sugar?' asked Brigid.

He shook his head. 'Not for me. Kidney problems run in my family.'

'Does your family live around here?'

'No, south-east. We're river people. I visit them as much as I can. And you? Where're you from?'

'Far west, originally. Near the coast. I've been away for thirteen years. Mostly up north.'

'I've not made it too far north, or over to the west coast. I want to, one day. Really keen to see red desert sands.'

'It can be spectacular up there, especially at night. The stars are so much brighter. Everything is brighter, really.'

'I do a bit of stargazing. Even know about constellations and such.'

Maggie said, 'I remember watching stars from Bethel and Omer's house. So many falling ones. Aunty Isabelle told me a story about a falling star. Do you remember that one, Victoria?'

Her sister put her book down, and reached for a scone. 'Of course, silly. It wasn't that long ago.'

Victoria spread jam on her scone. Gabriel handed her the pot of cream, and she politely thanked him. Meanwhile, Maggie talked incessantly to Gabriel. *He's supposed to be my friend,* thought Victoria, becoming increasingly annoyed at her sister. Brigid didn't notice the growing tension; she was too enthralled with the visitor. Gabriel was easy to talk to, and so patient with the girls. He soon had Victoria smiling, and Maggie listening intently. Brigid loved watching him with her daughters. They'd not been this happy since living with Omer and Bethel. They'd always had time to listen to the girls, and never talked down to them.

Iris had also loved being around Maggie and Victoria, but she'd babied them. Even so, Brigid knew they'd been missing Iris. And disliking how nasty Stefan was becoming. It was good to see them enjoying Gabriel's company. Brigid hadn't managed to get much of a word in. Still, she was surprised at how relaxed she felt around him. Except for the occasional discomfort of blushing whenever he beamed that beautiful smile her way.

'Mumma, can we?'

Brigid looked at Maggie, realising she'd missed hearing something.

Victoria said to her sister, 'Mum's too busy. Maybe just us?'

'I'm sure your mother can find time. Next Saturday, perhaps?' suggested Gabriel.

'What?'

'A film, mother. Gabriel has asked us all to go to the cinema with him,' said Victoria. 'You don't have to come if you're too busy.'

'That sounds like fun. Gabriel, it would have to be a Sunday, if you don't mind. I have one off every fortnight.'

'So a fortnight from today?'

She nodded. 'Shall we meet in town, for the matinee?'

192

'Okay. I'll ask my boss if I can borrow the truck, to drive you home.'

Maggie clapped her hands in excitement. She'd never seen a film before. The other children at school talked about them all the time. She couldn't wait. Victoria was quietly looking forward to going. The current film screening was a musical from a few years ago: a cartoon about a boy who lives in the jungle with animals that can talk. She'd stared wistfully at the poster, whenever she walked past the cinema on the way home from school. The boy character had skin similar to hers. She couldn't believe such a film would be popular, given how much the other children taunted her at school. Victoria had felt she really need to see that film, but hadn't asked her mother, as she knew money was tight. Now they were all going, with Gabriel. Which made it even more special for her.

***

Brigid took another look at the girls, to make sure they were really asleep, then left. She carried the two cups behind the cottage, where Gabriel was waiting. He was sitting on a thick wooden bench, watching moonlight dance on the water's surface. He'd taken a liking to that dam, even more so when he discovered it contained both trout and yabbies. A few days earlier, Gabriel had used his boss's truck to deliver slabs of wood. With the help of a friend, he'd made a bench behind the cottage, overlooking the dam. He had plans to fix up the old pier next. Brigid handed him a mug of tea.

'Thanks.'

'The moon is bright tonight.'

'Unna,' he said, taking a sip.

'What?'

'What what?'

She laughed. 'What's that word mean?'

'Unna? It can mean a lot of things, depending how you say it. Such as: yes; ain't it; I'm listening; cool; not gammon.'

'Gammon?'

'You don't know that one, either? It means when someone or something is false; a lie, or some trickery. You know, like pulling someone's leg. Or it can mean someone is tooting their own horn.'

Brigid nodded, and took a sip. She liked the stillness of the night, and being with him. In a short time, they'd become close friends.

He turned to her. 'Hey, how come you don't know those words? And same with other blackfella words I've used? I know there's different languages all over, but a lot of lingo has spread across the continent, amongst mob.'

'I probably heard some when I lived with my nana Vic and grandfather Albert. I just didn't pay attention. A lot of the time, I didn't know what people were saying. Most knew English as a second language, some only spoke in their language.'

'Your language too.'

'Not really. I was born out there, but didn't grow up there. My father was a black digger, and he died overseas when I was three. I didn't see that side of my family again until I was nineteen, when the twins were born. I grew up with my granny Maeve and mother. Margaret, my mother, remarried a white guy, and they had three boys. I was the odd one out at home. Same with school; the only black child there.'

'Was there no mob around?'

Brigid was about to say no, then she remembered: friendly faces who had often tried to talk to her, before Granny told them to stay away from her granddaughter. The nice woman who asked if she was okay, after children pushed Brigid into a mud puddle on the walk home from school. That woman had called her bub. That felt nice. Children, similar-looking to her, would hide in the apple orchard, waiting for her to come out and play. Granny had shooed them away, and told Brigid to stay away from them. She'd told Brigid that she might look like them, but she was not like them.

'My family, the one I grew up with, I guess they didn't approve of me talking with other Aboriginal people. Not even children.'

'Shame. What about the girls' father? Is he a whitefella too?'

'No. He was taken as a baby, along with his two older brothers. The government put him in a church-run children's home, where they taught them how to make things and ride horses. His older brothers were sent to work on a cattle station when he was ten. He never saw them again. Him and me, we weren't together for long. He left me, to go find family.'

'He left you alone with twins?'

'It wasn't like that. He didn't know I was pregnant. I didn't even know. And it was sort of my fault he left.'

'It's okay, you don't need to tell me. Relationships can be hard. And what the government has done to us, and our families, can make things even harder. It never stops. Loss and trauma, generation after generation, it tears us all up inside.'

Brigid nodded. 'Maybe one day I'll be ready to tell you more. If that's okay?'

'Sure. I'm not planning on leaving any time soon. Not when I've got this comfy bench, and a perfect view,' he said, looking at her.

***

196

Unlike previous afternoons, there were no fish biting that day. They'd all given up quickly. The girls were content playing in Gabriel's patched-up wooden boat, which was resting safely on the banks of the dam, while their mother and Gabriel talked. Maggie looked at them, sitting close together on the rug, and smiled. She was glad her mother liked Gabriel as much as she did. Victoria also glanced at them, hoping her mother didn't get in one of her moods. She was doing that more often. Working for von Wolff was upsetting her. This place wasn't good for any of them, even if they now had Gabriel as a friend. It was obvious Gabriel was doing his best. *Nothing is good enough for Mother,* thought Victoria. *She ruins everything.* Then Victoria felt guilty. It wasn't her mother's fault. Von Wolff wouldn't let them leave because of the money their mother borrowed to fix Maggie's teeth. If she had to blame anyone, it would be him.

Brigid stood up and gathered their belongings. With a frown, she lifted a corner of the picnic rug. Gabriel picked up a white sock and handed it to her.

'Thanks,' she said, with a smile. 'Maggie's always leaving things behind.'

'Why do you stay?' asked Gabriel.

Brigid frowned. 'We're leaving now. As soon as I get those girls out of that boat.'

'No, why do you stay here, working for von Wolff. He's not a good person.'

'Don't you think I already know that? I'm doing my best to look after my family.'

'What about looking after yourself? You deserve to be happy.'

'You don't have to pretend. I know you're repulsed by these scars, like everyone else. Working here is all I deserve.'

'No one deserves to be belittled, to be constantly talked down to. I've heard him, seen the way he treats you. You need to get out of here.'

'I can't, I owe him money. And anyway, I've got nowhere to go.'

'All those years of travelling, raising those girls on your own; you can leave, find somewhere better.'

Brigid sighed, and sat down again. 'I'm so tired.'

Gabriel shifted towards her and then stopped. Brigid followed his gaze, and saw Maggie running towards them.

'Mumma, Victoria went in,' she announced. 'You told us not to.'

'Since when does your sister do what she's told?'

Brigid walked towards the dam, with Maggie following. When they returned, a wet Victoria trailing behind, Brigid noticed Gabriel looking at a piece of paper. Getting closer, she saw it was a photo of a woman and three smiling children.

'Is that your family?' Brigid asked.

Gabriel nodded, before putting the photo in his shirt pocket. Brigid felt a pang. She didn't know what this feeling was. *Jealousy?* Surely not. She still loved Daniel. Even if she never saw him again, there would be no one else for her. Gabriel looked her way and his copper-flecked brown eyes flickered.

'My sister and her kids. My niece and nephews. I've been missing them lately. She's not been well,' Gabriel said.

Brigid nodded. And felt both a sense of relief and guilt. In the past six months, she'd got close to Gabriel. Closer than she had to anyone in a very long time. Brigid felt as if she could tell him anything and he would never judge her. Instead, he listened. He believed in her. Gabriel was the confidant Brigid had been longing for all her life. She'd just never realised that until now.

'Von Wolff is going into town tomorrow, isn't he?'

Brigid nodded. 'Yes, he usually goes on Tuesdays. And the city most weekends.'

'Can I call on you? While the girls are at school.'

Brigid laughed. 'That's sounds a bit formal. I have a chicken to pluck tomorrow, for von Wolff's dinner. If you don't mind blood and feathers, you can help me.'

*

The next day Brigid was trying to catch a chicken when she heard laugher. Hands on hips, she watched Gabriel enter the coop.

'That's not how you do it,' he said.

She stuck her tongue out at him. 'Bet you can't do any better.'

Gabriel reached for the brown chicken that had just eluded Brigid and was catching its breath close by. When it suddenly ran off, wings flapping in panic, Gabriel fell in the dirt. Brigid laughed loudly. He stood up, smiling boyishly at her. By joining forces, they rounded up that chicken and put it in a wooden crate.

A few hours later, clothes still covered in feathers, they sat behind the stone cottage. Cups of tea in hand, they watched the sun's reflection on the water in the distance. Brigid felt heat rise from him. She liked the way he smelt. She leant a bit more to her right, touching his side ever so slightly.

Gabriel said, 'I need to go away for a while. Nana rang me at work today. My sister and the kids need me.'

Brigid felt a coldness wash over her. Gabriel noticed her stiffen, and placed a hand gently over hers.

'I'll be back. Sissy needs to go to the city. Her kidneys are getting worse. So I'm going home to help look after her children. My niece and nephews are a real handful. Too much for my nana to look after.

Those boys take after their dad. He was such a risk-taker. He died attempting to jump the river on a motorbike.'

'Your family needs you, I understand. Do you miss them much?'

He nodded. 'Sissy and I have always been close. I want to be by her side in the hospital, but she insisted I look after her children. Our youngest brother, Charlie, will go to the city with her. It's been good to see him step up. Our mother died when he was a bub, and then our father shortly after. So I took on caring for Sissy and Charlie when I was a teenager. Nana helped, of course. It's only right I go back home, to help out.'

'Of course. Is she real sick?'

'Doctors are hoping a treatment called dialysis will work. And they've talked about a kidney transplant. Can you believe that? They can now put someone's kidney into someone else. Normally that type of care isn't offered to us mob, but there's this doctor in the city doing research, and they think Sissy might get into that.'

'Sounds serious. I do hope she'll be okay, and gets the help she needs.'

'I've been real worried about her. I've also been worried about you.'

'What for?'

'I want to take you away from here. The girls too.'

'Do you now? And who made you the boss?'

'Brigid, it's not safe here. You know that. Let me help you.'

'I've never needed help before, so what makes you so special?'

'Because I care for you. And your daughters.'

Brigid got up and took the cups inside. Gabriel followed her. She put the cups in the sink, ignoring him. He took a seat at the table, and waited. Patiently, as always. Brigid peered at him discreetly as she walked past to put the tea cannister back in the cupboard. Not for the first time, she noticed her heart skip a beat. *Damn my traitor heart,* she thought. Brigid knew she wasn't the only one to find him attractive. Whenever Stefan went to the city, she'd sneak away from work to visit Gabriel at the timber mill in his lunch break They'd wander down the road and sit with cool drinks outside the general store. She'd seen those white women flutter their eyelashes at him, acting all coy as they walked past him in the street. Brigid had also seen little looks of envy they'd thrown her way. Gabriel seemed only to have eyes for Brigid. She'd stopped comparing him to Daniel a long time ago. It just didn't seem fair. Both were attractive men. Still, those copper rays in Gabriel's eyes never failed to draw Brigid in. *Damn him,* she thought now.

'What are you thinking?' he asked.

'I'm thinking you're a fool.'

'Because I want to look after you? Because I care about you?'

'Because you assume I care about you.'

'Leave with me,' he said.

'We're not dating, are we?'

'Why do you think I've been hanging around here so much? It's certainly not for the trout in the dam.'

She blushed. 'I really like you. I don't know if I love you.'

'You don't have to.'

Brigid shook her head. 'We can't be together. Ever.'

'Why not?'

'Aside from the girls, people I love end up leaving me. They disappear, or they die. I've had my fill of heartbreak.'

'Everyone has to die someday. It's what we do with our time on earth that counts. We need to leave footsteps for the next generation to follow, like our ancestors did for us.' Gabriel closed the small gap between them and wrapped his arms around her. 'And being brave enough to let love in is part of living.'

She leant into his chest. She could hear his heartbeat. It was a warmth she'd not experienced for such a long time.

*

Brigid felt safe, like she'd found her place of belonging. As she had that moment she'd first seen Daniel. Danny, father of their children. Brigid squeezed out of Gabriel's arms, putting distance between them.

'No,' she stated.

Gabriel looked into Brigid's eyes and knew why she had said no. He'd felt the other man's presence come between them on other occasions.

'You can't wait for him forever.'

She shook her head. 'I've stopped looking for Daniel. It's debt that keeps me here. I owe Stefan money, from before Iris died.'

Gabriel said gently, 'The offer of leaving here, with me, still stands. You don't have to love me back. Let me help you as a friend. I can help you find work, so you can repay von Wolff. You don't have to stay here.'

Brigid looked up, and gazed into those damn copper-lit eyes. 'You need to give me just a little more time.'

'Fair enough. I'll be back, I promise. Until then, I'll write to you.'

***

'Mumma, Mumma, another letter,' shouted Maggie as she opened the door.

Brigid slowly untied her apron. Victoria frowned. Their mother was looking more exhausted each day. Von Wolff worked her far too hard; she no longer got off early enough to meet them on the road after school. And he was getting meaner.

Maggie handed the letter to her mother, who opened it. She smiled, then frowned.

'Well,' asked Maggie. 'Is he coming back? He's been gone for months; I miss him.'

Maggie sat at the kitchen table. Victoria walked over to the stove and added wood. She put the kettle on a hotplate, and fetched the tea leaves.

'Gabriel will be away for a bit longer,' replied Brigid. 'His sister has passed away.'

Maggie stopped smiling. 'Poor Gabriel. And those kids. The girl is not much younger than Victoria and me. I couldn't imagine losing you, Mumma.'

Victoria put a cup of tea on the table, in front of her mother. Brigid smiled at her. She was growing up far too quickly. She'd seen too much hardship and trouble in her twelve years. Especially the three years they'd been living in this stone cottage. Brigid knew they'd all had enough of being here. Even Maggie, who was usually so reluctant to travel, was eager to move.

Victoria said, 'Is Gabriel ever coming back?'

'Soon. He wrote in the letter that he has things to do there first. Then he's coming back to work at the timber yard for a bit more, as he needs to save some money. Then he'll go home, and help raise his niece and nephews. He's asked us to go with him.'

'To live with him?' asked Victoria.

'If that's all right with you, and Maggie.'

Victoria nodded, while Maggie chattered excitedly about living with Gabriel, and becoming best friends with his niece.

***

'Put that on,' he demanded, throwing a bundle of cloth at her.

Brigid stood up slowly, placing the scrubbing brush in the nearby bucket. She picked up the cloth von Wolff had thrown on the wet kitchen floor she'd been scrubbing. Brigid held it up, and saw it was a garment of rough material. Made from a hessian grain sack, this sleeveless garment could hardly be called a dress. Brigid looked at von Wolff, one eyebrow arched.

'Don't you be thinking of giving me any of your sass. Put it on.'

She shook her head. His closed fist hit Brigid's cheek before she even realised he'd raised it. She fell backwards, then quickly righted herself. Eyes glaring, she was prepared to stand her ground. His hand shot out again, this time grabbing her by the hair.

'Have it your way, then.'

He pulled her towards the door. Brigid's scalp ached as she resisted. Kicking the front door open, von Wolff dragged her out, onto the verandah, and pushed her down the stairs.

'Get up, trollop,' he ordered, walking down after her.

Brigid sprang up and took a step towards the cottage. Von Wolff grabbed her by a shoulder and yanked hard. Holding her firmly by the shoulder and upper arm, he steered her towards his studio. She tried to wriggle free, so he painfully tightened his grip, and she stopped resisting. When they reached the studio, von Wolff opened the door and threw her inside.

He tossed the hessian-sack garment at her again. 'Put it on, or I'll strip you and do it myself.'

Brigid began to slip it over her head.

Von Wolff barked, 'Don't just put it over your dress. Take the dress off. And your undergarments.'

She turned her back to him and did as she was told. While undressing, she saw purple marks appearing on her upper arm, where he'd held her roughly. Her face also smarted. Now wearing only the sack-dress, she turned around slowly. Von Wolff looked her up and down. She'd caught him staring at her before, but not like this. She held her head higher, looking him straight in the eye, defiant despite feeling fearful of his next move.

'Are you even aware of how damn alluring you are?' he asked, moving closer.

Brigid shied away, staring at him wide-eyed, nostrils flared.

'You're like a brown snake, backed into a corner, ready to strike its way out. And that scarring just makes you even more desirable.'

Von Wolff reached out, and ran a finger along the scars that snaked down Brigid's neck and along her shoulder. She flinched at his touch and tried to hide her pain as his hand skimmed over her emerging bruises.

He went over to his camera cabinet and, with his back towards her, said, 'Keep your head high. I like that.'

Turning around, he started taking photos. Moving around the room, circling her. She stared back at him stonily. She thought about her daughters, thankful that they would be at school for a few more hours. *It'll be over soon. There's time to clean myself up before they get home,* Brigid thought. *And late tonight, we'll leave here.* As the camera flashed, her thoughts drifted to Gabriel and that warm parting hug they'd shared. She ignored von Wolff, instead making overdue plans. Gabriel's address was on the letters he'd sent her. She would leave, tonight, and go to him.

Von Wolff put down the camera. 'Stay.'

He walked over to the record-player and, selecting a record, put it on the turntable. Brigid listened, letting the music wash over her. Its lyrics were hauntingly sad. Even the tune was sad. Fitting for how she felt right now. Feelings she would not let von Wolff glimpse. He took up the camera again, placing the cord around his neck. He picked up a footstool, grabbed Brigid by an arm, and dragged her out the studio door. Once outside, he placed the footstool under the apple tree that grew next to his studio. The tree had struggled this season, and only a few apples remained. Fruit so unappetising that even the birds had left them alone. The other apples had already fallen and were rotting on the ground. Brigid staggered when he shoved her, landing under the tree. She sat up, brushing leaves and squishy fruit from the side of her body. Her face felt gritty, covered in soil and debris. Von Wolff picked up a thick plaited rope that was lying by the studio door and, coming back to Brigid, made a knot. He then threw one end of the rope over the lowest branch. Using the footstool, he tied it securely to that branch. She frowned, trying to work out what von Wolff was doing.

'Climb up on the stool,' he ordered.

Brigid shook her head fervently, and stayed seated on the ground.

'Do as I say, and this will be over soon.'

She looked up at the rope, staring at the loop dangling above her. She considered running, but knew she'd get no more than a step away before he'd grab her again. Perhaps it was best just to get this over, then return to the cottage and start packing their bags. Her daughters would be home from school soon. They could be ready to make their escape at sunset. Until then, she just had to do what he demanded. Brigid got up, testing the stool with one foot before climbing up. Von Wolff then joined her on the stool. Brigid wriggled as he placed the looped rope around her neck.

He hit her hard on the back of her shoulder. 'Stop it. You'll just make it worse.'

Trembling now in fear, Brigid did as she was told. He stepped down, took up his camera and started to take photos. She kept very still, so as not to upset the stool she stood on. In her peripheral vision, she noticed a stunted apple hanging near her head. The rainbow finches that Maggie loved so much were flitting around in the branches of the tree. Looking upwards, she saw a solitary raven on an upper branch. *Only one, not three,* she thought with relief.

'Look directly at the camera.'

Brigid turned away, refusing to look at him. She saw a second raven land on a branch.

Von Wolff didn't notice the bird; he was too focused on Brigid. 'Your bronze skin, those dark-brown eyes. Your race might be flawed, but some of you can be attractive.'

Brigid still refused to acknowledge his presence, and pulled the rope away from her neck, scratching where it was irritating her skin.

'Put your hand down,' he commanded. 'I've often wondered what it is about you that makes you so interesting. You give the impression of being uncomfortable with your own body. Not the scars. Something else. As if even you reject your own skin.'

Brigid suddenly recalled a conversation from long ago. *You don't accept your own blackness,* Daniel had pronounced that day they fought. Brigid had no reply for him, all those years ago. Just a shrug. She had no idea what to say. After all, she was just a potato. A dirty potato. No more, no less. She now vividly remembered what Daniel had verbalised next: *If you can't love your own blackness, how can you ever really love me?* Much as she'd tried, Brigid hadn't forgotten the look of hurt on Daniel's face as he'd said that. She had carried the guilt of being the cause of his pain though the red desert, across rocky plains, among the spinifex, over ridges of various sizes and along the streets of country towns. She had carried it here, to this apple tree.

Von Wolff interrupted her thoughts. 'This isn't real enough.'

The jolt as he kicked the footstool from under her feet shocked her into movement. Her feet running in air, searching for a foothold. Looking around, it was if time had slowed. Finches were suspended in midair, wings flapping in slow motion. That lone apple near her head was falling, microsecond by microsecond, towards the ground. Brigid could hear the record still playing; the same lyrics over and over, as if the needle was stuck in a groove: *strange and bitter crop strange and bitter strange and strange.* Sensing something slip away, she looked down and noticed a flash of silver among the rotting apples on the ground. Placing a hand on her chest, Brigid realised her necklace was gone. Her grandmother's silver-encrusted apple seed now lay on the ground.

Granny, Brigid thought, *you were wrong. I'm not a dirtencrusted potato.*

An image of Granny Maeve appeared, floating among the finches: *You're my little potato, Birdie.*

No, Granny. This is me, in this skin. You were ashamed and tried to wash my blackness away. I cherished those family stories you told me, but there were gaps. None of those stories could reconnect me to Country, or the kin you and Mother didn't tell me of. None of those stories gave me the strength to stand against hate, and to be proud of my identity.

I kept secrets to protect you, Birdie. I do love you, forever.

I know you loved me, thought Brigid.

The image of her grandmother was replaced by Nana Vic. Brigid's nana smiled at her, and she felt a warmth spread throughout her body. Brigid noticed bright flashes before her eyes. Von Wolff was still taking photos, an eerie grin on his face. She pictured her daughters running towards her: toddlers, girls, teenagers. A single tear fell. Brigid knew she'd never see them become women.

Don't be afraid, said Nana Vic. *Your father is here to catch you. Grandfather Albert is here too. We'll show you the way.* Brigid looked at the tree again. It had changed form; parts of it were still an apple tree, like the ones that grew in her family's orchard, entwined with a bloodwood tree. Brigid thought of that tree her nana had shown her, near the rockpool. She noticed a bush coconut now hung on a branch next to her.

Tears streaking through the dirt on her face, Brigid felt as if she could no longer breathe. The finches that had been interrupted by the slowing of time began to dart around. As they flew away, another raven landed in the apple tree. Now there were three large black birds acting as witnesses. Brigid heard a chorus of cherished voices: *Come on, Brigid, it's time to go.*

ELEVEN

From inside the cottage, Maggie saw the birds again. Three large black birds perched in the nearest gum tree.

She remarked, 'Did you know they're not really crows?'

Victoria shook her head and climbed into bed, even though it was only early afternoon.

'People call them crows but they're actually little ravens.'

'How was school today?' asked Victoria, uninterested in birds.

'It was okay, I guess. I hate going without you. Is he very mean to you?'

Victoria turned her head towards the wall. Not before Maggie had seen tears forming in her eyes. Maggie went over to the bed and climbed in. She put her arm around her sister's shoulder, and they lay in silence.

***

'I don't believe she left us. He's lying,' whispered Maggie.

Victoria nodded. 'She would never.'

'I don't want to do this any more. I hate posing for him.'

Von Wolff turned around. 'Stop talking. Or I'll send you to that orphanage, and they will not be as tolerant as I am. Sister Marie locks disobedient children in a cage for days, without even a sip of water.'

They reached for each other's hands, and held on tightly. Victoria glanced over at the photos of them hanging from string along one of the walls. She hated them. Almost as much as she hated von Wolff. On display at the moment were the photos from when he'd made her wear nothing but a small cloth around her waist, while Maggie was outfitted in a fine lady's dress from a bygone era. Victoria had been made to hold a spear, one foot resting on her other thigh. She'd felt like one of those herons down at the dam, standing on one leg, without the dignity they possess. Von Wolff had then made her stand over Maggie, who was on the ground, pretending to have fainted. Later, Victoria cried late into the night, with Maggie beside her in bed, softly singing lullabies until she fell asleep. A week later, it was Victoria who comforted Maggie, with stories, until she fell asleep. That day, Maggie had been made to dress in men's clothing. A white linen shirt and pants, and a pith helmet. Von Wolff had shoved a pipe in Maggie's mouth, then made her hold a rifle in one hand and a thick chain in the other. The chain was attached to the neck of her sister, who was, once again, semiclad. The photos were always developed in black and white. Depicting the twins as a caricature of black and white.

'The way he makes us pose, that's not who we are,' Maggie had sobbed that night. 'I would never hurt you, ever. I hate him so much.'

In the stone cottage, which was the furthest from von Wolff they both could get, every night Victoria and Maggie wished for Gabriel to return. They believed he would help them find their mother. She would not have left them willingly. They knew that with all their heart.

***

'He's back,' announced Maggie, as she walked into the cottage.

Victoria got up off the bed, quickly pulling her dress down over her thighs.

'What's that, Victoria?'

'Nothing. I got scratched when walking too close to the rosebushes up at the house.'

Maggie frowned, sure her sister was not telling the truth. She pictured the cane that had recently appeared in von Wolff's studio.

'Did he use the stick again?'

'Who's back?' said Victoria, as if she'd not heard Maggie's question.

'Gabriel.'

Victoria smiled. At least, it appeared to be a smile. Maggie had not seen her sister smile for some time. Maggie felt guilty. At least she could still go to school, even if under strict instructions about what she could and couldn't say. While Victoria went nowhere. She cleaned von Wolff's house and cooked his meals, and was forced to participate in photo sessions in the studio on weekends. The rest of her time was spent in the cottage. She was not permitted to leave the property.

Victoria lifted the lid of a pot on the stove, picked up a wooden spoon and stirred. Maggie fetched two plates, and watched as Victoria served the stew. Looking at bits of meat and vegetable clump onto her plate, Maggie instinctively winced. Victoria tried her best but she wasn't a good cook. Not like their mother. Maggie knew that von Wolff also disliked her sister's cooking. Sometimes Victoria would come back to the cottage, after serving his dinner, with a bright-red mark across a cheek. Maggie knew not to ask. Instead, she'd silently fetch a cool cloth and gently wipe Victoria's face before applying lanolin.

'Gabriel can help us,' Maggie asserted.

Victoria shrugged, then sat at the table. They both ate in silence.

Maggie put their plates in the sink. 'The rainbow birds have gone. So have those ravens.'

'I noticed,' replied Victoria.

'Victoria, he's back. He can help us find Mumma.'

'It's too late. She's gone.'

'Don't say that. I'm going to talk to Gabriel tomorrow. I'll stop off at the timber yard after school.'

'It's too risky. Von Wolff might notice you're late and get angry.'

'I'll be extra careful, because I know he'd probably take it out on you. He never raises a hand to me.'

'Don't speak about it, Maggie. Please.'

***

Victoria recognised the truck parked near von Wolff's studio. It was the one from the timber yard. Gabriel had borrowed it from his boss a few times, to give them lifts home from town. Removing another bedsheet from the line, Victoria squinted, trying to see who was unloading wood from the truck. A man turned around, catching her gaze. Gabriel. He began to walk over, before she waved him back. He stopped, immediately understanding. He returned to his work, and she to hers.

*

Later that day, as the sun set, Victoria and Maggie were pulling in the yabby pots at the dam. They heard a whistle and looked over towards some nearby bushes.

'Wait here,' said Victoria, as she ran towards the sound.

A few minutes later she returned. 'It's Gabriel. Just letting us know he'll see us at the cottage later tonight, when it's safer.'

***

They heard a soft rap on the window by their bed. They threw off the bedcovers, both fully dressed. Victoria opened the door, and Gabriel slid into the darkened cottage. He seemed to fill the room. She had forgotten how tall he was. Stefan was a small man in comparison. Victoria remembered Omer as a large man, able to fill a room with his infectious laughter, but Gabriel was taller. Maggie lit one candle, and placed it on the table. In the shadows, Victoria put the kettle on. Maggie fetched mugs, and soon they were all seated at the table. Gabriel studied the twins' trusting faces and felt a pang of sadness. He wasn't sure if he should tell them now or later. Perhaps later would be best. Gabriel was still coming to terms with his recent discovery. Von Wolff hadn't even bothered to make a proper resting place, so it had not taken Gabriel long to find her a few hours earlier. He'd made sure Brigid was respectfully laid to rest, on the other side of the dam, before coming over to the cottage. Gabriel was trying to mask his feelings. The grief of finding Brigid was compounded by the horror he'd felt when realising the cause of her death. He had no idea how to tell Victoria and Maggie. Looking at their faces, he knew the last couple of months had not been easy for them. He decided to tell them later. First, he had to ensure their safety.

Gabriel put down his cup of tea. 'Can you be ready to leave this time tomorrow night?'

Maggie insisted, 'Our mumma is coming back, to get us. We have to wait here.'

'She's not coming back,' said Victoria. 'Is she, Gabriel?'

He met Victoria's eye, realising she needed to hear the truth. 'No. She's gone on.'

'You mean dead?'

Gabriel nodded. Maggie started to cry and Victoria put an arm around her shoulders. She waited until the sobs subsided, then helped her sister into bed. Gabriel watched her, a lump in his chest. She'd changed since he saw her last. Beyond the sorrow was something else. Gabriel berated himself for not insisting that Brigid and the twins leave with him. He could not have prevented his niece and nephews being orphaned, but he did blame himself for the twins losing their mother. He should not have waited so long to return. Victoria had always reminded him of Brigid. Now Victoria's eyes reminded him of that resigned look Brigid had when he'd first met her, a look that had slowly dissolved as they got to know each other.

Gabriel's shoulders slumped as he remembered that he'd never see Brigid again. Then he sat up straight, resolving to put thoughts of her aside for now. He knew now was not his time to grieve. He had to help these young ones. Get them away from von Wolff. Gabriel had gone into the studio earlier, when he was delivering timber, and seen those photos. Grotesque photos hanging on string throughout the studio. And he had seen the way his boss, Tony Bolt, had leered at those lurid images. When they'd dropped in at the pub on the way back to town, Gabriel had heard Bolt telling an out-of-uniform Constable Peters about the photos. Peters replied he'd already seen them, many times. Peters and Bolt shared their sudden appreciation for the arts over a few beers. Feeling sickened from overhearing some of this conversation, Gabriel resolved to get Victoria and Maggie far away from men like them. And away from von Wolff.

'You need to be ready to leave tomorrow night, Victoria,' he said when she returned to the table.

She nodded. 'I'll pack tonight. It's his card night tomorrow, so his mates will all be here, drinking.'

'Good,' said Gabriel.

'Not good. They're loud and scary when they drink. And von Wolff, if he hasn't passed out by the time his friends leave, gets angrier. We hear him shouting, breaking things, late at night. Making a bigger mess for me to clean up the next day. I worry that one day he'll make his way over here, to the cottage. I'm not a child any more. I'm thirteen now. I know things. I'm not sure I can protect Maggie if he tries anything.'

'One more day, I promise. I'll get you away from here.'

***

Victoria had watched them arrive. Constable Peters and Mr Stevens from school were in the first car. And then a car she'd not seen before pulled in. Victoria recognised Mr Bolt, Gabriel's boss, as he got out of the car and walked into the studio with a handful of beers. She'd normally be dismayed that Father Paddy was not joining them, but tonight would be her last here, so it didn't matter how drunk and unruly they got. Victoria glanced at their bags tucked under the table. She knew von Wolff never came to the cottage; still, she didn't want to take any risks. She'd acted normal all day, despite a high level of anxiety. And insisted that Maggie went to school. Now, they were both dressed, ready to go. They were just waiting for Gabriel to arrive. Maggie had extinguished the lantern and candles. She wanted von Wolff to think they were sleeping.

'Did you hear that?' she whispered.

Victoria shook her head.

'There's people out there. I heard footsteps.'

Thinking it was Gabriel that Maggie had heard, Victoria went to the door. She opened it, just a little bit.

Maggie stood beside her. Frightened by what she'd seen, Maggie ran over to the bed. Victoria shut the door quickly and put the latch on.

Maggie whispered, 'Birdmen.'

Don't be silly,' said Victoria.

'You saw it too. They had feathers instead of hair. And feathered feet.'

Victoria went to look out the window above the sink. It was dark, except for the lights coming from von Wolff's studio. Maggie got out of bed and stood next to her. They kept watching, hoping to see Gabriel approaching.

'Look,' whispered Maggie, pointing.

Victoria saw three figures moving from behind the studio. They were little more than shadows, until one walked into a sliver of light.

'See, Birdmen,' said Maggie.

Victoria watched the three stealthily enter the studio. Maggie clung to her sister when the shouting started. They both jumped as gunshot was heard, followed by more shouting, and then frenzied yelling. When flames and smoke started pouring out of the studio, everything went quiet. Victoria counted shadowy figures leaving the studio: one, two, three. And then she counted three men running from the flames: Peters, Stevens, Bolt.

'Where's von Wolff?' Maggie asked.

Victoria shrugged. Indifferently, she watched the studio go up in flames. The photographic chemicals turned the flames blue. Then they heard someone turning the door handle behind them, and two short knocks. Victoria went to the door and lifted the latch. Gabriel entered the cottage, breathless. Maggie handed him a glass of water, which he drank quickly. As he put the empty glass on the table, Maggie reached over and pulled a long, thin grey feather out of his hair. She'd seen ones like this before.

Maggie held it up in front of Gabriel. 'Emu?'

He nodded.

'Are we free now?' asked Victoria.

'Yes,' replied Gabriel.

'Then let's go,' declared Victoria, as she pulled the bags out from under the table.

Gabriel reached out to take one.

'Not that one,' said Maggie.

He picked up another one, while Maggie clung tightly to the battered old suitcase their mother had been reluctant to give up. Victoria went to their mother's bed and, pulling back the covers, revealed her great-grandfather Albert's gun. She picked it up and walked over to Gabriel, handing it to him carefully.

'Here,' she said. 'You can carry this. For now.'

224

'I can't see anything.'

'Listen instead.'

'All I hear is the waves. They're so loud.'

'How about now?'

'What did you do? The waves are not so loud.'

'Can you see now?'

Victoria shifted a foot. 'I see you, Aunty Isabelle. At the edge of the inland sea. Are you really there?'

'Yes, I'm here.'

'I hear something. It's a story, flying by. I remember that voice. She told us stories, that old lady. She was much older than you, Aunty.'

'And now? What do you see?'

'Another old lady. She's standing under an apple tree. She has kind eyes. I bet she knows some good stories.'

'And now?'

The girl froze.

'You can say, come on.'

'It's our mother. She's with that old lady. She looks happy.'

'It's okay to cry.'

'No. The bad man might hear.'

'He's gone. The bad man can't hurt you any more.'

'Are you sure?'

TWELVE

The rules were simple: stay away from roads, duck down when told to, and never wander off alone. Most days they travelled together. Sometimes Gabriel would tell them to keep walking in a straight path, while he disappeared into the bush. As the sun set, he'd always find the campsite that Maggie and Victoria had set up. He'd usually throw a freshly butchered emu or kangaroo next to the campfire. While they slept, Gabriel would stare into the flames, remembering that night of the fire. If von Wolff hadn't panicked, it could have turned out differently. There had been no intent to kill him. Justice had been on Gabriel's mind. Instead, von Wolff died in agony. Gabriel could still picture him, arms outstretched like a fiery starfish. The fire was von Wolff's fault. He'd knocked over a candle when he tried to punch Gabriel. The candle, which von Wolff used to light cigars on card nights, had fallen onto a bench where he'd earlier spilt a bottle of raw alcohol. He'd been experimenting with it as a final rinse when processing some film, and hadn't bothered to clean up the spillage. The studio had gone up rapidly. Von Wolff would have died quickly, even if in extreme pain.

As the days went on, Gabriel no longer reflected on that horrifying image. Instead, he thought of Brigid as he stared up at the stars, unable to sleep. Maggie and Victoria also thought of her and, slowly emerging from their recent trauma, would share childhood memories around the campfire. Gabriel would warm his hands by the fire, feeling his heart thaw as he listened to them speak fondly of Brigid.

***

The girls huddled under a scrawny tree, not much more than a bush. Water poured through the leafless branches, making both of them shiver.

'I hate this,' murmured Maggie.

Victoria nodded, not even bothering to ask what exactly Maggie hated. Instead, she wondered if Gabriel would be able to find them. All this rain would surely have washed away their footprints. She heard a rustling to the left of them, and put a finger to her mouth to hush her sister. Victoria stood up and peered at the low bushes that surrounded them. A figure of a man appeared.

Maggie jumped up. 'It's Gabriel!'

She ran to him, giving him a hug.

He grinned. 'You two look like drowned rabbits.'

'And you're not even slightly wet,' remarked Maggie, letting him go.

Victoria frowned. 'How come?'

Gabriel replied, 'I walked between the rain.'

228

'What?' said Victoria, at the same time as Maggie said 'How?'

He smiled. 'It's easy, once you know how.'

Victoria responded, 'This just a silly story. No one can walk between rain. It's just not possible.'

'It is possible, if you believe it is.'

'Show me then,' insisted Victoria.

***

The old man handed Maggie a chipped enamel plate, and then one to Victoria.

'Eat, it's good tucker,' he said.

They spooned up the stew, tasting it gingerly. It was good. Soon they were asking for seconds, and he laughed goodheartedly as he refilled their plates. Gabriel finished eating, and took out his tobacco pouch. He was down to just crumbs and had no papers left. He started rolling a smoke using a scrap of paper. A younger man handed him a pouch and, nodding thanks, Gabriel rolled a proper cigarette. Gabriel went to hand back the tobacco pouch, but was told to keep it. The man picked up a guitar and started strumming. The older man cleared his throat and began to sing. Maggie and Victoria, feeling warm and bellies full, climbed under their blankets and were soon asleep.

'They're looking for you, brother,' commented the old man. 'I seen your picture in the papers; they said you killed a man.'

Gabriel nodded. 'I expected them to. I was stupid. I dropped my wallet, so it wouldn't have been difficult for them to work out I'd been there that night. I didn't kill him, though.'

The old man picked up a stick, and stirred the fire. 'Since when do they care if we didn't do what they said we did.'

'True.'

'Them young ones will slow you down.'

'They keep up. Not once have they complained in the past four months. Still, I know this is no life for them.'

'What're you going to do?'

Gabriel shook his head. 'I don't know. I can't go home. No doubt the police have been keeping an eye on my family. All I know is I need to keep these young ones safe.'

The younger man pointed his chin towards the sleeping girls. 'They're not yours, are they? Where's their mob?'

'I'm looking out for them,' said Gabriel. 'Their mother never told me where they're from. She told me lots of things, but she kept some to herself. I don't even know what her family name was.'

'Devlin,' declared Victoria, from behind them. 'Our mother's last name was Devlin. Same as ours. I think her mother's name is different. Brown with an "e", maybe. I once saw that on a piece of paper, in our mother's suitcase. No address or anything, just that name.'

Victoria got up and went to sit by the fire, near Gabriel. She'd been slowly getting closer to him in the last few months. She still didn't like to be touched. Unlike Maggie, who would hold Gabriel's hand when they sat by campfires, and gave him goodnight hugs.

'Do you remember anything else, girl?' asked the old man.

Victoria frowned. 'Our dad's name is Daniel. Don't know his last name, or where he is. We never met him.'

'Don't forget about Aunty Isabelle,' chimed in Maggie, joining her sister by the fire. 'She's our father's aunt too. I don't remember the name of the place where she lived. It once was the shore of an inland sea.'

The younger man remarked, 'I know that place. Went there once, to visit a cuz who was working nearby, in the opal fields.'

Maggie said, 'Our friend Omer had a opal mine. We worked there sometimes.'

The older man nodded at Gabriel. 'Shouldn't be too hard to send a message up that way, to find out more about this aunt.'

'Bit hard to get a reply when I'm on the move,' remarked Gabriel.

'True,' replied the old man.

Victoria asked Gabriel, 'Why are the police looking for us? Is it because of the fire?'

Gabriel replied, 'Yes. There's no need for you to worry. I'll keep you safe.'

'And von Wolff? Is he really dead?'

'Yes.'

'I hope it hurt real bad.'

***

Gabriel had found the way Brigid was killed too painful to consider until Victoria had said those words: *I hope it hurt.* Although the sight and sounds of von Wolff's final moments were vividly burnt into Gabriel's memory, he was not sorry for what had happened. He knew it had hurt immensely but had no pity to spare for von Wolff. Gabriel was not a cruel man – he knew von Wolff had been.

Gabriel had planned on keeping the promise he'd made to his sister, and the promises he'd made to Brigid. In that last letter from Brigid, she'd agreed to leave with him as soon as the debt was cleared. That news had made him happy. He was finally able to believe that them all living together would not just be wishful thinking. His niece was nearly the same age as the twins, and the nephews not much older. Gabriel thought they'd have easily formed a blended family. All those dreams had been shattered when he'd returned to find Brigid gone. Gabriel instinctively knew that something bad had happened to her. Now he was on the run with her daughters, and not with her or his sister's children. Gabriel knew others would be taking good care of his niece and nephews. For now, Victoria and Maggie needed him more. And he needed them; they were his last connection to the only woman he'd ever loved. He vowed to protect them for as long as they wanted him around.

***

Gabriel crept up to the window, and peeked in. Same as the other windows: he didn't see anyone. There were no cars around, aside from a couple of rusted chassis and a truck with no tyres. He could safely assume no one was home. He didn't like to steal, but the girls had not eaten for two days. There were no more bullets for the rifle, and rabbit snares had not been successful. He went around the back, and put his hand on the door knob.

'Well, aren't you a big one.'

He turned, and saw a woman. She was about his age. Sunburnt face framed by red hair. Patchworked dress worn over men's jeans and rubber boots. Raised rifle. Gabriel put his hands in the air.

'Not going to shoot you, unless you do something foolish. How could I shoot a gift like yourself? You can put those arms down.'

Gabriel stood still, watching her every move. Two dogs came running towards her, before racing off to a bush. They jumped around, yapping wildly.

'What you got in there? You have friends with you?'

He shook his head.

'My dogs say different, and they never lie. Flush 'em out, boys.'

The dogs raced around the bush, frantically barking. Maggie and Victoria appeared from behind the bush, obviously nervous around the dogs.

Gabriel said loudly, above the barking, 'Call them off. You can see they're just girls.'

The woman lowered her gun. 'Those dogs won't bite 'em. Hey, kids, you hungry?'

The twins looked at Gabriel, who nodded. The woman walked to the door, and held it open as everyone entered.

She introduced herself as Janice as she made a big plate of sandwiches. When the plate was empty, she made more. And then milky tea. Soon the girls were sleepy, so she made up a bed. She insisted they stay when Gabriel told them to pick up their bags. Then, when the twins were asleep, she interrogated him. An hour later, the room fell silent.

'Six months, you say? That's a long time to be on the road with young'uns.'

'They travelled a lot with their mother, this was nothing.'

'So what's the plan? You want to call someone?

Gabriel looked at the phone on the kitchen wall. 'Is that okay?'

'Sure. I'll even give you some privacy. I've got chooks to lock up. The foxes around here are so sly, they even outwit my dogs.'

After Janice left, Gabriel dialled the only number he knew. The person who picked up called out for a child to go down the road and fetch old Mrs Crow. And soon he heard his nana's voice on the other end. By the time Janice had returned, Gabriel was sitting at the table again. He felt reassured that his nana was doing well, as were his brother, niece and nephews. He promised her he'd be home soon. When it was safe.

'All good?'

He nodded. 'Yes, thanks. How can I repay you?'

'No need. I just like the company. You can stay here for a few days, if you like. Rest up, get some meat on those bones. And let me give those kids a bath tomorrow. Oh lordy, do they need one. You too, handsome. Think I can even rustle up some clean clothes for you all.'

*

The next morning, while the girls were bathing, Gabriel took an axe to the woodpile. He split logs, and had soon chopped up enough to fill the woodshed. That night, he slept soundly. Each day he'd find new chores to do, to repay Janice for her kindness. The girls loved helping her with the chickens, and were experts at finding the hens' secret nests. Gabriel was on edge at first, always reminding the girls to stay out of sight. Soon, six months had gone by. Those months were easier than the previous six spent hiding in mallee scrub.

One morning, Gabriel asked if he could use the phone again. This time, his nana told him the police had stopped watching her place months ago. She felt it was safe for him to come home. And, just in case, his brother Charlie had built a hidden trapdoor covering a staircase down into the newly constructed cellar. Big enough for three to hide in for days, if need be. When he told Maggie and Victoria that it was time to leave, they were at first upset. Until they heard they would be going to live with Gabriel's family.

The next day, Gabriel had almost finished packing their bags, when Janice walked in. She looked concerned. He then heard the car doors.

'You all need to go hide in my bedroom wardrobe,' she told him, before leaving again.

He called the girls and the three of them picked up all their bags and belongings, then squeezed into the large wardrobe. With the door slightly open, they heard footsteps enter the house. They listened as Janice talked to at least two men. Gabriel's heart was racing. Ready to flee, if need be. Then he heard the front door shut, and the car leave.

'You can come out now,' called Janice.

Gabriel told the girls to stay in the bedroom, while he went to speak with Janice. She was picking up a girl's shoe that must have been dropped when Gabriel and the twins rushed into hiding.

'Lucky they didn't see this. It was the cops. Not the local one. Two detectives from the city. Useless bastards, all of them,' she said.

'What did they want?'

'You.'

'They know I'm here?'

Janice shook her head. 'They're doing door-to-door checks, asking about someone else. Some bloke who robbed the local bank at gunpoint. Then they asked if I'd seen anyone matching your description.'

'Why would they connect me to the robbery?'

'They didn't. I guess they're just killing two birds with one stone. You know, bringing up an older case while looking for the other guy. They're heading back to the city now, but I don't reckon its safe for you to be sticking around. One of my neighbours might see you or the twins, and connect the dots. Cops are telling people you not only killed that man, but kidnapped the girls after killing their mother. That bit of news will have people picking up the phone quick smart if they happen to see you.'

Gabriel looked down the corridor, relieved the girls were still in the bedroom and had not heard the conversation. *Will this ever end?* he thought.

'Come on, stop looking mopey. I'll put the kettle on, while you figure out a plan B.'

Gabriel phoned his nana, and told her it would take him longer to get home. A few more months hiding in scrublands wouldn't hurt them. Janice picked up a duffle bag she'd filled with fresh food and staples, and handed him a large box of bullets. Standing in the yard, bags ready, the girls gave her a hug. Then Janice demanded Gabriel give her one too.

'Been waiting for that since I first seen ya,' she said, with a wide grin. 'Go on, you lot. Get out of here, before you see me cry.'

***

Maggie and Victoria had been alone all day. They'd remembered to keep an eye on the sky, making sure they walked in the right direction. Gabriel had left them to go hunting, and given them instructions on where to meet up later.

Maggie stopped abruptly. 'That one has been following us the whole day.'

'Who?'

'Up there. See?'

Victoria squinted, looking up into a clear blue sky. She saw a bird circling, up high. It swooped down, towards them. She recognised it as a wedgetail eagle. Gabriel had told them a story about eagles, one night around a campfire.

Maggie remarked, 'He's looking out for us, until Gabriel gets back.'

Victoria nodded, and smiled. Her sister and birds. It was as if Maggie could communicate with them. Maybe she could. Victoria remembered their mother telling them about how her granny Maeve had taught her the language of birds. And how, when her mother wasn't too much older than they were now, she'd followed a little black-and-white bird. That's how their mother had met their father. Or so she'd told them.

Victoria was beginning to think she was too old to believe in stories. Their fifteenth birthday was nearing. She wondered if Maggie would even remember their birthday this year. Victoria was beginning to lose all sense of time. They'd been on the run for nearly two years. It was more than two and half years since they'd lost their mother. Now, the only times that mattered were sunrise and sunset; and only because Gabriel made them keep walking in between. Always on the move, just like those years with their mother. Sunrise: smother the fire, pick up your luggage, get walking. Sunset: collect wood, light the fire, fall asleep exhausted. Victoria hadn't minded the days travelling with her mother. This travelling was different. Everything was different without Mother.

Maggie interrupted her thoughts. 'I can hear more birds.'

Victoria listened. She couldn't hear a thing. Maggie stepped to her right and pushed through some bushes.

'Stop,' insisted Victoria. 'There could be snakes in there.'

Maggie kept walking, so Victoria followed. And then Maggie stopped abruptly.

'We need to go back,' she said.

'Why? I can hear those birds now. Don't you want to see what type they are?'

Maggie shook her head. 'We need to turn back.'

Victoria pushed passed her and kept walking. Maggie followed, pleading with her to stop. Victoria halted suddenly, causing Maggie to bump into her. They were on a tall cliff, with a large river below them. It was the biggest river they'd ever seen. Before then, they'd only known creeks.

'We need to leave this place,' said Maggie, pulling on Victoria's sleeve.

'Look at it. So huge. Like a big watery snake. I wonder where it goes.'

'We have to leave here.'

Victoria walked to the very edge of the cliff. Looking down, she whistled in amazement.

'This is a bad place,' Maggie declared. 'Can't you hear the screams?'

'What are you talking about? I can't hear anything.'

'You shouldn't be here,' announced a voice behind them.

They hadn't heard Gabriel approach. Victoria stepped back from the edge of the cliff and Maggie walked over to take Gabriel's hand.

Victoria. 'Why shouldn't we be here?'

Gabriel replied, 'Do you need to question everything, Victoria? Can you not just do as I ask?'

Maggie added, 'I told you it was a bad place, Victoria.'

'Let's go,' said Gabriel.

'How many died here?' asked Maggie.

'Hundreds,' he replied.

'How?'

'Men on horseback drove them off the cliff.'

Victoria felt shaking, as if she could feel the thunder of dozens of horses' hooves on the ground she stood on. She still couldn't hear anything, not like Maggie had, but she felt that shaking.

Victoria asked, 'Even the children?'

Gabriel nodded.

Maggie pulled on his arm. 'Let's leave this place.'

Victoria walked back to the clifftop and peered down. It was a long way. Under the cliff lay sharp rocks that had at some point tumbled from the cliff face. She imagined people falling, driven to their death by settlers on horseback.

'Why do they wish us dead?' she muttered.

Behind her, Gabriel responded, 'Because it's them who are uncivilised, not us.'

*

That night, further along the river, they made camp next to a circle of stones. Maggie had seen it first and asked Gabriel what it was. He explained the circle of rocks was a map, which had once been used to determine the position of the sun when it set at the equinoxes and solstices. To mark the seasons, so people knew which bush food would soon be ready to harvest. He told them the white rocks of various sizes had been carried there a very long time ago. Gabriel lit a fire close by, and while he was preparing their dinner, Maggie and Victoria sat in the middle of the stone circle.

Maggie sighed, 'I wish I knew all the names of the stars.'

'Given how many there are, that would be impossible,' asserted Victoria.

Placing warm damper and kangaroo meat on enamel plates, Gabriel said, 'I can show you constellations. Well, the few I know.'

After they ate, they all lay in the circle, looking skywards. Gabriel pointed out constellations, drawing lines in the air until the girls saw the ancestral beings for which each star collective had been named. Maggie's favourite was the Southern Cross, because it was actually an eagle's talon, not a flag, while Victoria was enthralled by the seven glowing sisters that Gabriel had told them lived in the constellation of the Pleiades.

'Look,' observed Maggie. 'A falling star.'

'Gabriel?' said Victoria, after the streaking light had vanished.

'Yes?'

'What does it mean when someone says "Didn't fall far from the tree"?'

'Who said that?'

'The bad man.'

Gabriel sat up. 'Do you want to tell me more?'

'He was yelling at me, as usual. This time he said I was too uppity. What does that word mean?'

Gabriel replied, 'Nothing wrong with being uppity. They might use it as an insult; I know it to mean a person of strength. One who won't bow down to them, won't tolerate their hate. Your mother was strong like that.'

'After calling me uppity, he said, "The apple doesn't fall far from the tree." It sounded mean, the way he said it.'

'Von Wolff was not a good person. His words are of no relevance. You should be proud of the tree you came from. You remind me a lot of your mother. I know she'd be proud of you, Victoria. Always. You too, Maggie.'

'Do you think she's up there, among those stars?' asked Maggie.

Gabriel replied, 'I reckon so. She's looking out for you both.'

Maggie pointed. 'I think she's that star there. The brightest one.'

***

Over the following weeks, they often saw the large river. Gabriel told them his nana lived beside one of the many smaller rivers that came off the big river. They were making their way to her house. Home was only a few weeks away, if they kept following the river. Gabriel told them the big river snaked towards the south much further, splitting many times, until it reached the sea. Maggie and Victoria had never seen an ocean, so they asked Gabriel lots of questions. Maggie imagined the sounds that seagulls would make, and thought of how wonderful it would be to see a sea eagle. Gabriel told them that if anything was to happen to him, if they followed the river almost to the sea, they'd come to a big city. Bigger than any town they'd ever seen. And there, he'd suggested, they could get help to find their family.

Days walking, evenings by a campfire, and nights sleeping under the stars were all too familiar for Victoria and Maggie. Gabriel found it easy travelling with them. Maggie had whined a little in the first few days, but she soon got used to the daily routine. It would have been enjoyable, if not for the absence of their mother. Victoria loved being outdoors again, and occasionally wandered off to look at things. She knew this worried Gabriel, so she was trying hard not to. Every time Gabriel had to leave them, to hunt for food, he would get them to recite the rules: stay away from roads, duck down when told, and never wander off alone.

*

It was Maggie's wandering off that caused trouble. They'd been walking through a thick coverage of scraggly trees, not too much higher than bushes, when Victoria heard cars.

'Is there a road nearby?'

Gabriel nodded. 'A highway. Just a few metres to our left. We need to be careful and stay under cover.'

'Where's Maggie?'

They looked around and couldn't see her. Gabriel made a bird noise, their secret call. There was no response. They went towards the road, making sure they could not be seen in case a car went by. Gabriel told Victoria to duck down, behind a bush near the side of the road. He'd caught sight of Maggie, on the other side. Telling Victoria to stay put, he ran quickly across the road.

'Maggie, what are you doing?'

She turned around. 'I saw some rainbow birds. I've not seen any since Mumma disappeared. I had to get a closer look.'

'Don't wander off. I've told you that before. Let's get back to your sister.'

Telling Maggie to duck down until he called for her, Gabriel walked to the edge of the road. After a few minutes of waiting, Maggie heard a car approaching.

'Damn,' muttered Gabriel. 'Keep down, Maggie. And don't move until I say so.'

Maggie could see Victoria hiding on the other side of the road. Gabriel started running in the same direction the car was travelling. Victoria and Maggie watched the car speed by, siren blaring. Gabriel stopped running and put his hands on the back of his head, elbows extended. The car stopped, and two policemen got out.

'Lean on the bonnet,' one instructed.

Gabriel did as he was told, and the officer searched his pockets.

'Where's your wallet?'

'Lost it,' replied Gabriel.

'Got any identification?'

Gabriel shook his head.

The other policeman, who was stouter and older in appearance, asked, 'Why were you running, boy?'

'No idea,' replied Gabriel.

'Are you sassing me?'

'No, sir.'

'He looks familiar, Sarge,' said the younger policeman.

The older man asked, 'How so?'

'Like a photo I saw on one of the wanted lists. Murder, I think.'

'You sure?'

'Yeah, that murder that happened up north from here, about two years ago. Victim was named von Wolff, I think. They reckon a darkie did it.'

'You know anything about that, boy? Do you know this von Wolff?'

Gabriel shook his head. 'Don't know anything, sir. Just walking home. Been at my cousin's place the last few days. My woman is going to tear strips off me when I get home.'

The sergeant said, 'Call the station, Kuper. See if you can get a description of the man they've been looking for.'

The young officer walked over to the car and picked up the car radio. While he was talking, Gabriel scrutinised the road, relieved that Maggie and Victoria had listened and remained hidden.

'What's your name?'

'John.'

'And last name?'

'Smith, sir.'

'John Smith? You think I'm an idiot, do you? Wise guy,' the sergeant shouted as he hit Gabriel across the side of his head.

Gabriel saw the top of Victoria's head and willed her to duck down again. The other policeman returned.

'Sounds like this guy is that boong wanted for von Wolff's murder. Gabriel Crow.'

'Smith, eh? Funny bugger,' remarked the sergeant as he hit Gabriel again.

*

Victoria and Maggie kept on waiting, just as they'd been told to. Long after the police car had left. Long after Gabriel had gone. They looked at each other in silence, eyes peering from between bush branches. They waited. As the sun was setting, Victoria stood up. Maggie ran across the road, into her sister's arms.

'I'm sorry, so sorry. It's all my fault,' Maggie sobbed.

'There's nothing we can do. Crying won't bring him back.'

Maggie stepped back. 'He's not ever coming back, is he?'

Victoria went to fetch their bags. Gabriel didn't have much, but his backpack had things of use in it, so she shouldered it. And then she picked up great-grandfather's rifle and slung it over the other shoulder. Victoria started walking and, with no other option, Maggie followed.

***

They'd been following the river for weeks, just like Gabriel had told them to. They weren't quite alone. An eagle hovered above them most days. Maggie was adamant that it was the same eagle they'd seen over their campsite a while back, before Gabriel was taken. Victoria wasn't too sure, as they'd walked a long way, but Maggie had no doubts. She would often see the eagle first thing in the morning, as if it was waiting for them to get moving. Sometimes it would stop, showing them something to eat or a safe place to rest. Eagle and girls followed the river as it snaked its way towards the ocean. Some evenings, looking up at the stars and recalling the stories Gabriel had shared, Maggie would become melancholy. She still felt bad about what had happened to Gabriel, firmly believing that it was her fault. Victoria would just tell her to stop talking about it, as there was nothing either of them could do. Silently, Victoria also thought it was Maggie's fault. She wondered how long they'd keep him locked up. She vowed one day to find out where they'd taken him, and to be there for him when he got out. If he ever did.

THIRTEEN

Even before opening her eyes, she could feel someone next to her. She settled closer, welcoming the body heat on a cold morning. After a while, she gently rolled over, so as not to disturb her sister. She studied Maggie's face and saw no trace of last night's terrors that had woken them both. During moments like that, her sister would call out for their mother. And in the dark, they would both often cry, wishing their mother was with them. Lying in bed, she appraised the place they were living in. It wasn't much but it was their refuge. She reflected on the day they'd found this place, as if they'd been led there, just as they'd been guided to other havens as they slowly made their way to the city.

First, the eagle had been their guardian. Not quite taking Gabriel's role, for a year that big bird travelled with the twins. She'd done okay providing Maggie and herself with fresh meat, with her great-grandfather's rifle and the help of the eagle's eye. The bird saw potential prey that she would have just walked past, unaware. Mostly small animals – rabbits, lizards, bandicoots – and sometimes wallabies, kangaroos, emus. Not every meal needed the rifle. She'd been aware the box of bullets Janice had given Gabriel wouldn't last forever. So wombats were always a welcome sight. She'd killed them with rocks, like he had done. She hated doing it, so she'd remind herself it was a matter of survival. After a few months, she'd got better at killing, skinning and gutting. Maggie did the cooking and washing up. And helped collect other foods. They'd raided vegetable crops and snuck into chicken coops for still-warm eggs. Most nights they'd slept outside, by a fire, just like when they'd travelled with their mother, and later with Gabriel. In the coldest part of winter, they found shelter in barns and woodsheds. Occasionally they'd have to run because they'd disturbed sleeping dogs.

She made sure people never spotted them. Maggie had argued with her on a few occasions about this, when spying a country town in the distance. She was tired of walking, sick of being cold and rain-drenched, and just wanted to sleep in a bed for one night. She'd try to convince her sister that they might meet a nice person who would help them, even for a little while, like Janice did. Or perhaps they could find Gabriel's grandmother, who would surely give them shelter. And perhaps she'd have news of where he was. Maggie reminded her that Gabriel had told them his family lived alongside one of the small offshoots from the river they followed. She would not budge. They were following that river to the sea. It's what Gabriel had told them to do.

Shortly after the wet weather had finished, they'd come across miles and miles of citrus orchards. They laughed as juice ran down their chins, and the liquid sunshine filled their bellies and chased away the winter gloom. With renewed hope, they filled up their bags with citrus fruit, and kept walking. The twins didn't know where they were heading; they just kept following the eagle, which mostly followed the winding river. The eagle left them as they stood on a hill one evening at dusk, looking at the countless roads and buildings below them. It was as if every town they'd ever gone past was here, in one spot. That night, watching the city lights in wonderment, Victoria had decided it was time to leave the past behind. In the morning, she told Maggie that she wanted to be called Tori from now on.

*

They'd waited until the next afternoon before making their way down from the hill, along the busy highway that led towards the city. Tori's first perception of the city was a multitude of noise, colour and movement. She had never seen so many people, or heard that much noise, and had felt overwhelmed. Tori put on a false sense of bravado, while Maggie had clung tightly to her.

When the after-work exodus began to dwindle, just before night cloaked the streets, they'd seen a promising sign. Maggie had noticed the skinny tabby kitten first. That young street cat was just like the one she'd loved many years before. So they'd followed it. They'd raced along unknown streets, pushing against the flow of people, until they'd came to a darkened side street. The kitten had stopped at a small street-level window in what appeared to be an abandoned building. It briefly turned around, as if waiting for them to catch up, then it jumped in through the open window. Making sure no one had noticed them, Maggie and Tori climbed in after it. From her pocket, Tori had taken out a small torch that had once belonged to Gabriel. The kitten had led them to a basement. It wasn't much, but through the weak glow of the torchlight, it had appeared dry. Past occupants had left behind an old iron bed with a ripped mattress, and an assortment of items strewn around the room. Tori had closed the window and checked that the door was locked. Allowing tiredness to overcome them, the girls had curled up together on the bed and drifted off to sleep. With a kitten resting at their feet.

From that first night, it hadn't taken much for them to settle in. After living most of their lives in open spaces, four walls and just one small window suited them. With no electricity, they would go to bed early every night. On the nights when sleep eluded them, they told each other stories to make the world a less frightening place. They would pretend that the shafts of light from the street lamps were moon rays. And they ignored the eerie shadows on the walls of the basement. Just as they ignored all the small unexplained noises in the night, which was most likely just the scratching of vermin and the creaking of the old building.

*

A rustling sound caught Tori's attention. She glanced towards the open window and saw a flurry of leaves flying past, caught up in a gust of wind that blew in, bringing Louis with it. His smile always seemed to arrive before he did.

'Hey, sleepyheads, you're missing a great day out here,' Louis said.

Tori sat up, slowly stretching her arms before swinging her legs out of bed. Carefully, trying not to disturb Maggie, she got up. She noticed Tabby Tomcat, now very much a fullgrown male, curled up at her sister's feet, as usual. Louis placed a battered canvas bag on a milk-crate table. He started pulling things out of his bag, and the rustling of paper woke Maggie. Sniffing the air expectantly, she pulled up a milk-crate chair, waiting to see what Louis had brought them this time.

'I have sugar donuts or yeast buns with raisins. Which do you want?' he asked.

Maggie picked up an almost-stale donut, eyes lighting up in anticipation of the sugary sweetness. Tori selected a bun, experience having taught her that they were generally not as stale. Louis picked up a bun too.

Louis often brought them the choicest bits of treats he could find, after lining up early at various charities and taking whatever leftovers were on offer. The twins had learnt a lot from Louis. He had shown them the best places to go for food, blankets and cast-off clothing. He showed them places and people to avoid, and how not to get caught by predators who roamed the city streets at night.

Maggie looked anxiously up at the ceiling. Muffled sounds of movement indicated the people who squatted in the floors above them were beginning to stir. Only a few would be awake at this time of day; most of the occupants rarely stirred before nightfall. The upstairs people left Maggie and Tori to themselves but would smile if they recognised them out in the streets. It was hard to really know if these friendly strangers were still neighbours, as people never seemed to stay in the squat for long. And every few months, streams of blue uniforms would pour through the building, roughly evicting people. Luckily, the police never bothered to go into the locked basement.

Swallowing the last of a second bun, Tori asked Louis, 'Hear of any jobs this morning?'

He shook his head. 'I was going to take a walk today, look for signs in store windows and such. Want to join me?'

'Sure. Just give me time to clean up a bit.'

'Okay. I'll wait for you in the park,' he said, before climbing out the window.

Tori rummaged through the bags of clothes near the bed, searching for something suitable for job hunting. There wasn't much to choose from, even among the second-hand clothes they'd recently got from the church. She selected a pair of black tailored pants and put them on. They were clean, although a bit worn in some places. The eggshell-blue shirt she put on, which always appeared oversized on Maggie, hugged Tori's body. She picked up a hairbrush and attempted to sort out the tangles in her unruly curly hair. Admitting defeat, she put the brush down and instead put her hair in a ponytail. She then searched for her shoes. When she found them under the bed, she realised they wouldn't be suitable.

'Can I borrow your sandals? Mine are too shabby-looking.'

Maggie nodded. Tori buckled up the sandals and headed towards the window.

'You'll be back before dark, won't you?' Maggie asked.

'Of course. Don't worry,' she replied, climbing out the window.

Once outside, Tori stood a while, taking in the sounds of the city. Their building was on the edge of the city, where concrete melded with parklands. Tori thought of how her sister didn't often go outside any more. On the rare times she did, she liked to stand on nearby parklands that were part of a wide green belt around the city. She'd enjoy the feel of sun on her face, while watching the tiny birds that flourished on the city fringe. Tori preferred to explore further afield, finding new sights in the heart of the city. And she liked discovering what was new on their block. Among the office blocks, new types of businesses were occupying the dilapidated buildings, breathing colour into the greyness. A bohemian flair was taking over this part of the city. Vegetarian cafés, tiny independent bookstores, second-hand clothes stores, basements full of records, and modern art galleries were sprouting up among offices. On weekends and most evenings, the nine-to-five crowd in hotels was replaced with an eclectically clad clientele seeking the next trend. Sounds of live music, guitar-dominated with an occasional sitar or bongo, would float out the doors of packed establishments and travel towards the twins' basement. Tori would often sit by the window, waiting patiently for the music to arrive. Sitting in the shadows, so as not to be seen, she would catch glimpses of people walking towards the music, or meeting friends at cafés and late-night galleries. She knew she could never join them. Even if licensed venues would let Tori in, Maggie didn't like to be left alone at night.

*

Walking towards the park to meet up with Louis, Tori recalled the first time they'd met. She'd been looking for food. Louis and food had become a pattern in her life. And she'd be the first to admit that the quality of city food had improved after he appeared. Maggie and she had been in the city for about half a year, and been having difficulties finding food. Hunting was out of the question. Tori had stashed the rifle safely out of sight. Gathering wasn't impossible, just not easy. There were no edible plants in the city, only water-hungry flowers and trees introduced from overseas. They'd finally discovered some fruit trees in the suburbs, on the other side of the parklands fringing the city precinct. It was bit of a long walk, so they made sure to collect as much as they could carry each time they ventured out there. There were plenty of trees with fruit draping over suburban fences, dropping produce onto sidewalks. If one didn't mind the small bites insects and birds had made. When the trees had stopped fruiting, they had to find other sources of food. Dogs made it too difficult to jump fences and raid backyard gardens. So they looked closer to their basement home. They discovered that local restaurants and delicatessens discarded a lot of food that was still edible. Maggie and Tori soon learnt where the bins with the best food were, and what days of the week generally yielded better finds. In those earlier months, Maggie had helped gather food.

The change in her sister had happened before she'd met Louis. They'd been a few blocks from their place, filling up a bag with discarded meals in the alley behind a cluster of restaurants. Neither of them had seen him approach. They looked up when they heard a yell, and saw a white-aproned man with a thin moustache running towards them. Maggie was the first to see the carving knife in his hand. She froze. Tori grabbed her hand, and pulled her along the alley, away from the furious stranger. As they disappeared around a corner, they heard him shout a warning that he'd better not see them going through his bins again. Maggie kept the tears in until they were safely home. She didn't stop sobbing all night. She stayed in the basement for weeks. And, even then, would only emerge after much coaxing and many promises from Tori. Louis was the only person, other than her sister, that Maggie would talk to.

Tori smiled, thinking of that first encounter with Louis. She was half in a large bin. Rear end protruding, as she struggled to keep her feet on the ground and not fall in. She had her sight on some roast potatoes that looked fresh and in relatively good condition. As she reached out her arms, the bin wobbled, and fell over. Head still buried in the bin, she heard laughter. Emerging with spaghetti embedded in her hair and a cucumber slice on her forehead, she looked around. A young man, not much older than herself, was amusing himself with the sight of her. Arms on hips, legs slightly apart, he reminded Tori of a book cover she'd seen in a bookshop window. That boy was dressed in green, with a fairy on his shoulder. And the book boy, of course, was not a young Aboriginal man with hazel eyes. He walked over and offered his hand. Tori let him help her up, and then proceeded to remove pasta from her head. Despite her being at first reluctant to speak with him, Louis soon had her talking. He was likeable, and not at all judgemental. He never pried, or pushed her to talk if she wasn't in the mood. Maggie instantly took to Louis when, a week later, Tori allowed him to see where they lived. Since then, he'd become their best and only friend in the city.

*

Tori jumped slightly when someone touched her shoulder. Turning around, she was relieved to see Louis.

'Quit the daydreaming. We need to find some work,' he said with a grin.

Tori smiled back at him. She couldn't help it. He had that type of infectious smile that could win anyone over, which was why he was usually able to talk his way out of any situation. Like Tori, he wasn't one for sharing stories of his past. She knew as little of him as he knew of her. If he'd been more open, he might have told Tori how he'd come to be in that southern city, far from home. And how much he missed his nan. Growing up, Louis had not seen much of his mother and father. They'd drifted from town to city to prison – and repeat. When Louis did see them, his mother usually had warm hugs for him. And his dad had words of advice. Words his father had never heeded himself.

Louis had been raised by his father's mother. She'd given him a good home life as a child, with homecooked meals, bedtime stories every night, help with homework, and visiting cousins to play with during the school holidays. And as those cousins grew, so did the territory they roamed. Louis, a natural-born leader, led his cousins into a series of adventures and harmless shenanigans. When Louis took up with some older boys, the cousins didn't follow. These adolescents had nothing in common with Louis and his cousins. They went to the type of school where students wore expensive blazers and shiny shoes, and stood for the anthem and a prayer each morning. Bored with a life mapped out by their distracted parents, they'd lured Louis into hanging out with them, barely containing smirks at the thought of their parents' faces if they saw their latest mascot. When away from the watchful eye of a stern but loving nan, there was more temptation for Louis and more risks taken. He never meant to cause any trouble; he never wanted to see that look of disappointment in his nan's eyes ever again.

Unlike his partners in mischief, who were represented by a team of Queen's Counsels, thanks to their parents' connections, Louis's latest bad choice could have earnt him his first stint in juvenile detention. He was acutely aware of what harm the revolving-prison-door life had done to his parents, and did not want to follow in their footsteps. So he took off before the police cars arrived. After a few months of aimlessly wandering towns and busy cities in the east, occasionally bumping into a parent or two, Louis headed west. He didn't make it far, instead stopping in a smaller, southern city by the sea. He'd been there a year before Tori and Maggie arrived. Since leaving home, he'd managed to steer clear of trouble; a caged life was not for him. Despite his determination, cold nights and hungry days sometimes made him itch to revive the bad habits he'd learnt from that gang of wealthy white boys. What stopped him was a strong drive to make something of his life.

When he met Tori, Louis became more determined. He didn't have a how, but he now had a who. Even before she'd removed the pasta from her hair, he'd fallen for her. A feeling of destiny had grown each day. Louis was soon imagining them living together in a rented flat. With Maggie, of course. And maybe a dog, if Maggie's Tabby Tomcat would agree to sharing space. Louis hadn't had a dog since he was a kid, when his dad, out on parole, gave him a chicken-chasing mutt that was more dingo than dog. Ten-year-old Louis had named that dingo/dog pup Dido. Louis wanted to get another dog, just like Dido.

These plans of his would take money to achieve. And having money would take a job. Louis had been looking for a while, but no one seemed prepared to hire a young black man who'd not even finished Year 9. Still, he had a dream and he was not one to give up easily.

*

With the sun's warmth on his back, Louis was feeling optimistic.

'Come on, Tori,' he said. 'Let's go job hunting.'

Tori, having no idea of her friend's big plans for the future, followed him. They set off along city streets looking for work. A couple of hours later, Tori suggested they give up for the day.

'What about that?' asked Louis.

Tori read the small sign in the window and shrugged. 'Maybe I can give it a go.'

'This might be your lucky break.'

She looked closer at the store. 'This place looks a bit posh.'

'You'd look great in those clothes, Tori. All the customers will be wanting to look just like you. And you have such good taste. You're sure to sell heaps.'

She took a deep breath and pushed the door open. As soon as she entered, she felt curious eyes turn in her direction. She ignored the two sniggering teenage girls browsing racks of clothes, and walked towards the sales counter.

Tori said to the woman behind the counter, 'I'd like to enquire about the vacancy. I'm very interested in fashion.'

The woman assessed her, slowly. Ignoring the girls' laugher behind her, Tori straightened her shoulders.

The woman raised an eyebrow. 'We don't employ your type.'

'What do you mean?'

'You know. Now get out of here or I'll call the police.'

As Tori walked past them, one of the girls muttered, 'Yeah, go back to the bush where you belong, lazy boong.'

The other girl laughed. Tori turned towards the other women in the store, gauging their reactions to that word that hung heavily in the air, hoping for a gesture of support. Instead, she saw them shift uncomfortably and look away. On one of the faces, she saw a look of disgust. Tori walked swiftly, head held high, out the door. Once outside, she let her shoulders droop. She saw Louis waiting a few doors down and walked towards him.

'You okay?' he asked, noticing the look on her face.

'Who would want to work there, anyway. Full of snobs.'

'What happened?'

Tori tugged on the sleeve of her shirt, noticing the frayed cuffs.

Louis said, 'What did they say?'

'I was told to get out. And some girls called me the b-word.'

'I have a word or two for them!' he stated, turning towards the clothes store.

'No, Louis. They're not worth the fuss. I'm okay, really.'

He stopped. 'I hate how they do that. They look at us as if we're dirty, or something. Like they're better than us. Well, they're not, and I'm going in there to tell them to quit being so rude.'

Tori looked at Louis, trying to see her friend as strangers might, taking in his dark-brown hair with an unruly fringe that fell over his hazel eyes. Tori hated being the target of slurs and having people look down at her, but it bothered her more when she saw people being rude to her friend. In addition to slurs, she'd seen other men try to throw punches his way. Louis wasn't scared to stand up for himself, or her. Unlike Tori, who preferred to avoid conflict. She had to stop her friend from going into that store, and letting them know what he thought. Neither of them could risk the police being called. She put a hand on his arm, squeezing gently. He looked at her, and settled down instantly.

'I know they're no better than us, Louis. I'm just not going to let them get to me.'

'You'll find something better than that stuck-up place.'

They both started as the sound of laughter drifted down the street towards them. They saw a group of five walking in a cloud of noise and colour. Tori and Louis turned away, not wanting any further trouble that day. The people got closer, and Tori snuck a look. One woman was dressed in a close-fitting linen suit of a vibrant shade of tangerine. The other three women were wrapped in layers of velvet, cheesecloth and flower-patterned fabrics, topped off with wide-brimmed felt hats. Patchouli, sandalwood and rose attar floated on the air, and their bangle-laden wrists jingled as they walked. All four women huddled close to the man in the centre of the group. Seeing him look in her direction, Tori turned away. All sounds of their approach seemed to cease midair. Even the jangling jewellery was silenced. Tori's heart raced as she waited for the expected slurs.

'You there, turn around.'

Against her better judgement, Tori turned and saw cold grey eyes appraising her. Feeling uncomfortable under the man's gaze, she gathered up a false sense of bravado and looked him over. Although she was tall, he towered over her. He was dressed in a black suit, with a salmon-pink shirt and darkgreen paisley waistcoat. A black velvet hat, so tall it was almost a top hat, and a silver-topped cane complemented his outfit.

He addressed her again: 'What's your name?'

Tori hesitated, wondering if she could ignore him and just walk away. She sensed Louis next to her and knew he would protect her, if needed.

'Come on, I haven't got all day,' the man said sharply.

Tori glanced at Louis. He was clearly uncomfortable at the way the man's companions were looking at him. As they giggled, pushing each other slightly, Louis turned away from them.

'Oh, what fantastic bone structure,' said one.

'Those lips are positively delicious. I would love to photograph him,' said another.

The first woman laughed. 'Oh, darling, we all know you really want to do something else with him. Face it, Ana, you're a failure as a photographer. Just be content with spending Daddy's money in the most pleasurable way you can.'

'You're so catty, Sybil. Remember all those pieces I sold at my last exhibition? They were practically running out the door.'

'Your father's business acquaintances were snapping them up, hoping to win his favour by being nice to his darling.'

'They were good photos. And at least I do something worthwhile with my time.'

'What's that supposed to mean?' asked Sybil, as she moved closer to Ana.

Stepping between them, the woman in the tangerine suit said, 'Come on, that's enough. There's shopping to be done.'

They laughed and wandered towards the clothes boutique from which Tori had just been evicted.

Sybil paused. 'Angie, are you coming?'

The fourth woman ran to join them. Fascinated, Tori watched them walk away. All that confidence. And their clothes were so spectacularly unusual. Like a flock of many-coloured birds. Tori was thinking how Maggie would agree with that description, until a tapping noise brought her attention back. The man was impatiently knocking his cane on the pavement.

'Well, your name?'

'Tori.'

'You look familiar,' remarked the stranger.

Tori shook her head, positive they hadn't met before. She would have remembered someone like him. He reached over, grabbed her chin and proceeded to position her head one way and then another. The woman in the tangerine suit came out of the boutique. She was striking. Tall and angular, with blue-black hair cropped short to frame high cheekbones. Tori wondered if she had also been asked to leave the store, and what slur those girls might have used for her. The woman didn't appear to be upset as she walked sensually towards the man, threading an arm into the crook of his.

'Not another project, Andrés,' she said.

Tori had only ever heard an accent like that on television, in shows made overseas.

Andrés responded, 'Always, Marcie. I need to stay one step ahead in this game.'

'Well, play nicely. This one isn't like your others, and she's so young.'

Turning back to Tori, he asked, 'Are you looking for work?'

Tori nodded, not sure where this was heading.

He pulled a small card from his top pocket. 'I own a photographic gallery. Here's the address.'

He turned and proceeded to walk slowly up the street with Marcie on his arm. The other three women flowed out of the fashion boutique and followed, chattering in their wake.

Tori examined the business card: *Galería de rebelde. Andrés Califa, proprietor.* There was a phone number, and an address on High Street. She handed the card to Louis and, with a frown, he passed it straight back. Tori had forgotten Louis couldn't read.

'It's his business card.'

Louis observed, 'That lot looked loaded with cash. Bet he'd pay well.'

'What do you think he wants me to do?'

'Don't know. Maybe he needs a cleaner.'

'Probably something like that.'

Louis stated, 'I don't like him.'

'He's a bit, I don't know, strange?'

'Yeah. And arrogant.'

'I suppose so, but I really need some work.'

'Maybe he has something suitable. I still don't trust him.'

'I can ask questions first, make sure it's something I want to do. Or I don't even have to go there at all.'

Louis watched Tori put the card in her pocket. 'It's up to you.'

Tori nodded. Even with Louis as a good friend, it was all up to her. Keeping Maggie safe. Providing them both with food and security. Finding work. Filling the space their mother had once occupied.

Louis said, 'Hey, if we hurry we can make it to St Martin's before lunch finishes. I'm sure we can talk them into letting us take some home to Maggie, as well.'

*

Later that day, Tori sat at the basement window, looking up at passing legs – a flood of people on their way home from work or heading to an early dinner in the city. Tori didn't notice the sounds of muffled voices and soft music that drifted from the floors above. She was thinking about her encounter with that man. She wasn't sure why Andrés made her feel uncomfortable. What she did know was that she needed a job. They couldn't keep living like this, in a dank basement, existing on discarded food. As the last piece of sunshine was replaced by the soft glow of street lights, she heard Maggie moving around. The old bed they shared creaked as her sister climbed into it.

'Will you tell me a story, Tori?'

'Sure, which one do you want?'

'One about Mum. A time when she was happy. When we were all happy.'

Tori walked over to the bed and got in next to Maggie. 'Okay, ready?'

Maggie nodded as her sister bunched up a too-thin pillow under her head. Tabby Tomcat jumped through the window, and settled on the bed too.

'Are we all ready now?' laughed Tori.

***

Tori hoped Maggie hadn't heard her stomach grumbling. She'd given her sister the last stale donut, pretending she wasn't hungry.

'Why don't we do something different today?'

Maggie looked up from the book she was reading. 'Like what?'

'Oh, I don't know. Perhaps a walk in the park?'

Maggie shook her head.

'How about we feed the ducks in the park?'

Maggie shook her head again.

'I noticed some newly hatched ducklings the other day, when I was walking past the pond with Louis.'

Maggie's eyes lit up. 'How many did you see?'

'About a dozen, swimming with their mothers on the pond.

If we took some bread, they might come close.'

'It's all gone.'

'I know a place where we can get all the free bread we can carry. And pies, sausage rolls, donuts.'

'Where?'

'The bakery on the other side of the park. Louis showed me the other day. They throw out all the unsold things at closing time.'

'He gets them from the bin? Are they yucky?

'Not if you beat everyone else to the good ones, on top. To do that, we'd have to leave now. And since when did you become too posh to eat binned food?'

Maggie shrugged. 'Can't you do it on your own?'

'You have to come too, so we can carry more. And then we'll stop off at the park, and feed the ducks before it gets dark.' When they'd finished feeding themselves and the ducks, Tori gathered up the bags of remaining pies and cakes. She estimated they had enough for about two days, if they weren't too stale before then. She put on her coat, and placed her hands in the pockets to warm them. She felt something, and remembered the business card Andrés had given her. As Maggie said goodbye to the ducklings, Tori thought about the job he'd offered her. She remembered the other studio she'd been made to clean. And how she'd been forced to pose for the camera. She could still feel von Wolff's presence sometimes, even though she knew he was dead. Tori would sometimes catch herself remembering the things he'd made them do. And how he'd threatened to send them to an institution if they didn't obey him. Tori had vowed never to let someone treat her like that again. Andrés didn't make her feel the same way von Wolff had, but she was still unsure about him. She'd found him unpleasantly fascinating: a peacock with a hint of malevolence. Tori didn't think she could bear being in a photographer's studio again, even if the work was just cleaning. Shaking away unwanted memories, she stood up and called out to Maggie. As they started walking towards their squat, the sun had begun to set and the sky was full of red, pink and blue. Halfway across the park, Maggie stopped in her tracks.

'Look at that sky, it's so pretty. Let's stop for a bit more,' she suggested.

She found a patch of soft lawn and sat down, looking up at the spectacular show the setting sun was putting on. Tori sat beside her. They were so enthralled they hadn't noticed the man's presence until they heard the music. He was of medium height and quite thin.

His jet-black hair fell down his back, held tightly in a single plait. Unobserved, Maggie admired his long mustard-coloured shirt with an embroidered firebird on the back. They watched him; first he stood like a starfish, then moved his arms and legs through the air as if dancing in water. As he moved gracefully in the dusk, the man sang a joy-filled song. Maggie and Tori could not understand the words, but the birds seemed to. The park had filled with small birds, darting in and out, making loops. The birds were like shadow puppets against the backdrop of the fading sunset. Maggie had noticed that the birds appeared the moment the man started singing, as if this was a normal part of their day – farewelling the day together, a harmony of dance and song.

He then took a reed flute from his pocket and put it to his lips. The birds settled on branches of nearby trees, heads bobbing side to side in rhythm. A lone bird swooped close to the twins. Maggie stood, and put an arm straight out. This small bird alighted on her arm, chirping merrily. Maggie stood still and smiled at the bird. Suddenly, the man stopped playing his flute, and turned to her. Maggie's bird flew away, joining the others that were settling in among branches and leaves of nearby trees. Maggie became aware of him looking at her. She smiled. He bowed, and then walked away.

***

The sun had well and truly risen, and Louis still hadn't shown up with breakfast. When they saw him yesterday, he'd promised. All the twins had were some rock-hard donuts they couldn't bring themselves to eat. They discussed where they might find more food. Some of the places they frequented were no longer safe. There'd been too many questions and raised eyebrows from those charities, prying about where their parents were, and if they needed help to go home. More than a few had not asked questions. Instead, they told the twins their problems would disappear if they'd just let the good Lord into their hearts. Maggie would get nervous with all the attention, so had stopped going. Tori told her that some charity people were fools and to just ignore them. Secretly, Tori also found them unnerving. They never questioned Louis, so she often asked if he could fetch them some food. Tori was certain they treated her differently from him, as they assumed she was just a girl. If they knew what she'd already been through in her life, or seen the way she handled a rifle, she was certain they'd stop patronising her. Their fussing just made it difficult for Tori and Maggie to get the help they really needed – food, not salvation.

Trying to distract herself from hunger, Tori set to work tidying their place. As she was sorting clothes, a card dropped on the floor. Tori picked it up, and immediately recognised Andrés's business card. Tori put it in her jean's pocket then picked up her sneakers.

'I'm going out for a bit.'

Maggie looked up from the book she'd been reading. 'Where?'

'High Street. To see if I can find leftovers in the alley behind the restaurants.'

Maggie nodded, returning to her tattered book. Tori laced up her shoes and then climbed out the window. When she got to the corner of the block, she heard someone shouting her name. Turning, she saw Louis running towards her. She didn't acknowledge his presence and kept walking. Tori crossed at the lights, with Louis following.

'Stop, will you. Where are we going?'

'We're not going anywhere. I am.'

Louis frowned. 'You're going to that guy's place, aren't you?'

'Yes, not that it's any of your business.'

'I should go with you.'

'I don't need your help. I'm just checking out what sort of job he has going.'

'Let me come too, and afterwards we can go back to your place for a feed. Look, I got lots.'

He held up three bags, grinning broadly.

'Where'd you get all that?'

'From the church over on Second Street, the one with the red roof. There's a new brother there. Brother Eddie is cool. He's like us. I told him I needed to get food for two friends, so he let me have extra.'

'Like us?'

'Yeah, he's a blackfulla. I think he's from the west coast. Or maybe up north. He's travelled a fair bit.'

Tori frowned. 'What did you say about us? You didn't say we were living in a basement, did you?'

'Of course not. Anyway, he's all right. I reckon we can trust him.'

'He can't ever know about Maggie and me. He'll send us to an orphanage, or worse. It's different for you. Guys don't get hassled by welfare and do-gooders like girls do.'

'You know I'd never make trouble for you. I'll do anything to keep you safe, and Maggie.'

Tori felt bad. Louis didn't know they were hiding from the police. He didn't deserve to be growled at. Louis was their best friend. Their only friend. Tori couldn't imagine how they would have adjusted to city life without him.

'Hey, thanks for the food. How about you take that to Maggie, and I'll see you there soon. After I talk to this photographer guy.'

'You sure I'm not needed?'

278

'Don't worry. I'll be fine.'

'See you soon, then.'

As he walked away, Tori called out, 'Hey, don't tell Maggie you saw me.'

*

Tori had no trouble finding Andrés's studio. No one could miss that garish façade. The brickwork and overly large front door were painted in vibrant flowers, butterflies, paisley and peace symbols. Tori stood by a wide window, peering in. She didn't see anyone in there but the sign said it was open. Taking a deep breath, she pushed the door, which set off a small bell.

'Hang on, won't be long,' she heard a woman's voice call out.

Tori stood near the door, looking around at framed photos on the wall, mostly altered objects and landscapes. Tori wondered how the photographer made that hazy, lurid effect and went to have a closer look. Hearing someone come up behind her, Tori turned and saw one of the women she'd seen with Andrés outside the boutique: the tall, stylish woman with the accent.

'Hey, it's you.'

Tori nodded, feeling unusually shy.

'You've come about that job, I suppose.'

'Yes,' stammered Tori.

'Don't worry. I don't bite. Andrés, though, that's a whole different story.'

'What?'

'Don't worry, hon. I was just joking,' she said. 'I'm Marcie.

And your name?'

'Tori, ma'am.'

She laughed. 'Just call me Marcie, honey. Does your mother know you've come here for a job?'

Tori pretended to be distracted, unsure of what to say. She felt a strong urge to tell this woman with the kind eyes and warm voice the truth. Well, part of the truth. The bit about her mother being dead, and how it was now up to her to look out for her twin sister. Instead, she kept quiet.

Marcie said, 'It's okay. Mothers don't need to know everything we do. Although, as someone older than you, if I was to give you any advice it would be to turn around and walk out that door.'

'Are you making things up again, Marcie?'

Tori turned around, and saw Andrés standing behind her.

'Just warning this girl about what a tyrant you can be,' replied Marcie.

'Not true, I'm a big softie,' he said.

While his attention was on Marcie, Tori studied Andrés. He was wearing a close-fitting topaz shirt with black leather pants. With the top buttons of his shirt undone, Tori saw a mass of pendants resting on his chest, hanging from chains and thin leather straps. Chestnut waves swept across his forehead, highlighting his cold grey eyes.

Marcie laughed, 'Soft? Ha!'

'Haven't you got things to do, places to be?' commented Andrés, raising an eyebrow.

'Yeah, yeah. I was just leaving.'

As Marcie walked out the front door, Tori was reflecting on how Andrés's mood had quickly changed. She then noticed he was staring intently at her.

'So, you came after all.'

Tori nodded, unsure of what to say, and feeling intimated being alone in Andrés's presence.

He blazingly looked her up and down. 'I suppose you want to know what I have planned for you?'

'I came about that job.'

'Good, let's talk business. I'm an artist. Those are mine on the walls. In addition to my photography, I exhibit other artists' works in my gallery. Come, follow me.'

Tori followed Andrés to the end of the long room and through a door. In this small room were tripods and camera cases. The room also had benches, with photos strewn all over them. Andrés opened another door and Tori peered into a darkroom, not much bigger than a closet. Tori recognised the smells rising from the trays of liquid. She suddenly felt apprehensive and moved away from the darkroom's entrance. Memories started rising to the surface: a flashing camera, leering grin, fire, screams. Tori pushed the images down again.

'I want you to model for me.'

'No, that's not the type of work I'm after.'

Tori started to walk away but he grabbed her wrist. She twisted her arm, freeing herself from his grip, and glared at him, nostrils flared.

'Feisty, aren't you?' said Andrés. 'Don't be so rash. I can offer an attractive rate of pay. And you look like you could do with some money.'

Tori hesitated, remembering how hungry she was some days. And how cold the basement got in winter. She knew Maggie wouldn't be able to work, so it was up to her.

'I'm looking for proper work, not modelling. Perhaps you have other things need doing around here. I could clean, answer the phone, do errands, anything.'

Andrés raised a hand to his chin. 'How about four hours a day, Monday to Thursday? Cleaning, mostly. And helping Marcie in the gallery. Maybe extra hours leading up to the next exhibition. You'd earn much more if you were to model for me, of course.'

'Those hours sound fine. When do I start?'

'None of us are early birds around here. Come back tomorrow at eleven, and Marcie will show you around.'

FOURTEEN

Their basement hideaway was quickly filling with little birds. Sketches that Maggie had done. She'd cut them out and hung them around the basement. With her first pay, Tori bought Maggie a gift. Remembering how much she'd liked drawing when she was younger, Tori gave her a tin of pencils and a sketchpad. While she was working in the gallery, Maggie seemed content with drawing.

'How do you remember the fine details?' asked Tori, putting on her shoes for work.

'I don't.'

'What do you mean?'

Maggie looked up from her sketchpad. 'I draw them from sight.'

'What?'

'I start my sketches in the park. Where there's lots of birds.'

'You go out when I'm not here?'

Maggie nodded, busily colouring in another bird. 'I go to the park most days. Sometimes I talk with the flute man. Occasionally I see Louis there. Most days, it's just me and the birds.'

'And you're not scared?'

'I'm not a baby. We're the same age, remember?'

'Well, you've been acting like a baby since we got to the city. I've been the one to find us food, get a job; while you hide in here, too scared to go out. And suddenly you're spending your days in the park, talking to a stranger, while I'm at work. When were you going to tell me?'

'Why do I have to tell you everything? You're not my mother!'

Tori scowled at the paper birds hanging around the room.

Maggie said, 'Sorry. I know you've been looking out for me.'

'I miss her too.'

'Maybe if we talked about her more? Shared good memories.'

'Perhaps later. I've got to go to work.'

'Sure.'

Tori hesitated before climbing out the window. 'Hey.'

'Yeah?'

'Just be careful, okay?'

As Tori walked through the park, on the way to the gallery, she felt even more confused. The park was already busy, and she couldn't imagine her sister choosing to spend time there, without her. For a long time, Tori had felt responsible for her sister. Even before they'd lost their mother, Maggie had needed looking out for. Sometimes when travelling, frustrated because she thought her sister was slowing them down on purpose, she'd pick a fight with Maggie. Afterwards, Tori would silently carry her sister's suitcase as they walked, and did the bigger share of collecting firewood when they'd set up camp. Back then, Maggie seemed to take her sister's help for granted, rarely acknowledging it. As she recalled those days, Tori suddenly remembered moments when Maggie hadn't needed her. When travelling with Gabriel, Maggie had turned to him whenever she needed anything. And at that tin-shed school, many years ago, Maggie had been confident and quite popular. Then, it was Tori who'd needed her sister's help, to stare down frecklefaced children as they called her horrible names.

One day, Tori had finally confided in her mother about what was happening at school. Brigid had hugged her and then told her daughter that she'd had the same problems. Tori asked what she'd done to make them stop being so mean. Her mother had replied that there'd been no one to turn to, so she'd just learnt how to shut it all out. Her family didn't understand. They weren't like her. She then told Tori that Granny Maeve had tried to make her feel better by telling her a story of potatoes nestled in earth. Later, at Tori's insistence, she'd told Maggie and her Granny

Maeve's story. They'd both asked what it meant. Their mother had replied that she'd never figured it out.

Thinking of those days, Tori recalled how Maggie had tried to protect her from hateful taunts. And afterwards, on the walk home from school, she'd talk about how silly those children were. The same blood flowed through Tori's and her veins. So if the children at school liked her, they had to like Tori too. Tori already had a differing, less hopeful, view of the world. She knew the way she was treated was always going to be different from how Maggie was treated. And she had quickly worked out why.

Now, standing on the kerb, waiting for a gap in traffic, images of their time at von Wolff's arose. Those months after their mother had gone, before Gabriel came back, when von Wolff had forced them to participate in humiliating photoshoots. Through von Wolff's lenses, Maggie and Tori were not sisters. It was obvious he did not see them as equals. He only ever gave Maggie two roles to act out: steely coloniser or distraught settler's wife. Back in their cottage, after being forced to pose for von Wolff, Maggie would cry herself to sleep. Tori was also only given two roles, but she had refused to let his obscene fantasies define her. No matter what he said or did to get under her skin, Tori knew she was neither a noble savage nor a tainted gin. She didn't know much of her heritage but, as she stood exposed in that studio, Tori had drawn upon the strength of the few black matriarchs she'd met. She'd lifted her head high and stared aloofly at the camera, while silently wishing von Wolff a painful demise. When that fire consumed the studio, Tori had taken a departing look at the destruction before following Gabriel, hoping her wish had come true. Once free of von Wolff, Tori had declared to herself that she would never allow someone to treat her that way again. And she'd vowed to take better care of Maggie.

Tori was confident she'd done a good job of looking out for her sister. Now, it was obvious that Maggie didn't need her protection any more. As Tori opened the gallery door, she accepted that her sister might not want or need her help. She also knew they both needed the money she was earning. For the rest of the day, Tori couldn't stop thinking about their futures. She didn't even complain when Andrés told her to polish the wooden floors of the large gallery, as that gave her lots of time to think. Mostly, she was curious about what had come over Maggie. Why was she suddenly willing to leave the basement?

*

Towards the end of Tori's shift, Marcie arrived. Tori stood up and stretched her tired muscles.

'Hi,' Tori said, picking up the bucket and rags she'd used to polish the floors.

'Looks good.'

'Andrés will still find something to criticise.'

'He's sure to be in a better mood soon. He just sealed the deal on a purchase of photos he's been negotiating for a while. Works by some famous guy who died a few years back. Apparently, the photographer was an old mentor of Andrés's, when he was first starting out. I haven't seen the photos. He's thinking this exhibition will be a big thing, so expect a few more hours of work.'

Tori walked towards the cleaning cupboard.

Marcie followed. 'Have you told your mother about working here?'

Tori shrugged as she shut the cupboard door.

Marcie observed, 'Not much of a talker, are you.'

'If there's no more work today, I'm off home.'

'And where is home?'

Tori shrugged again. 'Not far.'

'If you don't want to talk that's okay, but if you ever did, I'm really good at keeping secrets.'

Tori hesitated. She'd got to know Marcie over the past few weeks and felt like she could trust her. Besides Gabriel, Tori had never had someone she could confide in before. He'd always listened to her, and he'd known just what to say to make her feel strong enough to get through the loss of her mother. Gabriel had been supportive but Tori thought a female friend, just a few years older, would be like having an older sister.

She felt tempted to share a few secrets with Marcie, and ask for some advice. She knew that she and Maggie couldn't spend the rest of their lives in the basement of a vacant city building. Then Tori remembered she was a minor until her upcoming birthday, which meant she and Maggie could still be sent to a children's home. She couldn't be sure Marcie wouldn't tell the authorities about two parentless girls living in a basement. Tori couldn't trust anyone.

Tori said, 'I really need to be leaving.'

'Okay, hon. Just remember, I'm here if you ever need me.'

*

The next day was a Friday, and Maggie suggested they go to the park. Tori told her a different idea about spending the day together.

'Are you sure?' asked Maggie.

'Can't think of a better way to spend a pay cheque.'

Tori pushed open the door and they walked into the women's store. It was not as posh as the one where Tori had enquired about a job, but it appeared to be friendlier. Tori started flicking through clothes on hangers.

She held up a dress. 'This one looks your size.'

'I like this one,' said Maggie, holding up a blue dress with a bird motif along the hem.

'It's perfect for you.'

Tori selected a lime-green mini-dress, and together they went to the change rooms. As she was zipping it up, Maggie slipped into her change room.

'What do you think?'

'It looks really good on you. Let's buy it,' suggested Tori.

'Are you sure? We walked past a second-hand store. Maybe they have something just as nice.'

'If you like this one, I'm buying it for you. Call it an early birthday present,' Tori offered.

'I'd forgotten our birthday was soon.'

Tori saw herself in the mirror. The lime dress was very vivid and modern, like something Marcie would wear. Tori wondered if she was brave enough.

'That looks amazing on you,' noted Maggie.

'You think so? It's a bit bright. And short.'

'You have good legs.'

'Must be all that walking Mum made us do as kids, eh.'

Maggie didn't respond. Tori was too busy looking in the mirror to notice. They were both dressed in clothes befitting young women. Tori imagined their mother standing behind them, and wondered if she'd have been proud of how far her daughters had walked on their own. Then she remembered: they lived in a dank basement, with no dreams of their own to chase. What had she done to earn her mother's pride?

'She'd have been proud of you,' said Maggie.

Even though it was not uncommon for them to read each other's thoughts, Tori was surprised.

'Really?'

Maggie nodded. 'You remind me of Mum.'

Looking in the mirror again, Tori tried to visualise their mother, and wondered what they shared – beyond their skin and hair. Was it the way she held herself, back straight and head high? Strong, independent, fearless. Tori shook her head, thinking how foolish she was to act so proud.

She remarked, 'I'm sure Mum wouldn't be pleased to see us living in a basement. Or eating others' unwanted food and wearing their castaways.'

'Stop being so hard on yourself. Get that dress, Tori. You need some colour in your life.'

'I'm sorry about fighting with you yesterday.'

'It's okay. Everything will work out, as long as we have each other.'

'Together, forever,' said Tori. 'Now, let's buy these dresses. And matching shoes.'

***

Tori moved aside a pile of feathers. Waving a shoe in the air, she walked over to Maggie. Her sister was concentrating on finishing a sketch of green finches, so hadn't noticed Tori's frantic searching.

'Can you stop drawing for just a minute?!'

'What's up?'

'I can't find my other shoe. The new ones.'

'Did you check under the bed?'

'Yes, I did. All I found were more feathers. What's with all these blasted feathers?'

'We'll need them soon.'

'Why the hell will we need them?'

'For our new place.'

Tori retrieved her other shoe from under a pile of bird sketches. 'What are you talking about?'

'We can't stay here forever.'

'I know that. Which is why I'm working, so one day we can rent a place of our own. With running water, and electricity. And a bloody door,' groaned Tori, as she climbed out the window.

*

The walk to work had cleared Tori's annoyance. She entered the gallery quietly, not wanting to attract attention. Andrés had been in a bad mood the previous day, so she wanted to avoid him as much as she could. The light was on in the storage room, from where loud banging noises were emerging. Tori walked towards the sounds, and was relieved to find Marcie. She took one look at Tori and laughed.

'Don't look so scared, little bunny. It's just me in here. Andrés has gone out for a bit. His regular guy refused to do the frames for the next exhibition. Andrés was furious. He's gone to speak with another framer, so hopefully he'll return in a better mood.'

'What are you doing in here?'

'Looking for more packing tape. Andrés swore there was more in here, but I can't find a thing in this mess.'

'Do you want me to clean it up?'

'Later. It's my lunch break, and I'm taking you out.'

Tori started to protest, but Marcie took her by the arm and walked towards the front door.

'I won't take no for an answer. I want some company, and you're much more pleasant than Andrés. Besides, you look like you could do with a good feed.'

'We can't close the gallery in the middle of the day.'

'Watch me,' said Marcie, as she flipped the open sign to closed and locked the front door.

She led Tori to a café a few blocks away. Tori had never been in such a nice-looking place, and immediately felt uncomfortable. People at the other tables were staring, and she was sure she'd be asked to leave.

'Ignore them, honey. They're just jealous. Unlike those pasty lizards over there, we don't have to spend hours in the sun, smothered in cheap cooking oil, to get this gorgeous glow we've both been blessed with,' said Marcie. 'Now, what shall we order?'

Tori observed Marcie as she scanned the menu. Marcie was right: she was gorgeous. Perhaps the most beautiful woman Tori had ever met. Too many times people had called Tori 'black' in a tone that made it very clear they had disdain for her. Strangers seemed to treat her with either anger or disgust. Some even pretended not to see her. Marcie turned heads. Tori wished people would look at her that way. Not as an object to put in front of a camera, as she believed Andrés had in mind. Or to perversely mock, as von Wolff had. Looking at Marcie, Tori yearned for someone to look at her and see a beautiful, strong black woman. Growing up, it had always been Maggie who'd get compliments from strangers. Tori didn't want to look like her sister. She wanted to be like Marcie. She looked around the room, at the people openly staring at Marcie and her. She knew what they were thinking. She put the menu in front of her face to block them out, and slid down slightly in her chair.

'You're a beautiful young woman. Don't you ever let their small-minded views make you feel bad about yourself, you hear me?'

Tori blushed, finally feeling seen for who she really was. She sat up straight and held her head higher. That motion reminded her of how sure of herself she'd felt walking through the streets of that town in the desert, many years ago, with her mother and sister. She remembered how expertly her mother could disarm people with a well-aimed side-eye. Tori channelled that energy, and mimicked a look she'd seen Marcie give people: turning towards the other diners with a measured disinterest.

'Girl, that's how you do it. You sure are pretty when you let that confidence shine through. You could be a model, for sure.'

'I'm not interested in modelling. Anyway, in this country, models are always white.'

'Times are changing. If you want to be something, you go for it. You can do anything you want.'

'Wish I had your poise. I always feel like I'm looking through smudged windows at others living their best lives, while I have absolutely no idea what I want to do with my life.'

'What about your parents? Don't they encourage you to work out your own goals?'

Tori picked up the menu and held it in front of her face again. Marcie reached over and gently pushed it down.

'Tori, tell me about your family.'

Looking over at Marcie, seeing kindness in her eyes, Tori suddenly felt the urge to talk about her mother and sister. Then she remembered the look of resignation on Gabriel's face as the police took him away. She also recalled the sense of retribution she felt watching the fire at von Wolff's. And her mother's cries of pain when she'd been burnt by a different fire, after they'd been kicked off the coach. Then there were memories of wailing parents in that desert town, unable to stop their children being taken. So many things she'd rather not remember. She'd rather create a less painful past.

She said, 'My mum works evening shifts and my dad is away a lot because of his job. When I was little, we all travelled with him, so I never really had a chance to make friends.'

'Same here. My dad was in the army, so we moved all the time. It was hard.'

'I didn't mind too much. I preferred being on the move to living in boring country towns. My sister hated moving all the time. Now that we live in the city, I miss open spaces and she misses the birds.'

'A sister? Why haven't you mentioned her before?'

Tori shrugged. 'I guess it wasn't important.'

Marcie waited, but she sensed that Tori had shut down again. Marcie tried to get the waiter's attention.

'I'm starving,' she said to Tori. 'I hope their steaks are big and juicy rare.'

After ordering, Tori kept the conversation focused on trivial topics. And once the food arrived, they enjoyed it too much to talk. Tori hadn't noticed that the other diners had left, except for a couple in the far corner. Calling over the waiter, Marcie ordered glasses of champagne, ignoring his questioning look in Tori's direction. Tori sat up straighter, hoping he didn't ask how old she was. When the drinks arrived, she eagerly took a sip.

'Bubbles!'

Marcie smiled. 'Is this your first time?'

Tori nodded. 'It's not as sweet as I thought it would be.'

'There's different types. Next time, I'll get you a sweeter one. Now, tell me about your sister.'

'Her name's Maggie.'

'Older, younger?'

'We're twins, but I'm the oldest.'

'I always wanted a sibling. It must be nice to have someone to share things with.'

'Sometimes, but not always.'

'Do you do that thing twins do: tricking people about which one is which?'

Tori shook her head. 'She isn't really like me.'

'You're non-identical twins?'

'Most people don't even think we're related, let alone twins.'

'What do you mean?'

'It's hard to explain. There's lots of things about my life that are hard to explain.'

'You can tell me anything. I won't judge.'

Tori shook her head. 'You'd just get caught up in my troubles.'

'Is it about working at the gallery? You still haven't told your parents, have you? If you want, I can speak with your mother. Let her know I'm looking out for you.'

Tori dropped her head, feeling ashamed about the lies she'd just told about her parents.

Marcie offered, 'Any time you're ready, I'll be here to listen.'

Tori tipped up her glass, disappointed there were no drops of champagne left.

Marcie stood up. 'You drained that quickly. Come on, we'd better get back to work. If Andrés gets there before us, there'll be all hell to pay.'

FIFTEEN

It was the man with the flute who told Maggie about trees that devour men. Since then, she'd often stand still for long spans, one eye closed to reduce distractions, wondering if the tree she was looking at was the type that ate people. He hadn't told her what type of person the carnivorous trees found most appetising, so Maggie had that on her list of things to ask when she next saw him. Since watching him that first time, when he'd played a lullaby for the birds, Maggie often saw him in the park. Other than telling Maggie his name, Cetan was not one for talking. He would, however, share the occasional story. It was the tale of the man-eating trees that had most fascinated Maggie. That may have been because she'd spent most of her childhood living in places with a scarcity of trees. Or, more likely, because her home was now the tallest tree in the park. They'd only recently moved from the basement to the tree. It was a move Tori had not foreseen and would never have agreed to under different circumstances. Maggie had known change was coming, and she'd had enough time to collect feathers to make a comfortable nest.

For Tori, a loud banging one morning heralded the change of abode. Awoken by the sound, she climbed out the basement window to see what was making all that noise. She quickly returned, and informed Maggie that a big sign had been pounded into the small strip of dead garden out the front of the building, announcing that the block had been leased to a legal firm, with a grand opening imminent. At this news, Maggie had simply nodded and started bagging up the piles of feathers she'd been collecting.

'Didn't you hear me? This building has been leased.'

Maggie nodded. 'I know. I'm packing for the move.'

'Move? I'm not going anywhere. And even if I agreed, where will we live?'

'In a tree. Cetan showed me.'

'A tree? Don't be silly. And who the hell is Cetan?'

'The bird man, remember? The one who plays the flute for the birds in the park. You saw him that one time. He's my friend.'

'Friend? What other secrets have you not told me?'

'I'm not keeping secrets. You never listen to me any more.'

'Well, I'm listening now.'

'Now there's no time for talking. We have to pack.'

'I'm not leaving.'

'Oh yes you are,' came a voice from outside.

Maggie and Tori both looked towards the window. There stood a pair of legs, clothed in an expensive-looking grey suit and shiny black shoes. A face appeared in the street-height window. A disapproving face crowned by blonde hair.

'Who are you?' asked Tori.

'Charles Smythe-Worthington. I work for the firm that has leased this building. And you are trespassers. You have until close of business today to vacate these premises. Or else.'

Tori moved closer to the window. 'Or else what?'

'Or else I will have no choice but to call the police, and they will evict you. I'm guessing you're both underage, so child services will also need to be called.'

'No, don't call anyone. We're packing,' said Maggie.

'You'd better hurry then,' urged the man as he stood up to leave.

Tori reluctantly helped pack. It didn't take them long, as they didn't have much. Just some second-hand clothes, shoes and cooking gear they crammed into suitcases and bags. Battered luggage that had travelled a long way: up the coast, across red dirt to the inland sea. Newer bags given to them by Grace: taken to the place they'd lost their mother, then carried during those years of walking with and without Gabriel. And, finally, the city.

'Leave those,' Tori said, as Maggie lifted the bagged feathers.

'You'll be thankful I took the time to collect these.'

Tori knew it would be a waste of time to start an argument with her sister. Instead, she retrieved their great-grandfather's rifle from under the bed and wrapped it in a blanket. With one final look at their basement home, Tori and Maggie climbed out the window for the last time.

Out the front of the building, there was chaos. A cluster of bedraggled and bewildered people were staring at the sign. The other squatters were slowly coming to terms with impending eviction. Some went back inside to pack. Others called for action, confident they had a right to remain there. Mr Charles Smythe-Worthington promptly showed them the paperwork, then attempted to scare them into action with his solid grasp of property law. Soon, a stream of deflated people was exiting the building.

Tori spotted Tabby Tomcat across the road. 'We should grab him.'

Maggie looked where her sister was pointing, and saw the cat. Two cats walked up to him, giving him a nudge, before moving on. These cats stopped, and looked back at him, expectantly. Tabby Tomcat was looking straight at Maggie.

She laughed. 'Go on, off with you.'

'Are you sure?' asked Tori.

'He's a street cat, not a bird. He won't like living in our next house. Come on, this way.'

Confused, Tori followed her to the park then through it. When they neared the duck pond, Tori stopped.

'Where are we going?'

Maggie said, 'We're almost there.'

'Where?'

'The tree Cetan showed me. There's a treehouse there. He used to live in it. Now he lives on a houseboat. He told me I can have this place. Which is why I've been collecting feathers. For our nest.'

'Nest? You expect me to live in a nest?'

'Wait until you see it before you get all negative. Trust me for a change.'

Tori reluctantly continued to follow her sister to the base of a very tall tree, probably the tallest in the park. Its upper branches were abundant with leaf, perfectly hiding whatever was up there. From behind a bush, Maggie fetched a long stick with a hook at the end. She reached up and pulled down a rope ladder.

'Clever, eh?' she said.

Tori looked hesitantly at the ladder.

Maggie said, 'Don't worry, it's sturdy enough. Stay here for a bit. I'll climb up and send down a basket for our stuff.'

A few minutes later, a large cane basket on a rope dropped down. Tori filled it with some of their belongings. She tugged on the rope, and the basket disappeared into the upper branches. It soon fell down again, and Tori put the rest of their bags in the basket. Tori slung the rifle over her shoulder, grabbed the rope ladder and started to climb. Halfway up she felt a bit dizzy, which was made worse when she looked down. Tori clung tighter to the wobbling ladder and kept climbing. She finally reached a wooden platform and saw Maggie's hand reach down to help her up. After catching her breath, Tori appraised her surroundings. It was more spacious than she'd imagined. And, in addition to the wooden floor, there were walls and a roof woven from some sort of plant fibre. Shelves had been built on one side. Near a window on the other side was a low table with cushions surrounding it. Nearby was a cupboard with screen doors, perfect for keeping food safe from creatures. On top was a single-burner kerosene camp stove. And in the middle of the space, perched on a raised platform, was a massive nest. A bed made from soft plant fibre and feathers. Tori climbed in, to test the bed.

With a smile, Maggie remarked, 'It's comfy, isn't it?'

'It'll do.'

'Fussy. Wait until you see this, then.'

Maggie unhooked a rope that was attached to one of the walls, and gently pulled. It opened a large hatch in the roof. Tori could see blue skies.

Maggie said, 'Imagine the view on clear nights. Heaven will be our roof.'

'Like that time we slept in the stone circle, with Gabriel.'

'Do you remember the constellations? And the stories he told us?'

'Some.'

Maggie picked up a bag of feathers, and shouted, 'Incoming.'

Tori laughed as feathers fell on her. Maggie threw the other bags into the nest unopened, and climbed in. They both opened bags, throwing feather everywhere, and laughed. Once the bags were empty, they evened out the layer of feathers, filling any gaps in the nest-bed. Maggie then took a large sheet from one of the wall-shelves, and together they spread it over the feathers.

'Our quilt is too small for this bed,' remarked Tori.

'Don't worry. Cetan made us one, as a gift.'

Tori watched as Maggie retrieved a large quilt from the shelves. She reached out to touch it. It was the softest fabric she'd ever felt.

'Silk,' said Maggie. 'Filled with duck down.'

'So soft. I love the colours.'

'It's like a rainbow lorikeet.'

'Not just one. This is a whole flock.'

They spread the quilt out and both lay upon it. Arms behind her head, Tori watched the sky.

'Do you think you could get used to living in a tree?' asked Maggie.

'It beats living in a basement.'

***

Walking to work, Tori saw that little bird again. A black bird with a sprinkling of white feathers. She'd seen it a few times since they'd moved into the treehouse. The bird had started hanging out at the bottom of the tree, as if it was waiting for Tori. And it would often follow her to work. Despite its insistence, she hadn't taken much notice. Today, the bird was noisier than usual, trying to catch Tori's attention. When they walked past the almost-dead tree with the large hole in its trunk, the bird stopped and chirped loudly. Tori turned around and it fell silent. She turned to continue her walk to work, and the bird started chirping again. Tori kept walking, with the little bird hopping behind her, making frantic noises.

'What?' said Tori, turning around. 'I'm not the bird fanatic. Go bother my sister.'

The bird hopped about, making a noise that sounded like indignation. Tori shook her head and kept walking, ignoring the noise. She suddenly recalled she hadn't seen Louis for a while. He didn't even know where they'd moved to.

When she got to the gallery, she greeted Marcie and began to tidy up. She heard Andrés shouting in his studio, and looked over at Marcie.

Marcie shrugged. 'Who knows what's got him in a mood this time.'

Then came the sound of something dropping, or being thrown against a wall. A door slammed and a woman stormed past Marcie and Tori, straight out the front door.

'You're a shit model, anyway,' shouted Andrés, walking into the main gallery behind the woman.

'What have you gone and done now, Andrés?' muttered Marcie, as she walked towards the front door. 'Sonia, wait up. Are you okay?'

Andrés turned his attention to Tori. 'I wouldn't have to contend with stuck-up scrawny girls like that one if you'd just model for me.'

Tori shook her head and continued tidying the sales counter. 'It's just not my thing.'

'"Not my thing." Ha! You might pretend to be different, but you're just like the rest of them. The pretty young things who find their way here, looking for attention, craving fame.'

'Not me. I just want to work and get paid.'

'Modelling is work. And I need a model more than a clean floor.'

Marcie walked back in. 'Not everything is about you, Andrés, so stop pestering Tori. You've already upset Sonia. Give it a rest.'

'Are you playing big sister again? It's been a while since you've taken one of my girls under your wing.'

'Tori is not "your girl". None of the others were, either. Women don't exist for your sake.'

Andrés turned towards Tori, glaring. 'The storage room is a mess. I want to see it sorted by the end of today.'

Tori walked towards the room, glad to get away from him.

'Marcie, get on the phone to that useless agency and tell them to send me another girl. Tell them I want one who's had a recent feed, and is not strung-out. In the meantime, I'll be down the pub.'

After he left, Marcie went to the storage room. Tori was picking up boxes and placing them on shelves.

Tori said, 'He's such a pig.'

'In more ways than one.'

Tori picked up some discarded paper.

Marcie announced, 'I reckon it's time for a break. You put the kettle on, and I'll retrieve the whisky from Andrés's secret stash. Have you had coffee with a dash of whisky before?'

***

Maggie opened the sky-hatch and climbed back into bed. Tori pulled the quilt up higher, covering herself from the cool breeze.

'How big do you think those dinosaurs were?' asked Maggie, gazing up at the stars.

'What?'

'The dinosaurs that once lived in the inland sea. The ones Aunty Isabelle told us about.'

'Oh, right. Super big, I suppose.'

'I think they'd have still been graceful, even if they were huge. That they swam like ballerinas in that ancient sea. Do you think they would have been graceful?'

'Haven't thought about them since we were kids. I remember the idea of them scared me a bit. I even had nightmares about them for a while.'

'They didn't scare me. The tiny scorpions that lived in the dried-up seabed did,' said Maggie.

'I'd forgotten about those. Seems like I've forgotten a lot about those days.'

'Some things I'm glad to have forgotten. I also get worried that one day I'll no longer remember the good moments. Do you still see Mum's face in your mind when you think of her?'

Tori didn't reply. She looked up at the night sky, wondering if any of the faint stars above were the eagle's talon Gabriel had shown them. It was so much harder to see stars in the city. Too much light from street lamps and businesses. There was sometimes even lingering smog obscuring the sky. The park was less bright, so on clear nights they could see stars. On those nights, Tori would remember sleeping under the stars with her mother, Maggie by her side, a campfire warming them even on the coldest of nights. Sometimes she'd remember the night of the fire that had burnt their mother.

Maggie said, 'I can see Mum's face when I close my eyes and think of her, but I still worry that I'll forget one day.'

'You won't forget,' insisted Tori, scratching her arm.

'Why do you do that all the time?'

'What?'

'Lately, you've been scratching in your sleep. Or when you're sitting silently, with a worried look on your face.'

312

'No I don't.'

'You do. See, your arm has red streaks.'

'It hasn't,' said Tori, rolling away. 'Go to sleep and stop being annoying.'

*

The next morning, as she was brushing her hair, Tori stopped and stared in the small mirror on the wall. Moving closer, she turned her head to one side, gently touching her face. It was red, like a rash. It didn't feel sore, but it was noticeable. Tori finished her hair and put on her shoes.

'What are your plans for the day?' she asked Maggie.

'I'm going to an art class. Louis showed me this place where you can do free stuff. He goes there sometimes, to visit Brother Eddie.'

'You've seen Louis?'

'Yesterday, down by the duck pond. He said he'd been trying to find us. I showed him where we live now. Then he showed me the place that has classes, and introduced me to Brother Eddie.'

'He told me about that brother. What's he like?'

'Friendly. And funny.'

'You didn't tell him about Mum being gone or where we live?'

'I'm not silly, Tori. We talked about other things.'

'If you see Louis today, say hi from me. I've missed him.'

'He said the same. That he missed hanging out with you.'

'That's nice. I have to work, though.'

'You're always working. You should come to that place with me sometimes.'

Tori went to leave. 'Maybe after the launch of the next exhibition. Until then, Andrés has us doing extra hours. And he's grumpy as all hell.'

As Tori walked through the park, the little black-and-white bird followed her as usual. She didn't even hear its chirping; she was too deep in thought. She liked earning money, but the gallery was not a pleasant place to work. If she didn't have Marcie for company, Tori would have left a long time ago. Andrés wasn't just rude and demanding, he made her feel uncomfortable. Even when he wasn't in sight, she worried about what sort of mood he'd be in next time she encountered him. Andrés reminded her of von Wolff, especially the way he was after Iris died. Tori had begun to think that if she'd tried harder to make their mother leave that place, she'd still be alive. And she and Maggie wouldn't be living in a tree with no family, no place to belong.

Cheeks flushed from helping Omer round up the goats, Maggie and Victoria ran over to join Bethel on the bench under the olive tree.

'Is that the pottery jar you broke yesterday?' asked Maggie.

Bethel nodded. 'It made quite a noise, didn't it?'

Victoria asked, 'Why are you filling it with dirt? Shouldn't you be fixing it with glue?'

Bethel pressed down on the dirt, packing it tighter. 'Glue won't fix it. Not this time. This jar has been broken and patched up too many times.'

Victoria said, 'So what's the dirt for?'

Bethel made a small indent in the dirt and picked up a seedling. 'When patching doesn't work, then a new way of looking at the problem is needed.'

She planted the seedling in the pottery jar. 'The top part is broken beyond fixing, but the base is still solid. If I water this young seedling, one day it will reward me with flowers. I'll still remember the jar that once kept flour safe from mice, but I won't feel sad, as it's been reborn as a home for flowers.'

SIXTEEN

A few days later, Tori walked with Maggie to the community centre. She was hoping to see Louis there, as she'd still not seen him since before moving out of the basement. When they got to the centre, Maggie excitedly showed her sister the art room. Paint tubs and large pieces of cardboard were scattered on long tables.

'More people today than other times I've been here,' remarked Maggie.

Tori looked around; it was mostly women in the room, busy painting on the cardboard. Looking out the large windows, Tori saw children playing on the grass.

Maggie went up to a middle-aged woman sitting at a table. 'What are you doing, Aunty Gloria?'

'Making signs for the march tomorrow.'

'What's a march?' asked Maggie.

The woman stopped painting and stretched her back. 'It's a protest. Big mob of people coming together, to let the government know what we want.'

Maggie asked her, 'What is everyone wanting?'

'Our land back, mostly. Tomorrow's march is in solidarity with desert mob. They want to protect the

316

land around the inland sea, to stop more mining. That Country needs to be left alone, so it can heal.'

Maggie said, 'The inland sea? That's were my Aunty Isabelle lives. We stayed near there for a while, when we were younger.'

'Then it's your Country too, bub,' commented Gloria. 'Grab a piece of cardboard and start writing. You'll need a sign when you come to the protest tomorrow. What about your sister? She'll need one too.'

Tori raised an eyebrow. 'How'd you know we were sisters?'

'Twin girls are generally sisters.'

Others in the room chuckled, and remarked how alike they were. Maggie got some cardboard and found a place to sit. She was unsure what to write. Tori scowled, thinking they were all laughing at her.

'Don't be like that, bub,' said Gloria. 'Maggie told me she had a twin sister. Sit. Join in.'

Tori shook her head. 'I've got to be at work soon.'

'Okay, but come back soon. Don't be shame. We're all friendly here. Except for that old girl over there. You watch out for her.'

Everyone started to laugh, even the woman Gloria had pointed out. Tori smiled awkwardly. After saying goodbye to Maggie, she had a quick look around the rest of the centre, hoping to spot Louis. Not seeing him, she went to work.

*

The day went much too slowly. Marcie had called in sick, so it was just her and Andrés in the gallery. Luckily, he worked in the darkroom for most of the day, leaving Tori to sit behind the gallery counter in peace. Not many people had come in, so Tori flicked through a fashion magazine and tried not to watch the clock. Occasionally she'd catch herself scratching her arm, or unconsciously picking spots on her face. She'd noticed that it was usually during moments when her mind was filling with worry, or sadness. The hole her mother had left behind felt so big that Tori often imagined she was falling in, never to be seen again. Tori had also realised that she could stop the freefalling sensation by scratching. It felt oddly satisfying to free bits of skin. Like exhaling after holding one's breath for too long. That feeling disappeared whenever she looked in the mirror. Then she felt shame and disgust for the self-disfigured person she saw reflected back. The redness on the side of Tori's face also reminded her that she was motherless. The scarring was not as intense as Brigid's had been, but there was an obvious similarity. She knew Maggie had noticed this shape she'd unconsciously made on her face. Tori didn't want her sister's pity, and she didn't want to carry around this visual reminder of loss and grief on her face. The problem was – she didn't know how to stop herself.

Tori looked up when she heard someone walk in. Seeing who it was, she draped her hair over one side of her face to cover the redness.

'Hey, stranger,' said Louis. 'I hear you were looking for me earlier.'

'Was just wondering where'd you been. Why don't you visit any more? Scared of heights?'

Louis laughed. 'No, I actually like trees. I've been to your place a few times. You're just never there.'

'That's because I'm usually here.'

'How's it going?'

Tori stood up, and walked around the counter. 'It's just work.'

'I've been working too. Got a job at a supermarket, filling shelves at night.'

'Cool.'

'I can ask if they have any more openings.'

'What the hell are you doing?'

Both Louis and Tori turned around in surprise. Andrés stood at the other end of the gallery. He strode towards them, glaring at Louis. Tori fidgeted with her hair, while Louis stood up straighter.

Andrés said, 'You're not allowed to bother my girl while she works.'

'I was just asking when she's finished. We've got plans for the evening.'

Tori glanced at Louis, wondering why he was making things up.

'Next time wait outside,' ordered Andrés, before turning his attention to Tori. 'You can lock up, I've got an appointment.'

Andrés walked out. They heard his cane tapping on the sidewalk, fading away.

'Who does he think he is?' asked Louis. 'Stuck up bastard.'

'Shhh. He might come back and hear you.'

'I don't care if he does. Come on, let's get out of here.'

Tori closed the till before taking the money to Andrés's office. She put it in the bottom drawer of his desk. When Andrés wasn't around to open the safe, that's where Marcie and Tori had been told to leave the daily takings. Tori had tried to look in the safe once, peering over Andrés's shoulder. All she saw were large yellow envelopes and a small metal tin. Like a cigar box. She'd seen tins like that at von Wolff's. Standing in Andrés's office, it was almost as if she could smell von Wolff's studio. That stench of burnt cigar ends on the mornings after his friends had been around for their weekly card nights. That sickly stale odour had made unpleasant moments in front of von Wolff's lenses even more disturbing. Leaving Andrés's office, Tori shivered at the memory of von Wolff. And, not for the first time, chastised herself for taking a job in another photography studio, under the watchful eye of another disturbing man. Money didn't make it less disagreeable.

Tori turned off the main switches by the office door, plunging the gallery in darkness. She could make out the shape of Louis standing near the front entrance.

They walked out, and she shut the tall double door, turning a key in the lock.

Louis asked, 'He gives you a key?'

'Not because he trusts me. Andrés is lazy. This way, he can sleep in while someone else opens up the gallery. Marcie and I take turns doing the morning shift.'

'You work too hard. How about I take you out tonight? A friend of mine is in a band, and he's got a gig in a pub. It's not far from the park.'

'I don't know. I need to open the gallery tomorrow.'

'It's Sunday tomorrow and the gallery opens later. Come on, it'll be fun.

Tori heard a sound and, glancing towards a bush, saw the little black-and-white bird again. Not frantically hopping around this time, just chirping. Louis and Tori walked towards the park.

She replied to Louis: 'You'd have more fun without me. I'll probably just get tired early and want to go home.'

'Then I'd leave early too. I just want to hang out with you, Tori. We used to do things together.'

'Okay. I'll ask Maggie if she wants to come too.'

'Sure. How about I come to your place in about an hour?'

Tori nodded, and they said goodbye. She continued through the park, towards the treehouse, while Louis turned to the left, towards the duck pond. Not for the first time, she wondered where he lived. Tori decided to ask him tonight.

*

Tori put on the lime-green dress. It was the first time she'd felt daring enough to wear it in public. When Louis arrived, Maggie threw down the rope for him, and talked to him while Tori put her shoes on.

She looked over at Maggie. 'Are you sure you won't come with us?'

'I want to finish this sketch I've been working on. There's an exhibition I'm thinking of entering.'

Louis commented, 'That's so cool, sis.'

Maggie grinned. 'Hope I'm ready.'

'Of course you are. Your work is deadly,' said Louis.

'Shame job,' she said with a grin. 'Now, you two get going and leave me in peace.'

Tori and Louis climbed down the ladder. As they descended, Tori reflected on how Maggie's style of speaking was changing, and thought maybe it was because she was at the community centre most days. Tori tried to remember if Louis had ever called her sis. She didn't think he had, and it hurt a bit to think he now preferred Maggie's company. The bird was waiting at the bottom of the tree, again. Tori threw it some crusts she had in her pocket. She thought if the bird was going to hang around so much, she might as well be nicer to it.

The sun had set, so it was dark in that part of the park. Tori could see the soft glow of street lights in the distance, and the occasional car headlights. She liked this time of day. The park was usually empty. Except for soft sounds of night birds, a deep quiet would fall over the parklands and pond. Tori was never scared of walking in the dark. Not after all those years of sleeping under the stars, with her mother and sister by her side. Living in the park reminded her of those days.

Louis reached out and took her hand. Tori flinched, and he let go.

'Sorry,' he said. 'I should have asked first.'

'You surprised me. Also, it's not something I feel comfortable doing. Does that sound weird?'

'No, I get it.'

'What kind of music does your friend's band play?'

'Reggae. You heard any before?'

Tori shook her head. 'I've never really been out. And we didn't have much music growing up. Heard a bit of country and western at my Aunty Isabelle's. A few people had guitars, and others would join in, singing around the campfire. And there was folky-type music when we stayed with an old couple. The man, Omer, would play a string instrument that looked like a tiny guitar-box. I think my mum loved jazz and blues. She'd sometimes put records on while working, to try and cheer up Iris, the woman she looked after.'

'I reckon this is the first time you've ever told me anything about your family, or where you were before the city.'

'Well, you've never told me anything about yours.'

'I've got reasons.'

'Same,' said Tori, as they crossed the road.

The pub was already crowded when they arrived. People were spilling out into the street, smoking something that had an unusual smell. Tori recalled smelling it on Marcie a few times, when she came back from lunch breaks. Which had surprised Tori, as she didn't even know Marcie smoked. Louis led Tori through the crowd, gently pushing to make a path for them. They went out a back door, to a fenced garden.

'A garden in a pub?' remarked Tori.

'Yeah, they call it a beer garden. Great place to hang out in warmer weather.'

Over the tops of heads, Tori noticed the band's instruments in a far corner.

'They must be on a set break,' suggested Louis, looking in the same direction. 'Wait here, I'll get us some beers.'

'I'm still underage, remember.'

'So are lots of people here. No one cares.'

While Louis was gone, Tori took in the crowd. In the sea of denim and cheesecloth, she noticed some women were wearing mini-dresses, which made her felt a bit less awkward about her short hem. She also noted that, unlike other settings she'd been in, there was not the usual abundance of white faces. A man with brown curly hair walked past, and he lifted his chin slightly. Tori smiled awkwardly. She'd seen people do that to her before, in the streets, but was unsure of the right response. *Is it okay for me to give an upward-nod back?* she wondered. *Is it a type of acceptance?* Tori made a mental note to ask Louis. He'd know. Maggie might even know. Tori hated asking her sister. She knew she shouldn't feel that way, but it irked her that Maggie knew more than she did about these types of things.

Tori noticed Louis making his way cautiously towards her, trying not to spill their drinks too much whenever he got bumped in the crowd. He handed her a glass of beer. She sipped hesitantly. It tasted odd. Not at all like the champagne she'd had with Marcie.

'I'm not supposed to be drinking for a few more weeks.'

'We should do something fun. Maggie too.'

Tori shrugged. 'I'm not into birthdays. Maggie is, though. So perhaps we should, for her sake.'

'How about a day at the beach?'

'You mean, like, the ocean?'

Louis laughed. 'Yes. What else would I mean?'

'I've never seen an ocean. Is it far from here?'

'Never? Then you must. The nearest beach is only a short tram ride away.'

'I've also never been on a tram.'

'Well, that's two firsts to celebrate your birthday with. Make sure you get the day off.'

'I'll speak with Marcie, see if she'll do a double shift.'

A murmur rose from the crowd, and Tori noticed some men picking up instruments on the small stage.

'The band is back,' remarked Louis. 'I didn't introduce you to my friend. Next break I will.'

Tori smiled to acknowledge she'd heard, not wanting to shout over the increasing noise. She looked over at the band. People towards the front of the crowd had started to dance, and others were swaying.

'Cool music, unna?' said Louis.

She nodded. Tori didn't mind it at all, despite the loudness. She even felt an urge to move, but dancing in public was something she was too scared to try. Louis moved, and was facing her, blocking her view of the band. Over his shoulder, she saw a man with bleached blonde hair, worn in short dreadlocks, pushing through the crowd towards them. He stood behind Louis. Tori saw Louis grimace before he turned around. The white man in dreads gave him a nod.

'Is this your missus?' he then asked.

Tori blushed in annoyance, and looked away.

'Barry, this is my friend Tori. Tori, Barry.'

Tori said, 'Hi.'

'Call me Bar Jah. All my friends do. If you're not his woman, how about a dance with me?'

Tori shook her head. 'I don't dance.'

'Come on, sugar,' he cajoled, reaching for her hand.

She backed away, obviously uncomfortable. Barry took a step towards her.

Louis said, 'She said no.'

'Keep out of it, kid. She doesn't really mean no. They never do. It's just a game they play.'

Louis clenched his fists. 'Barry, stop it.'

'It's Bar Jah, mate.'

Louis laughed as Barry stared threateningly at him. Tori moved closer to Louis, leaning her shoulder into his.

Barry noticed the closeness of their bodies. 'Thought she wasn't yours.'

'I'm not an object to be owned,' Tori asserted. And I'm absolutely not interested in dancing or anything else with you, mate.'

Barry muttered 'bitch', and Tori felt Louis tense. A shout was heard from a far corner. A rowdy group of young men were beckoning Barry over. As he walked away, Tori exhaled.

'I could have handled that myself,' said Louis.

'And I can look after myself. Thanks anyway.'

'I was so close to losing my temper. Barry is such an arse. Why are white guys with dreads always like that?'

'I've never met someone like him before,' remarked Tori.

'He annoys me so much. Such a pretender. I'm sorry he was so disrespectful to you, Tori.'

'What are you apologising for? He's the one in the wrong. Let's forget about him and listen to the music.'

Standing by her side, he could feel warmth filling the short gap between them. He thought about the way she'd just stood so close to him, in defiance of Barry, and imagined what it would be like to hold her hand. He took a sip of his beer, remembering that she'd told him earlier she wasn't comfortable holding hands. He suddenly felt ashamed, telling himself he was no better than Barry for even having such thoughts.

Tori turned and smiled at him. 'I really like this music. Thanks for asking me out.'

Louis's reply was interrupted by someone calling Tori's name. She turned around and saw Marcie walking towards her.

'Well, look at you. That dress is stunning. And I thought you didn't go out.'

Tori blushed. 'I don't. Louis asked me.'

Marcie said to Louis, 'I remember you. In the street that day. Before Tori started working at the gallery. I'm Marcie.'

Louis nodded hello. Then Marcie and Tori started talking to each other, mostly complaining about Andrés. Louis's ears pricked up. He wanted to know how Andrés really treated Tori, as she never properly answered his questions. They didn't say anything of interest, so his attention moved back to the band.

'Oh, there's my friends,' commented Marcie.

Louis and Tori looked in the same direction as Marcie. A group of people stood to the side of the stage, laughing loudly.

'I'll see you at work tomorrow,' said Marcie. 'Oh, I forgot. Ana's having a party soon. Do you want to go? You can bring Louis.'

'I'll think about it,' replied Tori.

After Marcie left, Tori asked Louis what he thought about the invitation. He looked at the group of people Marcie had joined, and commented that her friends seemed cool, so maybe it would be a fun party.

*

When the band finished, Louis insisted on walking Tori home, even though she thought it wasn't necessary. She changed her mind when he offered to show her where he lived. She was surprised to see him walk through the park, almost to the treehouse.

'Where are we going? I thought you were showing me your place,' she said.

'I am. It's not much further.'

He walked towards the duck pond, and stopped at the tree with the large hole in the trunk. 'This is where I live.'

Tori looked up. 'I don't see a treehouse.'

'Not up there, in here.'

He crouched down and climbed into the hole. After a few moments, Tori saw a light flickering. Louis stuck his head out of the hole, holding a candle.

'You coming in? It's safe.'

She edged closer, looking into the hole. Louis moved aside for her.

Tori hesitated. 'Maybe another time. In the daylight.'

Louis tried to mask his disappointment. 'It's comfortable in here.'

'I've got to go. Maggie's probably getting worried. See you tomorrow, perhaps.'

'I'll walk you home,' offered Louis, climbing out.

'No, don't bother. You can almost see my place from here. Thanks for the great night. Bye.'

Once she got home, Tori went straight to bed. Maggie was already asleep, clearly not worried about her. Tori thought over her day. Andrés's anger towards Louis. That creep Barry. And Louis. She hadn't seen him in a while, and something felt different between them. Tori wondered if she'd overreacted when Louis had taken her hand in the park. She'd always liked him, as a friend. Now she wasn't so sure. She pondered if it was possible to like someone in a different way. To want to be more than friends but still not interested in hand-holding and other gestures of romance. Tori caught herself picking spots on her face again and put her hands under the bedcovers.

*

The next morning, the redness on her face had spread a bit further. Tori draped her hair over that side of her face, hoping Maggie wouldn't notice. She left for work with just a mumbled goodbye. Tori now often wore her hair over that side of her face, and wore long sleeves even when it wasn't cold. She'd didn't think anyone had noticed that an occasional scratch had become obsessive behaviour.

Maggie had noticed. And long ago realised what the redness reminded her of. Same side of the face. Same shape and size. Maggie knew who was on her sister's mind, and wondered if she should say something. She too had been thinking about their mother more often.

When Tori got home from work, Maggie made pancakes with strawberry jam for dinner. They both loved pancakes, as a food connected to good memories of living in the hut on the gibber plains. Their mother would bring home tins of jam from the general store she worked in, and often cooked them up a big pile of pancakes for dinner. She'd told them pancakes were for any time, not just breakfast. She showed them how to make the batter just right, and flip the pancakes just so. Now, in the treehouse, pancake-making had become Maggie's specialty.

'Here you go,' said Maggie.

'Thanks for making dinner. Best thing to happen all day! Stuff kept going wrong at work, and Andrés unfairly blamed me. Marcie is better at standing up to him than I am.'

'Is that why you're stressed and, you know, doing that scratching thing again.'

'I'm not.'

'That redness has gotten bigger. Do you think you should see a doctor, before it scars? Maybe get some ointment?'

'Just drop it. I'm all right.'

'You could be allergic to something. Maybe it's this treehouse.'

'Stop prying. It's really none of your business.'

'I care for you. We used to talk more, share our worries.'

'I said drop it. I'm tired. I've worked all day to get us money. Don't hassle me.'

'Sorry.'

'Pass me the jam.'

Maggie handed her sister the jar of jam and a knife. She knew there was no sense pushing her. And besides, Tori was right. It wasn't her business.

SEVENTEEN

Tori had snuck out not long after sunbreak. Despite it being so early, she saw that black-and-white bird. She usually saw it when walking through the park. It always followed her, often stopping at Louis's tree. She hadn't seen him since the night they'd gone to the pub together. A few times, on the way home from work, she'd almost visited his place. It was a new feeling that made her keep walking past, that made her unsure of herself. For now, she had to get home before Maggie woke up. Tori wasn't sure Louis would remember their birthday plans, so she wanted to still do something special for her sister. Since their mother had died, birthdays were no longer fun for them. Tori had been looking forward to this one, given Louis's promise to show her the ocean for the first time. A living one, not a bed of rocks where an ancient sea had once been. She was still planning on going, with or without him. When she got back to the treehouse, she was glad to see him waiting at the bottom.

Tori climbed up the rope ladder, and placed a brown paper bag on the table. 'Breakfast time.'

'Do I smell warm donuts?' asked Maggie.

Tori nodded. 'Fresh from the bakery oven.'

Louis, Maggie and Tori sat on the cushions around the low wooden table, and ate while discussing their plans for the day. Then, gifts were exchanged. Tori gave Maggie a wooden box with birds painted all over. Inside were pencils of many colours. And for Tori, there was a pair of platform shoes. Tori tried them on immediately and walked around.

'They look good on you,' remarked Maggi. 'I'd trip if I even tried them on.'

'They're really not difficult to walk in. How did you afford these?'

'I sold some of my drawings. A friend of Brother Eddie's bought them. Offered to let me put more in his café. He's going to frame them first, then take some of the money when he's sold them.'

'This is so exciting.'

'I'm a real artist now.'

'Soon to be a famous artist,' remarked Louis.

'I don't know about that. I just like drawing.'

Tori said, 'You're really good at it. Wish I had some type of creative talent.'

'You'll discover yours one day.'

Louis glanced at his watch. 'We'd best get moving if we want to catch the next tram.'

*

As they walked, Maggie talked excitedly. She wondered if it was warm enough to go swimming, and then decided that she didn't care if it was as she was going in regardless. They'd packed towels but not lunch. Louis told them he had that all sorted. Tori wondered what he had in mind, as he wasn't carrying anything. Maggie's excited chatter didn't stop on the tram. She had to point out anything of interest as they travelled along the track.

When they got off the tram, it was Tori's turn to be overexcited. She smelt the salt air as she stepped down the steps and onto the pavement. She didn't need Louis to lead her to the beach. The sea was calling her. She could feel the waves pounding in her chest long before she saw the vast blueness.

'Come on, Maggie,' she said, taking her sister by the hand.

They hurried along the pavement, both eager to see what lay ahead. To see what was beyond the long wall of hessian and coastal shrubs in front of them. Tori stopped suddenly.

'What's wrong?' asked Maggie, with a look of concern.

Tori clutched her chest, struggling to breathe. The waves' rhythm had taken charge. She recalled that time Aunty Isabelle had taken her and Maggie to the site of the inland sea, insisting their mother stay behind at the camp. There, Aunty had taught her how to listen to the ancient sea, even if it was no longer visible. It had taken her a while. Rather than hear with her ears, she'd felt that sea deep in her being. She'd forgotten its rhythm. Now, beside this living ocean, she felt it again, knocking the wind from her lungs. When her breath returned, she knew it would forever be in tune with the waves.

Maggie and Tori held hands as they stepped off the pavement and onto the sand. Then they rolled around, laughing, throwing yellow sand in the air, not caring about dry seaweed becoming entwined in their hair. Louis smiled at the sight of them acting like children. Then the three of them ran along the beach. They found an abandoned bucket and made a big castle. Maggie decorated it with shells and feathers they'd collected on the beach. She then took a dip. Almost.

*

The water was cold, so she didn't dare go in past her knees. Exhausted, they stretched out on dry sand.

After catching his breath, Louis told them to wait there, and he walked off. When he returned, he was carrying a wicker basket and a picnic rug. Maggie spread the rug on the sand. He placed the basket in the middle, and opened the lid.

'Where did you get all this?' asked Maggie. 'Look, Tori, it's a feast.'

Louis replied, 'I came down here a few days ago, and ordered it at a local café. The lady there was super helpful when I told her how it was your birthday. She also made me promise to take you up there for ice cream before we went home today.'

'Thanks,' said Tori.

'It was really no problem.'

Soon they were all too full to take another bite. Tori and Louis covered the leftover food, while Maggie stretched out on the blanket, feeling the sun on her arms and legs.

'Don't get burnt,' warned Tori.

'Stop fussing.'

Louis suggested, 'Let's go for a walk.'

Maggie shook her head. 'I'm much too full. I might rest for a bit, then sketch some gulls. I brought some paper and my new pencils, just in case.'

'What about you,' asked Louis, looking at Tori.

She nodded and got up, brushing crumbs off her legs. They walked to where the sea lapped the sand. Side by side, they strolled along the water's edge. Louis knew Tori's hand was close, but he no longer had an urge to reach out and take it. If Tori was only interested in friendship, that's what he would give.

'You're really quiet. What are you thinking about?' asked Tori.

'Just enjoying this. Sun, the waves, watching you and Maggie enjoying your first encounter with the sea. I needed a bit of happiness.'

'Something up?'

'Just feeling a bit homesick lately. When I came down here a few days ago to arrange the picnic lunch, the sea reminded me of home.'

'Your family lives nearby?'

'Far from here. My nan lives close to the ocean, over on the east coast. Growing up, I lived with Nan.'

'Where were your parents?'

'Prison, mostly.'

'That must have been hard on you.'

'I was just a baby when they first went in. Got used to them coming and going. Nan made sure all that didn't upset me too much. And my parents aren't bad people. They never hit me or anything.'

'What are you doing here?'

'I did some dumb stuff; not like my parents, but still bad. I left before the police could find me. I never wanted to see that look on my nan's face, the disappointment, like my dad had caused.'

'Would you ever go back?'

'One day. I want to see Nan again. And hang out with all my cousins. If they've forgiven me for taking off. What about you? Have you got family to go to?

'Not really. We grew up with our mother. I don't know too much about family. We met Aunty Isabelle when we were staying near a mining town. She's my father's aunt. And Maggie and I were born on Country, where our great-grandparents live. I suppose they've both died by now. We lived with them until we were four. Our mum also spent her first years there. Her mother is white, and her father was black. He died in the second big war, when she was little, so she didn't have memories of him. Or her nana Vic and grandfather Albert. I don't really remember anything of the time we spent with them.'

'Where's your father?'

Tori shrugged. 'Never met him. I'm not really sure he's alive any more. It's just a feeling I've had for a long time. I think my mum had that feeling too. It made her stop trying. That, and the accident.'

'Accident?'

'Can we talk about something else? It's a day of happiness, remember?'

Louis fell silent, not wanting to push Tori. He was glad she'd opened up to him a bit, and relieved that she listened to his past, without judging.

***

A few days after their birthday, Tori was feeling annoyed at herself for telling Louis so many personal things about her family. Those things were supposed to remain secret, known only by her and Maggie. Tori had noticed she was picking at her skin more. Since the day at the beach, whenever she caught herself scratching she would take a deep breath and feel the rhythm of the ocean. It worked, most of the time. This morning, it wasn't working.

'Don't get mad,' pleaded Maggie, approaching Tori as she lay on their bed, 'I got you a gift.'

'Our birthday is over. What is it?' asked Tori, looking at the small jar in Maggie's hand.

'Bush rub. Gloria, the Elder you met at the centre, gave it to me. She told me it was for you. To stop the itching and heal your skin. She said it won't fix whatever it is worrying you, but it's a start. She wants you to come see her.'

'Busybody. I don't need her hoodoo goop. It even smells awful.'

'Don't be rude. I like how it smells. Like the grasses that Aunty Isabelle would pick and boil up in a large pot. She must have been making bush rub.'

'I don't care. It's primitive stuff. Complete nonsense.'

'You used to be more open. You believed everything Aunty Isabelle told you.'

'I was just a kid then. Everyone has to grow up some day.'

'Being at that gallery so much is making you forget what little we did learn from family. The stories that Nana Vic and Aunty Isabelle told us. The things Grandfather Albert showed us. We both need to hold on to all that. It will make us stronger, connect us to our Country and mob, even if we're far from them.'

'Don't tell me what I should do. Have you seen a mirror lately? You're not exactly black.'

'No need to be so cruel. I know what I look like. I also know who I am, where I come from. What and who I've lost. And I've seen how mean people are to you. Way back, since we were kids, I knew they treated you different because you're darker. I saw how much it hurt you. I fought in the schoolyard for you. I don't know what to do now we're grown up.'

Tori turned away.

'I'm going out,' mumbled Maggie, picking up her art gear.

'Yeah, hanging out at that centre like a pretender.'

Maggie stopped before climbing down the rope ladder. 'I'm not the coconut, Tori.'

***

Marcie reminded Tori about the party she'd mentioned. It was at Ana's parents' house. Marcie warned her that Ana's family threw large parties, the type you need to dress up for. Tori had never been to a formal event, so she was disappointed when Louis didn't share her enthusiasm. She talked him into going, and offered to go op-shopping with him for suitable clothes. She'd found a black lace dress for herself that she could dress up with costume jewellery.

When they got to Ana's place, Louis felt uncomfortable in his second-hand clothes. He was not one to usually care about appearances, but the other guests were clearly wearing expensive outfits. He didn't like standing out. Tori noticed he was tightly clutching an empty glass.

'Let me get you another one,' she offered.

Louis nodded. At least the drinks were free. And the lavish spread of food was interesting. He wandered over to the buffet table, and picked up a cracker with tiny black dots lumped on top.

'I see you have a taste for caviar,' purred someone behind him.

Louis turned around and saw a woman looking him up and down. She appeared to be slightly older than him, and expensively dressed.

'It's an aphrodisiac,' she said. 'Not that you'd need any help, I'm guessing.'

Louis turned away and, ignoring her, picked up a devilled egg.

344

'Did I make you blush?' she murmured.

He did his best to look uninterested, hoping she'd move on. He took a bite of the egg, chewing slowly.

She whispered, 'Why won't you play with me?'

'What are we playing?' asked Tori, as she handed Louis a drink.

The woman turned her attention to Tori. 'Oh, look at you. Those eyes. The bluest of blue jewels, in a sea of black. Sebastian, come here darling.'

A man walked over. 'What, Stephanie?'

'Look at this one. Isn't she so divine!'

'Very much so,' replied Sebastian, looking at Tori. 'Do you model?'

Tori shook her head. 'I work for Ana's friend Andrés. Doing odd jobs at the gallery.'

Stephanie asked, 'And he hasn't got you in front of the camera? Andrés must be off his game.'

'He's asked me a few times, but I'm not interested.'

'What about acting? I could introduce you to a few contacts of mine,' offered Sebastian.

'No, thanks. I'm okay with the work I've got.'

'Sweetie, your looks are far too divine for you to be wasting your time as a mere cleaner. Let my Seb hook you up.'

'I'm doing okay, truly.'

Louis asked, 'Have you tried these devilled eggs, Tori? They really are divine.'

Stephanie's attention shifted to the front door. 'Ah, Felicity's here. Seb, darling, we really must ask her how she found Venice.'

After they'd left, Tori muttered, 'Why were you rude to them?'

'I'm not interested in talking to people like them,' said Louis.

'What's that supposed to mean? They seemed nice.'

'That wasn't nice.'

Tori frowned. 'They were just talking to us. It's what people do at parties.'

'Why do you let people treat you like that?'

'Like what?'

'Like you're some sort of exotic animal.'

'Don't be ridiculous, Louis. They were just admiring the colour of my eyes.'

'They only made a big deal because they hadn't seen blue eyes with skin like yours before.'

'And what's wrong with my skin?'

'Nothing. My point is that, to people like them, you're an oddity. A collectable, even. Those two didn't care about you or me. The way they sexualise our skin, our youthfulness, but want nothing to do with us as real people, is perverse.'

'What nonsense. Have you been hanging out with the same people as Maggie? Her head's also full of nonsense lately.'

'You mean being with our people, at the community centre? You should be hanging out there too, not with these shallow toffs. Learn about your culture and stop chasing things you can't have.'

'I'm doing all right making my own friends.'

'They'll never let you in, no matter how hard you try or how exotic-looking you are.'

'I'm here, aren't I?'

'You might be content with being their sideshow freak, I'm not. I'm a man, not an object to be collected. A proud black man.'

'Why do you have to make this about colour? I don't hear anyone else here doing that. You're the one who's judging others, not them.'

'Let's go,' suggested Louis.

Tori shook her head and took a sip of her drink. Louis put down his glass and walked out.

'He's right.'

Tori turned around and saw Marcie.

'Stephanie and Sebastian see us as collectables. They want their friends to think they're liberal-minded because they talk to people like us, but they actually think we're below them. Put a fancy ribbon on racism, and it's still racism,' she said.

Tori shook her head. 'You're wrong.'

'I've been around people like them a bit longer than you have, Tori. Back in my own country, I fought in the streets for black rights. I know what racism looks like when I see it.'

'You sound like Louis. He sees it everywhere, even where it doesn't exist.'

'He's a smart young man. Why aren't you following him?'

'I'm my own woman. I don't run after anyone.'

'Honey, there are moments when it's important to stand up for your principles, and there are moments to stand up for friends. Are you sure it's not pride making your decisions?'

'I'm not a baby, I make my own choices. Right now, I choose another drink.'

Tori stayed longer than she'd intended, and had more drinks than she should have. She was aware that Marcie floated nearby, keeping an eye on her, and that just made her want to drink more. Tori began to feel light-headed and unsteady on her feet. Finally, she drifted towards the front door, carrying her high-heeled shoes.

'I've called a taxi. We can share a ride,' said Marcie, appearing by her side.

Tori waved her arms around. 'I don't need your help. I'm walking home.'

She stumbled outside, knowing Marcie was still watching. From out of the darkness emerged Louis.

'I don't need your help, either,' shouted Tori, before tripping over and falling in a low hedge.

Tori let him pull her up. Silently, they walked towards the parklands, back to the treehouse. She almost stumbled a few times. Louis stood nearby, steadying her if needed. At the foot of her tree, Tori grabbed the ladder. It wobbled. Or she wobbled. Her foot kept slipping out of the foothold. In frustration, she threw her shoes in a nearby bush. Louis went to get them.

'Leave them,' Tori shouted. 'You and Marcie think I need help, but I don't. I was fine before I met you, and I'm doing just fine now.'

'Tori...'

'Go away, Louis. And don't bother coming back, ever.'

He watched in silence as Tori climbed the ladder, standing ready in case she fell. When she'd disappeared from sight, he retrieved her shoes from the bush.

'Tell us another story, Aunty Isabelle.'

'Only if you promise to remember it forever. Can you do that? Forever is a very long time.'

The girls nodded. They'd promise anything for a story. She picked up a stick and prodded the fire, as the twins waited expectantly.

'Okay then,' said their aunty, 'this is a long one. Goes all the way back, and all the way forwards, and a little bit of now. That old sea over there, the one many can't see...'

'The one trapped underground,' said Victoria.

'It's there, under the red dirt, but it's not trapped. That briny mother has sent her children far and wide, to travel further than you or I could ever imagine. Droplets of that sea can be found within sun-warmed rock pools, not too far from here. Some are carried along by snaking rivers, others nestle in shallow puddles in green fields of almost-ripe grain. Dewdrops ride on the wings of birds, eager to taste enticing fruits and spices in faraway lands. Thirsty wisps of clouds travel far and wide, growing fatter and fatter, until they can hold no more moisture. As they spill their loads over land and sea, this generative liquid is eagerly absorbed. The sea travels far, changing form many times, but never once does it forget where it came from.'

'What about the creatures, Aunty?' asked Maggie. 'The ones that lived in that sea long time ago. Do they live on too?'

'Yes, because everything is connected. Even people. We've all soaked up that ancient sea. We reconnect with it every time rain caresses upturned faces. Rain carries the essence of those creatures. It keeps them alive. Water is infinite – not even a single drop can die. Water connects us to all that is, was and will be. We are all one; kin to ancient seas.'

EIGHTEEN

Maggie put down her art bag, and placed Tori's shoes in the box they kept their shoes in. She then looked in the food cupboard. Maggie had noticed her sister sitting by a window, but was adamant she was not going to be the first one to say hello.

Without turning around, Tori asked, 'Where did you find those?'

'Your shoes? Louis gave them to me. I stopped by his place just now.'

Maggie waited for Tori to say something. When she didn't, Maggie began to prepare dinner. She normally liked the absence of people-noise, as it meant more of a chance to hear birdsong, but she'd had enough of Tori's loaded silence. In a manner unlike her, Maggie noisily made dinner. She shut the pantry door a little too heavily. She placed the tinned beans on the table a bit too abruptly. The knife she dropped landed much too loudly.

'Quit it,' demanded Tori.

'You quit it.'

'What? I'm just sitting here, minding my own business.'

Maggie glared at Tori. 'You have no problem telling other people what to do.'

'What are you on about?'

'You, telling Louis to stay away from our treehouse. You had no right to do that. He's my friend too. And this is home for both of us.'

'Oh that. He was annoying me. Always telling me what to do and think. Guess I just had enough.'

'He cares for you. It's what friends do.'

'Nah, being controlling is not friendship.'

'You're a hypocrite. If you're so against people controlling you, why are you working at that gallery? The owner sounds like an arrogant bully.'

Tori got up. 'Louis is quite the tattletale. Where I work has nothing to do with him, or you. I make my own decisions.'

'After all that effort trying to make Mum leave that abusive von Wolff, you end up working for a similar man. That's what you decide for yourself?'

'It's not the same. This time, no one is in danger.'

'Are you sure about that? Something's bothering you. The marks on your face are proof that everything's not okay.'

'Get off my back.'

'You need to quit that job. I don't want to lose you too.'

'Enough!' yelled Tori.

Maggie watched in silence as Tori grabbed a coat and shoes, and climbed out of the treehouse. It was raining, but not heavily. Tori didn't even notice. She strode through the park, annoyed that Louis and Maggie were ganging up on her. Tori didn't feel as if she had any options. They needed the money that her job provided. Sure, Andrés was unpleasant to work for, but Tori knew how to keep out of his way. She was furious that her sister didn't trust her judgement, didn't realise that she could fend for herself. On the edge of the park, Tori stopped. The rain was beginning to fall more heavily. She was unsure if she should turn back or find shelter elsewhere. Thrusting her hands in her coat pocket, Tori felt a piece of paper. She took it out and read it under the street lamp. It was Marcie's address. She'd given it to her a while ago, and said she was there if Tori ever needed someone to listen.

*

Tori looked at the three-storey brick building. It was difficult to see through the rain. Most of the curtain-less windows showed lights from inside, so she hoped Marcie was also home. She opened the main door and walked up the stairs to the third floor. There was a strong odour in the stairs and hallway, like soggy clothes that needed airing. Tori rechecked the piece of paper for the flat number. She knocked on a door and immediately regretted being there. She heard voices, so she knew Marcie wasn't alone. Tori heard a door shut, and then footsteps.

'Hey, this is a surprise,' said Marcie, opening the door.

Tori nodded, not knowing if that meant she was a welcome sight. Marcie opened the door wider and beckoned her in. It was a small flat, with not much furniture. The kitchen and lounge were in the one room. Tori saw two doors, which she assumed led to a bathroom and bedroom. One of the doors opened and a tall woman walked into the room carrying a small suitcase. She smiled at Tori, put down her luggage and walked over to Marcie. As she embraced Marcie, and kissed her passionately, Tori stared. Not because of the loving kiss, but because this woman's hair was the blackest of blacks that Tori had ever seen. When they parted, Tori realised she'd been staring, and blushed.

'Simone, this is Tori. From the gallery.'

'Marcie told me about you. I'm glad she has company at the gallery. I don't like the thought of her working alone with that creep.'

'It's not that bad,' Marcie remarked.

Simone turned to Marcie. 'Please think about what we talked about earlier. I can use my staff discount to get you home. And I can put in for a transfer, just do domestic flights.'

'When are you back this time?'

'I have a longer stopover than usual, so a week.'

'I miss you already.'

'Then say yes to going home,' pleaded Simone, as she walked through the front door.

'I'll think about it. I promise.'

Marcie sighed as the door shut, then turned to Tori. 'You're soaked!'

'It's really wet out there. Thought I'd get washed away walking here.'

'Let me get you something to change into, and then we can dry those clothes,' said Marcie, walking towards the bedroom.

While she waited, Tori looked around. There didn't seem to be many personal items, no knick-knacks or photos. Even though her mother had discouraged Maggie and her from wanting personal belongings, due to their transient lifestyle, Tori thought other people's places were full of such things. A small silver photo frame on a side table caught her eye. Tori picked it up. She thought the woman, who appeared to be older than her mother had been, had kind eyes.

'That's my mother,' said Marcie, as she handed Tori some clothes. 'Do you want to get changed in my room?'

Tori nodded, and went into the bedroom. Like the rest of the apartment, its furniture was simple. There was a framed photo of Marcie and Simone next to the bed. Laughing, hair blowing, with the sea behind them. Tori put on the pants and jumper that Marcie had given her, and picked up her wet clothes.

When Tori went back into the other room, Marcie hung the clothes in front of a small radiator. Steam rose immediately, carrying a smell of dampness and pine needles. Tori suddenly thought of her sister, and felt a pang of guilt for leaving her during a storm. The increasing instances of arguing with Maggie also niggled at her. Tori was aware she usually started these fights. Lately, she didn't feel able to control her emotions. Her mum had always known what to say to help Tori through occasional exasperations. Now, alone, without such guidance, annoyance was too often becoming fury.

'Take a seat, make yourself comfortable. I need a drink. You want one?'

She nodded, and settled into an old armchair. It had a throw rug on it, covering worn parts, but was still comfortable.

Marcie handed her a drink. 'Gin and tonic. There's no lemons.'

Tori took a sip, and Marcie settled on the small couch.

'I hope you don't mind me dropping in like this,' said Tori.

'Not at all. Good timing, really. I get a bit glum every time Simone leaves, so it's nice to have some company.'

'Have you had this place for long?'

'A year or so. The rent is hard to keep up with. Simone gives me a bit, but as she's not here often I don't like her paying more than what's fair. As you know, Andrés doesn't pay well. I don't have a work visa, so he takes advantage of that. I also do hair. When I moved here, Simone and I quickly realised no one knows how to treat natural hair, like ours. With her job, grooming is important, so I did Simone's hair. Others asked where she'd got her hair done, and my little home-based business started from there. I could do your hair, if you want.'

'I'd like that. Other than my mum, when I was little, no one has done my hair. It gets knotty so easily.'

'I can cut it so it's more manageable. And make up a treatment to give it some gloss. Does your mother use treatments?'

Tori looked down. She was on the verge of crying, something she refused to do, especially in front of others.

'What's up, hon?'

'I feel bad. For lying to you. My mum isn't around any more. Neither is my father. It's just me and my sister.'

'Where are your parents?'

'We never knew our father. Our mother tried to find him. She spent years looking and hoping. She died before we could find out more about him, or any family.'

'I'm sorry. Was this recent?'

Tori put down her empty glass and looked out the window. It was now night-time, and a nearby street lamp was trying humbly to be noticed in the pouring rain. She hoped the rain wasn't causing Maggie any problems in the treehouse. There was a corner of the roof that let water in, drops just missing their bed. Tori knew Marcie was waiting for a reply, but wasn't sure how much to share. What would she think about them living in a tree, in a public park? Tori glanced at Marcie and reminded herself that she could trust her.

'Our mum was murdered when we were twelve. I've never told anyone that before. We've got some family, somewhere. My twin sister and I live in the park, in a treehouse. Before that, we lived in the basement of a vacant building near the park. Both places enabled us to be out of sight, and to stay safe. We were worried for a long time that someone would try to put us in an orphanage. We've heard of those places, and how they treat kids like us. Now that we've turned eighteen, no one can put us anywhere.

'Honey, that's a lot to be dealing with. Have you two been alone since your mamma died?'

'Mostly. Gabriel helped us escape but the cops got him.'

'Escape?'

'Yeah, he got us away from the man who killed our mum. That man died when his studio burnt down, but it was an accident.'

'Studio?'

'Yes, a photographer's studio, at his home, in the country. We moved there when Mum got a job looking after the man's wife, Iris. After his wife died, he got meaner. I tried to get Mum to leave. She was always a good mum to us, but it was like she had no hope left. After she died, he made us do horrible stuff. Lately, I've been wondering if he made Mum do those things too.'

'Do you want to talk about what he did?'

'I prefer to forget it ever happened.'

'Is there anything I can do to help?'

Tori thought for a while, then replied, 'Can I sleep here tonight? I had an argument with my sister.'

'Sure. I can make you up a bed on the couch. Do you want another drink? Have you had dinner?'

'If you don't mind, I just want to sleep.'

'I'll get a pillow and quilt.'

'Marcie?'

'Yes?' she said, pausing in the bedroom doorway.

'Don't tell anyone, please. All of that is a secret.'

'You can trust me.'

'And can we not talk about it again?'

'Not if you don't want to.'

Returning with her arms full, Marcie made up a bed on the couch. Tori climbed under the quilt as Marcie walked towards the light switch.

Tori said, sleepily. 'The other day, at Ana's party, I was horrible to you. I'm sorry.'

*

Marcie could hear Tori talking in her sleep in the other room. Even though Tori had not shared the details, she felt horrified thinking of her mother being murdered. And sad for Tori. Marcie knew how difficult it was to grieve the loss of a parent. She could not even begin to imagine the pain of having a parent taken by a murderer. Marcie thought back to the last time she'd seen her parents, still upset she'd never had a chance to say goodbye to her father.

Marcie remembered how the letters from him had gradually changed. The longer the conflict went on, the shorter and less frequent were his letters. And there was something else. It began with doubt. A questioning hidden between the lines of scrawled ink: should their nation even be involved in this war? He'd watched his fellow soldiers, and the way they treated both the enemy and allies, who, unlike him and his battalion, had in common an ancestral connection to the battleground. Then he began to notice little signals. Did men wearing the same uniform as him still not see him as an equal? And then came the delayed recognition: his own nation may have given him that uniform but they still didn't see the man within. Marcie had already begun her own questioning, but her father's letters confirmed for her that the fight for civil rights was essential to their freedom. She never had the opportunity to speak of these things with her father. He had been shot by 'friendly fire' on foreign soil, killed by his compatriots.

Marcie channelled her grief into action. Participated in anti-war marches and the civil rights movement. Her mother eventually heard rumours of Marcie's relationship with a militant activist and became concerned. She'd already lost a husband on the front line; she wasn't going to lose her only child. After a heated argument, Marcie moved out. One day, Marcie noticed an intended non-violent protest had become an out-of-control skirmish with the police. Even when away from the action, she felt engulfed by a rising chaos. Then, her boyfriend was shot dead by the police, when walking home from his grandmother's house. Packing her bag, Marcie flew as far away as she could. At first, she didn't keep in contact with her mother. Recently, they'd begun to exchange letters. Her mother had not shared bad news, but Marcie could read between the lines. Her mother was sick and needed her. And Marcie needed to be home. In her adopted country, she'd noticed subtle political shifts around her, and recognised the fire in the belly of black peoples fighting for rights. In some ways, it was similar to the fight she'd run from. She also knew that although she could give support, this was not her fight. Sitting alone in their bed, with the faint aroma of her lover's perfume on the pillow, Marcie knew Simone was right – it was time to go home.

After Marcie finally drifted off to sleep, Tori's sleep-talking was drowned out by the downpour outside. As Tori tossed and turned, her dreams filled with wondrous beasts. Dream-Tori recognised she was on Aunty Isabelle's Country, on the shore of the inland sea. As the rain fell, the ancient seabed filled, covering the red dirt. Tori noticed shadowy figures in the turbulent waters. Enormous flippers, slithery tails, long reptilian necks, teeth sharp as daggers. Big to gigantic aquatic creatures swam in this ancient sea. Tori took a step back from the shore as some of these shadows came closer, to swim in the shallows. A long beak, filled with sharp teeth, emerged. The beast flipped its head, revealing a large squid-like creature between its teeth. It opened its mouth wide and the prey disappeared down its gullet. It went to grab another, but a large reptilian bird swooped down, grabbing it before escaping the toothy-beaked water beast. Tori twitched in her sleep, reacting to this dream of carnage. Outside, the rain came down even harder, its sound penetrating her dreamscape.

Tori thought she heard Aunty Isabelle's voice. She couldn't find her. She turned towards the sea, marvelling again at the magnitude of the beasts. Especially the size of their stomachs.

She heard her aunty say, 'You are safe here, this is your Country too. They won't eat you.'

In her dream, Tori felt a longing for family: *What might have been if Mother hadn't made us leave our father's Country?* Perhaps he returned and they'd all be together now. Tori heard Aunty Isabelle's voice again: 'He didn't. He would have, if he could.'

A small, brightly coloured bird appeared, fluttering over the turbulent sea, as if teasing the beasts within. One creature broke through the water, snapping at the small bird, which nonchalantly floated out of reach. Mesmerised by the bird's dance, Tori's thoughts drifted: *Is Maggie safe?* The sea was expanding rapidly, water engulfing more arid land as the rain fell. Dream-Tori turned around and saw the treehouse. There is no sense of distance or geography in dreamscapes, so of course she didn't wonder why this urban tree and the inland sea were so close together. The unusual bird flew towards the treehouse, as if moving between the raindrops. Tori followed, becoming more and more soaked as she walked. Standing on a small hill, she saw that the park's pond had flooded and was almost surrounding their tree. The rain-loving ducks were nowhere in sight. The downfall was too heavy, even for them. Tori shouted, knowing Maggie wouldn't be able to hear her. The rain was too loud. Arriving at the tree, the bird flew up and up, until it was hidden from view in the dense foliage. And Tori woke up.

She checked her clothes hanging by the heater; they were almost dry. She got changed and turned off the heater. Finding a pen and piece of paper, she scribbled a note. Then she quietly left the flat. Standing in the doorway downstairs, Tori looked into the darkness. The street lights were feebly attempting to shine on a dreary night. In the dim light they managed to cast, Tori noticed the street was flooded. Water was gushing towards already full gutters, causing waves to rise and hit the pavement. That rain was not looking like it would stop any time soon. She suddenly thought of Gabriel, and what he'd taught her about rain.

*

Maggie was awake when Tori returned to the treehouse. Curled up in bed, listening to the rain, seemingly unafraid of the storm surrounding her.

'The pond has nearly reached the foot of our tree,' remarked Tori, taking off her soaked shoes.

'I had a peek just before. That rain is certainly heavy.'

'Tell me about it!'

'You're not even wet?'

'I walked between the rain.'

Maggie sat up in bed. 'Like Gabriel?'

Tori nodded. 'I remembered what he told us.'

'That's so cool. I want to try that, but not tonight. This nest is too cosy. The sound of rain has put me in the mood for thinking, and remembering. Just now, I was remembering stories. I'm not sure, but I think our great-grandmother told them to us.'

'Nana Vic? Can you remember that far back? We were just babies. All I know about back then was the little bits Mum told us about Nana Vic and Grandfather Albert.'

Maggie said, 'I know it sounds impossible, but I do remember. Just snippets of stories being whispered over us as we fell asleep. Of a colourful snake, starry sisters, and a bit more. I can't remember much of the stories, and what I can recall will one day be gone, just like Mum.'

'The stories will stay alive as long as we keep remembering and sharing them. Do you remember what Aunty Isabelle told us about raindrops?' asked Tori, as she climbed under the quilt of feathers.

'I think so. Something about duality of the collectiveness and individuality? And how it's represented by seas, which are made up of countless tiny drops.'

'And through the cycles of rain, everything is connected. We're linked to all, even ancient seas and beasts long gone. Which means Mum isn't really gone.'

'I guess not. Then neither is Father. Nor Nana Vic and Grandfather Albert, Aunty Isabelle, Gabriel, Bethel and Omer. Dead or alive, we're still connected.'

'With all that rain out there, flooding everything in sight, I reckon there's quite a few souls who want to make sure the living know they're still here.'

'I like that thought,' said Maggie. 'Perhaps they can do it with a little less rain.'

'Earlier, I dreamt about weird aquatic dinosaurs, like the ones Aunty told us lived in the inland sea ages ago. Probably because of all this rain.'

'Louis's place would be flooded. Is he okay?'

'I didn't go there. I'm sure he found somewhere dry. I went to Marcie's flat. She let me sleep on the couch. Then I had that dinosaur dream, and came back to see if you were okay.'

Maggie took her sister's hand. 'Thanks for caring.'

'I'm sorry I said those mean things when you were only thinking of my safety.'

'What happened at von Wolff's has left its mark on both of us, but we can't let those memories tear us apart.'

'I miss her so much.'

'Me too. Sometimes, when I look at the stars, I know Mum is still watching over us.'

***

Maggie picked up a placard and handed it to her sister. Tori turned it over to read the words.

'Did you make this one?' Tori asked.

Maggie nodded and picked up another one. 'If you don't want to carry that one, you can have this.'

Tori said, 'No, I like this one. The message and the design are good.'

'I made it for you, just in case you changed your mind.'

'You actually came,' said Gloria, as she walked past them. 'That sister of yours was worried you wouldn't.'

Tori shrugged. 'Had a day off, so thought I'd help. If that's all right?'

'Of course, bub,' replied Gloria. 'More people, the better. This bloody government has to start listening. We need to protect Country, make sure it's cared for. Not just for our mob but everyone. And for future generations. Gubs need to understand that we, the

First Peoples, know the right way to respect land, waters and skies. We will keep on demanding land rights, until they do the right thing.'

Gloria walked over to another table and greeted the older people seated there. More people were walking into the community centre's main room, picking up placards or greeting friends and kin. A few said hello to Maggie, who then introduced Tori. Everyone was really welcoming, but Tori felt overwhelmed and muttered shyly in return.

'The bus is here,' shouted a young boy, running into the room.

'Come on, then,' Gloria announced loudly. 'Time we were moving. Someone remember to grab the flag.'

Two men walked over to the far wall, and took down the gigantic black, yellow and red cloth that hung there. They folded it between them, and went outside. Louis arrived as the last of the placards were being carefully placed in the storage compartment on the side of the bus. The bus was old-looking, with large patches of rust. Tori noticed how rust and paint-fade had been covered up by a patchwork of painted designs all over the bus. Similar styles to the paintings people did in the community centre. There were also small black, yellow and red patches on the bus, like the cloth that had been on the wall of the centre. Maggie spotted Louis, and ran over to him. When Tori joined them they went to board the bus together. A line of people was moving slowly up the stairs and down the aisle.

'Looks like there's no seats left,' observed Tori.

Maggie pointed. 'There's two.'

Following Maggie, Tori sat next to her, with Louis standing in the aisle. The bus kept filling up and, after lots of goodhearted jostling, Louis had less space to stand.

Tori stood up. 'Here, you sit down.'

'No,' he replied. 'You sit.'

'I will. On your lap,' Tori laughed. 'If you don't mind, that is.'

'Okay,' he said, sliding into the seat.

Louis turned to Maggie. 'I'm not squashing your arm, am I?'

'I've got plenty of room.'

'How about you?' asked Tori, as she sat down. 'I'm not squashing you, am I?'

'Nah, I'm fine. Your bum is a bit bony though,' he said, with a smirk.

'Shut up!' laughed Tori. 'That's my comb.'

Maggie commented, 'Bet it's not your comb, Tori. You do have a bony bum.'

'Hey, twin. We're supposed to stick together.'

Maggie smiled. 'Sure.'

Louis exclaimed, 'How was that storm? My place got flooded out.'

'Oh no,' said Maggie. 'Do you want to stay at our place?'

'I've got somewhere new to live.'

Tori asked, 'Where?'

'Brother Eddie is letting me stay in his spare room. I do gardening and stuff instead of paying rent. It's pretty good there.'

'Cool,' said Maggie. 'I like him.'

Louis nodded. 'Yeah, he's been helping me a bit. I'm thinking of writing to my nan. Tell her I'm sorry. Brother Eddie reminded me how important family is. Culture gets lost if we don't stay connected to kin and Country. And without connection, we can get sick.'

'She probably misses you,' noted Maggie. 'I wish we knew where our mum's family lives. I hate being so alone. Other than Tori, of course.'

'Maybe Brother Eddie can help you. He's really good at finding people. He even gave me news about my mum and dad. Eddie visits prisons and chats to mob from all over. My parents have been putting word out, looking for me, and it travelled all the way here.

Mum's getting out soon. Maybe she'll stay clean this time and we can spend time together.'

'Mothers are important. I hope it works out for you,' said Tori.

Louis had an urge to take Tori's hand because she sounded so sad, but he remembered how she hated being touched. Feeling her weight against his body, and trying hard not to focus on her body warmth, Louis was unsure how he felt about her being so close. She'd initiated it, but he still was uncertain. Not for the first time, Louis pondered how hard it was to understand Tori. How difficult she made it for him to show how much he cared for her.

'What's that noise?' asked Maggie.

Tori listened. It was a distinctive thrumming, getting louder. She felt her heart beating in unison.

Maggie looked out the window, seeking what was making the noise. 'Deadly.'

Tori looked too, and saw a line of motorbikes overtaking the bus. A loud cheer came from passengers, followed by clapping and whistles. Tori watched the bikes go past, and noticed most of the riders had the same patch on their leather jackets or denim vests: a black fist raised. Some also had the black, yellow and red design on their clothes. She'd never seen that many motorbikes in one place before. After the bikes had passed, a lone police car went by.

'Hope they behave,' muttered Louis.

'Who?' said Maggie.

'Cops. They love making trouble for mob. And seeing that many blackfullas on bikes probably has them itching to start something.'

The bus began to slow, and then stopped. They looked out the window, and saw a river in the distance. After waiting for the aisle to clear, and giving way to older people, they fetched their placards from the storage compartment. They then followed the crowd across the grass. On top of a knoll, Tori paused. From where she stood and right up to the river, there was a sea of black. And black, yellow and red.

'How good is that sight?' declared Gloria, who'd walked up behind Tori.

'What's that design lots of people are carrying, and wearing on their clothes?'

'That's our flag, bub. The flag of proud sovereign peoples.'

'So many people here,' remarked Tori.

'Unna. Let's join them,' said Gloria, as she walked down the hill.

Maggie ran past. 'Hurry up, Tori.'

Tori and Louis followed Maggie. She led them towards the front of the crowd, but it was too dense to get through. They instead found a place to one side. The crowd fell silent as an Elder welcomed everyone to Country. And then the crowd clapped when the next speaker took the microphone. Tori listened closely, as the sound was being distorted by the audio equipment, and the words were often drowned out by people clapping. She had never felt this type of energy. People seemed so happy and confident. Children ran through legs, and out to the sides of the crowd, where there was more room to play. Their screams of laughter carried on the soft breeze. Tori then noticed blue uniforms scattered on the perimeter. So many police officers. She turned around, hoping none of them would recognise her or Maggie from a missing persons poster.

Tori still didn't quite understand what the protest was about, but she noted Louis and Maggie were nodding while listening to the speeches. She saw the crowd suddenly part, like an ocean being cut into two, waves held back on both sides. Down the middle walked a white man in tiny pink shorts, a white figurehugging T-shirt and long white socks. He carried himself with confidence, and it was obvious people respected him.

'Who's that man,' Tori asked, nudging Louis.

He turned around briefly. 'The Premier, silly. He's not one of those gammon ones. He's on our side.'

As the sea of people closed behind this unusually attired charismatic politician, Tori turned her attention back to the stage. A different person was speaking now. Saying something about land rights and sovereignty. Tori thought she should ask Maggie what it all meant later.

'Brother,' said a man, clasping Louis hand.

Louis smiled. 'Billy. Good to see you, bro. Where you been?'

'Around. You going to the concert after?'

'I reckon so. See you there?'

The man nodded and walked off to talk to a nearby group.

'What concert?' Tori asked.

Maggie replied, 'There's some bands on, in a park not too far from here. That park is closer to our place, so we can walk home after.'

Tori asked, 'So you're planning on going?'

'Sure,' said Maggie. 'It sounds like fun.'

Louis noted, 'I think Aunty Gloria's wanting to speak with you, Tori.'

Tori looked in the direction Louis indicated, and saw Gloria beckoning her over.

'Did you want something,' asked Tori, as she got closer.

'You need to come to the centre soon, so we can have a yarn. Are you using that bush rub I sent home with Maggie?'

'Sometimes.'

'Use it every day. It will heal your skin quick as, but it won't heal your spirit. We need other treatment for that.'

'Nothing wrong with me.'

'Who you trying to fool? I've got eyes, girl. You've let years of fear grow into rage. This inner unrest needs fixing, just as much as the tracks you've dug into your own skin. I know your mum's dead and you don't know where your father is; Maggie told me. That's a lot of grief and loss you're carrying, bub. It's time you worked on healing, before you push everyone away. So you come and see me; I'll help you.'

'I don't need any help. Especially not silly snake-oil cures.'

'Would you just look at this?! No-culture kid thinks she knows it all.'

'Don't be rude.'

'Rude? Look at you, on my Country, thinking you can get all mouthy at an Elder. You might not be from here, but you still need to show some respect.'

Tori looked away, and saw glimpses of river between gaps in the dispersing crowd. She suddenly thought of the river Gabriel had shown them. She remembered the many weeks they'd followed that river with him. He'd walked slower when he noticed they were tired. He showed them where to find food, and how to prepare it properly. Told Maggie and her stories at night. Taught them about stars. Always patiently teaching them, and keeping them safe. And then he was gone, and they'd kept following that river. *This isn't where we belong,* Tori thought. *Where is our place?* Gloria noticed a shadow of sadness flit across Tori's face.

'Go on with you then,' she said, softening her tone. We'll yarn next week.'

As Tori walked back to Louis and Maggie, she flipped her hair down to cover her face. Louis noticed the change in her demeanour as she approached, and again had an urge to reach out.

'Are you coming to the concert?' called out Maggie, when she saw Gloria walking up the hill, towards the bus.

'No. These old bones are much too weary. I'm heading home. Nukkan ya.'

'Nukkan, Aunty,' said Maggie.

'Why'd you call her Aunty?' asked Tori.

'It's a sign of respect.'

'If you say so.'

'Hey, don't be like that,' asserted Louis. 'Aunty Gloria is an Elder, and it's proper to show her respect.'

'Says you,' muttered Tori, walking away.

Maggie called out to her sister, 'Come on, we're going to that concert. You promised not to argue any more, remember?'

Tori shrugged, and walked back to them. 'Let's go then.'

Louis had been quiet as they made their way to the concert, and immediately disappeared once they got there. Tori had noticed his silence, and suspected he was annoyed with her. On reflection, Tori knew she'd been rude, even if she didn't mean to. Perhaps Gloria was right; she had to deal with the past, to heal herself. She sat on the lawn listening to the bands, while Maggie went to talk with some friends. Tori glanced at her sister, wondering why she was always popular. She'd also been the popular one at the country schools they'd gone to. Tori had noticed at the centre today, and then the march, how accepting people were of Maggie. Tori remembered times strangers had sneered at her, ignored her or, worse, threw slurs her way. Growing up, she'd sometimes felt jealous of Maggie. Even if some people didn't believe they were twins, Tori thought they were both attractive, in their own way. Despite that, her sister didn't get treated the same way, made to feel like she didn't belong. Even today, Tori felt like an outsider. She knew Gloria was right: she didn't know enough about culture and being respectful. Or, thought Tori, perhaps she didn't like being in her own skin.

Maggie sat down at the same time Louis appeared.

'Seen Marcie over there?' he said, pointing his chin to his left.

Tori shrugged. 'I'll see her tomorrow, at work.'

Louis frowned, and turned towards Maggie. They began to talk about the huge crowd at the protest, and the speeches they'd heard. Both claimed that this day was a turning point in history, the time for finally achieving Aboriginal rights. When the last band finished, Tori got up and headed towards home. Maggie said a quick goodbye to Louis, but he insisted on escorting them back to the treehouse. Once they got there, Maggie pulled down the rope ladder.

'Can we walk for a bit more?' Louis asked Tori. 'I need to tell you something that's been on my mind.'

She hesitated, then nodded. At the pond, they sat on a bench. Tori could hear ducks in nearby bushes, settling after their disturbed slumber. Louis picked up a pebble and threw it. In the dark, the series of ripples it made as it skimmed across the pond were hard to see.

Louis shifted slightly. 'Why do you have to be so unfriendly to people lately? And what's with being rude to Aunty Gloria?'

'I don't know. Guess I just feel uncomfortable being around those people.'

'"Those people"? What's that even mean? Are you ashamed to be black?'

Tori watched the moon's reflection on the pond. 'I hate how people treat me bad because of my skin. How they don't accept me.'

'Yeah, I hate that too, but this is our mob you were being rude to. Today was all about our people, our futures. You're the one who's not being accepting of others.'

'It's not that. I don't know what's going on in my head. Today made me think about people I miss. Sad thoughts, mostly. I'm sorry. Didn't mean to take it out on anyone, truly.'

'Do you mean your mother? Maggie told me what happened.'

'That was supposed to be kept quiet,' declared Tori, standing up. 'I'm going to have words with her.'

'Stop. Sit down. It's her story too. You both lost your mum. Maggie has a right to grieve. Keeping loss a secret isn't how you get through grief.'

'Gloria said something similar to me today. She thinks my sadness has become rage.'

'Aunty is wise,' said Louis. 'She can help, if you let her.'

'She offered. I'm not ready, though.'

Louis put his hand by his side, accidently brushing Tori's hand. She quickly moved it.

'Why do you do that?' asked Louis.

'What?'

'React like you've been burnt whenever people get too close. It's like touching repulses you, or something. Or is it just me that you do that to?'

'I'm just not into touching.'

'Have you always been like that? If you don't mind me asking,' Louis said softly.

Louis saw a single tear rolling down her cheek, the moonlight making it shimmer like quicksilver.

'I've heard him yelling, seen the way he treats you. Has Andrés done anything else to you?' Louis asked.

Tori scratched her left wrist. Louis had noticed her scratching before. His parents had sometimes scratched, and had marks on their arms. Louis was sure Tori was not like them. Then again, that Andrés, or some of the people who hung out at his gallery, could have introduced her to intravenous drugs. Louis became even more concerned, but knew from experience that prying was not how to help someone with addiction.

Tori said, 'I know you care about Maggie and me, but I'm okay.'

'Maggie told me some other things. Not much, just a bit. She mentioned you'd been living with an old guy, a photographer, and it was him who killed your mother. I got the feeling there was something else Maggie wasn't sharing. Did that man hurt you?'

382

'What do you mean?'

'You know. Like, did you touch you and...'

'Did he molest me? Did he leave me broken? Is that what you're wanting to hear?'

'Something made you dislike physical closeness.'

Tori stood up. 'There's more than one way to break a girl.'

Louis shook his head as she stormed off. He was annoyed with himself. This was not how he envisaged the conversation going. As he walked back to Brother Eddie's place, Louis decided to talk it over with him in the morning, to get some big brother advice. Being the friend Tori needed wasn't easy.

***

Tori opened the jar of bush rub and noticed it was almost empty. She thought about how she could get more without the awkwardness of asking Maggie or Gloria, because it was obviously working. Shrugging, Tori smeared some on the side of her face and then her left wrist. Maggie yawned, so Tori quickly put the jar away.

'Are you on morning shift?' asked Maggie, from their bed. 'A bit early, isn't it?'

'No, you slept in.'

Maggie got up. 'Did you eat?'

Tori shook her head. 'I can grab something on the way to work.'

'See you later, then.'

Tori said goodbye and climbed down the tree. She noticed the black-and-white bird had returned. She had been wondering where that little bird had disappeared to. She'd hoped it had found love and was starting a family, and not fallen prey to a street cat. It followed her until she reached the edge of the park, and then flew off.

*

Hardly anyone had come into the gallery all morning. Tori watched the clock, willing it to speed up to the time Marcie was due to relieve her. Even though she'd expected Marcie's arrival, Tori jumped when she walked through the door.

'I'm here,' Marcie called out.

'Me too,' declared Ana, following her.

Sybil and Angie then walked in, carrying large paper bags.

'Not seen you for a while,' Tori remarked to Angie.

'I've been busy,' replied Angie.

Sybil put down the bags she'd been carrying. 'Go on, show her. I know you just can't wait to show that rock off to yet another person.'

'You're just jealous,' Angie claimed.

Tori asked, 'Show me what?'

'My engagement ring. Isn't it just the dreamiest diamond ever,' Angie said, holding out her hand.

'Who's pouring the drinks?' asked Marcie.

Glasses appeared, as did a bottle of champagne.

Marcie looked at Tori. 'Where's sour puss?'

'Andrés? He's gone out. Won't be back until tomorrow.'

'Great,' said Sybil, as she shut the front door and turned the sign to closed.

'Hey, wouldn't it be fun to play dress-ups? Andrés has a trunk full of props in the studio,' said Angie.

They picked up the bags and walked towards the studio, leaving behind a trail of spilt champagne. They quickly rummaged through the large trunk, trying on different items. Angie sampled every hat, before settling on a pink one with white bows. Marcie found a fake moustache and teamed it with a top hat. Sybil, wearing a glittering gown that she couldn't zip up all the way, bowed to Marcie before sweeping her away in a waltz.

Ana asked, 'Do you mind if I take a few photos?'

Everyone nodded, except for Tori. She took off the purple boa she'd put on, and put it back in the trunk.

As she walked towards the door, Marcie said, 'You don't have to be in any photos. Just hang out with us.'

Tori nodded. She then smiled as Angie and Sybil made silly faces in front of Ana and the camera. Marcie refilled Tori's glass.

'I've been wondering about the name of this place,' Tori remarked.

'Galería de rebelde?' asked Ana.

'Yes. What's it actually mean?'

Ana responded, 'Rebel Gallery.'

'Why not just write that on the sign?'

'Because Andrés is a phoney,' offered Marcie.

'He has some talent, though,' remarked Ana. 'As a photographer myself, I can say that about his work.'

Marcie commented, 'Sure, but he's still ridiculous.'

Sybil asked, 'Tori, do you know his name isn't even Andrés Califa?'

'It isn't?'

'No, it's Andrew King. He thinks Andrés sounds artier, or something,' said Sybil.

'I told you,' said Marcie. 'A huge pretender.'

'Hey, I changed my name too,' declared Ana.

Angie countered, 'You shortened it, that's not the same thing.'

Tori asked Ana, 'What is your name?'

'Anastasia.'

'I like that. It's pretty,' said Tori. 'I shortened mine too.'

'What's yours?' asked Angie.

'Victoria. I was named after my grandfather's mother. I never got to meet him, but I was born the same place he was. Same place my mum was born.'

'Where's that?' asked Sybil.

'In the desert, somewhere north-west. Don't remember much. I was just a baby when we left there.'

'Why don't you ask your mum?' suggested Angie.

Marcie noticed the look on Tori's face, and swept in with more champagne. 'Who's hungry? This bubbly needs something to go with it.'

Sybil helped Marcie get cheeses, dips and crackers out of the bags, and set it all up on the benches in the studio.

Ana grinned. 'Annndreeew would be livid if he saw all this mess.'

Marcie laughed. 'He won't find out. We can easily get rid of all signs of this little party before we leave.'

'Tori, be in a photo with me,' pleaded Angie. 'It will be fun. Pretty please.'

'I'm not sure,' Tori replied, feeling slightly inebriated.

Angie handed her a bright-red wig. 'Come on, just for a laugh.'

Tori put the wig on. It was long and straight. She then picked up a gold dress and put it on over her clothes.

'Straight hair suits you,' remarked Angie.

Marcie picked up a cracker and cube of cheese. 'So does Tori's natural hair.'

'Sure,' said Angie. 'I didn't mean anything rude or, you know...'

Marcie smiled. 'Don't sweat it, Angie.'

'Tori, stand a bit closer to Angie. Now smile. That's it,' said Ana, from behind the camera.

At first, Tori felt self-conscious as Ana took her photo. She soon relaxed, though, and tried to copy Angie's poses. After a while, Ana put down her camera and filled up her glass. They sat on props in the studio, talking all at once. Tori's head started to spin, as much from the noise as the alcohol. Tori went over to the counter, thinking food might sober her up a little.

'Tori,' said Sybil, taking a small zipped bag out of her large handbag, 'I can show you how to cover that redness on your face.'

Unsure at first, Tori agreed. After Sybil covered the inflamed skin, she applied make up to Tori's eyes, lips and cheeks. Once done, Sybil handed Tori a mirror. Ana picked up her camera and took a few photos. Tori didn't even notice, she was too busy looking in the mirror.

'You're glowing,' smiled Ana.

Tori smiled. 'I can't believe this is still me.'

'It's you, honey. Radiantly beautiful. You shine all the time, you just haven't noticed before,' said Marcie.

'What the hell is going on!'

They all jumped. Andrés stood in the doorway, scowling at the mess. Angie and Sybil scurried about, picking up the clothing scattered around the room. Andrés didn't even notice, as he was glaring at Tori. She took off the red wig, hoping he'd stop staring.

'Modelling is not my thing,' Andrés said mockingly to Tori.

Marcie said, 'Leave her be.'

'You stay out of this,' Andrés bellowed.

'No, I won't.'

'And I'm not staying out of this, either,' claimed Ana, hands on hips.

Andrés turned towards Ana, his upper lip curling in a sneer.

Ana lifted her chin. 'You act as if you've made it, but you're still that boy in patched hand-me-down pants, watching from afar, hoping we'll let you play with us. It wasn't because your mother cleaned our houses that we didn't invite you to join us. You were cruel and selfish then, just like now.'

'Shut up.'

'I won't, Andrew. If it wasn't for me telling my father how good your photos were, you'd be working for a picture-framer or something less artistic. It was his generosity that allowed you go to art school. It was my family that opened a door for you into the arts circle, and helped you set up your career.'

'It was my hard work and skills that got me here.'

'And where is here, Andrew? My father owns this building. One word from me, and he'd evict you.'

'You wouldn't dare.'

'Wouldn't I? Managing my own gallery might be a bit of fun. Plus, the studio space and darkroom are bigger than what I have at home,' observed Ana, putting the lens cap back on her camera. 'I know a few people who'd help me get started.'

'Count me in,' said Angie. 'That's if I'm not too busy being a blissful newlywed.'

Sybil suggested, 'Maybe you could give Andrew a job, Ana. Cleaner, perhaps? His mother probably taught him the trade.'

'Or a model,' said Angie, picking up a boa and draping it around his shoulders.

They all started laughing. Andrés pulled off the boa and threw it across the room. It knocked over an open bottle of champagne, which spilt onto the ground, making them laugh even harder.

'You stupid trollops,' shouted Andrés.

'Trollops?' said Ana. 'This isn't the nineteenth century, Andrew. I think you mean divine divas.'

'Or sumptuous sirens,' declared Sybil.

Angie added, 'I quite like beautiful belles.'

Andrés opened his mouth to speak, but turned around and left instead. The sound of the front door slamming set them off into uncontrollable laughter.

The wind whispered through the bloodwood tree, bringing story after story. A warm breeze gently teased the old woman's hair: Tell this one; don't forget this one; they need to know this. *She lifted the blanket, tucking it under the chins of the sleeping toddlers. Victoria wriggled, an arm reaching out from the cocoon her great-grandmother had made, fist clenched. And then she settled back to sleep.*

Nana Vic leant back against the trunk of the tree. Lines of deep red ran down the trunk, dried sap holding the memory of past wounds. Scattered at the base were remnants of desert apples, the tasty grub inside having been eaten by others who'd sat here recently. Someone had once told her these grubs didn't taste like coconuts, but Nana Vic wouldn't know if this was true, as she'd never seen or eaten a coconut. Having never left Country, there were a lot of things that she'd not seen.

'You have to see all the things for me,' she whispered to Victoria. 'You're a wanderer, just like your grandfather. Just like that stubborn mother of yours.'

Victoria grunted in her sleep, causing her nana to laugh softly.

Nana Vic turned her attention to Maggie. 'And this little bub, she'll go with you, taking the stories with her. Don't worry if you forget them, dear Maggie. As long as you carry these stories, you and your sister will be all right.'

NINETEEN

Entering the gallery, Tori heard raised voices coming from Andrés's office. She knew it was Andrés shouting, and the other voice was Marcie's. Tori put her ear on the office door.

'You can't, Andrés. It's morally repugnant, and probably illegal.'

'I bought the negatives off a cop, so of course they're not illegal.'

'No doubt a corrupt cop. And did you ask Ana? I didn't think so. Did you steal her photos?'

'She left the negatives here, after using my darkroom. Ana should be grateful her work will be exhibited alongside such a famous photographer's work.'

'He was clearly a degenerate. Those photos are exploitative of minors. And that photo there, that's a goddamn lynching. You purchased crime scene photos from a crooked cop. How can you even consider exhibiting these?'

'Don't be so closed-minded, Marcie. It's art.'

'It's really not. Put these on display, and someone will call the police.'

'I can control access to the small gallery. Only invited guests will be able to see this exhibition. It will be all right.'

'How? Nothing about this is all right. And what about her? Imagine how she'll react when she sees these."

'Keep your mouth shut and she won't know.'

'You've gone too far this time, Andrew. These photos are repulsive depravity.'

'These images were his finest work. They need to be seen, to be contemplated. I owe a lot to him. His work inspired me when I was just beginning. I was even fortunate to have been mentored by him, for a short while.'

'I don't care about that degenerate. I care about those girls. Distorting blackness for his macabre exoticism is disturbing. This won't go unnoticed.'

'Get off your soapbox. Your black-power nonsense won't work here. Our blacks are too lazy to rise up.'

'You're a racist bastard, Andrew.'

'Isn't it time you were leaving? Your shift is over.'

'I'm leaving now. And going straight to the authorities. If you won't listen to me, then maybe some time in a cold cell will help you see reason.'

Opening the door, she saw Tori a few feet away. Whatever they'd been fighting about in the office, Tori noticed that it had made Marcie agitated.

'Hon, don't go in there. And don't go near the small gallery. Promise me you won't.'

Tori said, 'Why not?'

'Just trust me, okay? I'll make sure he's punished for this.'

Marcie walked to the counter and retrieved her handbag. She opened a drawer, and collected the personal items she stored there.

'I'm not coming back here. I'm done with him. You need to get out of here too.'

Tori shook her head. 'I can't. I need the money.'

'I'll give you money, anything you need to get away from that evil man. Go home, to your family.'

'I don't know where they live. All I have is my sister.'

'Look, I'll help you get away from here. I've got something urgent to do first. Meet me at my place after work. Okay?'

Tori nodded. Marcie picked up her bag and hurried out. Walking past the office, Tori heard Andrés on the phone. His voice was muffled, but Tori heard him say something about "dealing with" Marcie. She crept over to the small gallery and turned the handle. The door was locked.

'You stay out of there,' barked Andrés, from his office doorway. 'If I find you anywhere near that space, you're fired. Understand?'

Tori nodded, and looked at the floor. She'd never seen him this agitated before.

'I'll be out for the rest of the day. Lock the front door when your shift is over.'

*

Tori went to Marcie's flat after work, as promised. She knocked a few times but no one answered. The door opposite opened slightly, and an old woman peered out from the crack. The woman opened the door wider and stepped into the corridor.

'She's gone. They took her away.'

'Pardon?' asked Tori.

'The police. They took her. They made a right mess of the place when they searched it. They must have found what they wanted by the time two men in suits arrived, because they all left shortly after, taking Marcie with them.'

'Do you know where they took her?'

'No idea, but I don't think they plan on letting her return. I heard them tell Marcie to pack her belongings. Maybe she overstayed her visa? Can't imagine her doing anything criminal. She was a good neighbour.'

***

Tori was surprised to see Angie already in the gallery when she arrived for the morning shift. Before she could say anything, Andrés came out of his office.

'You're to work a full day today, to show Angie how to manage sales. She'll be taking over Marcie's shifts.'

'It will be so much fun working together,' said Angie breezily.

Tori frowned. 'What about Marcie?'

'She's gone. You're both to stay out of the small gallery. View ing the works in there will be by invitation only. I've hired people to help at the launch, so there's no need to come to that. I'll be in my office all day and I don't want to be disturbed.'

Angie whispered, 'What a grumpy boss.'

'Always rude, occasionally shouty.'

'We'll soon show him how to treat women.'

'If Marcie couldn't sort him out, not sure we can. Angie, I'm really worried about her. I went to her flat last night. A neighbour told me the police took her away.'

'Really? Maybe Ana can make some enquiries. Her family is friends with lawyers and important people.'

'Simone might know something?'

'Yes, we could get a message to her through Simone.'

'Marcie and Andrés had a big fight yesterday. I think it was over that upcoming exhibition in the small gallery.'

Angie whispered, 'It's so weird he's told us to keep out. We should look in there, when he's not around.'

'The door is always locked now. And I need this job, so I'm not doing anything that will get me fired.'

'If you change your mind, I know how to pick locks. For now, you'd better show me what I need to do around here.'

'It's not hard,' said Tori. 'This gallery doesn't get many visitors.'

'Probably because of grumbles over there,' suggested Angie, looking towards the closed office door.

'Tori, I need some help,' stated Ana, walking into the gallery.

Tori noticed Ana was flustered, which was most unlike her.

Ana said, 'The negatives, from that day we dressed up, I can't find them.'

'Where did you see them last?' asked Angie.

'Here. I developed the film in Andrés's darkroom. Mine is getting repainted at the moment. I was sure I took them home with me.'

'You were told not to disturb me today,' grumbled Andrés, as he walked out of the office. 'Oh, it's you.'

Ana said, 'I've lost some negatives. Have you seen them?'

'You left them in the darkroom. I put them in my safe. Wait here, I'll get them.'

*

The rest of the working day was uneventful. Tori had enjoyed working with Angie, but it wasn't the same as the times she'd spent with Marcie. She'd let Angie go home early, after Andrés had left for the day; she needed that last hour of silence. After locking the front door, Tori was surprised to see Simone at the nearby bus shelter.

'Simone! Is Marcie here too?'

'That bastard had her deported,' Simone said. 'He dobbed her in for running a hairdressing business in the flat. Marcie didn't have a working visa, so Immigration put her on a plane today.'

'Is she all right?'

Simone nodded. 'We were planning on leaving the country, anyway. It won't take me long to pack up our flat. I've got a work transfer, so I'll be joining her soon. She wanted me to tell you something before I left.'

'What?'

'She was only allowed a quick phone call, so it's a bit confusing. Something about she tried to tell the police about those photos, but no one would listen. She warned you to stay out of the small room. Do not look at those photos, but the evidence to get justice is in that room and the negatives are in the safe.'

'I don't understand.'

'Neither do I. Was hoping you would. Marcie insisted you have to get the police to go in that room.'

'I'm confused. I wish Marcie was still here. She was one of my few friends.'

'You should leave too. He's a horrible person. Go home, Tori.'

'I don't have a home.'

'Everyone has a home; you just haven't found it yet.'

***

The community centre appeared to be empty. She was about to leave when she saw a figure going past the window. She went outside and walked down the side of the main building, towards the big shed out the back. The door was open, so Tori peeked in.

'You can come in. I won't bite.'

Tori saw Gloria up the back, opening what appeared to be an enormous oven.

'These should be cooked just right,' she said, picking up oversized tongs.

Gloria reached in and pulled out a large urn. She placed in on a circle of sand, and went back to the oven. After pulling out three more pieces of pottery, she put down the tongs. She wiped sweat off her forehead with the back of her hand.

'Once they're cool, I'll paint designs on them. Lizards, snakes, birds, wattles. Like the ones over there.'

Tori looked at urns and pots of many sizes on a bench. 'Did you make all these?'

Gloria nodded. 'With that potter's wheel.'

Tori went over to look closely at the wheel, before sticking her finger in a clump of clay that was in a bucket next to it.

'Would you like to learn?'

'Is it hard?'

'Not really. Like everything, just takes someone to show you the way and a bit of practice.'

'Would you show me?'

Gloria sat down on a stool. 'I could, if you promise to listen. Do you?'

Tori nodded, already imagining her first urn. Wide and tall, with an eagle painted on it.

'Can you show me other things too? Like you mentioned at the protest?'

'First, you need to call me Aunty. That's respect. That's our way.'

'Yes, Aunty.'

*

When Tori left an hour later, she felt exhausted. She knew there was a lot of work ahead of her, but she felt more confident, and hopeful. Tori understood now that she'd let grief and loss simmer, unaddressed, for too long. Now she felt ready to let go and start to heal. Deep in thought, she hadn't noticed Louis until she almost bumped into him.

'Look out,' he laughed.

Tori took a step back. 'Sorry.'

'No harm done.'

'I mean sorry for the other day. When we were sitting by the duck pond after the concert, and I walked off in a mood.'

'Oh, that.'

'I know you were just trying to help. I shouldn't have been so rude to you. I'm not ready yet, but one day I'll tell you more things from my past.'

'You don't have to, but I'll be around if you ever need someone to talk to.'

'Hey, do you want to come to our place for dinner tonight?'

Louis nodded. 'Walk there now with you, or should I come over later?'

'Now is fine.'

They talked all the way there, filling each other in on things they'd been doing recently, until they reached the park. Tori noticed the little black-and-white bird before she heard it. It hopped along, following them. She smiled. That bird had grown on her.

'Louis,' asked Tori, when they'd reached the bench at the duck pond.

'Yes?'

'There's something I want to clear up.'

Louis sat down. 'Okay.'

'I get the feeling that you like me,' she said, sitting next to him.

'Of course I do, we're friends.'

'No, I mean like like.'

Louis fell quiet, gazing at the ducks on the pond. One made a V-shape in the water as it swam quickly towards him. *Probably expecting bread,* Louis thought. He was glad that Tori had been the one to bring up this difficult subject and not him, but he was anxious about how the conversation would go.

'I do have feelings for you,' he said softly. 'I've really tried not to, because I think you don't have similar feelings for me.'

'There's nothing wrong with liking me in that way, it's just I'm unsure about these types of things. I don't know what romance or attraction feels like. I don't think I can have those types of feelings, for anyone.'

'Can we still be friends?'

'Of course,' Tori answered.

Louis picked up a pebble and skimmed it across the pond. Tori watched it bounce across the water's surface one time, two times, three. Even after the pebble sank under the water, the ripples created circles within circles at those three places. The patterns reminded her of a painting she'd just seen in the art shed at the community centre.

'I went and spoke with Aunty Gloria today. She's going to help me learn not to be so angry and defensive.'

'Aunty is good with that sort of help. She helped me see what I need to do. Brother Eddie helped too.'

'What are you going to do?'

'Well, I just got some good news. My nan wrote back. She wants me to go home, and I want to be there.'

'When do you leave?'

'Soon. Eddie's helping me with travel arrangements.'

Tori watched a duck and her ducklings climb up onto the grass and waddle towards them. She suddenly had a pang. She didn't know what it was, but it made her chest hurt. Tori instinctively put a hand over where the pain was.

'Are you okay?' asked Louis, looking at her with concern.

She nodded, the pain having vanished as quick as it had appeared. 'Just anxiety, I guess. Gloria talked about how worry or fear can feel like physical pain, and told me to focus on the thoughts I might have had just before the pain.'

'I used to get those too. Before I had Gloria and Brother Eddie teaching me new ways of dealing with things.'

'I want to meet this brother. Maybe he can help me find my mother's mother. Maybe he can help me get home too.'

'If anyone can, it would be him.'

'I hope so. For now, let's get that dinner I promised you.'

As they walked towards the treehouse, Tori didn't notice the small bird that landed on the grass beside her bird companion. And she didn't notice them fly off together.

TWENTY

Angie was frivolous, chatty and spontaneous. So unlike Marcie. Tori couldn't share her thoughts freely with Angie, as she had begun to do with Marcie. The way the world treated them was too different. Angie wasn't even aware of these differences. She seemed to have no idea that inequality or oppression existed, let alone an awareness of racism. Angie mostly talked about her upcoming wedding, which wasn't of much interest to Tori. Still, Tori liked Angie and listened to her expanding plans.

When Angie walked out the door earlier, she'd whispered to Tori that Andrés was in one of his foul moods. It was now nearing closing time and Tori still hadn't seen him. She had a sudden thought that perhaps he'd gone out by the back door. She got up and went towards the office. She could hear Andrés's voice. He wasn't speaking loudly, but Tori could still tell he was annoyed about something. There were no other voices, so Tori assumed he was on the phone. She put an ear to the door. Andrés said something about not giving back the negatives, which puzzled Tori, as he had already returned Ana's negatives. Then he said, to the person on the other end of the phone, that he'd paid good money for them and would not pay a single cent more.

He raised his voice: 'No, I won't tell you where they live, Peters. And stay away from here. I don't need you distracting my employee.'

Tori tried to think where she'd heard the name Peters before.

Andrés laughed into the phone. 'Are you attempting to blackmail me? Your position doesn't scare me, Senior Sergeant Peters. I have contacts higher than a cop.'

Tori heard Andrés swear and slam down the phone. He was muttering to himself and walking around the office. Tori hurried back to the sales counter, in case he came out and found her eavesdropping. She suddenly remembered a policeman named Peters. Constable Peters had been a friend of von Wolff's. Tori shuddered. Not just at the unwelcome thought of von Wolff, but also of Peters. She'd never liked him. The way he'd look at her always felt wrong. The way he'd sometimes watch Maggie had unnerved her more. If this police officer was the same Peters, then Tori knew she had to make sure he'd never find out where she and Maggie lived. Tori looked at the clock and was relieved to see it was closing time. She shouted goodbye to Andrés and locked the front door, before running down the street. She had to find Louis; he would know what to do.

The community centre was locked when Tori arrived, so she asked some children in the playground if they knew where Brother Eddie lived. It didn't take her long to get there. Tori saw Louis leaving the house just as she turned the corner.

'Louis!' she called out.

He turned. 'Hey. How'd you find me?'

'Wasn't hard. I need to talk with you. It's urgent.'

'Do you want to come in? Eddie's out.'

Tori followed Louis inside. He showed her to the lounge room, and went into the adjacent kitchen.

'What's up?' he asked, returning with two glasses of water.

'I overheard something just now and it got me worried. Andrés was speaking on the phone to a cop called Peters. Something about negatives.'

'I don't get it.'

'I need to tell you some other things before it can make sense. It's not going to be easy telling you this, or listening to it.'

A while later, Louis felt overwhelmed. He'd offered a few times to listen to whatever had happened to her in the past, but this was not at all what he'd suspected. And now she wanted his opinion. Louis felt this situation was beyond him. Tori sat quietly, eager for his response.

He suggested, 'I think someone needs to look in that room. Marcie warned you not to go in there. Perhaps I should.'

'Think it should be me who does.'

'I know nothing I say will change your mind, so I'll go with you. When?'

Before Tori could answer, the front door opened.

'Are you home, Louis?' came a deep male voice.

'In here, Brother. With a friend.'

*

The moment Eddie saw Tori he remembered a photo of a young woman and a promise made. A promise to a grieving mother, in the west, where he'd once lived. Mrs Browne had heard she had twin granddaughters while keeping vigil at her youngest son's side. The accident that had befallen her son Patrick was tragic. Patrick, a local member of parliament, had made promises to a developer who wanted to build a country retreat. He'd offered to sell him the land the family orchard was on. He became frustrated when he wasn't able to, as his grandmother's cottage and the orchard had been left to his sister Brigid. Their mother had not heard from Brigid in many years. Still, she refused to go through the legal process of declaring her deceased. So Patrick intended to sell the orchard behind his mother's back.

The developer and his senior executives had driven up from the city on the west coast to see the land. When Patrick began to show them around the property, he'd felt peculiar rumblings under his feet. Even if he'd known this movement was his grandmother turning in her grave, Patrick wouldn't have reconsidered his intentions. The rumblings were soon joined by tree branches loudly creaking. Seeing the worried looks on the visitors' faces, Patrick had assured them everything was fine, but they'd run to their cars yelling at their chauffeurs to take them back to the city. His plans ruined, Patrick punched the nearest tree. The shock as the shower of apples pelted him was short-lived, as a large red apple had struck Patrick on the temple, knocking him to the ground.

Hours later, Patrick's parents had found him under a pile of apples. His mother stayed by Patrick's side, as his father went to call an ambulance. It was then that Patrick confessed to his mother. It was not the shady deals he had done as a politician, nor the many lies he'd told as a child, that was on his mind. It was telling his sister to never come home. Patrick knew how much Brigid needed family, he'd heard it in her voice, but still he'd told his sister that no one wanted her around. His mother had cried as he confessed, and cried some more when Patrick told her that she had twin granddaughters. By the time Patrick had taken his last breath, she had no more tears to cry.

A week after Patrick was laid to rest, Margaret told a novice brother about her son's confession. She'd shown him a photo of her daughter, and believed her granddaughters would be just as beautiful. Brother Eddie had promised to find Brigid and her daughters, and to bring them home. He'd never forgotten this promise made many years ago. This young woman before him was the spitting image of the woman in the photo. He could now complete that promise he'd made to Mrs Browne.

***

Tori paused to look at her sister, sitting alone on a long metal bench, surrounded by an eclectic assortment of bags. Tori had told Maggie not to worry, that she'd be back in time. Tori glanced up at the large clock on the bus station wall, then took off. Running around the corner, she bumped into Louis.

He asked, 'Where you going in such a hurry?

'I've got something to do before we leave.'

'What's so important? Your bus leaves in just over an hour.'

'I know, so I don't have time to talk. You can join me or wait with Maggie.'

'Let's go, then.'

The city streets were almost empty, as was often the case for late Sunday afternoon. Tori raced ahead, intent on seeing what Andrés had in the locked room. When she got to the gallery, Tori went down the back alley. She stopped under a small window that was slightly ajar.

When Louis caught up to her, Tori said, 'I left that unlocked yesterday. If you give me a leg-up, I can climb in, turn off the alarm and let you in the back door.'

Louis put his hands together, palms up, for Tori to step on, then hoisted her up. She didn't take long to pull the window open and wriggle through. Louis stood by the door, waiting for her. The alarm went off, just for a few seconds.

She opened the back door. 'Oops. Hope no one heard that.'

Outside the small gallery, she turned the handle, hoping Andrés had forgotten to lock it. Cussing, she tried to find something to break open the door open.

'Move aside,' urged Louis, taking out a thin piece of wire from his pocket.

Tori expressed surprise at how quickly Louis picked the lock.

'Don't ask,' he said, grinning.

Tori entered the windowless room first, turning on the lights. She stood frozen, with a hand still on the light switch, eyes wide. Louis glanced around the room.

'We need to get out of here. Marcie was right. You shouldn't be looking at these photos.'

Tori shook her head. 'I have to.'

Louis stayed by the door as Tori walked further into the room. Closest to the door were the photos Ana had taken of her. Tori eyes moved to the next image. Beside a large blackand-white photo of Tori, taken by Ana, was a black-and-white shot of Brigid. She guessed von Wolff had taken this. She stared at the image of her mother. Although she was much younger than Brigid had been when this photo was taken, the similarities were uncanny. Including the shape of the scarring on their faces. Tori's hand unconsciously went to her cheek. It felt hot, and she began to feel dizzy and unsteady on her feet. Louis moved quickly to stand behind her, lifting a hand towards her back. He paused, uncertain, then placed his hand on her shoulder.

'Thanks,' she whispered, straightening herself again.

Inhaling, Tori moved to the next photo, with Louis by her side. It was a picture of her, Maggie and their mother. She thought von Wolff must have taken a candid shot, as they wouldn't have been so carefree if he'd been in sight. Tears rolled down Tori's cheek. She raised a hand, touching the glass that imprisoned this happier moment from her past.

The next photos were a series of four photos of her mother, most likely taken on the same day, as she wore the same dress. Tori examined her mother's expression. Brigid's eyes were ablaze with a steely hatred, as she stared into von Wolff's camera lens.

Tori instinctively stood straighter, head held high, as she'd done as a child; as she'd seen her mother do many times. Despite that look of strength, in these photos Tori also saw weariness in her mother's face. Tori wiped away a tear. She suddenly recalled all the times she'd blamed her mother: for not leaving von Wolff, for leaving them. Gabriel had tried to convince Tori that her mother did the best she could. That it was debt that had kept their mother trapped; and that von Wolff had threatened to have them put in an orphanage if their mother left. He tried to get Tori to see things differently, to see from her mother's point of view. To forgive.

Tori then thought about Andrés. How mean he was to her. How she had known many months earlier that she should leave, that she deserved more, but still she didn't leave. She thought of the way he'd fetishised her and Marcie, while also treating them as below him. After he'd got Marcie deported, Tori no longer had a friend to lift her up. Instead, she'd begun to believe that the way that Andrés and Stefan had treated her was what she deserved.

'I understand now,' she whispered. 'I know how they grind us down, until we begin to forget who we really are. Until we hate being in our own skin.'

Tori walked out the door, returning shortly after.

Louis asked, 'What's that?'

'Chemicals from the darkroom. The really flammable type, I hope. Have you got a light?'

'What are you planning to do?'

'To burn this place down, of course.'

'Don't do it, Tori.'

Louis and Tori looked towards the doorway. Maggie stood there, catching her breath.

'What are you doing here?' asked Tori.

'I was worried you'd miss the bus. I had a feeling you'd come here.'

'You're just in time to watch this all burn,' remarked Tori.

'No, you can't fix the past by repeating the past.'

'I can try, and have some fun while trying.'

'Let's just go. Leave all the bad moments behind,' pleaded Maggie.

'Look at us. Do you not see us on these walls? The past won't let me have some peace until these images are destroyed.'

'That's not us. It's just a wicked man's false image of us. We are not these photos.'

Louis said, 'Listen to Maggie, please.'

'Why? She has no idea how much this hurts,' replied Tori, indicating the photos on the wall.

Maggie walked into the room. 'Don't I? That's my image up there too. Did he not also treat me appallingly?'

'It wasn't the same. It's never been the same.'

'Look again at the photos. Can you remember all the many times I cried myself to sleep? Do you really believe that von Wolff didn't cause me pain as well?'

Maggie stood next to Tori, as she moved to the next set of photos. And then the next. Each one took Tori back in time, to a place she'd resisted revisiting. There she was, dressed as von Wolff's vision of a noble savage: leaning on a spear, her foot resting on her bare thigh, hair unruly, face painted in a mockery of culture. Sifting her gaze, Tori noticed her sister in that same photo: sprawled on the ground, white gown ripped at the bodice, exposing a hint of skin over a whalebone corset. Then she looked at the next photo: Maggie was in a white safari suit and pith helmet, with a false moustache and holding a large antique rifle, while she sat on the ground at her sister's feet, bare from the waist up, heavy chains around her neck.

'He tried to portray me as victim to your villain, or conqueror to conquered. White against black. Sister against sister,' whispered Maggie. 'Am I not an Aboriginal woman too? Or do you see me as he saw me?'

416

'No, of course not. I know it was tough on you, but you can't know what it was like for Mum and me.'

'I'm not saying I know how it felt, but I saw how hard it was for you both. Like in that town on the gibber plains, when we were younger. The townsfolk accepted me because they saw me as white, like them, while they barely tolerated you and Mum. I saw all that. I knew how much you were hurting. It hurt me too. We're twins. The same blood flows through our veins. Same blood as our mother and father.'

Tori shouted, 'You don't know what it's like to be in this skin!'

'I know I haven't experienced racism, like you have. If I could, I would willingly punish everyone who hurt you, and who hurt our mother. I don't know what it feels like for you to walk in such an intolerant world, but I have been beside you since we took our first breath together. I know that doors shut in your face will stay open for me. Slurs thrown at you will rarely be said to me. The way people ignore my identity is painful, but unlike you, I'll never be discriminated against because of the colour of my skin.'

Tori took Maggie's hand and squeezed it. 'I'd forgotten how you stood up for me in the school playground. You were so little and so fierce.'

Still holding hands, they moved to the next images. While they were examining the photos, Louis collected the bottles of chemicals Tori had placed on the ground, and walked towards the door. He was surprised to encounter Brother Eddie standing there, an expression of sorrow on his normally serene face. Eddie reached out and squeezed Louis's shoulder gently, giving him a nod. He then walked into the room, the twins unaware of his presence. Eddie scanned the walls, visibly shocked by the images. Each photo was seemingly worse than the other, as if Andrés had laid out a path of ascending depravity. Eddie noticed that the twins now stood before a black curtain on the wall. Tori's hand reached out, to lift the veil.

'Stop,' said Eddie firmly.

They both tried to blink away the horrors they'd seen, before refocusing on a friendly face.

'Come on, let's leave this behind,' he suggested.

Maggie moved towards Eddie, still holding her sister's hand. When Tori did not budge, Maggie stopped.

Eddie said firmly, 'Don't look under that cloth, Tori. It won't bring your mother back. It will just scar you.'

Tori shouted, 'Am I not already scarred? My face might have healed, but I will always carry the scars of what that man did!'

Maggie went to Louis, who was still standing in the doorway, while Eddie walked towards Tori. Standing not too close, giving her the space she needed. The pain he saw in her eyes almost brought him to tears.

Taking a deep breath, he remarked, 'With time, all scars fade. Pain is forgotten. Right now it might seem impossible, but you will know happiness again, one day.'

'Don't patronise me.'

'That's not my intent.'

'Then get out of the way, so I can look at the remaining photos.'

'You've seen enough.'

'I need to look. Our mum needs a witness.'

'Then let me do it.'

Tori paused, thinking. She then noticed the concern on Louis and Maggie's faces.

Tori sighed. 'You must tell me what you see. Promise?'

Eddie nodded. Tori went to stand with her sister and Louis. The twins stood either side of Louis, his arms around their shoulders, as they huddled in silence. Eddie reached for the curtain. Lifting it, he was noticeably shaken. His eyes scanned photo after photo, each more horrific than the last. Eddie's thoughts raced: *How can I keep the promise I just made? How does one describe a mother's lynching to her own children?*

As he walked towards them, Eddie hid his thoughts while the girls scanned his face for a sign of what was under the curtain. Having seen all these photos, he knew they'd survived experiences no young person should have to endure.

'What's under there?' Tori asked.

Eddie inhaled. 'Photos of your mother.'

Tori whispered, 'Do they show how he killed her?'

'Yes. I'm so sorry.'

Tori took a step forward, then stopped. 'I don't need to see them, do I?'

'No, you don't,' said Eddie. 'I will ensure your mother gets justice.'

'Justice was already served,' opined Tori. 'Von Wolff is dead.'

Maggie reached up, took a frame off the wall, ripped off the back and removed the photo. She held it up for Tori to see. It was the candid shot of them with their mother, the one of them smiling. Tori also selected a photo, of just their mother. Not the defiant pose, the image of her with a serene expression.

'This reminds me of Mum from our campfires and openroad days,' remarked Tori.

'I know I often whinged about the walking, but I actually liked those days. That when Mum and you were the happiest.'

Once everyone was back in the large gallery, Eddie found the switch and turned off the lights in the smaller room. The sun was setting, which reminded Tori they had a bus to catch.

'We need to get back to the station.'

'First, tell me how Andrés got these photos,' Brother Eddie said.

'It was that cop, Peters,' said Tori.

'The one who was friends with von Wolff?' asked Maggie.

'I'm sure it was the same Peters.'

'Do you know where Andrés keeps the negatives?' asked Eddie.

Louis chimed in: 'Tori, didn't Simone give you that message from Marcie, about how the police need to check the safe in Andrés office?'

Tori nodded in reply to Louis, then asked Eddie, 'Why do you want the negatives?'

'The photos made me realise you were the twins that I'd been told about.'

'Yes, you already told us about the promise you'd made to our mum's mother,' remarked Tori.

'No, there's more. You see, I met a man called Gabriel. Two years ago, while working as a prison chaplain. He told me a bit about a murder, and a fire. And how he'd been framed. Mostly, he spoke of twin girls he was worried about.'

Maggie cried, 'You saw him? Was he all right?'

'He'd been hoping to get out, so he could find you two. Instead, he was sentenced to a long term in prison. For double murder, arson and kidnapping. Peters had testified that Gabriel purposely set the studio on fire, to kill von Wolff. He declared the motive was to stop von Wolff telling the police that Gabriel had killed your mother.'

'What a liar. I always hated Peters,' said Tori.

Maggie added, 'Gabriel would never hurt anyone.'

'I know,' said Eddie. 'These photos and the negatives might be enough to get Gabriel a retrial. And get Peters charged with perjury for the false testimony. At some point, you might both need to return as witnesses.'

'We would do anything for Gabriel,' declared Maggie. 'For our mum to have justice, the name of her killer must be known.'

'What about Andrés?' Tori asked. 'Can you make sure he pays too?'

Eddie responded, 'Perhaps he'll be charged for possession and intent to display those photos. Leave this to me. You two have a bus to catch.'

422

Maggie hugged Eddie. 'Thanks for everything. You're amazing. First you found our grandmother, and now you're going to help free Gabriel.'

'Thanks,' said Tori.

Eddie smiled. 'It wasn't much at all.'

'It truly is everything. We now have a place to belong, and a grandmother to love us. How can we ever thank you, Brother Eddie?' asked Maggie.

'Just keep being deadly,' he said, grinning.

Tori and Maggie hugged him as he chuckled.

'Come on,' urged Louis, 'or you'll miss that bus.'

*

They left by the back door, and walked along the side of the gallery. As they neared the end of the street, Louis beckoned for Maggie and Tori to stop. Peeking around the corner, they saw Andrés talking to two police officers.

'Thank you, but I don't need any help,' said Andrés. 'I appreciate the gesture, but I'm sure that noise was nothing of concern.'

'We need to check it out. The person who called also reported seeing someone climb through a window,' one of the officers insisted.

'I can deal with this,' argued Andrés, just as the front door of the gallery opened.

'Ah, this saves me ringing the station,' said Eddie, as he walked outside.

Scowling, Andrés turned away from Eddie and noticed people-shaped shadows at the corner of the building. Louis grabbed Maggie and Tori by the hand, and started running. The police officers had followed Eddie inside, so no one noticed Andrés leave. Louis tripped over the lid of a rubbish bin. Andrés caught up to them, and hit Louis hard on the legs with his cane. As he raised his arm, preparing to strike again, Louis yelled at Maggie and Tori to keep running. Tori reached for Andrés's cane, but Maggie pulled her away.

'This way,' she called, leading Tori towards the park.

Andrés turned, watching them escape. Louis got to his feet, and ran across the road. He soon caught up with Maggie and Tori.

'This is the wrong way,' insisted Tori, stopping to catch her breath. 'We need to get to the bus station.'

'Trust me,' said Maggie, as she kept on moving.

She stopped in front of a narrow tree, close to their recently vacated treehouse. 'This is the one.'

Puzzled, Louis and Tori examined the tree. With hardly any upper branches or foliage, it was bare at the top. At its base was a spiderweb of reedy roots and spiky branches.

'Hide behind that bush,' suggested Maggie, pointing.

With a shrug, Tori did as she instructed, with Louis reluctantly following. They watched as Maggie stood in front of the tree, facing outwards. Andrés appeared, panting from the chase.

'Run,' shouted Tori.

Maggie stood her ground, grinning at Andrés. When he was an arm's length from her, Maggie jumped to the left. With an expression of disbelief on his face, Andrés tripped over a tree root. His foot was jammed in one of the snaky roots. He tugged on a trouser leg, trying to free himself, but instead became entrapped in the spiky branches that spread out at the tree's base. Maggie, Tori and Louis watched with fascination. As if he was stuck in quicksand, any attempt Andrés made to free himself resulted in further entanglement. Sounds of annoyance soon became muffled panic, as he disappeared in a web of tree roots.

'I was right,' remarked Maggie.

Louis looked at her with a puzzled expression. 'About what?'

'He's the type of man a tree like this would eat.'

'What?' asked Tori.

'Ever since Cetan told me that story about man-eating trees, I've been wondering what type of man they eat.'

Andrés had stopped moving, but the sound of muffled swearing could still be heard.

'Do you think he's okay?' asked Tori.

Louis responded, 'He's swearing, so he's obviously still breathing. I'll tell Brother Eddie where he is, so the police can fetch him.'

'Don't forget to do that before you catch your bus home in the morning,' suggested Tori.

'Or, maybe not. That skinny tree sure looks hungry.'

'Maggie!' laughed Tori and Louis together.

***

As the bus drove west, into the eventide, no one noticed the snake of many colours emerge from the landscape. If any of the passengers had looked out the left window, really looked, they'd have noticed that the undulating, barren ranges were moving ever so slightly.

Tori peered out the window and caught the last of the sun's light. Looking at the hills in the distance, for a moment she imagined they were a large snake, moving across the land. Tori smiled to herself, remembering the story her mother had told them about the gigantic serpent that had protected her as she'd walked through the desert, before giving birth on her father's Country. As the bus moved west, Tori felt an uncomfortable mix of sadness and hope. She pulled back the sleeve on her left wrist, but stopped herself before scratching her skin. Instead, she pulled a chain out from under her shirt and held the pendant tightly.

'Where'd you get that necklace,' asked Maggie.

'I found it on the ground outside von Wolff's studio.'

'It's the one Mum always wore.'

Tori nodded, letting the pendant lie on her chest.

'I've not seen you wear it before.'

'I wasn't ready until now. You don't mind I have it?'

'Mum would've wanted you to wear it.'

Tori smiled, and closed her eyes, giving in to the soothing motion of the bus.

Her sister said, 'I packed us some food. Do you want an apple?'

'Sure.'

Maggie handed her sister the reddest of red apples, keeping one for herself.

Tori took a deep breath of the apple. 'I've always loved that smell,' she remarked.

'Then you're probably not going to mind living in an apple orchard.'

'Not going to mind at all,' she said, grinning.

Raising the fruit to their lips, they both took the biggest of bites.

'I have to follow that bird, Mother. I promised Granny Maeve.'

Brigid closed the suitcase, and looked around her bedroom. She'd packed almost everything she owned; there wasn't much she was leaving behind.

Margaret said, 'I've been reflecting on a few things since Granny died. I used to be angry at her, thinking she took over raising you, but that's not true. She stepped in because I wasn't there for you. Your brothers took up so much of my time, but that's no excuse. I should have been more attentive to your needs. More understanding of how hard it was for you, having neighbours and peers who wouldn't accept difference. I didn't know how to teach you to withstand that type of hate. That's something your father would have shown you. Still, I saw what he'd gone through. How much people hurt him with their prejudices. I should have wrapped you in love. I regret not having properly prepared you for the world you're about to venture out into.'

Brigid put on Granny Maeve's apple-seed necklace, and picked up her suitcase. Margaret remembered that suitcase. She'd carried it with her own hands, when saying farewell to her own mother.

'I will be back, Mother,' Brigid said. 'I promise.'

AUTHOR'S NOTE

Where the Fruit Falls is a work of fiction. Before this story was written, the characters, places and events existed only in my imagination. There are, however, a few cryptic references to historical events and policy eras embedded in the narrative. The Aboriginal characters I have conceived are not intended to portray any specific First Nations peoples. The characters' affiliation to Country and kin do not depict real places or peoples. Aspects within the narrative are not based on actual Aboriginal cultures, practices or knowledges, such as Songlines. Due to past roles, which involved frequent travel, this novel was imagined and written in every state and territory of Australia. The places I've been to may have influenced me to create realistic settings, but the fictional geography exists only in my imagination.

I respectfully ask readers, reviewers and educators to be aware of how they read and respond to this work. I invite non-Indigenous readers to reflect on perceptions, myths, biases and worldviews that often unconsciously filter how we read and respond to works of fiction. And to uncover the truth and call for action that often lies hidden in fiction. I purposely applied elements of magic realism to this narrative; to assist readers in understanding our collective pasts in a different way, and to perhaps reimagine a more just and truthful present and future.

430

I started writing this story in 2012. I've been through a lot of life events since then, both enjoyable and challenging. To have completed the manuscript, and watch it become an actual book, feels incredible. I realise that dreams, persistence and hard work are not the only factors that made this happen. As acknowledged on the following pages, I had support.

ACKNOWLEDGEMENTS

I acknowledge First Peoples, and their Country and histories, that inspired me to write this book. I live and write on unceded Kaurna land, so specifically express respect to Kaurna people. I give my respect to Aboriginal and Torres Strait Islander Elders and changemakers – past and present. Particularly Martu matriarchs within my own family, now gone but not forgotten, whose lives and visions continue to inspire me to keep walking and never give up.

I'd like to thank my family, especially my three children and my mother, for tolerating the writing process and all the times I was mentally absent whilst physically present.

I wish to thank Kate Pickard, Eleanor Hurt and Nicole van Kan at UWA Publishing, a small but mighty team. And express my admiration for Terri-ann White, who helped grow UWAP into a treasured Australian publisher. Thanks to Nicola Young for editing my manuscript and Alissa Dinallo for the cover design.

I'm grateful to the judges of the 2020 Dorothy Hewett Award who selected my manuscript; thank you Terri-ann White, Elfie Shiosaki and James Ley. And to the Copyright Agency for funding this vital pathway for writers.

Thanks to First Nations Australia Writers Network for ongoing support, including selecting my manuscript for the 2018 FNAWN/ACT Writers Centre First Nations Writers Scholarship, to participate in Hardcopy. Both this scholarship and the Hardcopy masterclass program were funded by the Australia Council for the Arts.

Much thanks to Jessica Alice from Writers SA for sending me to Ceduna for a residency in 2018. The Writers SA's Writers and Readers in Residence program, funded by the Australia Council for the Arts, gave me space to finish my manuscript.

A shout-out to the SA First Nations Writers group. Especially Dominic Guerrera, photographer of my author bio shots, taken at Living Kaurna Cultural Centre.

Much gratitude to Sally Morgan for reading my manuscript and gifting me a perfect quote for the book's cover.

Thank you to the numerous people, including respected authors, who encouraged me to keep writing – even when giving up seemed the sensible option. And to the doubters left in my past, who expressed the view that I'd never be a real writer – revenge is much sweeter eaten cold.

Lastly, thanks to reviewers, librarians, booksellers and readers. A story doesn't truly exist until it is read and heard. Readers breathe life into books.

Made in the USA
Coppell, TX
01 June 2021